''I won't have you playing with my emotions,'' Belle said.

''Can't you believe that I find everything about you fascinating?'' Morgan whispered. ''That I'm about to shock your sensibilities by kissing you until you can't think about anybody but me.'' He dropped his head and kissed her forehead. ''I'll give you exactly until I count to ten to walk away from me. If you're still here, I won't be responsible for what happens.''

''One.''

Belle stared into his midnight blue eyes, hypnotized by his gaze.

''Two.''

Prudence told her to run as fast as she could away from Morgan. She had to protect her emotions by getting out before she drowned in her forbidden needs.

His lips nuzzled her temple above her left ear as he continued counting. ''Eight.'' Long fingers tangled into the hair at her nape and tingles sizzled down her back. ''Nine.'' Belle's knees grew weak and her feet felt as if they were nailed to the floor. ''Ten.''

Desire surged through her with the force of a hurricane and she gave up trying to fight her emotions. She lifted her face to his. ''You win. Kiss me.''

His lips slid across her cheeks. ''Are you sure? Once I start, I won't be able to stop short of full possession. I want you, Belle—all of you.''

He was giving her a way out—a chance to protect herself. But Belle had sheltered her emotions for too long. She needed to feel a man's love, if it was only for one night. ''I've never been surer of anything in my life.'' Her heart thundered in her chest. ''Make love with me.''

Books by Jean Wilson

SWEET DREAMS
MY MARIAH
COULTER'S ANGEL
CHRISTMAS HOMECOMING

Published by Zebra Books

CHRISTMAS HOMECOMING

Jean Wilson

Zebra Books
Kensington Publishing Corp.

http://www.zebrabooks.com

ZEBRA BOOKS are published by

Kensington Publishing Corp.
850 Third Avenue
New York, NY 10022

First Printing: November, 1999
10 9 8 7 6 5 4 3 2 1

Printed in the United States of America

*Dedicated to my husband Don
for making every Christmas special.*

Prologue

New Orleans,
November, 1894

When a door closes, God opens a window. Isabella Jordan studied the letter that had arrived days ago. Was this the window she and the children had been praying would open?

The door had literally been slammed closed in their faces when Mr. Robinson had passed away. After living in his mansion on Prytania Street for more than twenty years—first while her mother was housekeeper, then as housekeeper herself— Belle couldn't remember living anywhere else. The elderly bachelor had been more than an employer, he'd been like a father to her and grandfather to her daughter and the foundlings they'd taken in.

In his will, Edgar Robinson had named Belle as his heir. She'd been delighted, until his attorney had informed Belle that her benefactor had lost most of his estate in bad investments. The remaining assets had to be sold to satisfy his creditors. She and the children were forced to vacate in less than a week.

Now this legacy from James had come as if on the wings of an angel. Surely it wasn't a ruse, or some kind of perverse jest.

Signed by Corbett Hayes, Esquire, the letter seemed legitimate. Her long-absent husband, James, had passed away in some place called Paradise, Colorado, and left his entire estate to his wife. She dropped the letter to the small writing desk, one of the few remaining pieces of furniture in the house. In a day or so, it too would be sold.

James was dead. If it weren't so tragic, it would be humorous. He'd been dead to Belle since the morning after their marriage. After they'd spent the night making love, she'd fallen asleep. When she woke, she found herself alone in the bed at the St. Charles Hotel. James Jordan had disappeared, taking her meager savings and few pieces of jewelry with him. He'd left her penniless, brokenhearted, and pregnant.

In the intervening seven years, she'd given birth to his daughter and hadn't seen hide nor hair of him until days ago. With the seventh year approaching, she had contacted an attorney about having James declared legally dead. That was no longer necessary.

According to this Mr. Hayes, James had passed on and left her his estate, an unexpected legacy. A gift from heaven, as Jerome would say.

The seven-year-old mulatto boy believed that his guardian angel had promised God would help them. That He would perform a miracle. Belle almost laughed. True, she believed in God and in angels, but she also believed that God helped those who helped themselves. She'd certainly tried work; now she had to accept that a miracle had come to bail them out.

She had decisions to make. Should she contact his partner, a man named Morgan Travers, and let him buy her out? Or should she make the trip to Colorado and check her legacy out for herself? Whichever she chose, she wanted the children settled in their own home by Christmas. They loved the holiday, and they deserved a home and security.

Her thoughts were interrupted when Rosalind raced into the study dragging three-year-old Beth behind her. At six, her daughter, Rosalind, took her responsibilities to the young orphan seriously.

"Mama, Officer Cannelli is here to see you. Rory's in trouble again."

Belle looked up to see the Italian police officer standing in her doorway, his beefy hand clutching Rory by the back of the boy's shirt. Her heart sank. She'd promised that she would keep an eye on the youth, and Rory had assured her he would stay out of trouble. She shot an angry glance at the boy. He had the decency to drop his gaze to his scuffed boots.

"I warned you, Mrs. Jordan. This one is a bad seed. You mark my words, he'll end up in prison within a year." The officer frowned at the boy. "You can't trust these Irish."

She ignored the slur against the youth's heritage. "What did he do now?" Standing, she faced the officer.

"I never did nothing." The boy struggled against the big man's hold. Red hair tumbled into his green eyes.

"Nothing? Mr. Katz caught him with a pocket full of apples from his fruit stand."

"I didn't steal 'em."

The officer released Rory. "Then how did you get them?"

The boy locked his mouth and shot a defiant glance at the policeman.

Belle moved closer and turned her ward's face with a hand under his jaw so their eyes met. At thirteen, he was nearly as tall as she. Surely the Irish lad would grow into a tall, handsome man. And a good man, if she had her way. He wasn't bad, just mischievous and greatly in need of a strong hand. "Rory, where did you get the apples?"

"I bought them from a boy."

"What boy?"

He shrugged. "I don't know him. He just asked me if I wanted some apples. I thought Rosie and Beth would like them."

"Ask him where he got the money? He probably stole it, too."

She ignored the harsh accusation. "Officer, will you please tell Mr. Katz that I'll be by and pay him for the apples? Then I'll deal with Rory."

"You're taking a chance, ma'am, no telling what this boy will do. Especially without a man in the house." Cannelli shook a finger at the boy. "You better obey Mrs. Jordan, boy. Or I'll slap you in the hoosegow."

Belle escorted the policeman to the door. Since Mr. Robinson had died, the officer had kept an eye on the house and on Belle. She suspected that the widower would have called on her given a hint of encouragement. "Thank you, officer."

He hesitated in the doorway. "I understand that you'll have to leave the house, Mrs. Jordan. Where will you go?"

She'd wondered about that for the past month. Until the letter from the lawyer had come, she'd had no idea where she and the four children would go. Now, thanks to an absentee husband, she had not only inherited a place to live, strangely named Eden House, but also half interest in a silver mine and a cattle ranch.

"West," she said, her mind made up. "As soon as I sell the rest of the furnishings, we'll take a train to Paradise, Colorado."

Chapter 1

Paradise, Colorado
three weeks later

Morgan Travers clamped his teeth down on his cigar and stared out of the window. Paradise had grown in the seven years since he and James Jordan had arrived. With the influx of miners and ranchers, the town had evolved from a single street to a small town, complete with mayor, council, and sheriff's office. Behind him Corbett Hayes, the attorney he didn't trust any further than he could toss a stallion across a river, shuffled papers on his desk

Now James was dead. He turned back to Hayes. "I've been gone for two months buying cattle for the ranch. I came back to learn that my partner has been killed in an accident, and now you tell me that James left his entire estate to a *wife?* Hell, I didn't even know he was married. And he was my cousin."

Morgan and James had grown up together. They'd lived

together, loved the same women, and worked the same schemes. For the past seven years they'd been partners in the Paradise enterprises.

In the years they'd been together, James had never mentioned a wife. If any man steered away from marriage more than Morgan did, it was his cousin. So where had this so-called wife come from?

The whole thing was preposterous. Morgan doubted the woman even existed. It sounded more like a scheme cooked up by Hayes and some woman he'd hired to swindle Morgan out of his own property. Businesses that were only now becoming prosperous.

The lawyer cringed under Morgan's hard stare. "I didn't know about her either. The wife was his secret. A few months ago, James gave me some sealed documents. He said they were to be opened only in the event of his death. After the accident, I read his will. Of course, I was shocked. Like you, I expected him to leave his share in J & T Enterprises to you, or perhaps to Louise. Instead, he bequeathed all his worldly goods to his wife and left her address. I wrote to her, like I'm legally obligated to do."

"If I'd have known any of this, I'd have bought James out years ago." Morgan caught a glimpse of the six o'clock train as it pulled into the station. He ignored the array of passengers who disembarked—a couple of men, families, and a woman with four children. He glimpsed his reflection in the glass. With news like he'd returned home to, he was certain more silver had crept into his black hair. At the rate he was going, he would be completely gray before his next birthday, his thirty-fifth. "Give me her address. I'll write and buy her out."

"Travers, I doubt that will work."

Morgan shot an angry glare at the lawyer. "Why not? You know something you haven't told me?"

Hayes tugged on the tight collar of his shirt. "In order to probate the will, I had to make an inventory of the estate. It seems that with the closing of the mine and what you've spent on cattle, you have very little cash on hand. You can sell the ranch, or Eden House.'' He paused and twisted a pen in his fingers. ''I'll be willing to take one off your hands. You can buy the woman out, and not have a partner.''

''And have only half of my own property? No thanks. I'll deal with her my own way.''

''If you aren't successful, I can buy out her half, and we'll be partners.''

Morgan studied the tip of his cigar. Was it better to deal with the devil he knew than one he didn't? Knowing Hayes, Morgan would take his chances on the woman. If she was legitimate. ''No, thanks. Mind if I see the will?''

The lawyer opened a lower drawer and removed a document. ''It's all legal. I don't think you can contest it.''

Dropping into a leather side chair, Morgan studied the document. It looked like James's signature and had been notarized by a judge in Denver. Morgan had seen the signature often enough on their many contracts and papers. He studied the terms. Sure enough, his partner had left everything—which amounted to half of everything Morgan had given his blood and sweat to build—to a woman in New Orleans.

Mrs. Isabella De'Lery Jordan was now an equal partner in all his enterprises.

If James had married a woman in New Orleans, it had to have been at least six or seven years ago. As far as Morgan knew, their trip back in '87 had been the only time his cousin had visited the city. What puzzled Morgan more than anything was that James had never mentioned a wife. If he hadn't acknowledged her up until now, when had he developed a conscience?

''I suppose I can write and make an offer,'' he said. ''Wouldn't hurt to learn exactly what she wants.''

''Too late.'' A sly look crossed the lawyer's face. ''I got

a letter yesterday that she's on her way here to claim her inheritance.''

"Here? To Paradise?" Now Morgan knew that something wasn't quite orthodox. Hayes seemed awfully pleased with the turn of events. For years, the lawyer had been trying to get in on Morgan's and James's enterprises. They'd never trusted the man, and hadn't wanted a third partner. "When will she arrive?"

"Any day now."

Morgan cursed under his breath. If he'd been here before Hayes had contacted the woman, he might have had control over the situation. Now his only recourse was to prove that the woman who showed up wasn't the widow Jordan, and send her packing.

"Let me know when she gets here. I want to talk to her before she makes contact with anybody else." Morgan grabbed his battered hat from the chair and shoved it onto his too-long hair. After weeks on the trail, he hadn't bothered with hair cuts or shaves. He'd come directly from the ranch when he'd learned about James's death. He hadn't expected the news to be nearly so grim.

"Where can I reach you?" The lawyer stood and started for the door.

"For the next few days I'll be at Eden House. Louise isn't taking the news about James's wife very well."

Corbett shook his head. "I suppose it was a shock, but I had to tell her about the situation."

Knowing the way word spread through a small town, Morgan supposed that everybody in Paradise knew about the "wife" before he did. "Let me know as soon as you get word."

Morgan and Hayes stepped from the doorway onto the board-walk into the growing dusk. The yellow glow of lamps streaked from the windows of the businesses still open. As Morgan approached his horse, he caught a glimpse of a woman racing toward them.

"Mr. Morgan, Mr. Corbett, come quick. Miss Louise said to fetch you right away." Abby, the young woman who worked at Eden House, skidded to a stop. Her face was flushed, and her braids in disarray. She twisted her apron in her hands.

Without bothering to ask questions, Morgan issued an order. "Get the sheriff, and have him meet us there." He leaped into the saddle and spurred his horse toward the edge of town. Hayes mounted a little slower and followed at his heels. Only something serious would cause Louise to fetch help. The woman prided herself in being able to handle any situation that came up. Morgan paid her very well to take care of Eden House. She'd been James's mistress and had stayed on and run the business after his death.

Minutes later he reached the large white house a half mile outside of Paradise. Men—customers—gathered on the lawn, gazing at the front door. They gestured toward Morgan. As he jumped to the ground, he snatched his rifle from the holster. Hurrying up the steps, he stumbled over trunks and travel bags blocking the doorway.

Expecting a confrontation with a rowdy cowboy or outlaw, he threw open the door. His finger on the trigger of the rifle, he dropped to one knee and stopped cold. The sight that greeted him was worse than facing a half dozen armed bandits.

Two women stood toe to toe, facing each other with murder in their eyes. From experience, he knew there was nothing worse than a cat fight.

"Louise, what the h . . ." His words died in his throat. The contrast between the women was startling. Louise wore a gold embroidered silk wrapper, showing quite a bit of bosom, while the other woman was wrapped in a flowing black wool cape.

He dropped his gaze to the four children who surrounded her. A boy nearly as tall as she, a girl huddled in a navy coat, a colored boy with wide brown eyes, and a toddler who had her face buried in the woman's cape.

Both women swung their gazes in his direction. The newcomer flashed a startled glance at him. She gasped, and spread her arms to protect the children. "You intend to shoot an unarmed woman?" Her voice croaked with fear.

"No, ma'am." He released his grip on the weapon. "Who are you?"

Louise waved her arms, and the wide sleeves of her wrapper fluttered in the air. "She claims she's James's wife."

The woman wrapped an arm around the young girl's shoulder. "I am. Or was. Since he is dead, I am his widow."

"Mrs. Jordan?" Hayes arrived a second after Morgan. He stepped forward, a small derringer his hand. "I'm sorry for this poor reception. I should have met you at the station."

Her gaze shifted to the lawyer. "May I ask who you gentlemen are?"

Morgan growled deep in his throat. "I'm Morgan Travers, and this is Corbett Hayes."

"The partner and the lawyer?" Her hair was covered by a hood, with loose strands of brown hair plastered to her cheeks. The plain woman was as out of place in Eden House as were the children cowering behind her back.

Just when he was about to gain control of the situation, the door again burst open. Sheriff Dan Sullivan dropped to one knee, his shotgun aimed at the innocent woman. She squealed and turned to cover the children with her body. At that moment the smallest child let out a howl that rattled the crystals on the chandelier.

Sullivan came to his senses and let out a string of expletives. The older boy stepped forward with his fists clenched. "You hurt Miss Belle, and you got to deal with me."

If it weren't so serious, Morgan would have laughed. A slender youth against three armed men. The boy's coat was too big, and his pants too short. A knit hat covered red hair that curled around his narrow shoulders. "It's okay, boy. Nobody's going to do anything to Mrs. Jordan."

The sheriff stood and lowered his gun. "You brought me

out here to arrest a woman and four kids? What did she do? Come to drag her husband home?''

Nothing but disrupt a most profitable business enterprise. ''It was a mistake, Dan. This is Mrs. Jordan.''

Dan shoved back his hat and studied the woman. ''James's widow? And his young'uns?''

Mrs. Jordan lifted the youngest child in her arms. The youngster's cries had quieted to soft wails. With a tilt of her chin, the woman shot an angry glance at Morgan. ''Sheriff, I'm glad you've come. Arrest these people. They're trespassing on my property.''

Morgan looped the rifle over his arm. ''Like hell we are, woman. You're the intruder. You've disrupted my business and sent my customers away.''

The sheriff backed off. ''I don't get between husbands and wives, and I won't interfere with partners. Send for me if one of you kills the other.'' With a wave of the hand he was gone.

The woman handed the wailing child to the oldest boy and stepped toward Morgan. By the sparks of fire in her brown eyes, he knew that if she had a gun she would plug him right between the eyes. ''I happen to own this establishment, in spite of its disgraceful purpose. I intend to make my home here, so I suggest that you and these people vacate the premises.''

''Half, lady. You own half interest, I own half. And we aren't going anywhere. You can take rooms at a hotel.'' Hands clutched into fists, he leaned forward and met her glare eye to eye.

''I'm not going anywhere.''

Corbett Hayes stepped between them. ''Let's sit down and discuss this like reasonable people. No use threatening anybody. We can settle this problem if we keep our heads.''

''You're responsible for this mess, Hayes. You should have waited until I returned before you contacted her.''

''Calm down, Travers. I'm sure Mrs. Jordan doesn't want

to cause trouble. Let's go into the office and talk.'' The lawyer doffed his hat and bowed. ''Mrs. Jordan, this way please.''

She stood her ground and continued to glare at Morgan. ''These children are hungry. Does this 'house' have a kitchen?''

Morgan signaled for Abby, who'd been watching the confrontation from the shadows. The young woman served as seamstress and maid for the ladies in his employ. ''Take them to the kitchen. See that they get something to eat.''

''Yes, sir.'' Abby approached Mrs. Jordan. ''I'll take care of them, ma'am.''

The woman turned to the youngsters. ''Go with the lady. Rory and Rosalind, keep an eye on Jerome and Beth.'' With covert glances at Mrs. Jordan, the children followed Abby to the kitchen. Mrs. Jordan turned to Louise. ''Madam, and I believe that is your occupation, will you have your ladies, and I use that term loosely, prepare rooms for us? We'll be living here.''

''Over my dead body, you will,'' Morgan ground between his teeth. His temper was a hair's breadth from exploding.

She faced him boldly. He had to give it to the woman, she had guts.

''Mr. Travers, that can be arranged.''

Behind him, the ladies giggled. They'd never seen anybody best Morgan either at the poker table or in a debate. He shot a quelling glance at them. The ladies had tied the belts on their wrappers, and were sitting in a row like prim schoolgirls.

Hayes offered his arm to Mrs. Jordan. She set her fingers on his forearm and allowed him to escort her to the office. Louise shrugged and followed at their heels with Morgan at her side. He didn't know how he was going to handle the woman. She had every right to be there—if she was legitimate.

Under her skirt and petticoats, Belle's knees knocked like the drums in a marching band. She was fortunate to walk down the hallway without crumbling to the floor. The two women on the davenport stared at her with mild amusement in their eyes. As soon as she'd entered the foyer, the madam, Louise, had dismissed the men from the premises. For that small favor, she was grateful.

Eden House was a large, elegant house, beautifully decorated and quite lovely. Crystal chandeliers with dozens of candles lighted the foyer. Gilded sconces lit the hallway. Silk flocked paper lined the walls. She spotted the gaudy red velvet divans in the parlor, and large gold-trimmed mirrors. In spite of its beauty, the house's intended use was far from attractive.

From the moment she'd entered the door, she'd felt as if she'd delivered the children into a true den of iniquity. So far, nothing had come out as she'd expected. Between the women in their skimpy attire and that horrible Mr. Travers, her welcome was far from what she'd hoped for.

The lawyer patted the back of her hand. "Don't worry, Mrs. Jordan, I'll protect your interests," he whispered.

Her heels clicked on the shiny wood floor. "Thank you." Of the men she'd met since arriving in Paradise, Mr. Hayes was the only gentleman among the bunch. Yet, she didn't trust attorneys. She was convinced that Mr. Robinson's lawyers had cheated her out of her inheritance. That was something Mr. Hayes and Mr. Travers were not going to accomplish.

She lifted her chin a notch and entered a room at the end of the hall. Behind her, Mr. Travers and the madam whispered between themselves. Although she was far outnumbered, Belle refused to be intimidated. Mr. Hayes helped remove her cape and held a chair for her. Morgan Travers settled behind a wide desk. For an instant, she wondered if that had been James's desk—if he'd managed this business from this room. Never in her wildest dreams had she imagined that James had willed her a bordello.

Mr. Travers plucked a cigar from a shiny humidor and stuck a lit match to the end. She knew he was trying to unnerve her.

It wasn't going to work. Her stomach knotted, but she refused to allow her trepidation to show. With slow nonchalance she was far from feeling, she tossed back her hood and tugged the kid gloves from her hands. Brushing her fingers along her temples, she tucked a stray lock of hair behind her ear. Louise took the chair beside the desk, while the lawyer settled in a leather chair that matched the one on which Belle sat.

Boldly, she studied her adversaries. The woman was very beautiful, in a hardened, worldly way. Her blonde hair was piled on her head with a single long curl trailing down her cheek. Belle was afraid that if the woman made one quick move, her overly ripe bosom would burst right out of her wrapper. The front opening showed an immodest amount of a silk-stockinged leg. Louise's gaze was locked on Belle, as if trying to peel away the layers of her skin and see what lay underneath. Mr. Travers, for his part, studied the glowing tip of his cigar. Belle resisted fanning her face to dissipate the stinking smell of the cigar.

The contrast between the men was striking. Mr. Travers stood half a head taller than Mr. Hayes, his shoulders wider, and his gaze harder. While the lawyer wore a finely tailored gray suit, Travers looked as if he'd ridden into town from his ranch—correction, *their* ranch—without bothering to shave. He'd tossed a wide-brimmed, dusty hat onto the desk, and his too-long black hair tumbled into his thick eyebrows. Dark whiskers shadowed his lower face, giving him a devilishly dangerous look. Under a brown leather jacket, he wore a faded chambray shirt with a blue bandanna tied at his thick throat. He leaned back in the chair and propped his long denim-clad legs on the desk. The soles of his scuffed boots met her gaze.

The silence lasted for long seconds. Belle took advantage of the moments to gather her courage, something she was far from feeling. She bit her lip to keep from being the first to open the dialogue.

The lawyer broke the silence. "Mrs. Jordan, I apologize for our rude welcome. I hope you'll accept our condolences on your husband's death."

"Mr. Hayes," she said, stemming her growing discomfort. "My husband abandoned me nearly seven years ago. I quit grieving for him when my daughter was born. Until I heard he'd passed on, I'd planned to have him declared legally dead."

Mr. Travers rolled the cigar around in long blunt fingers. "How many of those youngsters are his?" Blue eyes as dark as midnight bore into her.

"Rosalind, his daughter, is six." It took all her strength to remain calm under his hard stare. The other children's parentage was none of his business.

"How do we know you're telling the truth?"

"How do I know you aren't trying to cheat me out of James's share of your enterprises?"

"Mrs. Jordan," Hayes said, "I can assure you I'm looking after your best interests."

"I'll bet you are," Morgan Travers said around the cigar between his lips. "James was my cousin as well as my partner and he never said a word about a wife. Do you have proof that you're who you claim to be?"

She leaned forward. "Mr. Travers, I'm not surprised you're skeptical. I don't know why he deserted me following our marriage, or why he chose to conceal my existence. I have a copy of my marriage certificate and a photograph that was taken on my wedding day." Digging into her handbag, she pulled out the envelope she'd guarded for nearly seven years. "This should prove I'm James Jordan's widow."

The lawyer took the envelope from her fingers. He scanned the document and photograph, then handed them over to Mr. Travers. "It looks legal to me."

Belle leaned back in her chair and waited. The woman they'd called Louise leaned over Morgan's shoulder. She glanced from the photograph to Belle and back again. "That's James and the woman sure looks like her."

Morgan studied the photograph. "It could be a fake."

She had taken more of the man's rudeness than she could stand. "Mr. Travers, I don't have the time or strength to argue with you. I've come a long way, and I'm exhausted." Standing, she snatched her documents from his fingers and slammed them to his desk. "We can let a court of law settle this problem."

He jerked his feet from the desk and stood. The man towered over her, making her feel small and insignificant. "That's an excellent idea. Meanwhile you can stay at the hotel."

He had no idea of her limited funds. Quite simply, until she got some of James's money, she didn't have the funds to rent rooms at the hotel. "I have no intention of leaving this house. They say that possession is ninety percent of the law. I'm staying here."

The lawyer stepped between them. "Morgan, Mrs. Jordan has proof that she's James's widow. Give up. She's your partner, unless you're ready to made a deal."

"Deal? Sell out? Not on your life. I put too much of my heart and soul in this to give it up to some stranger."

Belle sincerely doubted the man had either a heart or a soul. "Mr. Hayes," she said, another idea taking root. "Please draw up the necessary papers naming Mr. Travers and me equal partners. I assume this house and the other property are half mine."

"According to the terms of his will, James left you everything he owned," the lawyer said.

"Good. Meanwhile, I'll fetch the children, and we'll select our rooms for the night. Tomorrow I'll decide which half of this house I want."

"Morgan, do something." Louise grabbed the obnoxious man by the arm. "I have a yard full of customers, waiting for us to allow them back in. We're losing a fortune."

Morgan shot a look at Belle that threatened to reduce her to ashes. "We'll close down for the night. Then I'll settle this with Mrs. Jordan tomorrow."

"The girls won't like that."

"I don't like it either, but it looks as if we're stuck with this crew for the night."

Belle folded her arms over her chest to stop her hands from trembling. Her stomach was quivering, and her knees were mush. "This crew intends to stay. And we have no intention of living in a house of ill repute. Which I'm assuming is the purpose of this place."

Morgan leaned toward her, his gaze inches from hers. He smelled of cigar smoke and leather. A different kind of excitement sizzled through her. "Lady, this is a whore house and it's important to this town. I'd hate to be in your shoes if you tried to shut it down."

"I cannot have these children living under the same roof with that kind of immoral behavior."

A smile lifted one corner of his mouth. He looked like the devil incarnate. "That's up to you. We're staying. And tomorrow evening we're opening for business. If you want to subject your children to our depraved activities, it's entirely up to you."

For Belle and her children, it was no choice at all. She ignored his vicious slurs and directed her gaze to Louise. "If you'll be so kind as to direct me to the unoccupied rooms, I'd like to settle the children for the night."

With a resigned shrug, the woman led the way from the office. "I'll have Abby make up rooms for you."

"Thank you." Belle left the men staring after her and followed the madam to the kitchen.

Her heart sank. She wasn't wanted here. The environment was all wrong for the children. Unfortunately for them all, she had nowhere else to go. It was either stay in this place, or sleep in the streets. The children deserved better. Belle had swallowed her pride and stood up to a wicked and obstinate man.

She hoped Jerome's guardian angel was on duty that night. They needed all the protection he could give.

This place was named all wrong. Eden House was more like Hades Hall.

Chapter 2

Morgan snapped the quill pen in two and wished it were the obstinate woman's neck. She'd bested him, and he hated to come out second best in any confrontation. Louise had returned moments earlier and had poured drinks for him, Hayes, and herself.

"Did you know he was married?" he asked, swirling the amber liquid in his glass. Funny, he remembered that Mrs. Jordan's eyes were exactly the same whiskey color. Her eyelashes were long, and her skin as pale as porcelain. But she was the most bull-headed creature he'd ever encountered. Any other woman would have melted under his stare. He cursed her under his breath. She'd ruined a profitable evening for him and the girls. It had been his responsibility to run off the men who'd been customers, plus the others who'd simply heard about a commotion and had hoped to see some excitement.

Louise tossed the liquor down her throat in a very unladylike fashion. But she never claimed to be a lady any more than

Morgan claimed to be a gentleman. "No. A man rarely discusses his wife with his mistress."

Hayes stared at the photograph lying on the desk. "He was a fool to leave her. Isabella is very pretty."

Morgan snorted. "Pretty? I supposed if she ever smiled. As far as I can see, she has the disposition of a mule with a burr stuck in its hoof."

"I believe her." Louise refilled her glass from the decanter on the sideboard. "The older girl looks like James—same blue eyes and dark hair. In fact, Morgan, she could pass for your child."

A shiver passed over Morgan. "Believe me, I've never set sight on that woman until tonight. I've been very careful to prevent such a disaster."

"Well, Travers, looks like you have a partner." The glass of liquor didn't hide the lawyer's calculating grin. "With children."

"I can make a trade. She wants this place, I can give it to her and keep the rest of the property." Morgan sipped the whiskey and felt the burn clear to his stomach. He'd felt the same reaction from the minute Hayes had informed him of the woman's existence.

"As her lawyer, I'd have to advise her against it. The ranch and mine are far more valuable than this place."

He slammed down his glass; the liquor splashed on the portrait of the woman and Jordan. "She doesn't know that. And when did she hire you?"

"James did, and I'm obligated to respect his wishes and protect his widow's interests."

Louise glared at Morgan. "If you give her Eden House, what will happen to me and the girls? You know she'll throw us all out on our bottoms and wash her hands of all of us."

He rubbed his forehead at the growing headache. "You're right. As much as I hate to admit it, Eden House is our most prosperous business until the ranch turns a profit. The cash is keeping me afloat. I can't afford to shut down the house. And I sure won't give her the ranch."

Morgan loved his ranch, while James preferred the house. As a boy raised on a dirt farm in Alabama, Morgan had dreamed of owning his own place to breed cattle and raise horses. The other investments were only a means to that end. He'd planned to eventually sell his interest in Eden House, and live full time on the ranch. The silver mine was nearly played out and he'd shut it down. Now he couldn't give it away.

"She may own half the land and the cattle, but the horses are mine. James wasted his profit on jewelry and a fancy buggy. The rest he gambled away. I invested in livestock."

"Mr. Hayes." The sultry feminine drawl came from the open doorway.

Morgan cringed. He'd hoped to be free of the woman for the night. He needed time to consider his options. She'd removed the cloak and wore a dark maroon travel skirt. The jacket nipped in her waist, and the skirt flared around her feet.

Corbett surged to his feet. "May I be of assistance, Mrs. Jordan?"

She shifted her gaze to Morgan seated behind the desk. He refused to show even a modicum of manners.

"I believe I forgot something." Stepping into the room, she retrieved her photograph from under Morgan's glass. With a frown, she shook off the drops of whiskey. "My marriage certificate, please." She stuck out her fingers.

Reluctantly, Morgan shoved the document toward her. "Hope I didn't ruin it."

"You didn't." With a tilt of her nose, she turned back to Hayes. "Mr. Hayes, as my husband's attorney, I would like a conference tomorrow."

"Certainly, Mrs. Jordan. You're welcome at my office at any time." He bowed gallantly. His dandified manners made Morgan sick.

"I'll be there first thing in the morning." She started to

leave, then turned back. "By the way, I would appreciate a complete inventory of all James's assets, the value, and exactly what I have inherited. I would also like to know if I can sell my half of the enterprises."

At that, Morgan leaped to his feet. "He'll tell you that James and I signed agreements giving each other first refusal if we wanted to end the partnership. And I have no intention of letting you sell out to anybody except me."

She stepped closer, her eyes blazing amber fire. "Are you offering to buy me out?"

"I'm thinking about it."

"Present the offer to my attorney and I'll give it my consideration." In a swirl of her skirt, she strutted from the room, the faint fragrance of lavender trailing behind her.

Morgan was torn between strangling the woman and getting stinking drunk. He dropped to the chair, knowing he would do neither. He had to keep a cool head if he wanted to retain his businesses.

"You can always marry her," Louise stated, her tone bland. "That's one way to keep her in line."

"Marry? I don't want James's leftovers." He noticed the pain in the woman's eyes. She and James had been lovers since he'd hired her to operate Eden House. "I spent most of my childhood taking the blame for my cousin's mischief. I've bailed him out of more tight spots than I care to remember. I sure don't want to spend my life supporting his kid."

"She has a point, Travers," the lawyer threw in his unwanted advice. "Mrs. Jordan is an available woman, and a fine looking one at that. When word gets out she's inherited James's estate, the suitors will be lined up from here to Denver." From the look on his face, Morgan believed that Hayes would be first in line.

"I value my freedom too much. I lived all my life with hand-me-downs, and I won't take some other man's discard. And I surely don't intend to get involved with a shrew like that one."

"Like it or not, Morgan, you're already involved. I have the feeling she'll have her nose in every aspect of your businesses. And if she marries somebody else, you may not like your new partner any better." Louise shot a glance at the lawyer.

Hayes picked up his hat and started for the door. "You can escort her to my office tomorrow. We'll figure out something."

The lawyer left, and Morgan sagged back to the chair. Louise sank into the chair across the desk from him. She waited until they heard the front door close before she spoke. "You'd better keep your eye on Hayes. More than once he tried to buy James's interest. He could just be your rival for the hand of the widow Jordan."

"I told you, I'm not a young swain out to win some woman's hand. I'll figure a way to buy her out, fair and square."

"Good luck, Morgan. From what I see of her, you're going to need it."

That he wasn't about to deny.

As Abby escorted Belle and her charges to a bedchamber, Belle struggled to remain calm. She didn't want to upset the children any more than they'd already been. Thanks to her arrogant partner and impulsive sheriff, they'd been frightened half out of their wits. Now they found themselves in an overly ornate room, fancier than the downstairs parlors.

She wondered whose room it had been, and if it was where a woman entertained her male friends. Abby had generously shown her to the bathing room that boasted a large footed tub and running water. Belle and Rory had helped carry hot water up the rear stairs, and she'd seen that all the children had baths. The young woman had also helped her drag her trunks and bags up the wide staircase.

Although she hadn't taken inventory, she was certain the house had at least ten bedrooms. Downstairs were parlors, a study, kitchen, dining room, a library, and other rooms she would discover the next day.

Afraid to let the boys out of her sight, she had pallets made up for them in the connecting dressing room. The girls shared the wide four-poster bed with Belle. As they knelt to say their prayers, they gave thanks for a safe journey, and a warm place to stay.

Rory mumbled, not convinced that they were better off in Paradise than in New Orleans. He murmured that it was too cold, and he didn't like Paradise. Belle tried to ease their fears, but she had too many of her own to be convincing. Although she was certain right was on her side, she fully expected her partner to toss her right out into the cold, children and all.

After setting the lock, she tied the key on a ribbon around her neck, and shoved a bureau in front of the door. No telling what kind of depravity went on under this roof. She certainly didn't want the children subjected to that kind of corruption. When sleep came, her dreams were haunted by bright blue eyes, and a handsome devil in the form of Morgan Travers.

Belle rose early the next morning, while allowing the children to remain in bed a while longer. She shoved the bureau aside and unlocked the door. Before going down to prepare their breakfast, she took a quick glimpse at the boys. Rory lay on his stomach, snoring softly. As soon as the door clicked, Jerome opened his wide chocolate eyes.

Belle knelt down beside him and brushed her fingers over his curly hair. "You can sleep a little longer. I'll be back as soon as your breakfast is ready."

The youngster caught her fingers in his small hand. "Miz Belle, can I talk to you?"

"Of course, Jerome. You can tell me anything."

"I saw Earl last night."

With a smile she settled on the floor to hear the child's story.

Before the boy's mother had died, she'd told him that when she got to heaven, she would send a special angel to look after him. He'd named the angel Earl, and believed that Earl spoke to him and guided him. He claimed that Earl had led him to Belle.

"That's fine."

"He talked to me." His voice was soft with awe. "He said that we should be lights in the darkness and that the light will guide us just like it guided the Wise Men to Jesus." He lifted his gaze to hers. "Miz Belle, will we be here for Christmas?"

She wrapped an arm across his narrow shoulders. A bordello was certainly no place to raise children, but she couldn't lie to them. If Morgan Travers had his way, they would be out in the cold without a roof over their heads. "I'm not sure where we'll be. But I promise we'll all be together."

He hugged her around the waist. "That's all I want for Christmas. To be with you and the others."

"Didn't Earl promise you a home? You'll always be with us." She kissed him gently on the forehead. "Now, get some rest. I'll call you when breakfast is ready."

"Thank you, Miz Belle." He dropped his head to his pillow. "I almost forgot. Earl said to tell you that God heard your prayers, and you'll get exactly what you want for Christmas."

"You thank Earl for me next time you see him."

Rory rolled over and opened one eye. "You still talking about that angel? There ain't no such things as angels. You was just dreaming." He punched his pillow and buried his face.

Tears glimmered in the dark-skinned boy's eyes. "I wasn't either dreaming, Miz Belle. Earl is real. He talks to me. It ain't no dream."

It was a continuing battle between the boys. Jerome had a deep-seated faith, while Rory was a doubter. It wasn't hard to understand, considering that the Irish lad had watched both his parents die of the yellow fever and had survived by his wits

32 *Jean Wilson*

until Belle and Mr. Robinson had taken him in. Theirs was the first home he'd known.

"I believe you, Jerome. Ignore Rory. Some day, he'll believe, too."

Belle left the room, not as convinced as she'd tried to sound. True, the other prediction had come true, but this about Belle getting her Christmas prayer answered confused her. The only thing she wanted was a home for the children and herself.

As she stepped into the hallway, another thought struck her. When she'd started the proceedings to have James declared legally dead, she'd thought about remarrying to give the youngsters a father. But that was impossible. She didn't want to be tied to a man who would dominate her and possibly abuse the children. Since she'd inherited this house and other property, she didn't want a man to snatch it away from her as James had stolen her meager savings.

That morning, she decided not to use the rear stairs, but to stroll down the main stairs like the lady of the manor. Her heels tapped lightly on the shiny wood steps, and she brushed her hand along the mahogany banister. The house was beautiful, if on the gaudy side. She stuck her head into the parlor and found it empty, as were the library and the other rooms.

The morning was very quiet, as the women must still be asleep. For a second she wondered where Morgan Travers slept—and with whom. She shoved away the thought. What he did was none of her business. The only thing that she cared about was taking possession of her inherited property.

Grateful for the time alone, she set out to find food for breakfast. To her surprise, the pantry was well-stocked. She was sure that Abby was responsible for the housekeeping and for keeping the kitchen in fine condition. The evening before, she'd prepared a delicious meal for the children on the spur of the moment.

First off, she put a pot of coffee on the stove. While it brewed, she mixed up a batter for pancakes. Searching further, he found a can of maple syrup, jams and preserves. While giving the children a chance to rest, she settled at the table with a cup of coffee. It wasn't as rich as the chicory blend he'd grown accustomed to in New Orleans, but it would serve to bolster her waning courage and get her ready for her next confrontation with that heinous Morgan Travers.

He certainly was a handsome devil with his black hair and blue eyes—and devil he was. The man wanted nothing more than to cheat Belle out of her inheritance.

"Smells good. Mind if I have a cup?"

Her heart skipped a beat. She jerked her gaze from the cup to the man entering the door. It was as if her musings had conjured him up out of thin air. He tugged a black hat from his head and slid his arms out of a leather jacket. His clean-shaved cheeks were rosy and he looked as if he'd just come from the outdoors. Belle clutched her cup to keep her hands from trembling. The man was too big, too handsome, and too intimidating.

"Be my guest." If he expected her to jump up and serve him, he had another thought coming.

He grinned. "I believe you're *my* guest."

His arrogance irked her clear to the bones. "Have you forgotten that I own half of this house?"

"Not for a minute." He dropped his jacket on the back of a chair, then filled a cup from the pot heating on the stove. Turning a chair around backward, he straddled the seat. "Not bad coffee," he said after taking a sip. "Better than mine, but not as good as they serve in New Orleans."

"Have you been to New Orleans?"

He nodded. "A couple of times. James and I were there about six or seven years ago."

She shivered. "At about the time we married."

"We spent most of our time in a house like this. Of course, James didn't say anything about getting married."

Belle really didn't want to hear about her husband's sordid

past, yet she'd always wondered what had happened to the rogue. "You're really his cousin?"

"We grew up together, and got into trouble together. I had no idea he had a wife."

She'd long ago gotten over the pain of desertion. "Were you running from the law?"

He laughed, a warm masculine sound. "We managed to stay one step ahead. In New Orleans, we decided to pool our limited resources and come to Paradise. The silver mine was our first success. Then this house, then the ranch. What will it take to buy you out?"

"I'm not sure I want to sell. I like this house, and I promised the children we'd be settled by Christmas."

"You can't keep those children here. This isn't the right atmosphere for kids. We have men coming through here day and night."

He hadn't told her anything she hadn't already considered. "Then change the atmosphere. Keep the men out, and turn the house over to a more respectable use."

"Mrs. Jordan, this place was built to be a whore house. That's what your husband intended—in fact he ran it personally. He selected the girls, he kept order, served the drinks, and collected the money. James liked it. He lived here, while I mostly stayed at the ranch."

With every word he spoke, Belle felt the heat rush to her face. "After James left me, I didn't believe he lived as a saint. What you've said doesn't surprise me in the least. Or that Louise was his mistress."

He lifted a thick black eyebrow. The action emphasized the thin scar that ran from the corner of his brow to the top of his ear. It made him look even more wicked. "How did you know?"

"Mr. Travers, I am not stupid nor am I blind. I saw the way she looked at me when I introduced myself as Mrs. Jordan. I wouldn't be surprised if she was in love with him, and he forgot to tell her he had a wife."

"He didn't tell anybody."

She took a sip of the coffee, now grown cold. "I don't understand why he left his estate to me. If he'd cared at all, he'd have contacted me years ago."

"I suppose he had a fit of conscience. Until now, I hadn't thought he possessed one. James was the most totally selfish person I knew. He loved himself to the exclusion of all others. That included his wife and mistress."

Belle studied him through a fog of unshed tears. It hurt to hear how little she'd meant to the only man she'd ever loved. A man who'd killed the love of a vulnerable woman with his selfishness and greed. "Nobody ever told me how he died."

"An accident. His buggy turned over and killed him outright. I suppose that's the way he would have wanted to go. Quick and without lingering." Morgan stood and picked up his jacket. "Thanks for the coffee. I'm going to change. We'll head over to the lawyer's office in about hour, if you can be ready by then."

"Make it an hour and a half. I have to feed the children and see that they're settled."

With a nod, he disappeared the same way he'd come.

Morgan paced the front foyer waiting for the woman to descend the stairs. He'd thought the swift ride in the cold air would calm his ravaged nerves. All it did was give him time to think about the strange situation into which they'd all been thrust.

To be fair, he didn't fault the woman for wanting her inheritance. His cousin had wronged her, and she deserved some recompense for the way he'd treated her. But not at Morgan's expense. He had to come up with a plan to get her and those children out of the house. Or he would be stuck with a partner worse than the last one.

His heels clicked on the shiny floor. The house was inordinately quiet. It was too early for any of the girls to be up and around. Only Abby showed her face before noon. Louise had hired the young woman to take care of the clothes and supervise the house. It wasn't only Isabella Jordan who took in strays. Abby had come begging for a job when her father had been killed in a mining accident. Louise had taken the girl in, given her a place to live, and put her in charge of the household.

Eden House had turned into an enterprise that employed far more than the women who entertained the men. Daily, Mrs. Franklin, a widow, came in to cook and clean. Her teenaged son cleaned the yard and tended the horses. Abby stayed in a small chamber near the head of the rear stairs. She was a jewel, freeing Louise to take over where James had left off.

Morgan was reaching into his pocket for a cigar, when he spotted the hem of a navy skirt on the top stair. He stopped and stared. The woman lifted her skirt, giving a view of a nicely turned ankle. His gaze lifted to the round womanly hips, nipped-in waist, and a fitted jacket flaring over a full bosom. A white bow filled the high neckline of her blouse. A small feathered hat sat atop her upswept hair, and a sheer veil shielded her eyes.

A disturbing need gripped his gut. The woman was quite a fine specimen of femininity. Morgan cursed the unwanted desire that could only lead to trouble. If he wanted a woman, at least three willing, experienced ladies were asleep upstairs.

She pulled on her kid gloves as she neared the lower landing. "I'm sorry I'm late. I wanted to make sure Abby could remain with the children until I return."

He ground his teeth until they hurt. "Mrs. Jordan, the children will be as safe at Eden House as in your arms."

"I'm sure you're right, Mr. Travers. I wanted to be certain they wouldn't need anything while I'm gone." At the last step, she paused. Glancing over her shoulder, she troubled her lip with her teeth. On a sigh, she turned back to Morgan. "Shall we go? I have several questions for Mr. Hayes."

"Anything you want to know, I'll be glad to inform you."

"I wasn't aware that you're a lawyer." She moved gracefully across the foyer to the door.

He bit his tongue to hold back an angry retort. "I'm not. Even better, I know every dime and every asset in the partnership. Believe it or not, I have no intention of cheating you." Opening the door, he gestured her outside.

"I'll decide that after we talk to Mr. Hayes."

Morgan grabbed her arm and pulled her to a stop. She lifted her surprised gaze to his. "Be careful around Hayes. He looks after his own interests before those of his clients."

Her cheeks pinked. "I've had my own encounters with lawyers. I don't trust the lot of them."

Dropping his hand to her elbow, he guided her to the steps. "We agree on one thing. Let's see if we can find other common ground."

Belle seriously doubted they would see eye-to-eye on many subjects. She allowed him to assist her into the elegant little black buggy trimmed with brass fittings. He settled on the narrow leather seat and clicked the reins. The matching black horses took off at a trot. His shoulder brushed her as he guided the horses down a narrow road.

At first she almost hadn't recognized the man. Today he wore a black suit that fit his muscular body to perfection. A stiff white shirt and high collar with gray and black necktie enhanced his dark good looks. He wasn't wearing gloves, and his bare, callused fingers twisted in the lines, handling the frisky team with expert ease. In place of the scuffed boots, he wore highly polished shoes. The disreputable cowboy had transformed himself into an elegant businessman. In spite of wearing her best navy suit, Belle felt dowdy and plain beside him.

Lifting her chin a notch, Belle struggled to calm her racing nerves. The man managed to unnerve her with a mere glance from the corner of his eyes.

"I suppose this buggy belongs to you now, Mrs. Jordan, along with the horses."

She slanted a glance at him. "Did they belong to James?"

He nodded. "He was driving this rig when he was killed. It overturned and he died instantly."

A chill raced over her. She gripped the side to keep her balance. As the horses picked up speed, her heart beat a loud tattoo. Only then did she realize that they were headed out of town, not into it. He took a turn, and the vehicle tilted to the side. "Mr. Travers," she yelled. "Please slow this thing down."

He laughed, the sound carried away on the wind. The chill air cut through her suit as if she were wearing nothing. "Scared, Mrs. Jordan?"

"N. . .no." She held her hat in place with one hand and clutched the side with the other. "We're going the wrong way."

"Are we?" He tugged on the reins and the horses slowed. "I wanted to give you a tour of the mine and the ranch."

The man was as degenerate as she'd suspected. He wanted to frighten her into accepting his offer and leaving. Belle determined to show him that nothing he could do would force her to leave until she was ready. "I would like to go directly to Mr. Hayes's office, if you don't mind. If the buggy and horses belong to me, I would appreciate your being more considerate of my property."

"Would you like to drive?"

Belle didn't want to admit her lack of anything, but she didn't know the first thing about handling a team. In New Orleans, she was able to take a streetcar or hire a cab wherever she went. "You can drive, just be careful. I may decide to breed these horses."

At that he laughed louder. "You don't know anything about animals, do you?"

"Very little."

"You can't breed these horses. They're geldings."

Her face pinked more from embarrassment than from the cold air. "Oh. What a waste."

"My sentiments exactly." He turned the team and retraced their route, only this time at a more sedate pace. "If you stay, I'll teach you how to handle a team."

She gritted her teeth. "I'm staying, Mr. Travers. You might as well get used to me. I'll be around for quite a while."

"That's what I was afraid of."

Chapter 3

I'm rich. Belle tried to stem her excitement when Corbett Hayes read James's will. She crossed her fingers in the folds of her skirt. Those same words had crossed her mind when she'd inherited Mr. Robinson's estate. Then in the next breath, the lawyer had snatched everything away from her.

"I have the estimated value of the property." Mr. Hayes slid a sheet to her and one to Morgan. "It's rather a conservative estimate since I'm only the lawyer, not an appraiser." He lifted his gaze to Morgan, who'd said little since they'd entered the office. "Does it look accurate to you, Morgan?"

"Yeah." He shoved the paper back to the lawyer.

Belle studied the figures. She owned a large, elaborate house on the outskirts of town, a silver mine, and thousands of acres of land. She turned the paper over, looking for the catch, the debts that would snatch it all away from her. "I own all this? Free and clear?"

"No." Morgan shot her a hard glance. "You own *half*. I told you I own the other half."

She shivered under his chilled gaze. "I didn't mean to insinuate anything else. I only wanted to know if there are any liens, or debts against the property."

"Only what we owe the girls, the housekeeper and ranch hands. And unless we let them get back to work, we won't be able to meet our obligations." He snatched a cigar from the humidor on the lawyer's desk without so much as asking permission.

"You do have some money in the bank, don't you, Morgan?" Hayes leaned forward with his elbows on his desk.

"Some. Enough to cover the expenses at Eden House and the ranch. We don't have any cash to spare."

Belle's heart sank. Without cash, she would be forced to remain at Eden House and put up with the goings-on of the occupants. Unless she was able to put the house to better use. "Mr. Hayes, can you draw up the documents making Mr. Travers and me equal partners?"

"As long as I'm the managing partner." Morgan crossed an ankle over his knee and chewed on the unlit cigar.

"*Equal* partners." Belle fired an unwavering cold glance at her disagreeable partner who wanted nothing more than to unnerve her. "I intend to operate the enterprises just as my late husband did."

Hayes covered his mouth to hold back a cough. "Mrs. Jordan. You don't know what you're saying."

Morgan barked a humorless laugh. "You intend to run Eden House? James interviewed the girls, he kept order, and decided which man went with which girl, and he collected the money." A wicked glint danced in his midnight blue eyes. "And he slept with any and all."

"Travers." Hayes leaped to his feet and braced his fists on his desk. "Is it necessary to remind Mrs. Jordan of her husband's indiscretions?"

"Just telling her the truth, is all. If she wants to be an equal partner, she'll have to carry her share of the load."

Heat rushed to Belle's cheeks. She was tempted to pick up the glass paperweight from the desk and bash in the man's thick skull. Never in her life had any human being provoked her to as much wrath as Morgan Travers. "I'll carry my load, Mr. Travers, as I've done since the day my husband ran off with my savings and left me expecting his child."

"Exactly what do you think you can do?"

"I'm a fine housekeeper and a qualified bookkeeper. I'll handle the books, while you do the physical labor."

The lawyer settled back to his chair. "That seems reasonable, you share the chores, and the profits."

Morgan shot the lawyer a distrustful glance. It was clear there was no love lost between the men, and Belle blamed it on the abominable man who was now her partner.

"If there are any profits. How can we expect the men to frequent Eden House when it's full of kids and a widow?"

Belle had taken all of his abuse she could tolerate. "Mr. Travers, we can find another use for that hell hole, one as profitable and more respectable."

He jabbed the cigar toward her. "Like what, Mrs. Jordan? A home for wayward girls? An orphanage? Sorry. The house stays as is. And that's my final word."

"Mr. Hayes, is Eden House half mine?"

"Yes. The title is in Morgan's and James's names. I'll have it changed to yours."

"Good. Mr. Travers can do what he wants with his half of our estate. I'll run my half in my own way." She stood and tugged her gloves over her shaking fingers. "As soon as you draw up the papers, I'll sign them." She glared at the rude man who remained seated.

Hayes got to his feet and took her elbow. "I'll look after your interest, Mrs. Jordan. I'll draw up the documents and deliver them to you at Eden House."

"Thank you, Mr. Hayes, it's a pleasure to meet a gentleman." She started for the door. Behind her back, Morgan snorted like an angry horse. Pausing, she looked back over her shoulder. "By the way, are the horses and fine carriage mine?"

"Yes. They belonged to James, so now they're yours." The lawyer's hand stroked slowly from her elbow up her arm.

"Good. Could you arrange to sell them for me? I'll pay you a commission, of course."

Morgan surged to his feet. "No need for that. I'll take them off your hands."

"For how much?"

"I'll work out something fair. Don't worry, Mrs. Jordan, I won't cheat you."

She nodded. "I hope so, Mr. Travers." Turning to the lawyer, she stuck out her hand. "Thank you, Mr. Hayes."

Instead of shaking her hand, he lifted her fingers to his lips. "It's my pleasure to help a lovely lady. If there's anything I can do to serve you, please send for me." His hand lingered on hers much longer than was proper.

The man had been nothing but kind and courteous, yet Belle wasn't sure she should trust him. She shoved aside her doubts, and smiled. "I'll do that." Stepping onto the boardwalk, she walked toward the buggy tied at the hitching post.

From the corner of her eye, she spotted Morgan stop and speak to the lawyer. "Don't get any ideas, Hayes."

"I don't know what you're talking about. I intend only to see that the lady's interests are protected."

"For her, or for yourself?"

"It's my responsibility as her attorney to see that her husband's wishes are carried out."

Morgan slammed his hat on his head and stalked toward the buggy. Hayes trailed at his heels and when he approached Belle, he offered a hand up. Morgan ignored the pair and climbed into the seat. Belle accepted the lawyer's help and settled beside the man who was her business partner. She gripped the side and waited for him to drive in the same reckless fashion as when they'd come into town.

This time, he took off at a more sedate pace.

"Mr. Travers," she said.

He acknowledged her with a grunt.

"Do we have an account at the general store and the mercantile?"

"Yeah."

"Good. Then stop there. I have to pick up a few things."

"Mrs. Jordan, I'm not your private driver. I have work to do."

"Mr. Travers, since this is still my conveyance and my horses, you can stop right here, and I'll drive them myself." What could be so difficult about clicking reins and letting the horses pull the buggy? If he could do it, so could she.

He tugged the team to a halt, handed her the lines and leaped down to the ground. "Just don't kill yourself until you make a will and leave your share to me."

Her mouth agape, she watched him stalk away. He crossed the street, climbed to the boardwalk and slammed into a saloon. Belle opened her mouth to call him back, but by then he'd disappeared into the dim interior.

"Of all the rude, ill-mannered louts." She picked up the lines as he'd done and shook them gently. The horses simply stood their ground and turned to stare at her. "Go." Either they didn't understand English, or they were deaf. Aware that people had stopped to stare, she decided to wait until later to test their hearing. For now, she would go to the general store and purchase the items she needed to settle into Eden House. As she'd seen Morgan do, she tied the lines to the hitching post. The rest she would learn later.

The woman provoked more emotion out of Morgan in five minutes than any other woman in his entire life. He threw down the jigger of whiskey, and let it burn all the way to his gut.

Normally, he wasn't a drinking man. However, in the past twenty-four hours he'd drank a year's supply.

From his table near the window of the Pair-a-dice gambling saloon and bar, he watched the prissy Mrs. Jordan sashay from Peterson's General Store to Norman's Hardware, Feed and Grain. After leaving each store, a delivery boy loaded her purchases into the buggy. He hated to see the bills she was piling up on him.

Sweep Baker, owner of the saloon, settled in the chair beside Morgan. Since the saloon didn't hire girls for the upper rooms, the gambler and Morgan got along as well as could be expected. Until his marriage a year ago, Sweep had been a regular customer at Eden House. When Morgan wanted a game of chance, he frequented the Pair-a-dice. They were friendly competitors.

"So that's James's wife," the gambler said, setting a bottle of his best whiskey on the table. "Not bad looking."

The woman, who'd caused more than a few bar patrons to question Morgan about her, left the hardware store and approached the buggy.

Morgan grunted. He wasn't in any mood to discuss the woman he wanted to forget. "I suppose."

"Did you know about her?"

Refilling his glass, he lifted it to his lips. "No. My cousin was a man who kept secrets."

"I understand she's your new partner." Sweep adjusted the gray necktie under his black coat. His purple waistcoat set him apart from most of the other businessmen in town. That and the diamond on his little finger.

"Does everybody in town know all my business?"

Sweep laughed. "You'd better keep an eye on her. When word gets out that she's an heiress, the men will be lining up to court her."

"I'm glad you're married. You would be first in line." Morgan's gaze followed the woman in question as she approached the buggy.

"What about you, Morgan? Are you in line?"

He choked on the whiskey. "Never. She may be pretty on the outside, but that woman is as stiff as an old maid corset."

As he watched, she loosed the lines and climbed into the buggy. Morgan had a good mind to let her try to handle the frisky team on her own. She snapped the lines, and the horses took one step. Several men had stopped to stare. Everybody knew James's fancy rig. And they all knew he'd been killed when the horses had run away and overturned the buggy. His conscience prickled.

"Oh, hell." Morgan threw down the glass and strode from the saloon, letting the doors swing angrily in his wake.

By the time he made it across the street, the horses had decided to head for home, taking off in a trot. Morgan quickened his pace and leaped into the seat. He grabbed the lines from her fingers. "Woman, are you trying to kill yourself?" Expertly, he guided the team down the middle of the street and around the oncoming wagons.

"They wouldn't listen to me. These horses are as stubborn as old mules." She folded her arms over her chest and stared straight ahead.

"So are you," he muttered under his breath.

"I heard that. Insulting me will get you nowhere."

He slanted a purposely leering glance her way. His gaze dropped to the top of her bosom, the fullness not hidden by that high neckline or large bow. The thought of what lay beneath those garments sent a surprising shot of desire through his gut. He'd been on the trail too long if she had this kind of effect on him. "What about flattery, Mrs. Jordan? Will that get me into your good graces?"

Pink tinged her cheeks. "Mr. Travers, from you I'm afraid flattery is another form of insult."

Morgan was beginning to think the woman had no good graces. He turned his gaze back to the road, aware that looking at her was doing strange things to his libido. "Call me Morgan. May I be so bold as to call you Isabella?"

"I prefer Belle."

"Pretty name. Sorry, that sounded like flattery."

For the first time, she smiled. "I'll forgive you this time."

As he'd expected, the woman was striking when she smiled. "Looks as if we've made a little progress. Why don't we call a truce? If we're going to manage our enterprises together, we could be a little less hostile." He hoped his offer would pacify the woman. Yet, he had no intention of letting her stick her pretty nose in any of his business.

"As long as you're ready to accept me as an equal, I won't stand in your way as you manage our affairs."

"Deal." He stuck out his hand to her. Almost reluctantly, she accepted his gesture. Her hand was small and soft, but her grip was strong and firm.

He drove the buggy to the rear of the house near the stable. Jeb, the handy man, rushed out to meet them. Morgan leaped down and came around to assist Belle. He ignored her offered hand and set his hands on her waist. She let out a startled cry as he lifted her to the ground. For a moment longer than necessary, he held her to him. Her body was soft and inviting. Unwanted needs shot through him.

She lifted her gaze to his. He hadn't noticed how her eyes flashed with specks of gold. Her mouth opened in a surprised gasp that invited a kiss.

"Mr. Morgan."

Jeb's voice snapped Morgan out of his temporary stupor. Belle jerked out of his grip. He turned to the young man. "Belle, this still-wet-behind-the-ears puppy is our jack-of-all-trades. His mother is our cook and housekeeper. Jeb, meet Mrs. Jordan. She'll be staying at Eden House."

"Yes, sir." The young man doffed his hat. "I met the young'uns. The boys have been following me around all morning."

From the shadows of the stables the two youths appeared. The tall, slender youth led the way, the dark-skinned boy a few feet behind. "Miss Belle, they sure got a lot of horses. Jeb said he would teach me how to ride."

She gathered the younger boy in her arms. The older one slanted a wary glance at Morgan. "That's fine. If we're going to live here, you'll both need to learn."

"I'll teach them when I have time," Morgan said. "Now help Miss Belle with her packages."

"I hope you don't mind, but I charged my purchases to Eden House. I'll pay for them out of my share of the profits."

Morgan nodded. "I'm going to check out the ranch. I'll be back this evening when it's time to open." He held up his hand to stop her expected protests. "If we want any profits to pay your expenses, we have to operate Eden House as always."

She merely shrugged. "Of course. You did say this house is half mine, didn't you?"

"Yes. That's what the agreement says. I'll sign it as soon as Hayes draws it up."

"Thank you, Mr. . .Morgan. I'm looking forward to tonight." She turned to follow the boys.

He caught her arm. "Belle, keep the youngsters upstairs tonight. We don't want to corrupt them with our immoral activities."

"Don't worry, Morgan, I'll keep them on my side."

"Good." He opened the door for her. Did she say *on* her side, or *by* her side? It didn't matter as long as she didn't interfere with Louise and the girls.

"By the way, Morgan, which room is yours?"

His eyes grew wide. He lowered his voice to a whisper. "Are you planning to join me there tonight?"

"Curious is all."

"I have an apartment with a private entrance down the hallway off the kitchen. Be sure you knock before you come in."

With a wink, he tipped his hat and headed to his apartment to change.

Belle spent the better part of the day putting her plan into motion. With Abby's help, she inspected every room on the first floor and the sleeping chambers on the second floor. Louise and the girls weren't very happy to be roused out of their beds, but they realized that Belle had stepped in and taken her place as the owner of Eden House.

As she saw it, she had as much right to the house as Morgan and his girls. She and the children needed a decent place to live. And thanks to James, she had such a home.

With the assistance of the maid, Mrs. Franklin, a widow who came in daily to cook and clean, and Abby, they cleaned rooms and shifted the residents to their new quarters. She and the children would reside in the west wing, while Louise and the girls would be separated from them in the eastern side of the house. For herself, she chose the large corner room, the farthermost down the hall. Abby informed her that the chamber had once been her husband's. That seemed only right, as he'd deserted her so many years ago. She arranged for Rosalind and Beth to share her room, while Rory and Jerome slept across the hall.

Louise warned her she had better watch out for Morgan. He would have his say about her new rules and regulations. Belle told herself over and over she had every right to do this. After all, she owned half of Eden House.

The girls grumbled and complained as they moved their belongings to their newly assigned quarters. Belle felt it important that they were placed as far away as possible from the children. Thankfully, Eden House was large enough to afford them all their own privacy.

Louise had informed her that they opened their doors at five o'clock. The madam ignored Belle and went about her own business, readying the parlor for the customers.

After the children had been fed, Belle escorted them to their rooms and left them with Abby. With the expected confrontation with Morgan, she wanted them as far as possible from the parlors. Not to mention the semi-clad women who were now waiting for the coming explosion.

Belle troubled every nail on her hands waiting for Morgan. Jeb had informed her when he'd returned his horse to the stable and gone to his apartment. Now she paced the foyer waiting for his entrance.

She peeked out the windows and saw several men lounging near their horses on the front lawn. Checking the watch pinned to the collar of her white shirtwaist, she knew she had only minutes before the expected encounter. For a second, she was tempted to remove everything she'd spent the afternoon setting up.

Heavy footsteps on the polished floor announced Morgan's arrival. He stopped cold in the foyer. His gaze shifted from Belle to the signs she'd posted on the doors of the parlor and to the rope she'd draped down the center of the staircase. On one side she'd written "Eden House," and she'd named the other half "Hades Hall."

"What the hell is going on here?" he demanded. He placed his hands on his hips and glared down at Belle.

From the corner of her eye she spotted Louise staring at her and the girls covering their laughter with their hands. Belle's bravado melted under his fiery gaze. "Nothing. Your employees are awaiting your arrival, and I'm going to retire to my chamber."

He snatched the signs she'd printed, and tore them in half. "Is this your handiwork?"

She squared her shoulders. "Mr. Hayes explained that I own half of this house." Ignoring her trembling stomach, she gestured to the room. "I'm taking possession of my half."

Chapter 4

Morgan should have suspected she'd given in too easily. Never in his wildest imagination had he expected her to do something so preposterous. The woman had actually run a rope down the middle of the house.

"Your half? You divided the house in half?"

She lifted her chin and returned his glare. "Yes. The children and I will take the west wing; the women can have the east. I've measured and made sure everything is equal. They can have the front parlor; I'll take the rear. You have your office, and I'll use the library. Of course, we'll be forced to share the kitchen."

"Woman, you are out of your mind." He dug his nails into his palms to keep from wringing her pretty neck.

A flush swept over her face. She twisted her hands in her navy skirt. "Half a house is better than no house at all."

Seething, he grabbed her by the shoulders and turned her toward the stairs. "You had better hide in your half before I lose what little control I have left."

She glanced over her shoulder. "You have to admit this is best for the children."

He took one menacing step and she took off at a run. Lifting her skirts, she scurried up the stairs, carefully staying on her side of the rope. It was the dumbest thing he'd ever seen. A grin threatened at the corners of his lips. To actually attempt to divide the house in two equal parts. She had grit; he had to give it to her. Morgan was certain lack of time was the only thing that had stopped her from erecting a brick wall down the middle of the house.

"I told her you wouldn't like it," Louise said, coming to stand at his side. Her strong cologne teased his nostrils and made him sneeze. The memory of Belle's soft lavender fragrance drifted through his mind.

"I don't, but I'll let it go for tonight. We have customers waiting. I can deal with her tomorrow. Open the doors."

More customers than usual crowded into the parlor. Morgan played host, supervising the girls and keeping order. He suspected that many of their visitors were simply curious as to Belle's part in the house. They asked questions about the children and the widow. Morgan sidestepped their curiosity. What went on in the west side of the house was none of their business.

In spite of the crowd, the girls found themselves with few paying customers. By midnight, Morgan shut down the player piano and cleared the parlor. Only the men with money to go upstairs were permitted to stay. To make sure nothing untoward happened, Morgan personally escorted them to the girls' rooms, and he remained at the head of the stairs until the last of the customers departed.

In the silence of the early morning, Belle entered the kitchen. She'd slept little, worried about Morgan's reaction to her dividing the house in half.

He'd been so angry, she expected to see steam pouring from

his ears like a locomotive. Belle didn't care. She'd been as angry at his lack of concern for the children's welfare. If she had someplace else to go, she wouldn't stay under this roof one more minute. However, according to the inventory Mr. Hayes had provided, James had left her little cash and lots of property. She owned thousands of acres of land, but only one house.

Belle put on the coffee, and waited for it to brew. Thanks to the loud, jarring piano and raucous voices from the parlor, she'd been awake half the night. For additional security, she'd locked the door and shoved a bureau in front of it. She'd advised the boys to do the same.

While she waited for the coffee, she mixed up the pancake batter for the children. At the general store, she'd inquired about the school, and planned to escort the three older children to their classes. They'd been out of school long enough. She wondered if the people in Paradise would be more tolerant of Jerome than those in the south. He'd attended the Negro school in New Orleans, while Rory and Rosalind had gone to the white school. The little colored boy was sweet and intelligent. He deserved as fine an education as the others.

Before coming downstairs, she woke the children and told them they had to prepare for school. Rory protested he was too old, but after a mild rebuke, he obeyed.

She'd just put a stack of pancakes on the kitchen table when the four youngsters crept into the kitchen, still in their night-clothes. As the child did every morning, Beth ran into Belle's arms for her morning kiss. "Mama," she called. Belle scooped the little girl into her arms and gave her a big hug. Since Belle was the only mother the child knew, the little girl followed Rosalind's lead and accepted Belle as her mama.

Rosalind and the boys settled at the table, and Belle set Beth in a chair. "You'll have to eat up to make school on time."

Rory groaned. "Do I have to go, Miss Belle? I'm already smarter than them."

"That isn't saying much, Rory, since they're all much younger than you." She cut up a pancake for Beth, and handed the child a spoon.

"You'll never regret your education, boy." The raspy male voice came from the doorway.

Belle's heart sank. She wasn't ready to face Morgan. And she certainly didn't want a confrontation in front of the children.

He entered the room, his hair mussed and his jaw in need of a shave. Today he again wore a faded plaid shirt and canvas trousers. He reached for a cup and filled it from the coffeepot Belle had left on the stove. Lifting his gaze, he flashed her a lopsided grin. "You said we can share the kitchen."

Her heart fluttered. In spite of his disreputable appearance, the man was better looking than he'd been in the elegant black suit. The rough clothing enhanced his dangerous good looks.

"Help yourself." She didn't like the catch in her voice when she spoke to him. Belle set a plate in front of each child and willed her hands not to tremble under his stare.

"Got enough for a hungry man?" he asked, taking a chair beside Jerome.

With a nod, she piled the remaining pancakes on a plate. The children stopped eating to stare at Morgan.

"I don't believe I've been officially introduced to these youngsters. I'm Morgan." He smiled and nodded to the children.

"These handsome young men are Rory McGinnis and Jerome Johnson. The little one is Beth, and this is Rosalind." Her daughter dipped her head, and studied the food on her plate. "Honey, Mr. Morgan is your father's cousin. Maybe he can tell us something about the family."

Morgan frowned. "There isn't much to tell. Your grandparents died a long time ago. Then, your father and I both left Alabama when we weren't much older than Rory. Reckon I'm the only kin you've got."

Rosalind lifted expectant eyes to Morgan. This was the first real news she'd had of her father. "Are you my uncle?"

"No, honey, Mr. Morgan is a cousin." Belle poured syrup on Beth's pancakes. From the look on his face, she doubted that Morgan wanted to get close to the children.

"You didn't have to go to school?" Rory asked. "Looks like you did okay to me. Miss Belle said you own a silver mine and a ranch."

Morgan leveled a hard look at the boy. "I wish I could have stayed in school. In the coming years, a man will need a fine education if he wants to get ahead."

Relief flooded Belle. She whispered silent thanks for his unexpected encouragement. "Now hurry along. You don't want to be late your first day."

Jerome and Rosalind hurried their breakfast and darted for the door.

"I'll be up in a minute to help you get dressed. Rory, eat up."

The youth shoveled the remainder of his food into his mouth, then burped loudly. Belle knew when he was trying her patience. She set her hand on her hip and gave him her hardest stare. Rory shuffled out of the room in no hurry to get dressed for school. Morgan watched the exchange, but remained silent. He ate his pancakes and sipped his coffee.

Belle wiped Beth's mouth and lifted her from the chair. "You'll stay with Miss Abby while we go to the school." The little girl twisted her fingers in the chignon at Belle's nape. "You'll have such fun."

"No want Abby. Want Mama." Beth buried her face in Belle's shoulder.

Morgan lifted a questioning gaze to her. She read his thoughts, but chose to ignore them. Like most people who didn't know the child's background, he wanted to know if Elizabeth was her natural child. She didn't owe him or anybody else an explanation.

"Mrs. Jordan," Morgan said, surprising her with his formality. "I'll have Jeb hitch up a wagon and drive you and the children to the school house."

His offer shocked her. She'd expected to walk across town with the children in tow. "Thank you. We'll appreciate it. It's rather chilly this morning and I'm not quite sure of the school's location."

"You own half of the stable, so you might as well get some use out of it. Unless you plan to run a rope down the middle of the yard, too."

The man was as unpredictable as the Louisiana weather. One day he ran hot, the next cold, and then as furious as a hurricane in summer. Today, he was as warm as a May breeze.

"Tell Jeb we'll be ready shortly." Carrying the baby, she raced from the room. Her heart was thumping wildly, and her skin heated. The strangest sensations came over her whenever he was in the same room as she. She put the disconcerting thoughts aside. Belle had too much to deal with to bother with a good-looking man. A handsome devil, she reminded herself. One out to steal her soul, or her inheritance, she was sure.

Leaning against the wagon, Morgan turned up the collar of his jacket against the chill wind that had whipped up within the past few minutes. He didn't have time for this. For the past two days he'd served as driver for Belle, and today for her passel of children. She'd told him that James had only one child, Rosalind. The girl resembled her father. But what about the youngest, Beth? Who was her father? Not James, for certain. The little girl had pale blond hair and sparkling green eyes. Her former employer? Or had Isabella taken a lover? Could be the lady in question wasn't the paragon of virtue she pretended to be.

The slam of the door snapped him out of his thoughts. As

leader of the pack, Rory led the way to the wagon. "Jeez, it's cold. Do we have to go to school?"

Belle shooed the younger children toward the wagon. She looked like a mother hen gathering her chicks. "Yes." She lifted her gaze to Morgan. Her hair was covered with a hood, and she gathered her daughter in her cloak's warmth. "Where's Jeb?"

"He had to run an errand for his mother."

"Who's going to drive us?"

"I will." Morgan offered her a hand up, then climbed up beside her. "I want to teach you how to drive. Sooner or later you're going to have to handle a team. You might as well start now." He handed her the lines, and covered her hands with his. For a brief second, he wished they weren't wearing gloves. A flash of awareness shot through him. He ignored the feeling and tightened his grip. "Just follow my lead."

They drove slowly down a back road to the schoolhouse at the opposite edge of town. Belle was a fast learner, and he could have released her hands, if he were any kind of gentleman. He rather liked being beside her, feeling her shoulder pressed against his and holding her hands.

By the time they reached the school yard, he had to loosen his collar against the warmth that flooded him. He helped her down and promised to wait for her. His own work was falling behind, but he didn't want to leave her stranded. Besides, they needed to talk about the crazy situation at Eden House.

The three youngsters scurried from the wagon. As the oldest child, Rory charged ahead. Rosalind clung to her mother's hand, while Jerome hung to the rear. Morgan knew there were few colored in the county, and he wondered how the sepia-skinned boy would be received in the all-white school.

Curious, he followed at a short distance. Children were arriving in wagons, horseback, and on foot. Due to the brisk wind, they hurried into the classroom for warmth. Morgan stepped inside the doorway while Belle approached the teacher.

She glanced back at him, and then flashed a smile at the teacher. How anybody could resist that smile was beyond him. If the teacher were male, each of her children would finish the grade with straight A's. Morgan shook himself. When had he become aware of her smile, and when did he let it haunt his thoughts?

Belle garnered her resolve against the austere expression on the teacher's long, stern face. "Good morning. I'm Mrs. Jordan. I'd like to enroll my children in school."

"I'm Miss Lessman." The woman, a few years older than Belle, frowned down at her. "You're *that man's* wife."

"No. That is Mr. Travers. I'm Mrs. Jordan."

"I meant the one who killed himself by driving too fast."

In two days word of James Jordan's widow had spread like a swarm of bees through the town. She chose to ignore the censure in the teacher's voice. Who James was and what he did had no bearing on the children.

"We've only recently arrived in town, and the children need to return to school. This is Rory McGinnis, he's thirteen, my daughter Rosalind is six." She tugged Jerome from behind her. "Jerome is eight."

Miss Lessman looked her up and down, then studied the children. "That one can sit over there," she said, gesturing to Rory with her right arm. Her gaze dropped to Rosalind. "The girl can sit right here in front. That one has to leave." She dropped her voice to a whisper. "He's colored."

"He is?" Belle feigned surprise. "Jerome, did you know that you're colored?"

The other students had begun to take their seats, snickering behind her back. What sounded like muffled laughter came from Morgan.

"Yes, ma'am. My mama used to call me sweet brown sugar. So I reckon I am." The boy lifted sad dark eyes. For too much of his young life, he'd known prejudice and bigotry.

Exasperated, she place her hand on the child's head. "His

name is Jerome, and he's very intelligent. He's well-behaved and he'll be a fine addition to your class.''

The teacher tilted her nose. ''Mrs. Jordan, I do not make the rules. I only enforce them. If you don't like the rule, you'll have to contact the school board. Now I have a class to teach.'' Her words were a clear dismissal.

Belle opened her mouth to protest, when a hand touched her elbow. ''Mrs. Jordan, we'll take it up with the school board.'' Morgan tightened his grip and tugged her backward.

''But . . .'' she began.

''Mr. Travers is right. Only the school board can change the rules. You'll have to take him home. The others may stay.'' The teacher turned her back and moved to the chalkboard.

''Let's go,'' Morgan said in a tone that brooked no argument.

Belle brushed Rory's cap from his tumbled hair, and gave him an encouraging smile. The boy had never been fond of school, but he would do as Belle said. ''Behave, and don't forget your manners.''

He squared his shoulders and strutted away, swinging his lunch bucket from his hand. Belle recognized his forced bravado.

Leaning over her daughter, she gave Rosalind a kiss. ''I'll come by this afternoon to pick you up.''

Tears glittered in the back of the girl's eyes. ''Okay, Mama. I'll be real good.'' She lowered her voice and said, ''I wish Jerome could stay, too.''

''So do I, darling.'' Her heart clenched as her daughter settled at a desk. Belle draped her arm across Jerome's shoulder and allowed Morgan to usher them from the schoolhouse. She knew the children were in for a tough time. As the newcomers, they would have to work extra hard to be accepted.

''They'll be fine,'' Morgan said in an effort to placate her fears. In spite of their differences, she was thankful for his support.

At the door she glanced back and shivered under the teacher's contemptuous gaze. Though she couldn't imagine why, the woman didn't like her one bit. Belle suspected that as the widow Jordan she was doomed to the suspicion of the good people of the town. Living under the roof of Eden House didn't help her reputation, nor did being seen so often with Morgan Travers. She suspected that his and her late husband's characters weren't the most esteemed in town.

At the wagon, he helped her into the high seat. Jerome scurried to the bed, and huddled under the blanket Morgan had brought for the children. "We'll continue our lessons as soon as we get back home," she said to reassure the child.

"Yes, ma'am. I rather stay where I can help you and Mr. Morgan. I'm a real good worker. I'll feed the horses, and clean up the stable, and run errands." In spite of his bravado, she noted the sadness at being left out.

Morgan grinned at the boy. The warmth in his gaze sent a tingle to the middle of Belle's chest. "I could use a helper. But you have to do your lessons first."

"Yes, suh, Mr. Morgan. I'll study real hard."

"I'll talk to the school board and see what I can do, Belle. I'm not sure if I carry much weight with the sanctimonious town leaders. They never much liked James and me. Or the women at Eden House, either. The men, well, let's say most of them have visited the house a time or two."

"Thank you, Morgan, I'd appreciate any help you can give."

"Here," he said. "Take the reins, it's time for another lesson. I might not be available to drive you back to pick up the children."

Without his hands on hers, handling the team was harder than it had seemed. When she slowed the horses to barely a walk, Morgan laughed. "They can go a little faster. We'll never get home at this rate." He covered her hands and shook the lines. "They're well-trained, so it takes little handling to make them go at whatever pace you prefer."

Her breath caught. "This is fast enough. What if I can't stop them?"

"Yell, 'whoa,' and pull hard. They'll understand what you want. Horses aren't stupid, they know their jobs."

She swallowed hard. His nearness and the touch of his hands had her heart pounding in time with the team's hooves. Was she so lonely that the first handsome man who came around made her forget the vows she'd made to keep her distance from a man who was not only related to him, but was exactly like James? She was too old to let her head be turned by looks and charm.

"Let me try again. With Jeb busy, I'll have to learn to arrange my own transportation. There are no streetcars or hansom cabs in Paradise."

He removed his fingers and she took a deep breath. He was right. As long as she kept a firm hand, the horses did her bidding. She breathed a sigh of relief when they reached the rear door of Eden House. Pulling gently, she slowed the team. "I did it."

"You did. A little more practice, and we won't be able to keep you home." He jumped down and came around the wagon.

She stood to climb down and tripped on her skirt. He caught her by the waist before she tumbled from the wagon. "Watch it." His hands tightened, and he lowered her to the ground.

"I'll be more careful from now on." She lifted her gaze. His deep blue eyes darkened to midnight. Lightning sizzled between them. The cool breeze chilled her face, but her insides heated to boiling. Her fingers rested on his jacket. Under the heavy leather, his chest was hard and firm.

Over the years, she'd avoided contact with handsome men, men who could break her heart as James had done. Now she found herself in the arms of the one man who could destroy both her life and that of the children. She came to her senses and shoved him away. "I'd better get in."

His face hardened, as if he, too, had realized that he'd made a mistake. "Jerome can come with me while I stable the horses." He climbed back into the wagon. "By the way, we have to talk. Meet me in the study in ten minutes."

Belle's stomach lurched. From the tone of his voice, she knew a confrontation was brewing. Morgan had made it clear he wasn't happy about the way she'd divided the house. She watched him drive off, with Jerome clinging to the sideboards. At least he hadn't blasted her in front of the children. For that small favor, she was grateful. However, there was no way he was going to run her and the children out of Eden House.

In spite of its notorious reputation, Eden House was her home and she intended to stay. Regardless of what Mr. Morgan Travers said.

Morgan didn't have time for this. He had a ranch to run as well as the house. Dealing with Belle Jordan took too much of his strength and was sapping his energy. She had him in a state of total confusion. He entered the house by the kitchen, where Abby was playing with the youngest girl. The young woman looked up at Morgan.

"Mrs. Jordan is in the study, sir," she said. "I'm looking after Beth."

He nodded his thanks, and headed for the hallway. He opened the study door to find the fire blazing and the room cozy and warm. Pausing for a moment, he watched Belle from the doorway. She was staring into the fire, a teacup in her hand. He couldn't deny the woman was lovely. Not for the first time, he wondered why James had deserted her so soon after their marriage.

"We didn't often use the fireplace in New Orleans. Only in the dead of winter. Mostly we use gas heat." She turned to face him.

Morgan started. He hadn't known she'd seen him enter. The woman must have eyes in the back of her head. He slipped out of his jacket and hooked it behind the door. "Compared to your sultry climate, this must be like the North Pole."

"It isn't too bad. We'll get used to it." She picked up the teapot. "Would you like a cup?"

"Mrs. Jordan, I need something a bit stronger than tea."

"Isn't it early in the day for liquor?" Her words held a definite hint of censure.

"I meant coffee. Do you happen to have any coffee in that pot?"

She frowned. "Only tea." Quickly, she poured a cup and offered it to him.

Grimacing, he accepted the cup and settled in the chair across from her. "I hate tea."

"The English swear by tea, but in New Orleans, we like our coffee laced with chicory."

"I know. It's as dark and thick as the Mississippi. At least we agree on one thing." He sipped the tea and studied her over the rim of the cup.

"Where's Jerome?" she asked, meeting his gaze without flinching.

"I left him in the stable. He wanted to spend some time with the horses."

"I'm not surprised. He loves animals. I had to stop him from bringing home every stray dog and cat in town." She set the cup aside and folded her hands in her lap.

"You seem like a fine woman, Mrs. Jordan. How did you happen to become involved with a cad like James?"

Pain sparked in her amber eyes. "You could call it the follies of youth, but I can't use that as an excuse. I was of an age to know better." She shifted her gaze to the dancing flames in the fireplace. The light reflected in her eyes, adding a golden sparkle behind her thick eyelashes. "I'd grown up as the daughter of a wealthy man's housekeeper. We were treated very well by Mr. Robinson, a kind, warm-hearted gentleman."

She bit her lip as if wondering how to go on. "After finishing

school, I took a clerk's job in Daniel Holmes's department
store on Canal Street. I met James when he came in to purchase
some shirts. He asked me to recommend a fine restaurant, and
invited me to dine with him.''

He chuckled softly. ''I'd wondered where James was spending his time.''

Her eyes glittered with unshed tears. ''He was handsome
and attentive to a twenty-four-year-old woman who'd resigned
herself to spinsterhood. He swept me off my feet. After just a
week, we married. You saw the photograph. I dragged James
into a studio on Frenchman Street.'' She let out a bark of bitter
laughter. ''It was all I had left when he disappeared the next
day with my life's savings.''

Morgan's heart twisted at the pain on her face. He remembered the days he and James had spent in New Orleans. He'd
spent his time gambling and looking for another scheme. ''I
suppose I'm partially to blame. I'd heard about Paradise, and
convinced James the mining town was easy pickings. We left
New Orleans together, and headed west.''

''I suppose he neglected to mention he'd married a wife.''

''Never a word.'' Guilt nagged at Morgan. He hadn't even
bothered to ask James where he'd been. When his cousin had
hesitated to join him, he'd convinced him that they could find
their fortune in the west. ''What did you do?''

''I went back to work, and when I learned I was in the family
way, I returned to my mother. She took me in, and when
Rosalind was born, Mr. Robinson insisted I stay. Not long
afterward, my mother died, and I took her place as the housekeeper. It was a safe, comfortable home for my daughter.''

He nodded. ''James is Rosalind's father. Who's Beth's
father?''

''I don't know.''

Morgan nearly choked on his tea. ''You don't know? Did
you have so many lovers you don't know who fathered your

hild? Was it your Mr. Robinson? You don't have any right
o look down your nose at these women, when your morals
ren't any better than theirs. In fact, they don't make any bones
bout what they are. While you pretend to be the paragon of
irtue.''

Chapter 5

The blood drained from her face. Angry shivers poured over her. Surging to her feet, she folded her hands into fists to resist the temptation to slap the smug look off his face.

"Mr. Travers, I shouldn't dignify your accusation with an explanation. Your assessment of my moral character is reprehensible. You admit you're responsible for my husband abandoning me, and now you have the unmitigated gall to accuse me of immorality?"

"I call them as I see them." He glared right back at her, his eyes as dark and foreboding as the depths of hell.

"Then perhaps you need eyeglasses." She spun away from him, too angry to hold a coherent conversation.

"Hold on." He caught her arm before she reached the door and tugged her to a halt. "What do you mean?"

"Please unhand me." She brushed his hand from her arm. "I don't know the identity of Elizabeth's father, because her mother died giving birth. She never mentioned his name, and I didn't ask."

His face blanched. "You aren't her mother? She calls you Mama."

She rubbed her arm to wipe away the tingles from his touch. "I'm the only mother the child has ever known. What do you suppose she should call me? Mrs. Jordan? Or Miss Belle, like the boys?"

He had the good graces to gesture to the chairs. "I apologize for my ignorance. Please sit down."

Belle struggled to regain her composure. Returning to her chair, she met his troubled gaze. "I met a young woman while I was doing a bit of charity work. She was staying in a hovel, with no food or heat. She was very ill and about to deliver a child. From the little she told me, she didn't have a husband or family. Mr. Robinson agreed to allow her to live with us. I took care of her, but she was too weak to survive childbirth." Her voice wavered at the thought of the loss of a young life. "I promised to take care of her child as if she were my own. I've kept that promise. There was no way I could consider sending that beautiful infant to an orphanage. With Mr. Robinson's help, and that of his attorney, we arranged that I should have custody of the baby. I'm her mother, and that's all anybody needs to know."

Morgan nodded, his eyes soft with understanding. "Forgive me for being so obtuse. What about the boys? How did you happen to find them?"

On a sigh, she refilled her teacup. "Rory's parents died of the yellow fever. He tried to pick Mr. Robinson's pocket. The police wanted to lock the boy away, but Mr. Robinson wouldn't hear of it. The boy was ragged and hungry. My employer offered to take responsibility for the boy, and we took him into our home. A few months ago, Jerome came to our door begging for food. His mother had died, and he didn't know his father. I couldn't let the child starve, so I offered him a home with us."

"Sounds like you had a house full of orphans. Did you also take in dogs and cats?"

She couldn't help smiling. "On occasion. Mr. Robinson regularly brought home strays to feed. I managed to find homes for three dogs and four cats before I left New Orleans."

"He sounds like quite a man, this Mr. Robinson."

"He was a wonderful gentleman. He allowed my mother to take me in when I was expecting and too ill to work. Could I do any less for the orphans without a place to go? I would take in a dozen children if I had the means. When my employer died, he left his estate to me."

He lifted a thick black eyebrow. "You're quite the heiress, aren't you?" The bullheaded man didn't even try to hide the reproach in his voice.

"I learned that my legacy was worthless. Mr. Robinson lost his money with bad investments. We had to sell the house and the contents to satisfy his creditors. I was left with barely enough to pay our passage west." Tired of his criticism, she stood. "Now if you'll excuse me, I'd like to get Jerome started on his lessons."

"One moment, Mrs. Jordan. We still have to discuss this situation with the house."

Belle had been anticipating and dreading the confrontation. "I thought I'd divided it fairly."

"Since you insist on staying here, we might as well get a few things straight. You're right, it wouldn't be good to subject the children to the goings-on at night. I've given your situation a lot of consideration. You can let them have the run of the downstairs during the day. At five o'clock, we open for business. You and the children can use the kitchen and the rear stairs. The girls and Louise will use the parlor and their share of the upstairs chambers."

His offer was much more generous than she'd expected. After all, she was the newcomer, the intruder in his enterprises. "That seems fair." She started to rise when the knocker sounded on the front door. "Who could be calling this morning?"

Morgan stood and headed for the foyer. "I'll find out."

Accustomed to answering the door, Belle followed at his heels. He snatched open the door, and stopped cold. "Hayes, what are you doing here?"

Disgusted with Morgan's continued rudeness, Belle shoved him aside. "Mr. Hayes, how good to see you." She flashed a smile to the lawyer. "Please come in."

Morgan grunted, but unblocked the doorway. Corbett Hayes removed his hat and entered the foyer.

"Thank you, Mrs. Jordan." He glanced at the stairway where the rope divided the house in half. Considering the number of men who'd frequented the house the past night, word of Belle's plan had spread throughout the town.

She took Corbett's arm. "We were having tea in the study. Will you join us?"

"Certainly, Mrs. Jordan. I would be delighted," he answered, offering his arm.

Belle placed her fingers on his forearm. With Morgan hot on their heels, she ushered the lawyer to the study. "Please sit down, Mr. Hayes. Would you care for tea?" Ignoring Morgan, who'd settled behind the large desk, she gestured Hayes to the chair Morgan had vacated earlier.

"I can't think of a better way to begin the day than with a lovely woman and a warm cup of tea." Lifting the tails of his coat, he took the overstuffed chair the faced the fireplace.

"Did you come over here for tea, Hayes, or did you have business to conduct?" Morgan plucked one of his sickening cigars from the humidor and stuck it into his mouth.

The man was doing his best to aggravate Belle, much like Rory did when he wanted attention or when Belle disciplined him. His juvenile behavior didn't faze her in the least. She filled a cup for Mr. Hayes and offered it to him.

"Thank you, Mrs. Jordan." He settled back and flashed a charming smile.

He was quite handsome, with his blond hair and pale gray eyes. Yet, he faded in comparison with Morgan's darker good looks. Together the men reminded her of the paintings of the devil and angel side by side. She wondered if this was an accurate comparison of the men. Was Morgan the devil she supposed, and Hayes the angel? From all she'd seen so far it certainly was possible.

Belle chose to ignore Morgan and turned her attention to Corbett Hayes. "Mr. Hayes, have you drawn up the partnership papers for Mr. Travers and me?"

He reached into his pocket and pulled out an envelope. "Here they are, exactly as you requested. A copy for you and one for Travers." Opening the envelope, he passed one copy to Belle and set the other on the low table between them. "All you have to do is sign them to make the partnership legal."

She studied the document, and glanced at Morgan from the corner of her eye. He surged from his chair and in a few long strides, snatched his copy of the paper from the table. Clamping his teeth on the cigar, he scanned the paper, while Belle studied every word, phrase, and paragraph.

The document simply named Mrs. Isabella Jordan and Mr. Morgan Travers equal partners in the Eden House and the J & T Mining Company and Ranch. There was no mention as to managing partner, or silent partner. They agreed to share equal liability and profits. Belle sighed with relief. At last she would have a bit of security for the children.

"It seems fine with me. How about you, Mr. Travers?" She stood and moved to the desk. Hayes jumped to his feet. Morgan dropped into his chair in his usual lack of manners. "May I use your pen?"

He slammed his copy of the agreement onto the desk. "You might as well. You're half owner."

Belle dipped the pen into the ink and with precise movements signed her name to the proper line. She passed her copy to Morgan for his signature. He plucked the pen from her fingers and scrawled his name next to hers. Then he signed his copy and shoved it to her with the pen.

"Thank you," she said in an effort to control her temper. It was just too bad that he wasn't happy with the situation. He was stuck with her, as she was stuck with him. Belle hoped she hadn't sold her soul to the devil. She felt as if that was exactly what she'd done.

Hayes approached and stood beside Belle. "I've also brought copies of the various titles to the properties. I've had James's name changed to yours. You now legally own everything that had been your husband's."

"Thank you, Mr. Hayes. If you'll send us a bill for your services, I'll see that it's paid promptly." She stuck out her hand. To her surprise, the lawyer took her fingers in his, and lifted them to his lips. His kiss was short, and much too personal for a business transaction. By the gleam in his eyes, she suspected that his interest was as much personal as professional.

"I'll take care of the fee like I always do." Morgan folded his copy of the document and shoved it into the desk drawer. "I'm sure you have other clients to see, Hayes. You can go now."

Belle shot an angry glance at Morgan. The man was too rude for words. "Would you care for more tea?" She caught the lawyer by the arm and ushered him back to the fireplace. Some devilment inside her made Belle invite the lawyer simply to irritate Morgan. "Perhaps you can fill me in on the activities in Paradise. I started the children in school today." After settling in her chair, she refilled Corbett's teacup. "Is there a church in town? We always attended services in New Orleans."

"I have things to do," Morgan growled. "You two can sip your tea and socialize. If you need me, I'll be upstairs with Louise." His heavy footsteps stomped down the hallway and up the stairs.

His words sliced through her heart. Belle didn't need a knock upside her head to know why he was going to see Louise. Obviously he had taken James's place as the madam's lover. That she cared for Morgan bruised like a stone in the shoe. What her irascible partner did was none of her affair unless it concerned their business.

"We have a church, and a fine minister." The sound of the lawyer's voice pulled her out of her thoughts. "I would be delighted to escort you this Sunday, if I'm not being too forward."

She forced her attention from Morgan to Hayes. "I would like that very much. I've met a few of the merchants, but I would like to become acquainted with the women in town."

"I'll be happy to show you around our fair community."

For the next few minutes, Belle halfway listened to the lawyer extol the virtues of the small town. Of course it didn't nearly compare with the ambience of New Orleans, but since this was now her home, she tried not to make the comparison. With the other half of her mind, she wondered about Morgan. The very idea that she would allow his whereabouts to enter her thoughts angered her. She smiled at the lawyer, and wondered how she could politely get him to leave.

"You're still here, Hayes? I thought you'd be out fleecing somebody else by now." Morgan's strong voice came from the doorway.

Belle jerked her gaze to him. Seeing him and hearing his mocking tone didn't bother her. What shocked her most was that he held Elizabeth in his arms. The little girl had her fingers twisted in his hair, and her face buried in his shoulder. Of all the men in the world, he was the least likely to befriend the young child.

"Morgan!" she called, annoyed by yet another show of poor manners.

"I found your youngest child looking for her mama." He

emphasized Belle's relationship with the child for the lawyer's benefit.

As if on cue, Beth stretched out her arms and called, "Mama."

Belle stood and raced to the door. In a way she was upset at the interference. On the other hand, she was grateful for the excuse to get rid of the lawyer. She liked the man, but found him on the boring side. As she reached for Beth, the child changed her mind and clung to Morgan's shoulder. "Want Morgie," she said.

Hayes leaped to his feet. "Travers is right. I have another appointment this morning." He settled his hat on his head, and bowed gallantly. "I'll pick you and the children up for church on Sunday at ten o'clock, if it's agreeable?"

"It's fine, Mr. Hayes."

He caught both her hands in his. "Please call me Corbett. I believe we're going to be very good friends."

"Thank you, Corbett. I appreciate your help." She slipped her hands free. The man was a little too sure of himself. She'd encountered too many lawyers in the past years to trust any of them.

Morgan stood statue still in the doorway, while Beth tugged on his ears and hair. "He's being well paid for his services."

"Let me show you out, Corbett," she said in an effort to soften Morgan's boorishness.

"He knows the way," Morgan said. "He's been here often enough. By the way, Hayes, Vivian was asking about you. You haven't been to see her in about a week or so."

Corbett's face pinked. "I've been busy."

Before Belle could usher the lawyer down the hallway, Morgan shoved Beth into her arms. The child protested with a loud squeal and refused to relinquish her grip on Morgan's hair. He yelped.

"Like Morgie," the child said, tightening her hold, refusing to leave the man.

"It's okay, sweetheart. Morgan likes Beth, too." He jiggled the child to quiet her protests.

Belle set her hands on her hips and waited until the door closed behind the lawyer. Unable to hold her temper another moment, she lashed out at Morgan. "Mr. Travers, that was the worst display of uncivilized behavior I have ever witnessed. Your rudeness is inexcusable."

A crooked grin lifted one corner of his mouth. "You come from a city and society noted for good manners. Paradise is different. We say what we think and damn the consequences."

"I do not believe that simple courtesy is territorial. You are rude because you choose to be rude. You show contempt for everybody around you." She reached out for the child. "I'll take my child, if you please. I don't want you to corrupt her with your language or impertinence."

He handed the child over to her. "I never claimed to be a gentleman. This should prove it."

With the child in her arms, he gripped her shoulders and pulled them both into his wide chest. His face lowered, and Belle gasped when she recognized his intent. He covered her mouth with his. Caught off guard, she opened her mouth to protest. His tongue slipped between her lips and stroked her teeth. Heat spread through her like an inferno. Her stomach trembled and her knees grew weak. She tightened her grip on the child, unable to either shove him away or draw him closer. Belle didn't know which she would do.

She'd never experienced a bold, all-consuming kiss like Morgan's. Even James, when he'd made love to her on their wedding night, hadn't made her blood sing as Morgan did. His thumb stroked her throat, and goose bumps spread over her skin. He ended the kiss, and stepped away.

Belle staggered, and Morgan tightened his grip to steady her. His blue eyes gleamed with passion. He was right, no gentleman would kiss like that.

And no lady would stand by and allow such liberties.

Stepping away, she glared at him. A devilish grin that said he'd gained the upper hand curved his lips. "That proves my point, Mr. Travers. You have the manners of a gorilla."

He swept his arm in an extravagant bow. "Thank you, ma'am."

Growling under her breath in ways a lady would never entertain, she stormed from the office, leaving him grinning at her back. The man unnerved her more than any human she'd ever encountered. Even the lawyer who'd clearly stolen her inheritance didn't infuriate her as Morgan Travers had. He'd done everything possible to infuriate her, and he'd done a darn good job.

Morgan's lips tingled from the kiss. He'd only intended to taunt her and irritate her. Little did he think he would be the one whose blood heated to the boiling point. Or that he would find himself yearning for more than a stolen kiss.

He cursed his unfulfilled needs. Isabella Jordan was the last woman with whom he wanted to become involved. Not only was she his cousin's widow, she was a shrew in the worst sense. To alleviate his frustrations, he removed the rope from the stairway, and rolled it up in a loop. He was sorely tempted to use it to tie the woman up to keep her out of trouble.

As he reached the top of the stairs with the coil of rope, he found Louise watching him. A wry smile danced across her painted lips. Below was the woman James had married, in front of him was the one his cousin had royally duped.

"Have you set the widow Jordan straight?" she asked. Louise stepped out of the shadows. To anybody who didn't know her, she looked like any respectable woman in the town. Her dark green dress was modestly cut, and her hair neatly coiled at her nape.

Morgan didn't want her to know that the woman had set him right on his ear. "I explained that she and the children can have the run of the house during the day. In the evening they are relegated to the rear parlor, the kitchen, and their half of the upper rooms.''

Louise laughed. ''She didn't strike me as a woman who would be easily dissuaded.''

''I can handle her.''

''Why don't you take her and those children out to the ranch? She won't be able to interfere if she's out of the way.''

''It wouldn't be proper for a woman out there alone with the men. You know the cabin isn't fit for four youngsters and a woman. Besides, she's enrolled the two older children in school. She'll teach Jerome here.''

''Sounds like we're stuck with the whole crew of trouble.''

''Temporarily, until I figure out how to get rid of them.'' He looked her over. ''You're up awfully early.''

''I got to sleep earlier than usual last night. Thought I'd see what the morning is like.'' She started down the stairs. ''Hope there's coffee in the kitchen.'' Pausing, she glanced at Morgan. ''We do have use of the kitchen, I understand.''

''Yes. Though you might have to move around a pack of kids to get to the table.''

''I grew up with a half dozen siblings. Reckon I can manage around three or four.''

Morgan paused to stare at her back, ramrod straight, and her chin held high. He hadn't thought about her past, that she might have family somewhere. ''I don't know much about kids. There was just James and I in a one-room cabin on that Alabama dirt farm. It was all that was left after the Yankees burned the plantation to the ground.''

''I wasn't much better off. I ran away with the first man that noticed I was a woman.'' The bitterness in her tone matched his own distressed childhood.

''I left home before I could shave.'' He fell into step beside her. ''Don't worry about Belle. Things will work out. After a while she'll realize they can't stay here and they'll leave.''

She tilted one shapely eyebrow. "It's Belle is it? And I understand you drove her and the children to the school house."

"I didn't want her to walk, and she didn't know how to handle the team."

By then they'd reached the foyer. "I'll take this rope out to the stable, then I have to run an errand. Enjoy your coffee." He glanced toward the end of the hallway and glimpsed Belle darting into the rear parlor. So she'd been spying on him and Louise. He hoped she'd gotten an eyeful. "On second thought, I'll join you in a cup before I leave."

Taking his offered arm, Louise looped her arm in his. "Why did I have to fall for James and not you?"

He laughed. "Because I'm a worse cad than he ever thought of being."

"Somebody had better warn Belle of that."

"I think the lady can handle things all on her own."

"I believe you're right. But can you?"

Belle hadn't seen Morgan since she'd spied him and Louise descend the stairs arm in arm. They seemed to be quite a cozy pair. Were they more than employer and employee? Did they share secrets? Had Morgan taken James's place in her bed? The idea of Louise with Morgan brought a jealous twinge to Belle's heart. Common sense chased away the unwanted emotion.

She touched her fingers to her lips. The tingles from his kiss remained and made her yearn for more. Never had she imagined that a kiss could be so all-consuming. Nor had she ever supposed that a man could make her heart pound and her brain turn to oatmeal. She chided herself under her breath. A man like Morgan was the worst kind of scoundrel. While bedding one woman, he'd been toying with another.

It would be best for all if she kept in mind exactly who and what Morgan Travers was. He was partner-in-crime with the husband who'd broken her heart and left his child without a father. Morgan would cheat her out of the home she valued and toss her out in the cold. Not only would she be hurt, but four innocent children would be left homeless. Belle had best guard her inheritance as well as her heart.

She shoved aside the financial records she'd been studying, and glanced at Beth asleep on the davenport. Not wanting to venture into Morgan's study, she'd made herself at home in the rear parlor. The records seemed in order, and it appeared that Eden House was operated at a profit. She didn't like it, but it looked as if they needed the income to keep the ranch operating until it could become solvent.

A headache threatened, but she refused to give in to the pain. In an hour, she would have to leave to pick up the children at school. She hoped their first day at school was successful. It was always hard to start at a new school especially in a new town.

The knocker at the front door broke into her reverie. Knowing that Mrs. Franklin and Abby were busy upstairs, she jumped up to see who was calling so early in the afternoon. If it was a customer, she planned to send the man packing with words that would burn his ears.

She snatched open the door. A vaguely familiar, tall, well-built man stood on the porch. "I'm sorry, Eden House is not open for customers." As she began to slam the door in the man's face, he stopped her with a hand to the door.

"I'm not a customer, Mrs. Jordan." He shoved a box toward her. "I'm Dan Sullivan."

Eyes wide, she stared at the man. Recognition dawned slowly. "Sheriff? Is something wrong? Did somebody send for you?"

"No, ma'am. I came to call on you."

"Call on me?"

"To offer my condolences. You know, for the loss of your husband. May I come in?"

"Yes, of course." She gestured the man into the house. "Please come into the rear parlor. I left my daughter sleeping on the davenport."

He removed his hat and fell into step at her side. "I brought you some candy."

"The children will enjoy it." She accepted the box, and nodded her thanks. Belle didn't understand what the man wanted. She'd only seen him once, and then he'd leveled his shotgun at her.

"I want to apologize, ma'am, for the way I acted when we first met. I didn't mean to scare you and those young'uns." He removed his jacket and hat. His brown hair was neatly trimmed, and his face was freshly shaved. He was rather nice looking, in a rugged way, exactly the opposite of Corbett Hayes, though he was several years younger. She guessed the sheriff to be a few years her junior.

"It was a terrible misunderstanding, Sheriff. I'm sure you meant no harm." *Except to blow me to kingdom come,* she thought. "Would you like some coffee?"

"That would be nice." He stood awkwardly in the middle of the room, his hat in his hand.

Feeling equally ill at ease, she hurried to the kitchen. "Abby, will you prepare a pot of coffee?"

"Yes, ma'am, I'll be glad to." The young woman rushed to the stove and filled a china pot with the coffee that she kept warm on a burner. "Do you want me to serve it to you in the parlor?"

"With two cups, sugar and cream, if you please." Belle hurried back to the parlor. The sheriff hadn't moved from his spot.

"Please have a seat, Sheriff Sullivan," she gestured to a chair beside the davenport.

"Thank you, Mrs. Jordan. Why don't you call me Dan?"

Belle returned to her seat at the secretary where she'd been working. An awkward silence hovered between them. "You didn't have to bring gifts or apologize. I understand you were only doing your job.''

''After that terrible reception, I wanted to properly welcome you to Paradise. I hope you'll enjoy staying here.''

At that moment, Abby entered the doorway. ''Here's your coffee, Miss Belle.'' She stopped cold when she spotted the sheriff seated on the wing chair near Belle. Eyes wide and her face pale, she set the tray on the table. ''What are you doing here, Sheriff Dan?''

''I'm calling on Mrs. Jordan.''

A long shadow darkened the doorway. ''Calling on Mrs. Jordan? What are you talking about?'' Morgan stomped into the room like a fiery dragon. He spun on Belle. ''What do you think you're doing, woman? First you're flirting outrageously with Corbett Hayes, and now Dan Sullivan.''

''Morgan, you made a scene this morning. Please dig up a modicum of courtesy,'' she ground between her teeth. To make things worse, the loud voices woke Beth and she began to whimper. Belle settled on the divan beside the child and rubbed her back. ''Look what you've done. You've upset the baby.''

''Your husband has only been dead for a few months. You should be in mourning.'' Morgan flopped down in the chair opposite the sheriff, leaving Abby staring at the confrontation.

Belle gritted her teeth to control her temper. ''James Jordan deserted me seven years ago. He's been dead to me for a very long time. I am not mourning him, nor do I intend to stop my life. I can allow whomever I please to call on me. I do not need your permission to receive callers.''

''Well, it's time to fetch the children from school, or have you forgotten?''

''No, I haven't forgotten a thing.'' Especially his rudeness. ''Sheriff, I'm sorry, I have to leave.'' She lifted Beth in her arms.

The child nearly leaped toward Morgan. ''Want Morgie.''

Morgan reached out and took the child from Belle. "See your suitor to the door and I'll go hitch up the team."

Not wanting to argue with Morgan in front of a guest, she offered her hand to the sheriff. "Forgive Morgan's rudeness, Sheriff. Please feel free to call on us at any time."

"Yes, ma'am, I'd like that real fine." Dan Sullivan took her slender fingers into his large, rough hand.

Leading him to the door, Belle glimpsed Abby standing in the hallway watching. The young woman's face was blanched, and her mouth pulled into a frown. Belle had no idea what had upset Abby. Whatever it was, she would have to deal with it later. As soon as the sheriff left, she would have to confront the detestable Morgan Travers.

Once Dan Sullivan was on his way, she hurried back to the rear parlor. To her surprise, it was empty. Abby had disappeared, as had Morgan and Beth. Setting her hands on her hips, she let out a huff of steam. Since it was nearly time to fetch the children from school, she draped her cape over her shoulders and headed for the rear door.

Because he'd disappeared didn't mean that Mr. Morgan Travers was off the hook. Belle had a score to settle with the man, and the sooner they defined their relationship, the sooner they could bring a bit of peace to the explosive situation.

Chapter 6

Morgan stopped the wagon at the kitchen door and waited. He'd behaved like a horse's rear end. It was pure devilment that made him torment Belle. For some odd reason, he didn't like the way Dan Sullivan had been looking at her. The sheriff had no business trying to court a newly widowed woman. Especially when Morgan's property was at stake.

He'd wrapped little Beth in a blanket and held her safely in his arms. Jerome was in the back, kneeling to peer over the seat.

Belle stepped onto the rear porch and stared at Morgan. Fire flashed in her eyes. He grinned, knowing she wouldn't lash out at him with the children within earshot.

"Here's your mama, little one," he said, loud enough for Belle to realize he held the child in his arms.

"What is Elizabeth doing here? I assumed she was with Abby." Belle reached out her hands to the child.

"I thought she would enjoy the ride. It's warmed up quite a bit, and I'll see that she doesn't get cold."

Belle glanced to the rear where Jerome was clinging to the seat. "I suppose it's all right. The others should be getting out of school any minute." Climbing beside him, she hugged her cape around her shoulders.

Beth laughed and wiggled in Morgan's arms. "All these youngsters should learn to drive a team and ride. I'll make a point to teach them." He wrapped his hands around the child's on the lines. "Say 'giddy-up,' Beth. Watch the horses go."

"Isn't she awfully young?" Her shoulders brushed his as the horses broke into a trot.

"No. Out here children learn to ride before they walk."

"Mr. Morgan, will you teach me, too?" Jerome asked, his voice soft with longing.

"Of course, son. You have to learn how to get around."

Belle huffed, but didn't say anything. He was certain she would have plenty to say if they were alone. That thought made him chuckle under his breath.

"May I ask what you find humorous?"

He lowered his gaze to the child in his arms. "Bethie and I are having fun, aren't we, sweetheart?" He glanced over his shoulder. The boy's sad dark eyes stared ahead. "Climb up here, Jerome, and you can give us a hand."

"Can I, Miz Belle?" he asked with hope in his voice.

She scooted over and gestured the boy between them.

"Over here, Jerome. Always drive from this side." Morgan shifted closer to Belle, giving the boy room at the end of the seat. His shoulder pressed to hers, and he gave the child plenty of room to join them. He held the reins and let the boy place his hands on the leather lines.

"If you get any closer, you'll be sitting on my lap," she whispered.

"Interesting proposition. One I might consider, if you're good."

She grunted and jabbed her elbow into his ribs.

"You know, Belle, you're starting to sound like an old steam engine."

They'd only gone a few feet, when Morgan realized he'd made a tactical error. With every sway, with every bounce, with every pounding of the hoofs, his arm brushed Belle's breast or his shoulder touched hers. And with every touch, his blood heated. Even the squirming child in his lap didn't stop the lust that surged through him. If he had half the sense of a jaybird, he'd have asked Jeb to escort her back to the schoolhouse. And he'd have hightailed it out to the ranch where he wouldn't be tormented with a beautiful woman—a beautiful unattainable woman.

Thankfully, the schoolhouse came into view before he made a total fool out of himself. The children were pouring out of the building. Little Rosalind raced to the wagon when she spotted her mother. Belle climbed down and wrapped her arms around her child. So much love gleamed on her face, it hurt Morgan to look at her.

"Rosie," Beth squealed and nearly jumped out of his arms.

Morgan's chest tightened. Seeing Belle with her children, the one she'd borne, and the ones she'd adopted, touched him in a heart he'd thought long dead. He purposely hardened his resolve. It wouldn't do to start having amiable thoughts about her. Until he found a way to get rid of her, they were partners. That was as far as he would allow their relationship to go.

He glanced at the older boy strutting toward the wagon with his hands shoved into his pockets. For all the world, the youth reminded Morgan of himself. The boy's arrogance didn't fool him a bit. He'd adopted the same swagger when the youngsters in school taunted him about being dirt poor. Not that they were much better off. Most of the families in rural Alabama were left destitute after the War.

Belle brushed her fingers over the little girl's hair. "How was your first day?" she asked.

The girl looked down at her shoes and shrugged her narrow shoulders. "Okay, I guess."

"How about you, Rory? Did you make friends with any of the other boys?" She straightened the knit on the youngster's head.

He stepped away, as if embarrassed by her attention. "Do I have to go to school? They're nothing but a bunch of bumpkins. They don't know half as much as me."

Belle smiled at the boy. "Yes, you have to attend school. It will get better. You'll make friends, and soon you'll be having lots of fun."

Rory looked up at the wagon and Jerome with the reins in his hands. "How come I got to stay in school all day, and Jerome gets to drive a wagon? It ain't fair."

"Mr. Morgan was teaching him, and I'm sure he'll teach you, too. I'll climb in the back with Rosalind, and you can sit up front with the men." She lifted her daughter onto the wagon bed and climbed in beside her. "See, we'll bundle up in these blankets and you can drive us home."

Morgan glanced over his shoulder, and handed Beth over to Belle. He didn't like the change in plans, but she was right. Rory needed to feel a part of something special. Besides, he needed the chance to cool off without Belle pressed intimately against him.

Morgan was noticeably absent when they sat down to supper, but Louise, Vivian, and Savannah joined Belle and the children. Somebody must have cautioned them, as they were modestly attired in simple gowns buttoned to their necks. Rosalind and Jerome ate quietly, while Rory couldn't keep his eyes off the lovely women. They spoke to him and teased him until his face turned as red as the strawberry jam he spread on his bread.

"Girls," Louise admonished. "I know you're delighted to

have such a handsome young man living with us, but mind your manners.''

Savannah, the more vivacious of the pair, pouted prettily. ''You know I've always liked younger men. When I worked in Atlanta, my best customers brought their sons to me so I could teach them the ways of the world.''

Vivian glared at her friend. ''Vannah, do you want Mrs. Jordan to toss you out on your ear.''

Belle groaned inwardly. In just three days, more had happened to upset her than in the entire past year. Now it was over Rory's initiation into manhood. ''I think we should wait a few years and see what happens.''

Louise buttered a slice of bread and presented it to Beth. Her action surprised Belle. All during dinner the woman had shown all the children an unusual amount of attention. ''Mrs. Jordan is right. He is a little young.''

''I think I'm plenty old enough.'' Rory dropped his fork and stared at the women who were so openly discussing his life.

Vivian reached over and cupped his chin. ''When you start shaving every day, sugar, we'll get together.''

The boy rubbed his jaw. ''I feel them whiskers growing right now.''

Belle groaned. ''You have lots of time to grow up. Now, eat your dinner, or you'll never make it.''

Sitting beside Beth, Louise took it upon herself to help the child with her meal. The young girl loved the attention, and before long was chatting in nonsensical jabbering. When Louise spooned mashed potatoes into the little girl's bowl, Beth grinned and began to laugh. Then to everybody's surprise, she spewed a mouthful of potatoes at the woman, the mess landing square in her face. All talk stopped. As if she hadn't done enough damage, the child dumped her entire bowl on the woman's lap. Beth clapped her hands and shouted with glee.

Belle leaped to her feet. ''I'm terribly sorry. Let me help

you.'' She reached for a napkin, but was brushed away by Louise's hand.

Instead of the expected anger, laughter glittered in the woman's eyes. ''I'll handle her.'' She turned to the child. ''You want to play, sweetie? How's this?'' She smeared a small glob of potatoes on Beth's face. ''Is this fun?''

The girl squealed with delight, and scooped up a handful of peas and tossed them at the woman. When she couldn't find anything else on her plate, Beth reached for her glass of milk. Before she could do further damage, Belle snatched it from her fingers. ''That's enough, Miss. We don't play with our food.''

Louise stood and picked up the little girl. ''Let's get cleaned up, love. Tell Mama you'll be good as new in a little bit.''

''Mama, Weezie fun.''

They could have knocked Belle over with a bubble. Who would have thought an experienced madam would have taken to a little orphan girl? She watched in wonder as Louise danced Beth from the kitchen. Their combined laughter followed down the hallway.

''What was so funny?'' Morgan appeared like a spirit out of the shadows.

Belle's heart skipped a beat. Surprise was how she accounted for the tingles that surged through her. Not the fact that it was the devastatingly handsome man who strolled into the kitchen and took a place at the table beside Belle.

''Beth and Miss Louise were playing with their food,'' Rory offered. ''Miss Belle would whop me silly if I did that.''

Morgan laughed. ''I'd like to be around to see that.''

''Rory, you know I've never struck you.'' Belle shook a finger at the youngster. ''But there's a first time for everything.''

''I know, ma'am. I just remember . . .'' He frowned and returned to shoveling his food into his mouth, ignoring all the table manners she'd drilled into him.

''That was the past, Rory. You're with me now, and nothing

will happen to you.'' She offered a comforting smile. The boy had said little of the years between when his parents had died and he'd come to live with Belle and Mr. Robinson. But she knew it had been difficult. She suspected he'd been working for a notorious pickpocket, who often beat his charges when they didn't bring home enough money.

She glanced at Morgan, who'd been studying them with unexpected interest. "From what I've seen of her, Miss Belle would fight the beasts of Hades to keep all you children safe."

Jerome looked up from his plate. "She's real good to us." The boy's serious dark eyes sparkled with love. Jerome was a loving, trusting child who believed his angel would protect him and everybody he loved. After all, he claimed Earl had sent him to Belle that fateful day. Then he'd been invited to stay and make his home with her.

Morgan's gaze swept over Belle. "I see how good she is." Heat glittered in his gaze. "Did you save any dinner for me?"

"I'll fetch your food, Mr. Morgan," Abby said, jumping from her chair.

From the corner of her eye, Belle noticed Vivian and Savannah exchange glances. With a shrug, the ladies returned to their meal.

Seconds later, Abby set a steaming bowl in front of Morgan. He dipped in his spoon and took a sip. Belle held her breath as he tasted. "Mrs. Franklin outdid herself today. This soup is delicious."

Savannah laughed. "Morgan, you should know Creole gumbo when you taste it. Mrs. Jordan made it."

The smile he flashed curled Belle's toes. "Mrs. Jordan, you're not only beautiful, but talented. What more could a man want in a woman?"

"I can think of a thing or two," Vivian whispered in a husky, provocative tone.

"I have the feeling that Mrs. Jordan can hold her own in

other ways, too,'' Savannah added. "Just this afternoon Sheriff
Sullivan came to pay court. He even brought candy.''

Vivian humped loudly. "And here I thought he was sweet
on me.''

"Really, ladies.'' Belle's effort to still their obvious jests
was interrupted by the shatter of a glass on the floor.

Abby jumped back, and covered her mouth with her fingers.
"I'm sorry. I didn't mean to be so clumsy.'' The girl's eyes
misted over and her face turned crimson.

Belle and Morgan leaped up at the same time and bumped
sides. "It's only a glass. Think nothing of it,'' she said. "I'll
get a broom.''

Morgan trailed behind her. "Careful you don't step on the
broken glass.''

"Mr. Travers, I can handle this. Go back to your meal.''

He snatched the broom from her fingers. "I said I'll help.''

Their hands brushed, and the fire that seemed to ignite whenever he came within three feet of her erupted into an inferno
within Belle. How could something as simple as a touch do
such strange things to her insides? Quite simply, she was losing
her grip on reality.

Abby stood to the side, while the others continued their meal.
Morgan swept the shards into a tiny pile, and Belle stooped
down and held a small dustpan. Within minutes the floor was
clean, and Morgan carried the glass to a trash barrel. By the
time they returned to the table the children had finished eating
and were watching the two pretty women, who were having a
private conversation between themselves.

Morgan settled back at his place at the table. "I'd like a
little more of that gumbo, if there's any left.''

Abby jumped as if snapped out of her stupor. "I'll fetch it
for you, Mr. Morgan.'' She scurried away and returned with
a bowl brimming with the succulent stew.

Belle returned slowly to the table. She'd eaten her fill, and
needed to put some distance between herself and Morgan. Her

reaction to him didn't make any sense at all. She began to clear away the empty plates.

"Sit down and relax, Mrs. Jordan," Vivian said. "Vannah and I will give Abby a hand."

"I'll help, too." Rory leaped up and picked up his empty bowl. It was the first time he'd ever offered to do dishes without being threatened. He followed behind the two pretty women like a puppy after a fresh bone.

The boy clearly was smitten. Belle would have to have a talk with him. Or perhaps she could ask Morgan to help. Sometimes a boy needed advice from a man. She sneaked a glance at Morgan. With his way of life, could she trust him to give virtuous and moral advice? She might just have to handle this chore herself.

"We'll help, too." Rosalind and Jerome slid from their chairs and trailed behind. That left Morgan and Belle alone in the dining room.

"I don't often bite, Belle. You don't have to be afraid." His wide smile showed sharp white teeth that too much resembled the wolf in the Red Riding Hood story. The wolf had told the little girl the same thing. And look what happened to her.

She laughed to hide her nervousness. "Do you ever bite, Mr. Travers?"

He lowered his voice to a husky whisper. "Only when I can't control my passion."

Heat colored her face and spread down her neck. She shoved back her chair to escape his all-knowing glance.

A slender finger to her cheek stopped her. "You're even prettier when you blush, *Bella mia*. Do you blush all over when you make love?"

Mortified not only by his indecent speech, but by her reaction to his touch, she slapped his hand away. "You'll never know."

Chin held high, she strutted down the hallway away from his deep, masculine chuckles that followed in her wake. "I wouldn't bet the ranch on that, Bella."

Again, he'd succeeded in provoking her, and again she'd fallen into his trap. Never again, Morgan Travers, she said under her breath. If she had someplace else to go, she would leave Eden House so fast the breeze behind her would form a tornado.

However, this house was the only home available to her. And Belle planned to make it a home if she had to step over his dead body to do so.

After the children left for school the next morning, Belle decided it was time to inspect the rest of the property she'd inherited. She hoped Jeb would be able to escort her to the mine and to the ranch. Surely Morgan wouldn't object to that.

She'd studiously avoided him the past evening. As soon as the kitchen was clean, she and the children went to their rooms to study and retire for the evening. The noise from the front parlor wasn't nearly as loud as the past evenings, and from her window she noted that fewer horses and buggies were lined up in the yard. Tomorrow was Saturday, and she hated to think of the commotion when the cowboys from the surrounding ranches reached town with their pay. Vivian and Savannah would have their hands full.

Abby entered the kitchen when Belle finished feeding Beth. She wiped the little girl's mouth, and gave her a hug. "Abby, would you mind Beth for me this morning? I'd like to go out and see the ranch."

Abby turned her head and continued frying bacon on the stove. "I'll be mighty busy today. I won't have time." The young woman's harsh tone surprised Belle.

"Then I guess I'll take her with me."

At that moment, Louise entered, modestly clad in a pink silk wrapper. A ruffle of wide lace extended down the entire front and danced around the hem. The woman was stunning. No wonder James had made her his mistress—as had Morgan.

"You're going out to the ranch?" Beth reached out her hands to the woman and squealed. Louise picked up the child. "Have you told Morgan?"

"I don't need Morgan's permission to visit my own property. I'll ask Jeb to drive me, or Corbett Hayes, or even Dan Sullivan might be able to escort me." Anybody but Morgan would do. Belle simply didn't trust herself to be alone with him.

The spatula clattered to the metal stove. Abby muttered an apology under her breath. "I'm sure getting clumsy."

"I'll be glad to watch the little one for you, Mrs. Jordan," Louise said. "We get along just grand."

Belle hesitated a second. Clearly the woman cared for the child and the child adored the fancy woman. "Thank you. I'll speak to Jeb when he returns."

A half hour later, Belle stepped out to the stable with her cape draped over her shoulders. She entered the darkened interior, a place foreign to her. The smell of animals and straw greeted her. "Jeb?" she called.

A tall figure stepped out of the shadows. "Looking for somebody?"

She'd hoped Morgan had already gone off on whatever business took him away every day. "Yes. Has Jeb returned from town?"

He propped a wide shoulder against a post. Clad in a heavy sheepskin-lined jacket, he looked as large as the horse standing in the stall behind him. "I sent him on an errand."

"Oh." She tugged on the cuffs of her gloves, not at all happy to be alone with Morgan. "Do you know when he'll return?"

"After he collects your children from school." He set down the grooming brush and reached for a feed bucket. "Mind telling me what you need?"

For a moment she hesitated in answering. By the time the young man returned, it would be too late to tour the properties. She certainly didn't want to be alone with Morgan for the hours she knew it would take. "I need a ride into town. Do you think you could hitch up a buggy for me?"

"What do you need from town? I'll be glad to fetch it for you."

On a sigh she gave up. "If you must know, I want to ask either Mr. Hayes or Sheriff Sullivan to show me around the area."

"The area? Or my ranch and silver mine?"

Setting her hands on her hips, she gritted her teeth to control her temper. *"Our* ranch—yours and mine. As you recall, it's mine as much as yours."

"As if I could forget what I see daily. If you want to go, I'll escort you. I don't want strangers snooping around my property." He lifted a hand to silence her. *"Our* property."

Chapter 7

Morgan hitched the pair of geldings to the fancy buggy. He wondered if he was making the mistake of his life. He'd thought a good night's sleep would help him get over the way Belle had felt in his arms, the way her lips had melted against his, the softness of her skin when he'd touched her. Sleep hadn't come, as all night long she'd haunted his thoughts. Lack of sleep and business worries had him cross and out of sorts.

His mood hadn't improved when Louise had informed him that Belle planned to ask Hayes or Sullivan to drive her out to the ranch. He couldn't let that happen. He didn't trust either man around Belle or on his property.

Now he was going to be alone with her for an entire day.

She sat prim and proper, her back as stiff as if she'd shoved a steel rod up her back. That alone got his ire up. Orneriness made him shift closer to her. He turned down the narrow road faster than normally, and leaned against her. She grunted, and clung to the side to keep from tumbling out. Just to make sure she was safe, he draped an arm across her shoulder.

"Sorry, the roads out here aren't like the city."

"Aren't you driving a bit fast?"

"You do want to return home before the children get bac
from school, don't you?"

"Yes. How much further?"

Truth be told, he had taken the short cut to the mine. "No
much. What do you think of your new home?"

With a shy smile she studied their surroundings. "Colorad
is absolutely beautiful. The mountains are so high and majestic
and the trees reach for the sky. Does winter usually come thi
early? The snow seems to be lower on the mountains ever
day."

He looked into the sky. The clouds had drifted from the north
and he wondered if they would have snow before nightfall. I
wouldn't do for him to get stuck out here with her overnight

"Actually, winter is a little late this year. We often have
blizzard or two before the first of December."

As if the gods wanted to play a prank on him, a flurry o
tiny snowflakes began to fall. He was sorely tempted to turn
around and head right back to town.

Belle huddled in her cape, her eyes wide with excitement a
the scenery. It would be a pity to return before she saw every
thing. If they turned back now, he would be forced to escor
her another day.

"Look at those beautiful fir trees," she said, her voice a
eager as a child's. "One would be wonderful for Christmas
We can set it up in the parlor and decorate it with popcorn
cranberries, and ribbons."

"Not in my house you won't." Morgan's hard tone brough
a frown from Belle.

"*Your* house? Have you forgotten so soon? I'll have a tree
in my half of that house. Plus decorations and everything else
to make the holiday special for the children."

He grunted. "Who ever heard of a Christmas celebration in
a whore house?"

By the flare in her eyes, he knew he'd hit a sore spot. "Morgan, those children were uprooted from the only home they'd ever known. I brought them over a thousand miles from their familiar environment and dropped them into a strange land. None of them had ever seen snow, or mountains. The fact that I've dumped them into a house of ill repute is of no consequence. I fully intend to give those children the wonderful Christmas they deserve. That includes a tree with all the trimmings."

"I don't believe in Christmas. As far as I'm concerned it's just another day of the year."

Her gaze narrowed on him, and if looks could kill he'd already be pushing up daisies. "Morgan Travers, I don't give a fig for what you believe. I love Christmas, and *my* half of Eden House will celebrate Christmas if I have to climb over you and your 'guests' to do it. The others are welcome to join us."

He grunted, surprised at the painful memories that continued to haunt him. "Don't look for me to join you."

"What could you possibly have against Christmas? It's a wonderful time of year. People are full of good will and joy. It's a time for love, for giving, for sharing."

He dared a glance at her eyes, as bright and shining as a child's.

"Didn't your family celebrate Christmas?"

"No. The old man used any holiday as an excuse to get drunk and beat the kids."

She laid her hand gently on his arm. The comforting touch did little to ease the pain of his past. "Did you grow up with many siblings? Did James? We married, but I knew little about him."

As much as he dreaded thinking about the past, he felt the need to tell her. He had so much in common with her young wards, it was uncanny. The team clopped along the rock road, and the wind whistled through the tall pines. Yet, he didn't notice the cold, or the wind. "Our mothers were sisters, only his mother married a neighbor, a man her father approved of. The plantation overseer seduced my mother, thinking he would take over the plantation. Her parents disapproved, but since she was expecting me, they allowed her to marry."

"You and James grew up on a plantation?"

He laughed, a bitter sound lacking of humor. "If you want to call it that. The Yankees burned the place to the ground, ravished the fields, and stole the livestock. I was born at the start of the War, so I never saw anything but the ruins." Memories of his home, the tall columns standing like lonely sentinels reaching up to the sky, flashed across his mind. "Most of the land had to be sold off to pay the taxes. We eked out a living on a few scraggy acres."

"I've seen some of the destruction of the War. So many fine homes were destroyed. So many lives were lost."

"As was a way of life. You should know a little about your daughter's heritage. James's father was killed at Vicksburg, and his mother died shortly after. By then our grandparents were gone, and James came to stay with us. More than a few times I wished my father had been the one to die. He came back a bitter, ruthless man who never was able to accept that the South lost and everything was different. He worked us like slaves in the fields until we couldn't take any more and we ran away."

"What happened to your mother?"

He hesitated, not wanting to remember how he'd found his beautiful mother lying in a pool of blood, a gun in her hand. On Christmas Day. He'd never been sure if she'd shot herself or if somebody else had done it. "She died right before James and I ran away."

"And your father?"

"I don't know, and I don't give a damn. He probably drank himself into the grave."

"Oh," she whispered.

By then they'd reached the entrance to the mine, now boarded up with "No trespassing" signs posted on the entrance. "This is the mine," he said, thankful to change the subject. He hated talking about his past, but somehow, he felt the need to share his life with Belle. "It's completely played out."

"Are you sure?"

"I wouldn't stop production if we weren't losing money."

He turned the buggy toward the ranch. "After I show you the ranch, I'll get you back to town."

The tiny snowflakes melted as soon as they touched the ground. He doubted they would be delayed, but he wanted to get rid of her as soon as possible. Being alone with this woman was dangerous to his libido.

Belle bit her lip, thinking about what Morgan had revealed about his past. His distressed childhood had carried him into adulthood. As had James's. Perhaps her husband's lonely and cruel childhood had prevented him from being the husband she'd expected. Without a mother and father to show him what a family was like, he was unable to commit to marriage and ran away before he got too close to a wife.

"Is it much further to the ranch?" She hugged her arms to her chest against the drop in temperature.

"No. We've been on my land since we approached the mine. I have 20,000 acres and plan to buy more. Sorry—*our* land."

Belle chose to ignore his sarcasm. She wiped the moisture from her face. The flurries had increased, and mixed with rain felt like tiny needles against her skin. She pulled the hood closer down on her face.

"We'll reach the cabin soon. We can get a bite to eat and warm up."

She studied the passing scene. Cows grazed on the brown grass in the meadows. "Are all these cows ours?"

"The cattle belong to the partnership. The horses are mine."

"How many do we have?"

"About a thousand. Hope to double that come spring."

"I see."

"Are you planning to run a line down the middle of the property and divide the cattle. One for you, one for me?"

"Is it necessary?"

"No, Belle. I won't try to cheat you."

"Thank you. I never dreamed James had been so prosperous. These cattle will insure his daughter's future."

Morgan let out a bark of laughter. "Left up to my cousin, you would have inherited a string of bawdy houses all over the state. I'm the one who worked his butt off to build up the ranch."

"Then I suppose I should thank you for your foresight in investing in such a legitimate and prosperous business."

He nodded. "I spent the summer building the cabin. It isn't much, but it keeps the men warm and sheltered until we sell some cattle. Come spring, I'll add a bunkhouse and other out buildings."

By then, a small cabin came into view. A few hundred feet away stood a large barn and several corrals. Smoke curled from the chimney of the cabin—a welcome sight for a woman chilled to the bone.

Morgan pulled the team to a halt at the door. He jumped down and came around to Belle. Before she had a chance to climb down, he reached up and lifted her to the ground. He stepped away quickly. "Go inside and get warm. I'll stable the horses until we're ready to leave."

With a nod of thanks, she shoved open the door. The interior was warm and inviting. She hurried to the large stone fireplace, grateful for the person who'd lit the fire. After a few seconds, she threw back the hood of her cape and studied her surroundings. The main room of the cabin served as kitchen, dining room, and parlor. It was clean and everything neatly in place. Two doors led off one wall, probably bedrooms. She wondered if Morgan often spent his nights here.

As if she conjured the man out of her musings, Morgan

appeared in the doorway. He stomped his feet on a rag rug, and slammed the door behind him. Approaching the fireplace, he tugged his gloves from his hands and dropped them on a table.

"Good of Vic to keep a fire going." He shoved his hands toward the glowing fire.

"Vic?"

"My . . . *our* foreman. I haven't had time to build a bunkhouse, so he and the other three cowboys live here." He gestured to the door at her right. "The other room is where I stay when I have to spend the night. Come spring, I hope to stay out here and personally operate the ranch. In addition to my building program, I'll take on at least a half-dozen more hired hands."

He hunkered down and dug into the fire with a long poker. His hat was damp, as was his jacket. She shivered more from his nearness than from the chill that had seeped into her bones.

Standing, he gazed down at her with warm, blue eyes. "You're soaking wet, Belle. Let's get you out of that wet cape." His fingers tangled with hers under her neck as he tugged on the ties that fastened the cape. Tingles raced up her arms. "If you plan to stay out here, you'll need warmer clothes. Next time we get into town, we'll have to see Nelson's Emporium about warm coats for you and the kids." One long finger brushed lightly along her jaw.

After the way he'd been so insistent that she leave, his kindness surprised her. "This was more than adequate for New Orleans."

"*Bella mia,* you aren't in the South. Things are different out here."

She swallowed down the nervousness at his closeness. "So I've noticed." In spite of her chilled skin, heat surfaced to her cheeks. The man could start a bonfire in the midst of a blizzard. At least with Belle. She took a step away from him before she did something foolish, like melting into his arms and sharing the heat of his strong, muscular body.

As if he, too, came to his senses, he swept the cape from her shoulders and hooked it on a peg on the wall. "This should dry here."

"Thank you," she said, hugging her arms to her chest.

"I'll get us some coffee." He slipped out of his heavy jacket and draped it over the back of a kitchen chair at the large planked table.

She shoved her icy hands back to the fire, hoping to still the trembling in her stomach. Why did she react this way to Morgan, when he was as much a rogue as the one who had deserted her on her wedding night? Only a fool would let the man into her life. For the sake of her and the children, she'd best keep their association on a strictly business basis. Until she found another place to live, she would guard her heart like the gold in a bank vault.

From the corner of her eye, she watched as he filled two mugs from a large pot on the cast iron stove. Sometimes he was gentle and kind, especially with the children; at other times he was an absolute cad. Belle never knew which way his wind would blow.

With a quick glance, she took in the remainder of the sparse furnishings. A worn settee fronted the fireplace, with two equally tattered easy chairs at either side. Calico curtains hung at the window, as if somebody had tried to lend a bit of décor to the austere interior.

Through the opening between the curtains, she saw that it had grown darker since she'd entered the cabin. White flecks of snow pelted the panes, and the wind whistled around the cabin. She bit her lip. "Morgan, shouldn't we be starting for home? The children will return from school and they'll be looking for me."

He slanted a glance at the window. "The weather is worsening. It isn't safe for us to try to get back to town today. It should clear up by morning."

"Morning?" She darted to the window for a closer look. "I can't stay here. I have to get back to town." Panic clutched at her stomach. The children needed her, and more than that, she didn't want to be alone with Morgan.

"Belle, I don't want you stuck out there in the middle of nowhere in a snowstorm. I've already sent one of the boys into town to tell Louise that you won't make it back until morning. She'll see that the children are well taken care of, and that they do their lessons and get to bed early."

"Morgan, you can't make that decision for me."

"Sorry, Belle. I already have. You won't do them any good if you get ill, or have an accident. I'll see that you get back safely as soon as the snow stops." He offered a cup of coffee, then pulled it back. "Your hands are like ice." Setting the two cups on the mantle, he cupped her hands between his big, callused palms. He lifted their entwined fingers to his mouth and warmed them with his hot breath.

Heat spread up her arms and settled in her chest. Tingles raced down to her stomach and beyond. Between his touch, and the intimacy of his breath, she felt the tremors deep in the secret place only one man had ever touched. His breathing grew raspy, and his lips touched her fingers.

"I'm already warm," she managed in a weak whisper.

"But your face is cold, too." Clutching her fingers close to his chest, he lowered his head.

His lips found her cheeks, now flushed from his touch. He trailed a row of gentle kisses down her cheeks, across her jaw, and to her mouth. She shoved against his chest to stop him, but her protests were lost in the needs that he inspired. Desires she thought had died years ago blossomed like a dormant lily bulb in the spring sunshine.

She opened her mouth in a weak order for him to stop. He accepted her protest as an offer to deepen the kiss. His tongue slid across her lips, sending longings deep into her heart. Of their own accord, her teeth parted, allowing him access to the warmth of her mouth. Tongues met and tangled. Breaths blended. Hearts pounded. Belle's head spun.

Morgan released her hands and slid his arms around her back. Her own fingers crept up his wide chest and rested at his throat. His pulse beat strong and hard at her fingertips. His day's growth of whiskers brushed her jaw in a delightfully sensual way. He dropped his hands to her waist, stroking her spine and cupping her hips. In spite of her skirt, petticoats, and his thick denims, she couldn't deny the pressure of his hard maleness against her soft stomach.

Lost in the pleasure of Morgan's kiss, she didn't hear the door open. Nor did she notice the three men who entered the cabin. A tiny groan escaped her lips when Morgan ended the kiss and lifted his head.

"Hope we're not interrupting anything, boss."

At the sound of the gruff male voice, Belle stiffened. She buried her face in Morgan's chest to hide her embarrassment.

"Not at all. Mrs. Jordan was chilled, and I was just warming her up." Morgan turned his back to the men. "Feeling better?"

All she could manage was a nod. He'd warmed her in more ways than she wanted to admit. Caught in a compromising position with her partner wasn't the best way to meet their employees. She dared a peek over Morgan's shoulder. The men had removed their coats and had moved to the kitchen, facing the stove. A young man, not much older than Rory, stared openly at her. The older man with a week's growth of whiskers tapped the youth on his head and signaled him to quit staring.

Morgan cleared his throat and turned with Belle to face their employees. He kept his arm draped possessively across Belle's shoulder. "Men, I'd like you to meet Mrs. Jordan."

Belle hoped they believed the pink in her cheeks was caused by the fireplace and not by Morgan's embrace. She forced a smile. One by one, the three cowboys removed their hats. The older man stepped forward. "So this is our new boss?"

"*I'm* your boss. Mrs. Jordan agreed to let me run the ranch." Before she could set him straight that she'd agreed to no such arrangement, he continued. "Belle, this old goat is Vic Nabor. He's foreman. The kid is Zack Miller, and the sour-faced hombre is Sven Jorgensen." The men all nodded and grinned. "I sent Les to Eden House to let Louise know that Mrs. Jordan and I will be staying the night."

The youngest of the trio choked on his coffee. "Sorry. Guess it went down the wrong way."

Morgan grinned and reached for their coffee that had cooled on the mantle. She accepted the cup. "Has the snow stopped? I really would like to return to town tonight. My children will miss me."

"No, ma'am," said Vic. "It came up so sudden like, I don't reckon it'll clear up until morning. It ain't safe to drive that fancy buggy in this weather."

The men shared a knowing glance as if to remind each other what had happened to James in the very same vehicle.

"Don't worry about the youngsters, Belle. Louise will see that they're safe. When the girls get through spoiling them, they won't care if you ever return."

She doubted that, especially her sweet, shy Rosalind. "Do I have a choice?"

Morgan shook his head. "I'll get you something warm to wear. You're still chilled." He retreated through the door to his room, leaving her alone with the cowboys.

Belle stood by the fire watching the men, who could do little but stare at her. She felt like a heifer on display at a livestock show. Moments later, Morgan held a large flannel shirt for her. She slipped her arms into sleeves that covered her hands. When he began to button the shirt for her, she brushed his hands away. "I can do it myself."

He nodded and turned toward the kitchen. "We're starved. Did you get anything started for supper?"

"It's Zack's turn to cook, but I put on a pot of beans to make sure we have something decent to eat." Vic lifted the heavy lid off the pot sizzling on the stove. The aroma of spices filled the room.

Needing to keep her mind off of Morgan and his plans for the night, Belle hurried to the kitchen. "I'll be glad to help. Allow me to prepare the rest of the meal."

"Let her help. Mrs. Jordan is a wonderful cook."

Coming from Morgan, the compliment touched her in ways she didn't want to examine. "If one of you gentlemen will show me around, I'll have dinner on the table in minutes. With four children tugging on me, I've learned to cook in a hurry."

"Four children?" Vic tilted a dark eyebrow. The man was several years older than Morgan and nearly as large. Gray tinged his brown hair. His brown eyes exuded warmth and his smile was inviting.

"Only one belongs to James," Morgan explained. "The others are adopted."

Young Zack rushed to her aid. "I'll be glad to help, ma'am."

"Thank you, Zack. If you'll show me where to find flour, I'll get started on the biscuits."

For the next half hour, Belle busied herself preparing the meal for the four men. From time to time, she glanced out the window. Sure enough, the flurries had turned to snow. Not a blizzard, but she had to take the men's word that it was dangerous to try to return to town. Yet the thought of spending the night in the isolated cabin with Morgan had her stomach in knots and her nerves on end. Surely he wouldn't try anything untoward with three brawny men as chaperones.

Yet, she wouldn't put anything past a scoundrel related to James Jordan. If her husband had broken her heart, there was no telling what falling for Morgan could do to her.

* * *

Having a lady in the cabin kept the bawdy male talk to a minimum. Morgan wasn't too happy about the way the three cowboys fawned over Belle or the way Vic openly flirted with her. After the meal was finished, to riotous praise for her biscuits—hell, he thought, anybody ought to be able to fix biscuits—they settled at the table for a game of poker.

Belle asked to join, and sat beside Morgan. "You sure you know how to play?" he asked. "We wouldn't want you to lose the ranch or the mine to one of these card sharks."

She laughed, a sound that settled in the middle of Morgan's chest like a song. "I can hold my own, Mr. Travers. You worry about losing your shirt." She rolled up the sleeves of his oversized shirt to her elbows.

"Leave the lady alone, Morgan. I've got the feeling she's full of surprises." Vic took the worn deck and shuffled. "Five card draw, nothing wild."

The men dug into their pockets and placed their meager coins on the table. Morgan did the same. "Can I lend you some money to get your started, Mrs. Jordan?" he offered.

She shoved her hand into the pocket of her skirt. "No, thank you, Mr. Travers. I have money of my own."

He glanced at the few coins in front of her. Maybe he should let her win a hand or two to save her morale. Morgan added his coin to the pot and watched Belle from the corner of his eye. Vic dealt the cards, and she held hers close to her chest. She bit her lip and thought for a moment when it was her turn to bet. She called, and asked for two cards. This time when it came to her, she raised by a penny. Sven and Zack folded, leaving Morgan and Vic to bet against her. Vic called, and Morgan decided to take it easy on Belle.

"Call," he said, turning over his two pair. Vic grunted and threw down his cards. As Morgan reached to pull in his winnings, Belle's voice stopped him.

"Does three of a kind beat two pair?" She turned over three fives.

"I reckon it does, ma'am," Vic said with a grin. "Looks like Lady Luck is smiling on Mrs. Jordan."

"Beginner's luck," Morgan murmured, taking the deck and dealing the next hand.

To his surprise, Belle played conservatively, calling more often than raising, yet she won every other hand. As the coins in front of the others dwindled, the money in front of Belle grew. Even Morgan, who prided himself on his skill at the tables, was being taken for a ride.

When the others were nearly broke, Vic threw down his cards. "Morgan, are you helping her beat us?"

"You know me better than that. There are two things I take seriously—poker and women. I don't believe in mixing the two, and I sure wouldn't let a woman beat me."

Sven gathered his remaining coins and shoved them into his pockets. "I cannot afford to lose any more. I am trying to help my family in Sweden. I think it is time to turn in."

"I'm broke." Zack shoved back his chair and headed for the bedroom he shared with the other three hired hands.

"Tell me, Mrs. Jordan. How did you learn to play poker? It don't seem like a pastime for a refined lady like yourself," Vic remarked.

"I'm interested, too, since we're the only ones left." Morgan picked up the deck and expertly shuffled the cards. He didn't like being bested by a woman, especially the woman who was his partner.

"I often had to serve refreshments for Mr. Robinson and his poker friends. Once in a while he asked me to sit in if he had to leave for some reason. I learned the intricacies of the game from some of the finest gamblers in New Orleans."

Vic laughed. "A New Orleans gambler. I should have guessed. Morgan, looks as if you've met your match."

He groaned. Morgan suspected he'd met his match in more

ways than Vic could imagine. "Looks like it's just the two of us. Want to take me on?" He dug into his pocket and threw additional coins on the table.

She smiled. "I'm game if you are."

For the next hour, the money shifted back and forth. When Morgan had what he thought was a winning hand, he bet big. Belle called, and more often than not, she won. When Morgan was all but cleaned out, he decided he'd been skillfully suckered.

"Hope word doesn't get out that a woman bested me at cards." He leaned back in the chair to study his opponent.

Belle stacked her winnings. "This should buy new coats for the children. We thank you, Mr. Travers."

Morgan stretched his arms over his head. "Reckon it's time to get to bed."

Her face paled. "Bed?"

"It's pretty late, and you'll want to head back to town early in the morning."

"Yes. I do, but where will I sleep?"

He opened the door to his bedroom. "Here, of course, in my room."

She looked around as if seeking for a way to escape the gallows. "Your room?"

"Surely you don't want to spend the night listening to Vic, Sven, and Zack snoring?"

"No, but . . . but . . ."

Unbuttoning his shirt, he gestured her into the room. "I don't snore."

Chapter 8

Hands on her hips, Belle planted her feet in the parlor. "You can't mean that we'll sleep together?" Surely the man was mad.

"Why not? We're kin by marriage."

Her temper sizzled to a hair's breadth from exploding. She glared at him. "Mr. Travers, I know you're a degenerate of the worst kind, but surely you cannot be serious?"

He laughed, a deep devilish chuckle that angered her. "You should see the color of your face. Just to prove I can be a gentleman, I'll sleep out here on the davenport. Just let me pick up a pillow and blanket, and you can have your privacy."

"Gentleman? You don't know the meaning of the word." Head held high, she entered the bedroom. A narrow bed covered with several quilts sat against one wall. A bureau and cloudy mirror and one chair completed the furnishings. She grabbed a pillow and blanket from the bed and tossed them at Morgan.

"If you get cold, just whistle. I know how to warm you up." He winked and returned to the parlor.

She slammed the door and leaned against it to gain control of her temper. Sleep with her. Of all the nerve. The man was tempting beyond understanding. But Belle had given in to temptation once. She didn't intend to get caught in that trap again.

Feeling her way in the dark, Belle located the chair and propped it against the door. She didn't trust Morgan Travers any more than she could find gold in an abandoned silver mine.

As she struggled toward the bed, a fist rapped lightly on the door. "Belle?" Morgan whispered loudly.

"What do you want?" she asked, as if she didn't know.

"Would you like a lamp?"

"No."

"You sure?" He paused. "Do you need help with those tiny buttons?"

"No. I do not need a lamp, and I'm quite capable of loosing my buttons."

"Then do you want to help me?"

His persistence was comical. "No. You're a big boy. You can undress yourself."

"If I get cold, can I come in and let you warm me?"

"If you get cold, add another log to the fire."

"What if *you* get cold?"

"I'll manage with the quilts. Good night, Morgan."

By the shuffle of feet, she assumed he'd given up and retired to the davenport. Sitting on the edge of the bed, she removed her shoes and rolled down her stockings. She slipped out of her skirt and shirtwaist, leaving her chemise and petticoats. Without a fire, the room was chilled. Since she didn't have nightclothes, she pulled on Morgan's large flannel shirt. The garment was warm and smelled like Morgan. On a sigh, she cuddled under the quilt. How was she expected to sleep when everything around her reminded her of Morgan? The pillow bore the clean scent of his hair, the bed was indented with the shape of his body, and his shirt was as warm as his strong, muscular flesh.

Closing her eyes, she tried to sleep. However, all she saw was Morgan's long, lean frame cramped on that lumpy davenport. She turned over and encountered the cold sheet. Shivering, she curled into a ball to get warm. She'd just begun to doze off, when another fist rapped on the door.

She sat up, hugging the quilt to her chest. The chair she'd shoved in front of the door scraped and a sliver of light slanted across the floor. "Belle?"

"Morgan, get out of here."

"I want to know if you need anything."

"We all need to get some sleep." Vic's loud harsh voice came from the other side of the wall. Belle jumped at the sound. "Either get in bed with her, or keep quiet."

He laughed. "Good advice."

"If you take one step into this room, I'll. . ." She couldn't think of a single threat that would affect the man. Without a weapon, her threats would be futile. "I'll tell everybody I walloped you at poker. You won't be able to hold up your head in a game."

Backing away, he pulled the door closed. "You win. I'll spend the night on the davenport. But don't blame me if you freeze to death."

She pulled the covers over her head. As tempting as it was, she would rather freeze than to give in to the temptation of being with Morgan. Her reputation would be in shambles, and her heart would fare even worse. Belle suspected she was getting feelings for Morgan, and that would prove a real disaster. No, it was better to freeze alone than to burn in the hell of her lust.

Morgan and the men were seated at the table sipping coffee when Belle entered the kitchen the next morning. She hadn't thought she'd slept a wink, but when she heard movement and voices, she realized that at some point she'd fallen into a restless slumber. Chilled, she'd dressed quickly and again bundled in Morgan's flannel shirt for warmth.

All four men looked up as she exited the bedroom. Before she could ask for the location of the primitive facilities, Morgan pointed to a rear door. Slipping into her cape, she followed his directions.

The snow had stopped, and although the sun had yet to rise, the day promised to be clear and cold. When she returned to the kitchen, a pile of eggs and bacon waited in the middle of the table. Someone had set a plate for Belle at the place beside Morgan. He looked up from his breakfast and stood. For the first time he showed a modicum of manners by holding her chair as she was seated.

"Thank you, Mr. Travers," she said, hiding the surprise in her voice.

"You're very welcome, Mrs. Jordan." He returned to his chair and resumed eating.

Conversation ceased, and the men devoured the meal in record time. Belle ate one egg and a single biscuit. "It's very good," she said.

"Thank you for the compliment." Morgan's voice startled her.

"You? Did you cook this?" He nodded. "I had no idea you could even make coffee." At least at Eden House he acted totally helpless in the kitchen.

"Boss has a lot of talents he keeps hidden," Vic said, lifting his cup in a toast.

"Mrs. Jordan is learning them one by one. I don't want to overwhelm her with too much too soon. Might frighten her away."

"There's little chance of that. I intend to stay and be a part of all our enterprises."

Morgan narrowed his gaze. "Belle, I already told you I won't have you interfering in my business."

She didn't want to make a scene in front of the hired hands, but she didn't want to back down from her rights and responsibilities. "And I explained that I want to be an equal partner."

He shoved back from the table. "I'm going to ride out and check the herd. Would you care to mount a horse and join me?"

"Not today. I want to get back to the children."

"Vic has to go into town for supplies. He'll drive you. I'll be back tonight." He shoved his arms into his coat. At the door, he glanced over his shoulder. "See that the youngsters stay out of our way. I'm looking forward to a large crowd and lots of business." Slamming his hat on his head, he stepped onto the porch and banged the door behind him.

The three remaining men exchanged glances. "Zack, you do the dishes while Sven and I hitch up that fancy buggy. Then get out and give Morgan a hand," Vic ordered.

Zack mumbled under his breath, but began to pump water into a pail.

"I'll be glad to help," Belle said. She stacked the plates and carried them to the sink.

Vic reached for his coat. "I'll be around in a minute with the wagon. You said you wanted to get back to Eden House."

"As soon as possible."

After filling the dishpan with hot water, Zack dumped in the dishes. "Reckon Vic won't be back until late, especially since he has an excuse to go to Eden House."

Belle paused in scrubbing a plate. "Why is that?"

"He's sort of sweet on Miss Louise. Since Mr. James died, he goes to see her every time he goes into town."

That was interesting news. Her husband's mistress and the ranch foreman. An unusual couple to say the least—a sophisticated woman and a gruff cowboy. And here Belle had assumed Morgan had stepped in and taken his cousin's place. Would wonders never cease?

Moments later, Vic drew the conveyance up to the door. Belle bid the young man good-bye and climbed aboard. The

ground was damp, but the sun began to peek over the mountains
in the distance. A light dusting of snow clung to the limbs of
the evergreens, making them sparkle like diamonds. Yes, one
of these would make a glorious Christmas tree for the children.
And Belle was determined to give them their holiday celebration
regardless of Morgan's dislike for Christmas.

The sight that greeted Belle when she entered the kitchen at
Eden House stopped her in her tracks. The four children were
all dressed and seated at the table. Sipping a cup of coffee,
Louise sat beside Beth. Vivian stood at the stove stirring a pot
of oatmeal while Savannah sliced bread at the counter.

Vic, too, halted in the doorway. His eyes grew wide and he
chuckled under his breath.

"Please control your humor, Victor, and shut the door.
You're letting in the cold." Louise gestured with her mug of
coffee. She wore a red velvet wrapper with feathers at the
neckline and wrists.

Belle's mouth gaped. What a sight they were. Vivian's modest silk wrapper in a vivid green matched her eyes. Her red
hair was twisted in a single long braid. Savannah was attired
in a plaid flannel robe tied demurely at her throat. Not only
were the three women up abnormally early in the morning,
they seemed to have everything under control.

"Mama." Rosalind was the first to leap from the table and
greet her mother. The little girl wrapped her arms around Belle's
waist. "I missed you. Miss Louise had to sleep with us, and
she fixed my hair."

The boys moved slower. "Miss Belle, are you okay?" Rory
asked.

"I'm fine and I missed you all." She hugged all the children
to her chest. "Have you behaved for Miss Louise?"

"We been real good," said Jerome, returning to his place
at the table. "Miss Viv fixed oatmeal for our breakfast."

Belle stared at the children. Usually, she had to force them ▸ eat the cereal that was good for them. "Then you'd better ɑt up before it gets cold." She removed her cape and draped over the back of a chair.

Vic had removed his jacket and settled beside Louise at the ᴧble. "Never saw you with a kid before."

"Never had any around here before. Beth and I have gotten ▸ be real good friends." Her smile transformed her into a ⴰfter, prettier woman than the one Belle had met days earlier.

As if she was tired of being ignored, Beth stood on the chair ᴧnd planted her hands on her narrow hips. "Where Morgie? I ᵥant Morgie."

Belle reached for the little girl. "Honey, he'll be back later. ʟow, you'd better eat your oatmeal so you'll grow up into a ᴧig strong girl."

After planting a kiss on Belle's cheek, the child held out her ʀms to Louise. It looked as if the women had everything under ⴰntrol. The children hardly missed Belle.

"By the way, Mrs. Jordan"—Savannah set the bread on the ᴧble—"you had a couple of visitors yesterday."

Her words surprised Belle. "I wasn't expecting anyone, and know few people in town."

Vivian spooned the cereal into the bowls. "You know this ᴧir. First Corbett Hayes and then Dan Sullivan showed up."

Savannah laughed. "Miss Belle has been in Paradise for ᴧbout a week and the three best-looking men in the territory ʀe courting her."

Vic grunted, "Three?"

"You're spoken for, Vic," Louise added with a grin. "The ʜeriff and the lawyer came looking for her. Meanwhile, she ꜱpent the night at the ranch with Morgan."

Heat rushed to Belle's face. "We were well-chaperoned by ᴛhree other men and I returned as soon as it was safe to do so. ʙesides, no one is courting me. We're simply acquaintances."

"And I'm the Queen of Sheba." Louise shot Belle a knowing glance.

Vic caught the woman's arm. "Queenie, you got time for a lonely cowboy?"

"Always." She kissed Beth on the forehead. "Be a good girl for Mama." Arm in arm, the couple headed for the parlor.

Thankfully, the children were too intent on their breakfast to understand the adult banter. The very idea that Belle had even one suitor was preposterous. But three? And certainly not Morgan. He was as unlikely a suitor as Prince Edward of England.

The day passed quickly for Belle. Supervising four rambunctious youngsters, she had her hands full. That evening, she saw to their baths, reminding them that they would all attend church the next day. She was grateful she'd been away when Corbett and Dan had called. She had more than enough to worry about with Morgan's unwanted attention. The other two men posed a complication she did not need.

After the baths, she loaded a basket with dirty laundry to carry downstairs for the laundry woman who picked it up on Monday. With a week's supply of clothing, the basket was piled nearly to her face. Belle felt her way to the rear stairs, taking one careful step after another. It wouldn't do to tumble down and break her neck.

Halfway down the steep stairs, she heard a noise behind her. A hand touched her back. Balancing her load, she was unable to see who had come up to her. Then the pressure increased, unbalancing her.

Everything happened quickly. Belle staggered from side to side on the narrow passageway. She tottered, struggling to maintain her equilibrium. For a second, she thought she had managed to save herself. Then her feet tangled in her skirts. The heavy laundry tilted, pulling her forward. The basket flew out of her hands, and she flailed her arms like a bird. As she reached the next step, her ankle twisted and she was propelled headfirst toward the bottom of the staircase.

As her feet flew out from under her, a hand caught her arm and pulled her backward.

"Hold it." Morgan circled her waist and pulled her back hard into his chest. "I don't believe you know how to fly."

Her breath came in short breaths and her heart pounded out of control. The basket bounced to the foot of the stairs, scattering the laundry all over the floor. She gasped at the possibility that it could have been her sprawled out, injured at best. Or worse.

Morgan turned her to face him. "You okay, Belle? You gave me a scare."

All she could manage was a nod. "I think so."

"Be careful when you carry a heavy load down these steep stairs. You could have been hurt." Was the concern in his voice genuine? How did he manage to be there at that very moment? She hadn't even known Morgan had returned. Unless . . .

"I don't know what happened. I was trying to be careful."

"You're okay now." His gaze was warm, and full of anxiety. He lowered his head, and touched his lips to her forehead.

She clung to his stiff white shirt, struggling to come to terms with her near tragedy. Lifting her gaze, she spotted Louise on the landing. The woman met her gaze, then slipped into the shadows. Belle gasped. Had Louise been responsible? Was she working with Morgan to get rid of her? Impossible. Louise had been more than friendly that morning when she'd returned. Or was it just a ruse to get Belle's guard down.

Shoving against Morgan's chest, she looked into his eyes. "I'm fine."

"No, you aren't. You're trembling like a flag in the wind." Before she could protest, he swung her up in his arms and started back up the stairs.

"Morgan, put me down. I'm not injured. I have to pick up the laundry."

He ignored her and continued to her room. "I'll get Abby or the children to clean up. I want to check your ankle."

"There's nothing wrong with my ankle." She wrapped her arms around his neck for balance. Her breasts pressed against his chest, and her legs rested on his arm.

"Then why did you trip?"

"Somebody pushed me."

Morgan kicked her door open and carried her to the bed. "Who would want to hurt you?"

Belle bit her lip to keep her suspicions to herself. She could think of several people in this house who wished she would leave—starting with Morgan himself. "I don't know. I suppose it was my imagination. Did you see anybody behind me?"

"No. I was headed to the kitchen when I saw you staggering. Thank God I was there right on time. You could have been seriously injured." He sat on the edge of the bed and cradled her foot in his big hand.

"Morgan," she objected to his bold manner. "You shouldn't be in my chamber."

"Belle, be quiet and let me check your ankle."

With deft fingers he loosed the laces on her shoe and tugged it from her foot. She leaned on her elbows to watch. He was partially attired for the evening with his white shirt and black trousers. Before the customers arrived, he would add a stiff collar, black cravat and his tailored jacket.

Carefully, he pressed a finger along her ankle. "Does it hurt?" The intimacy of their situation sent her heart pounding.

She flinched. "A little."

"Do you want me to send for the doctor?"

"No. I'll be fine."

"Then stay off of it until morning. If it isn't better by then, I'll fetch the doctor myself." Morgan shifted and turned toward her. He brushed her hair from her forehead. Heat glittered in his midnight blue eyes. "Be careful from now on." He lowered his head until his lips met hers in a kiss as tender as kissing a child.

She lowered her eyelashes and watched. His mouth pressed gently, then on a groan, he increased the pressure. Her arms stole around his neck, and he stretched out beside her. Their bodies touched, and Belle gave in to the delicious sensations that sizzled through her. She opened her mouth, and she realized that at the same time she opened her heart. Morgan wrapped his arms around her and slipped his knee between hers. Layers of clothing separated them, but Belle felt the heat from his body as if they were naked.

The kiss went on until Belle was breathless with longing. His hands roamed her back, his fingers danced along her spine. She was soaring above the ceiling, lost in the wonder of his touch.

Morgan ended the kiss and pressed his cheek to hers. "Lord, Belle, you feel so good."

Her heart was pounding so hard, she couldn't speak. She wanted the moment to go on and on. She turned to beg him to kiss her again, when a noise came from the hallway. The door flung open and the patter of footsteps raced across the rug. Belle and Morgan jerked apart.

"Mama," Beth jumped on the bed and landed on top of Morgan. "Morgie. Are you putting Mama to bed?"

Belle groaned. She lifted her head and spotted the other three youngsters trailing close behind. Rosalind sprung to the other side of the bed and brushed her hand on Belle's forehead. "Mama, Abby said you're hurt."

"I'm fine, thanks to Mr. Morgan."

Rory stood beside the bed, hands fisted, ready for battle. "What did you do to Miss Belle?"

Morgan sat up. "Nothing, boy. Now that you're here, you can tend to her needs. See that she stays off her feet until morning." He flung his legs over the side of the bed. "You children pick up the clothes she dropped, and ask Abby to fetch her some tea.''

At the loss of Morgan's warmth, Belle shivered. ''Morgan, that isn't necessary. I can get up.''

Rosalind plumped up her pillows. ''No, Mama. We'll look after you like you always do for us when we're sick.''

Beth rested her head on Belle's shoulder. ''I love you, Mama.'' The child looked at her with sparkling green eyes. ''Love Morgie, too.''

Morgan twined his finger in one of the child's golden curls. ''Morgan loves Beth, too. I'd best get busy. We're expecting guests any minute. Louise will be looking for me.''

His words reminded her of the accident. Had Louise and Morgan conspired to get rid of Belle? But how could a man be so tender and kiss with so much passion if he meant to do her in? And how did Abby know about the accident unless she'd seen it? It confused and confounded Belle.

Jerome caught Morgan's hand as he moved toward the door. ''Mr. Morgan, will Miz Belle be alright?'' The child's voice cracked and his eyes were dark with worry. For a youngster, the little brown-skinned boy had seen more than his share of tragedy.

Morgan clasped his fingers on the youngster's shoulder. ''Sure, son. Come down with me, and you can fetch Miss Belle's tea and some of those cookies she made today.''

Belle stared at him in amazement. If he'd been gone all day, how did he know that she'd baked cookies? Louise must have filled him in on her activities. But why, when the woman had spent the better part of the day in the parlor with Vic?

At the door, Morgan turned his head and smiled. It was all too confusing for Belle. Surrounded by the children she loved, she relaxed against the pillows and flexed her ankle. Pain shot up her leg. Maybe Morgan was right. It would be best to stay in bed until morning. However, she planned to attend church if she had to hobble on one foot.

* * *

Morgan saw that Abby and Jerome carried tea and cookies to Belle. For some odd reason, the young housekeeper refused to meet his gaze as he instructed her. When he'd seen Belle wobbling on the stairs, he'd caught a glimpse of blue that disappeared into the shadows. Abby was wearing a blue dress, but so was Louise. Had Belle been right? Had somebody shoved her down the stairs?

Sipping on a cup of coffee, he watched as the young woman bustled around the kitchen, her voice full of sympathy and concern. Abby had been with them for more than a year, and in that time, she'd become invaluable to the house. From time to time he'd seen her with Dan Sullivan, but it was clear, to him at least, that Dan viewed her as much too young to bother with. When the sheriff had come to Eden House, it was to see either Vivian or Savannah, not Abby.

Louise was another matter. There were any number of reasons the madam would want to get rid of Belle. Not the least was jealousy. She'd threatened to shoot James when she'd caught him with one of the girls. The other woman had been promptly fired and sent packing. Then there was the loss of earnings since Belle and the children had invaded the house.

As Abby and Jerome exited the kitchen, Louise entered, her flowing blue dress cut very deep at the neckline. For just a brief second, he wondered how Belle would look in such a gown. She would be stunning—a real man-killer. Morgan shoved the improbable thoughts aside and gestured her in.

"What happened to Mrs. Jordan?" She filled a china cup with the rich, dark coffee.

"Tripped on the stairs. Thankfully, I happened to reach her just in time to save a tumble."

The woman's silvery gray eyes studied him over the rim of her cup. "Lucky for her."

Was that suspicion in her gaze? Or was she trying to hide her own guilt? "Lucky. Are the girls ready for the evening?"

She let out a small bark of bitter laughter. "Sure, if we have any guests. The pickings have been getting slimmer and slimmer. At this rate, we might as well close up shop and move to Denver."

"We aren't going anywhere." He slammed the cup on the table, spilling the remaining coffee.

"What are you going to do about our Mrs. Jordan and her orphans?"

He shrugged. "Damned if I know." He offered his arm. "Your job is to make whatever guests we have willing to spend their gold on an evening at Eden House. Let's go make sure the fire is glowing, and the whiskey is flowing."

She laughed, this time with real warmth. "You're right, Morgan. You're more decadent than your cousin."

"Thank you for the compliment, ma'am. I try."

Chapter 9

Belle was more nervous than she'd expected as she prepared for their first visit to Paradise Community Church. As Morgan had predicted, her ankle was much improved; however, her mood wasn't the best for a Sabbath. Loud music and raucous laughter had drifted up the stairs into all hours of the night. From the amount of boisterous noise, they must have done a landslide business.

Sunday was Mrs. Franklin's day off, and Belle took it upon herself to prepare the midday meal. She seasoned a beef roast and put it in the oven to bake. After peeling potatoes, she placed them in a pot to boil. By the time they would return from services, the meal would be ready for the table. Since Abby was nowhere in sight, she assumed that the young woman had also taken the day off.

Breakfast was on the table by the time the youngsters stirred and appeared in the doorway. "Mama," Rosalind explained. "You were supposed to let us help you. How is your leg?"

Beth shrugged out of Rory's arms, and darted for Belle. "Mama all fixed. Morgie fix Mama."

She lifted the child high in the air. "Yes, I'm all better now." But had Morgan fixed her, or hurt her? "You children eat up, and we'll all get ready for church."

Dressed in his oldest plaid shirt and faded trousers, Rory plopped down at the table and grabbed a biscuit. "I ain't going to church."

Belle narrowed her gaze on the boy's show of rebellion. "You aren't going to church? Why ever not? We go every Sunday."

He shoved the unbuttered biscuit into his mouth and chewed slowly. Belle waited patiently for an answer. "I don't want to, is all. If those bunch of bumpkins are there, they'll snub us just like at school."

"Shut up, Rory. They're not all that bad." Rosalind showed an unusual amount of spunk for such a shy child. She darted a warning glance at Rory.

"What do you mean? Have you had problems with the other students?" It was the first she'd heard about trouble at school.

"No, Mama. It's just hard since we don't know anybody." Her daughter reached for Beth and set the child on a chair.

"You'll get to know them in time." She turned her gaze to Rory. "And you, young man, most definitely are going to church. Now eat your food, we have to be ready by ten. Mr. Hayes will be driving us to the service." She turned back to the stove and the scrambled eggs that were about to burn.

Rory made a face and stuck out his tongue. Belle caught his action from the corner of her eye. The others giggled and covered their mouths with their fingers.

"Can you please let me in on the jest? I didn't hear anything funny." She set the large bowl of eggs on the table.

"Nothing, Miz Belle. Rory likes to make fun," Jerome offered.

"Aw, I don't see why I have to go. I'd rather stay here with Mr. Morgan and take care of the horses."

She set her hands on her hips. As she'd dreaded, Morgan was proving to be a bad influence on the children. Especially the boys. "You will go, no matter what Mr. Morgan chooses to do."

"Miss Belle is right, boy." As was becoming his habit, Morgan appeared in the doorway without warning. "Don't use me as an example. Miss Belle will have my hide." Morgan strolled lazily into the kitchen.

Belle's heart twisted every time she looked at Morgan. How did the man manage to stay up the better part of the night and still look handsome and appealing in the morning?

"Morgie go church with us?" Beth held up her arms to Morgan.

He tossed the little girl into the air. "Sorry, little bit, we don't want the preacher to faint dead away, or the roof to fall in on the good people of Paradise."

Belle giggled under her breath along with the children. She had no doubt what he said was true. A man with his reputation as a gambler and brothel operator would shock the entire congregation. "Mr. Morgan has his own responsibilities."

He settled at the table with Beth on his lap. "How's the ankle this morning?"

"Much better." She lifted her skirt and flexed it to show him.

His brows tilted, and a smile curved his lips. "Mighty nice."

Only then did Belle realize she'd also shown a goodly amount of limb. She dropped her hem and returned to the stove. "Care for some coffee, Mr. Morgan?"

"Could use some. And those eggs and biscuits sure look good."

She quickly served him, and set about cleaning up the kitchen. From time to time she slanted a glance at Morgan. He shared his meal with Beth, feeding her and letting her feed him. Who would have thought he'd have taken so with the child? The others chatted with him, and even her shy Rosalind fell in with the light conversation.

"Aren't you going to join us?" Morgan asked.

"I've already eaten. Dinner is in the oven, and I'll finish it when I return home from church." She dunked the skillet into the dishpan.

"Am I invited to dine with you?" He wiped the milk from Beth's upper lip.

"Of course. It's as much yours as mine."

He frowned at her subtle reminder that they were still partners.

Rosalind looked up from her meal. "Miss Louise and Miss Vivian and Miss Savannah are nice. Can they come, too?"

"Of course."

It seemed that the women and the madam were becoming part of Belle's eclectic family. Along with Morgan.

"Too bad you hurt your leg, and couldn't come down last night," Morgan said, drawing Belle's gaze. By the wicked grin on his mouth, she wasn't sure if she wanted to know why.

"Mama had to rest, Mr. Morgan." Rosalind said. "And you said we weren't allowed downstairs after five o'clock except to go to the kitchen."

He laughed, a warm sound that ignited the fire in her blood. Belle reached for the empty dishes on the table. Morgan caught her wrist. Their gazes met and held. "Don't you want to know why I needed you last night?"

"You're going to tell me, aren't you?"

"We had a high-stakes poker game going, and you could have won a bundle." He turned her hand over and stroked his thumb along her palm. The fire that he'd kindled in her stomach burst into a full inferno.

"Miss Belle, you know how to play poker?" Rory stared at her with a new respect in his young eyes.

Morgan chuckled, and kissed her fingers. "Didn't you tell

them what happened out at the ranch when we were snowed in?''

She snatched her hand back. "They know we couldn't return home until the snow stopped and that the hired hands kept us company." How could she ever teach morals if the children knew she gambled with the best of them? "I do play an occasional hand of cards, but I'm hardly in Mr. Morgan's league."

He shrugged, as if to say he would keep her secret, if she wanted it that way. "I could have used some of this coffee."

"Did you win?" Rory asked.

"Son, I always win."

Belle hid her smile. "Always?"

"In a fair game." He winked boldly and Belle's pulse raced.

"When you finish feeding Elizabeth, send her upstairs. The rest of you had better hurry." She set her hands on her hips and ignored Morgan's knowing grin. "That includes you, Mr. Rory McGinnis."

Behind her back, the youngster grumbled, but she knew he would obey. Belle rushed to the security of her room to get away from Morgan's disturbing presence. Her heart pounded and her skin heated. He was the most impossible man, and she didn't need him to keep her from her purpose. Thankfully, the one place he wouldn't follow her was to church. She needed a few minutes of peace away from him and the impropriety of Eden House.

It seemed that the reputations of Eden House and her former husband preceded Belle to the church. As Corbett drove his elegant buggy into the churchyard, Belle wondered if she'd grown two heads. Women stopped in the middle of conversation and stared. Men studied her with open admiration. Children stopped running and pointed at the entourage in the wagon.

Belle held her head high. She and the children wore their Sunday best, clean, pressed apparel that was fashionable in the city. Nobody had any reason to look down their noses at her. She waited for Corbett to stop and help her down. With Beth in her arms, Rosalind at her side, and the boys trailing behind, she accepted her escort's hand at her elbow.

The clang of church bells welcomed the worshipers. Corbett escorted her up the steps where the minister greeted his flock. The sixty-something man brushed his hand across his nearly bald head as Belle approached. Corbett stopped and removed his derby hat. Her escort wore a smartly tailored suit and black overcoat. He offered a hand to the minister.

"Reverend Steward, I would like to introduce Mrs. Isabella Jordan and her . . . children." Corbett stumbled, not sure what to call Belle's charges.

She set Beth on the floor, and stuck out a hand. "I'm very happy to meet you, sir."

His gaze spread from her to Beth, to Rosalind, to Rory, and stopped at Jerome. "*Your* children?"

"Why, yes. And a handsome crew if I must say so myself." Not surprised at the prejudice, she ushered the youngsters into the building. "We're looking forward to your message."

"We'll sit back here," Corbett offered, gesturing to the second pew from the rear.

Clearly he didn't want his friends and associates to stare at him with the widow Jordan and her crew of orphans. His caution didn't prevent the assembly from gazing at Belle as if Jezebel herself had invaded their hallowed halls.

As the first notes of the piano vibrated through the building, a finger tapped her shoulder from behind. She glanced back and spotted Sheriff Sullivan directly behind her with Abby at his side. The man smiled and mouthed a greeting. With a nod, she acknowledged him, and returned her gaze to the minister.

For the duration of the service, Belle ignored the obvious dislike of the people surrounding her. Frowns and gazes darted to her throughout the service. Even the hymns, the prayers, and the sermon didn't soothe her spirit. The message was one of hell, fire, and brimstone. It wasn't her imagination that the preacher pointed his long finger at her, or that his words were directed at the sinners in the group. She had little doubt that he assumed she'd given birth to all four children, including Jerome.

When the minister pounded on the pulpit and shouted a warning for the sinners, Beth let out a yell. "Want Morgie," she cried.

Belle rocked the child to quiet her. "Hush, darling. You'll see Morgan later."

The little girl grabbed a handful of Belle's hair and caught the veil of her hat. "Don't like church. Want Morgie."

Around them women made shushing noises, while the children giggled. The minister's voice boomed above the din, and Beth screamed louder. Rory reached for the child, only to have her punch him in the eye. He yelled in pain, and Beth wiggled out of Belle's arms and streaked down the aisle toward the pulpit.

Jerome took off after the little girl, grabbing her by the waist as she reached the first pew. Beth wiggled and screamed louder. Her hat askew, Belle jumped up. Her face was heated with embarrassment. Their first visit to the local church had turned into a total disaster. One little girl had disrupted the entire service. As Jerome dragged the screaming child, Belle gestured the others to the door.

Rory and Rosalind stumbled out of their pew and raced for the exit. Obviously humiliated by the spectacle, Corbett whispered apologies and followed at their heels.

At the door, the minister's words hit her squarely in the back. "The devil's own spawn has invaded our presence. Pray that the sins of the fathers will not destroy their children."

Belle's temper erupted like a volcano. She turned to defend herself, when Corbett's hand fastened on her upper arm. "Let's go," he ordered, in a tone unlike the usually mild-mannered lawyer.

At his fancy buggy, she gathered Beth in her arms. The child laughed, as if pleased to have her way. "You're going to be punished, little girl. No dessert for you."

"Morgie give dessert to Beth." She set her jaw in a determined line.

"Oh, no he won't, Miss. Now get up here with the others." The children loaded into the back seat of the buggy. Belle turned to Corbett. "I apologize for what happened. She's never acted like that before. In New Orleans, I took her to church often. I hope this didn't embarrass you too badly."

He caught her hands in his. "I'll get over it, my dear Isabella. Children will be children."

His endearment surprised her. "May I try to make it up to you by inviting you to dinner at Eden House. I've prepared a beef roast, and it will only take moments to get it on the table."

"I would be pleased to dine with you." He helped her onto the high seat and settled beside her. Beth had quieted and was now laughing and tugging on Rory's cap.

Belle had hoped to fit into the society of Paradise, but now it looked as if she would forever be considered an outsider. As a housekeeper, she'd always been relegated to the fringes of society. It looked as if it was happening again because she was the widow of the notorious James Jordan—a man who had for years shocked their sensibilities with his sinful life. They had passed the sins of her husband to her and the children.

"Don't look so sad, Belle. I'll help you convince the good people of Paradise that you're as good or better than they." Corbett snapped the lines and the horses took off at a trot.

"I'm not sure I want to try. Besides, we might decide to leave Paradise." For the first time, she voiced her concerns for the future.

"Where will you go?"

"I don't know. If I decide to sell my interests in the businesses, I'll find someplace else to live."

"If you need legal assistance, don't hesitate to call on me. can assist you in locating a buyer for your interests."

She set her hand on the lawyer's arm. "I will, Corbett. And appreciate your kindness and support."

They entered Eden House through the front door. Beth ran ahead, shouting for Morgan. Belle and Corbett entered last. After removing their outerwear, she led the children and the lawyer toward the kitchen. Succulent aromas wafted in the air. Surely her roast didn't smell that good. She came to a surprised halt as they entered the kitchen.

Wearing an apron over his faded denim trousers and plaid shirt, Morgan stood in front of the stove stirring a large pot. Vivian was at the sink, and Savannah was headed toward the dining room carrying an armload of dishes.

"What is going on here?" Belle studied the array of pots on the stove.

Morgan glanced at her, then his eyes narrowed on Corbett. "Nice of you to escort Belle to church, Hayes. Reckon you'd better get on with your business."

Again Morgan's rudeness irked Belle. "I've invited Mr. Hayes to have dinner with us. He'll be staying."

Savannah smiled over her shoulder. "I'll add another plate to the table." Today the woman was attired in a simple calico frock with her black hair twisted in a conservative bun. Her appearance was a sharp contrast from the first time Belle had seen her only a week earlier.

As usual, Beth raced to Morgan and locked her arms around his legs. "Morgie, Beth don't like church."

Morgan set aside the large spoon and hunkered down to the child's level. "Why not? Didn't they sing and pray?"

"The man hollered at me. Beth 'fraid of him."

Belle knelt down to remove the little girl's coat. "It was only the preacher emphasizing a point. She isn't accustomed to such demonstrative sermonizing."

Her hands tangled with Morgan's as they both reached for

the buttons on Beth's coat. Their gazes met over the child'
head. His eyes grew warm, and heat sizzled through her. H
smelled of roasting beef and spices. The flowery apron coverin
his denims made him more human, less aloof, but incredibl
masculine. And as tempting as sin.

Beth fell into Morgan's arms, allowing Belle to loose he
coat. When she was free of her outer wear, Beth wrapped he
arms around Morgan's neck. As he stood, Morgan placed hi
hand at Belle's elbow and helped her to her feet. Tingles race
up her arm.

Rory stared openly at Vivian, her hands still in dishwater
She winked at the young man over her shoulder. "I could us
a little help from a handsome man," she said.

He jumped, and grabbed a drying towel. "Yes, ma'am. I'l
be glad to help."

Returning to the kitchen, Savannah glanced at Jerome, stand
ing alone near the doorway. "How about helping set the table?"

The youngster raced to help. The boy enjoyed being neede
and Belle was grateful to the pretty woman who took him unde
her wing.

Belle returned her gaze to Morgan with Beth on one arm
the other hand stirring the pot. "What are you cooking?" sh
asked.

"My specialty—rabbit stew. Vic brought in a couple o
rabbits he'd killed this morning. Thought we'd add it to the fin
dinner you've prepared. Looks like we'll need it, considering w
have company."

As soon as the words left his mouth, the rear door agai
opened, admitting Abby on Dan Sullivan's arm. "Add anothe
couple of plates to the table, Vannah," he called. "Looks a
if we're feeding the entire town."

Belle glared at him. "Come to think of it, that's an excellen
idea. For Christmas we should open Eden House and invite th
entire populace."

He shot her a hard glare. "We'll talk about that later."

"May I lend a hand?" Corbett asked.

"Why don't you wait in the parlor with Vic and Louise," Morgan said. "You, too, Sullivan. You'll both just get in the way."

"Since you have everything under control, I'll take Beth out of your way. Come, darling, let's go into the parlor and wait until Mr. Morgan has dinner on the table."

"You're deserting me?" Morgan grumbled.

"You go ahead, Mrs. Jordan," Savannah said. "We'll take care of everything."

Morgan grumbled under his breath. For a change, Belle felt as if she'd gotten the upper hand. It was a rare and heady feeling.

Morgan couldn't remember when he'd last sat down to a dinner as a family. Not that the odd collection of people were a family—with the exception of Belle and her children. The other individuals had come together strictly by chance.

The residents of Eden House usually ate alone in their spare time. Rarely had they gotten together for a real family-type meal. That is until Belle showed up and tried to make the house a home.

As they set the serving dishes on the large rectangular table, Dan Sullivan shifted away from Abby and held a chair for Belle. As if remembering his manners, the sheriff held a chair for Abby, seating himself between the women. Morgan spotted Hayes darting toward the table. Effectively thwarting his plans, Morgan plopped little Beth on the other chair beside Belle. "She was looking for her mama," he said.

Frowning, Hayes had no place to go but at the head, opposite Louise. Vic made sure he was seated beside Louise. The others found seats around the table. Morgan stood aside and inspected the table, laden with food. He counted chairs and, as he'd planned, there was no place for him.

"Looks like we'll have to share, little bit." He plucked Beth from the chair, and took the child's place between Belle and her young daughter, Rosalind. "You don't mind, do you Rosie?" he asked permission of the little dark-haired girl.

Shyly, she shook her head. "No, Mr. Morgan."

Lifting the girl's chin, he smiled down at her. "You know, Miss Rosie, I'm willing to bet you'll grow up even prettier than your mama."

Rosalind's cheeks pinked, and she giggled like a happy little girl. Until now, Morgan had rarely been near children. To his surprise, he found them interesting and charming. If he kept up being so nice, he was certain to ruin his bad reputation.

He set Beth on his lap and brushed his arm against Belle's. "You don't mind do you, *Bella mia?*"

"As long as she eats her dinner." She shifted to put some space between them.

Louise grinned. "You had better watch that young'un, Morgan. She likes to wear her food."

He laughed. "I can handle her. She's always a good girl for Morgie."

"Beth love Morgie." She threw her arms around his neck and planted a loud kiss on his cheek. His heart tumbled at the child's trust in him. More than anything he hoped he didn't disappoint her.

Conversation was lively and loud around the large table. Sheriff Sullivan directed his comments to Belle, inquiring about her stay in Paradise. Hayes ignored Abby, speaking over the young woman and the sheriff to Belle.

Morgan found the situation rather humorous. Both Corbett and Dan had been frequent "guests" at Eden House, yet around Belle, they were the most moral and righteous gentlemen in town.

Vic and Louise didn't seem to notice anybody else at the table. As for Morgan, he kept up a running dialogue with the four children. Occasionally Vivian and Savannah chimed in.

When the meal ended, Vivian served the pies she'd spent the morning baking. It was the first time in the year the woman had been with them that she admitted she could cook. Even Savannah was impressed, although she claimed not to know her way around a kitchen.

Louise and Vic served coffee in the parlor. Dan and Corbett fell all over themselves to escort Belle to the davenport. Sandwiched between the men, she reached for Beth, who climbed up on her lap. Savannah and Vivian stayed behind to clear the table, with the assistance of the three older children.

When the cups were empty, Corbett leaned closer to Belle. "Belle—I hope you don't mind my calling you by your given name—would you like to go for a ride in the countryside. It's quite lovely this time of the year."

Morgan stood. "That's an excellent idea. Why don't we all go out to the ranch? I promised to show the children my horses and cows. Should be an interesting afternoon."

"Morgan, I don't think . . ."

"Sure Belle, the children will enjoy an outing and I want to give them another driving lesson. You enjoyed spending the night out at the ranch with me a couple of days ago." He reached for her hand and helped her to her feet.

Her gaze shot daggers at him for the reminder of their near indiscretion at the ranch. "Really, Morgan."

"Belle, I hoped we could go alone," Corbett whispered.

Dan Sullivan leaped to his feet. "That's a fine idea. We can all go."

Chapter 10

Dusk was falling when the entire entourage returned to Eden House late that evening. Somehow Morgan had managed to manipulate them so Belle and Abby rode in the rear seat of the buggy with Corbett driving and Dan beside him. This was hardly what either man wanted. Abby was clearly unhappy. Belle suspected the young woman cared for Dan, but from the way he acted, the feeling wasn't returned. She hoped the girl wouldn't be too hurt by Dan's dalliances.

The children enjoyed the outing. Morgan allowed the boys to drive the wagon, and even Rosalind got her turn. Beth gloried in being in Morgan's arms.

As they left for their own homes, both Corbett and Dan asked permission to call on Belle. Although she wasn't interested in courting, inborn good manners would not allow her to be rude to either man. Neither man affected her the way Morgan did. Nor did they have the ability to fuel her temper the way he did at their every encounter.

She didn't like the way he'd used the children, mainly Beth, to aggravate her. If she didn't know better, she would think he was jealous. That was impossible. He may be attracted to her, but he certainly didn't have designs on her—except where it came to her share of their property. And she wouldn't get involved with a man like Morgan if he were the last male on God's green earth.

After sending the children up to their rooms to wash and change into bedclothes, she carried up a tray for them. The house was very quiet, as Eden House was closed on Sunday.

The busy day had taken its toll on the children. All four fell asleep the instant their heads hit the pillows. Belle covered them with their blankets and made sure a low fire burned in the fireplaces.

She returned the tray and dirty dishes to the kitchen. For a long moment she stared at the hallway that led to Morgan's apartment. The need to set things straight with the man over-ruled propriety. Although she knew it wasn't proper for a woman to go to a man's room unescorted, she took a tentative step down the short hallway. A sliver of pale yellow light came from under the door. Not sure if he was awake or sleeping, she knocked softly on the door.

"Come in," came the deep, raspy voice.

Her hand trembling, Belle twisted the knob and shoved the door open a crack.

At her first view of his private quarters, a shiver raced over her. If she had a lick of sense, she would retreat as quietly as she'd come. Morgan was a dangerous creature, as wild and untamed as the winter wind that whipped down from the mountains. Every time she came near him, she felt as if she was being swept away in an avalanche of emotions.

Belle took one step across the threshold. Her heart thundered so loud, she was afraid she would wake the entire household. She took a deep breath to bolster her nerve. If she didn't define their partnership and relationship, she would never be able to remain in Paradise or in the home she'd promised the children.

Flames flickered in the marble fireplace, illuminating a figure slouched in a large leather easy chair. A thin curl of gray smoke came from the cheroot in the hand drooped over the arm of the chair. A glass and crystal decanter sat on the table at his elbow. She took one cautious step forward. The thick carpet muffled her footsteps.

"Close the door, Isabella, you're letting in a draft."

Instincts warned her to bolt and run. Instead, she swallowed her trepidation and closed the door behind her.

"How did you know it was I?" she asked, struggling to gain the upper hand.

He laughed, and moved his hand to take a puff of the cheroot. "Who else would be sneaking into my room so late at night?" He rose and faced her with his back to the fireplace. Silhouetted by the light from the fire, he was as large and frightening as the devil himself. "I sort of expected you."

She leaned against the door in a show of bravado she was far from feeling. "Are you alone?"

"All by my lonely." He gestured to the room bathed in shadows. "Come in and join me. Care for a drink?"

"No, thank you. I do not imbibe."

He tossed down his drink and returned the glass to the table. "Do you have any bad habits, *Bella mia?*" *Other than tormenting a man nearly beyond his endurance?* He refilled the glass with the whiskey that continually reminded him of the color of her eyes.

She remained at the door, as if she could slink through the thick wood and disappear. He shook his head to clear away the cobwebs. For an hour he'd been staring into the fire, thinking about how she would feel in his arms, and aching for her in his bed. Was she real, or an apparition out of his dreams?

"A few."

"I know you gamble, and your temper is barely kept in check." He twisted the cheroot in his fingers. "Did you come to sucker me into a poker game?"

''No, I want to talk.''

He lifted his hands in surrender. She moved slowly, the pale light from the fire making her look like an angel stepping into the hell of his world. Loose tendrils of her hair kissed the cheeks where he longed to run his tongue. Her wrinkled gown nipped in at her waist and flared over her hips. His fingers itched to loose those buttons and learn the treasures hidden under the layers of clothes.

''What transgression have I committed now?''

''You embarrassed all of us today.''

''How did I do that? I thought I was the epitome of the gentleman today. I didn't attempt to accost you once.'' Morgan didn't try to hide the humor in his voice. He tossed the cheroot into the fire.

Her cheeks pinked as pretty as a baby's bottom. ''I'm talking about the way you treated Corbett and Dan.''

''So, we're on a given name basis, are we? When are you going to realize I don't give a damn about either of them?''

She stood inches from him. The aroma of lavender wafted from her hair, but she also carried the smell of cinnamon and pastry. His mouth watered to touch his tongue to her lips and learn their taste.

''Don't be so sarcastic. None of us were happy with the way you managed to ruin the ride to the ranch. Corbett wanted to escort me, and he ended up sitting with Dan.''

Laughter bubbled from his throat. ''He didn't look too happy, did he?''

''He was not. Neither was I.'' Her eyes sparkled with golden highlights. He was seconds from pulling her into his arms and silencing her with his kiss.

''Can't help that. Both Dan and Corbett wanted to sit with you. One of the two would be disappointed. And there was poor little Abby. I think she's sort of sweet on Dan, but he doesn't even notice her. I thought it was a fine compromise. Nobody was happy, but nobody was disappointed either.''

Except Morgan. He would have preferred both men go their own way. His attitude surprised him. He'd known many women, but never had he felt as possessive as with Belle.

"Morgan, I'm quite capable of deciding who I wish to be with. And who can call on me. They've both been very kind."

"Kind? Is that what you call it? Corbett likes your inheritance. And Dan, well, you are a fine-looking woman. Our sheriff is known as a skirt chaser. We give him an occasional free romp just to keep peace in the town."

"That was crude and unnecessary."

"Widowed a couple of months, and already you have two suitors. I won't have you marrying either of them."

"How do you intend to stop me?"

"I'll marry you myself if I have to."

She curled her hands into fists. He fully expected her to take a swing at him. "You pompous ass. You arrogant oaf."

"Are you through calling me names? I've been called worse. Stick around awhile, and I'll teach you how to really curse."

"You think a man can't be interested in me? That they're only calling on me for the property?" Her voice dropped to a husky whisper. "Am I so unappealing as a woman?"

"Belle, I've never seen a more desirable woman." He lifted his hands to her face. With gentle fingers, he brushed the hair from her cheeks. She trembled under his touch.

"Morgan, I won't have you insulting me or playing with my emotions." Her hands caught his wrists, stilling his movements.

"*Bella mia,* can't you believe that I find everything about you fascinating? That I'm about to shock your sensibilities by kissing you until you can't think about anybody else but me." He dropped his head and kissed her forehead. "I'll give you exactly until I count to ten to walk away from me. If you're still here, I won't be responsible for what happens."

"One."

Belle stared into his midnight blue eyes, hypnotized by his gaze.

"Two."

Prudence told her to run as fast as she could away from Morgan.

"Three."

She had to protect her emotions by getting out before she drowned in her forbidden needs.

"Four."

His lips nuzzled her temple above her left ear.

"Five."

Long fingers tangled into the hair at her nape.

"Six."

Tingles sizzled down her back.

"Seven."

Belle's knees grew weak.

"Eight."

Her feet felt as if they were nailed to the floor.

"Nine."

Desire surged through her with the force of a hurricane.

"Ten."

She gave up trying to fight her emotions and lifted her face to his. "You win. Kiss me."

His lips slid across her cheeks. "Are you sure? Once I start, I won't be able to stop short of full possession. I want you, Belle—all of you."

He was giving her a way out—a chance to protect herself. But Belle had sheltered her emotions for too long. She needed to feel a man's love, if it was only for one night. "I've never been surer of anything in my life." Her heart thundered in her chest. "Make love with me."

Morgan wondered if he'd died and gone to heaven. But he hadn't been good enough for that. He must be dreaming. If that were the case, he would simply take what heaven offered and rejoice in the pleasure of the moment.

He cupped her face in his big, rough hands. Her skin was as smooth as the finest satin and as pale as moonlight. His outh traced a line along her full, pink lips. She released his rists, and slid her hands along his shoulders. The touch of er hands to his body sent sparks of lightning through him. Her yes closed, heavy dark lashes rested on her cheeks. Everything out this woman fascinated him.

In the firelight, gold streaked through her brown hair, eminding him of the sunlight through the trees. He liked the ay her cheeks pinked when he touched her. She had curves ade to fit a man's hands, and he couldn't wait to feel her legs rapped around his while they loved each other to exhaustion.

He slipped his tongue past her parted lips. She gasped and pened her teeth. Taking advantage of her surprise, he reached to the recesses of her mouth. As if startled by his touch, she etreated, then eagerly met his probing tongue with her own lick touch.

Desire swept through Morgan like a tidal wave sweeping way everything in its path. She melted against him, pressing er full, soft breasts against his chest. Even through her gown nd undergarments, the taut tips burned into his flesh. Her tomach pressed into his rigid manhood, sending a groan from is throat into her mouth.

Morgan dropped his hands to her back, pulling her fully gainst him, showing without words how much he wanted her. Ie'd never felt this way about a woman before. He'd never et his body and emotions overrule his judgment. With Belle n his arms, he lost all track of time and place. It didn't matter hat she was his cousin's widow, she was woman—warm, ;iving, with the power to either destroy him, or heal the pain f a turbulent life. Either way, he was ready to take her and nake her his own.

Belle shoved her reservations to the back of her mind. She eeded Morgan. Needed to be held, to be kissed, to feel like woman. In Morgan's arms, she wasn't a servant, she wasn't mother, and she wasn't a widow. Belle was a desired and ensual creature.

Her fingers sought the buttons of his shirt, eager to learn the hard planes, the solid muscles and the warmth of his body. A tremor raced over her, the distant thought that she could be making the mistake of her life. His hands stroked her back, erasing the misgivings from her thoughts. All she knew was Morgan and the way he made her feel. Morgan and the touch of his hands. Morgan and the pressure of his body to hers. She felt the hardness of him against her stomach. His need was evident. The expectation that he wanted her sent her blood rushing through her veins like lava spewing from a volcano.

The kiss ended, and their harsh breathing blended with the crackling of the fire in the hearth. She slipped her fingers under his shirt, tangling them in the soft hair on his chest. He gasped. Belle pulled her hand back, afraid she'd committed some offense, done something wrong. "I'm sorry," she whispered.

His kisses continued down her neck to her throat. "Don't be sorry, *Bella mia,* I want you to touch me. It just felt so good."

The knowledge that she could please him sent shivers of pleasure through her. Her body was on fire and his skin was as toasty as a bedwarmer. His hands skimmed her waist; his thumbs brushed the sides of her breasts. The tips tingled and ached for his touch.

Deftly, she released the remaining buttons of his shirt and shoved it aside. His chest was wide and muscular, his stomach corded muscles. His hands moved nimbly to the back of her gown, working at the tiny buttons that ran down her spine. "Too damn many buttons." With one quick jerk, he tore open the gown. Buttons flew and pinged on the floor. Cool air chilled her back. Instantly, Morgan wrapped his arms around her, chasing away the cold. She didn't care that her gown had been destroyed; all she wanted was to feel his touch on her skin.

He pulled the gown forward and shoved it down from her arms. The garment pooled at her waist. With a swiftness that surprised her, the gown ended up on the floor in a puddle of petticoats.

"Why do women wear so many undergarments?" Morgan's mouth traced a line across her collarbones and down the valley between her breasts. "Were they created by sadists to torment men?"

She laughed at his grousing. "You should have to wear this."

"Let's see if we can get rid of this iron maiden." He turned her around, and before she could protest, the corset fell away. She couldn't deny the relief to be rid of the confining garment.

"What did you do?"

He tossed aside a jackknife and grinned. "I put the wretched thing out of its misery."

Morgan scooped Belle up in his arms and lifted her out of the garments. She wrapped her arms around his neck for balance. In a few short strides, he reached the bed. He whisked aside the coverlets and laid her down on the crisp white sheet. He came down with her. Propped on one elbow, he let his gaze drift over her. "You're very beautiful, Belle."

His softly spoken words matched the glimmer in his midnight dark eyes. With one long finger, he brushed aside the strap of her chemise and planted a gentle kiss to her shoulder. His day's growth of whiskers rasped against her skin, adding to the erotic sensations from his touch.

She sifted the silky black strands of his hair through her fingers. Belle couldn't believe how wonderful it was to touch a man, and be touched by him. For so long she'd kept aloof from men, afraid to give her heart, afraid to admit her needs. Being married yet not having a husband had kept her as alone as a spinster. Now Morgan had broken through the barrier she'd built around her heart. She only hoped he didn't shatter her dreams along with her reserve.

Morgan couldn't believe how wonderful Belle felt in his arms. Shivers of desire passed over him. He couldn't remember ever needing a woman as badly as he needed this one. That she'd come willingly to his bed excited him beyond endurance. His lips followed his hands, and his tongue traced a damp path across her chest. The deep valley between her breasts invited his kiss.

Her fingers twisted in his hair, cradling his face to her bosom. His tongue snaked out and tasted the soft flesh. He covered one breast with his hand. The taut nipple pressed against his palm. Carefully, he rolled the bud against his palm. Fire sizzled through him. She groaned, and his tongue grew more aggressive. He covered her other breast with his lips. His tongue stroked and probed through the soft batiste fabric. She squirmed and urged his head closer. Teeth nibbled on the pebbly nub. If possible, he grew harder. He'd never felt like this, never wanted a woman more.

He took a deep breath and lifted his head. The dampness from his mouth left her garment as transparent as glass. "Let me see you, Belle, all of you."

His soft inquiry had Belle's senses racing. She didn't know how to respond. Was it proper to remove all her clothing? Or should she insist on total darkness. The only light in the room was from the fireplace, yet it was enough for her to see every line and emotion on Morgan's face. He didn't wait for an answer. Morgan reached for the hem of her short chemise and tugged it to her thigh, past her hips and over her head. Tossing it aside, he turned his stare to Belle. With only her thin underdrawers remaining, she blushed under his close scrutiny and crossed her hands over her breasts.

"Don't hide, sweetheart. You're lovely."

"Morgan, don't tease me. I'm not a maiden. I've birthed a child."

"That only makes you more desirable." He lifted her hands from her body and pressed them to his chest. "Feel my heart. It's beating as fast as a stallion in a race. I would never jest about something so precious."

As if realizing her nervousness at being seen naked, Morgan returned his attention to her face. His kisses started as tiny pecks and nips. The pressure increased until Belle was lost in the thrill of a man's passion. Their tongues met and tangled. Her body grew warmer, and delightful sensations settled in the secret place between her legs.

She returned his kisses, uncaring of what he must think of her. At some point her drawers disappeared. Before coming to his room she'd removed her stockings and wore only thin slippers on her feet. They, too, flew across the room along with Morgan's shirt and trousers.

Belle nearly came to her senses when he lifted himself from her to remove his winter underdrawers. Only then did she get the full impact of his glorious male body. The man was magnificent in his glorious masculinity. A thin sheen of sweat gave him the sleek appearance of a bronze statue. He was all man, primitive in appearance, and strong in action. Emotions ran wild in her heart. Feelings that had begun the moment she'd seen him burst into full bloom in her heart.

Belle loved Morgan. The realization made her gasp. He stopped the kisses that were even now probing her stomach. "Have I hurt you? I didn't mean to be so rough."

"No, please don't stop." If he had any idea of how she felt, he would surely laugh. Love had no place in his life. For the moment, Belle was satisfied to take what he had to offer, and give herself in return. She was on fire, and only Morgan could quench the flames.

He traced a row of kisses down her stomach and along her legs. Her hands searched his body as far as she could reach. She loved touching him, hearing his sharp intake of breath when she reached a particularly sensitive spot. It was a glorious and heady feeling to know she could pleasure him as he pleased her.

As Morgan kissed and licked his way back up to her body, she wondered how much more of his sensuous ministrations she could bear without going mad. Every nerve tingled, her skin glowed with a life of its own. Her body cried out for release.

He paused at the junction of her thighs and parted her legs with his knee. Hovering above her, he met her gaze, his eyes voicing an unspoken plea. Her breath caught at the desire and passion that passed between them. His manhood was hard and ready. Her body was warm and opened to him of its own accord. "Yes, Morgan. Now," she pleaded.

Morgan needed no further invitation. It had been hell holding back, but heaven anticipating the glory of her body. Inching forward, he probed gently, entering slowly, giving her time to adjust to his size. Belle sighed, and Morgan caught the sound with his mouth. Joined with her, as one, he began to move inch by inch until he filled her silken sheath. Perspiration beaded on his forehead in his effort to please her before he pleased himself.

Here was a woman worth pleasing, a treasure worth seeking. His tongue stroked the inside of her mouth in time with the movement of his hips. Her tongue met his and her body arched to meet him. Legs tangled, they set a rhythm as old as time and as new as freshly fallen snow. He felt the tremors deep in her and heard the groaning in her throat. Her release came swiftly, and he knew he couldn't hold back. With a few final deep thrusts, he took the fullness of pleasure, knowing she had received as much as he.

He dropped his forehead to hers, giving his heart a chance to slow to normal. *"Bella mia,"* he whispered. His mind blanked out any conversation. What could he say? That she'd given him a wonderful gift? That she'd reached something inside him no other woman had ever touched? That he was on the verge of falling in love? His mind rebelled at the thought. Not love. Never love. It was pure old sexual attraction between two lonely people—pure and simple.

She brushed the hair from his forehead. "Is something wrong,

Morgan?'' Her face was flushed, and her eyes shiny with passion.

"Wrong? What could be wrong after making love with the most exciting woman I've ever met?" He kissed her gently on the lips. "Am I too heavy for you?" Morgan shifted slightly and rested his weight on his elbows.

"You were frowning."

"I don't want to let you go."

Her fingers danced slowly down his spine. A new burst of desire surged through him, and he knew he couldn't release her, not yet. This time the kiss was hard and demanding. She met his lips with demands of her own. Within seconds Morgan was harder than before and thrusting inside her with renewed vigor. He wrapped his arms around her and flipped over so he was on his back with Belle straddling his hips.

She gasped, and shoved against his chest. "Morgan, what are you doing?"

He cupped her buttocks and held her tight to his body. "Watching you while we make love. I want to know if you turn pink all over when you reach your pleasure."

"I don't know about color, but I grew so hot, I thought I would burst into flames." Slowly she began to move, until he was fully encased in her warmth. He shifted his hands to cup her breasts, thumbing the peaks into hard buds. Her hair had come loose of the pins, and draped her shoulders like a thick veil. If Delilah had looked like Belle, Samson would have shaved his head bald long before he did.

She increased the rhythm, until both reached the top of their private mountain and plunged over as one.

Belle lay quietly in Morgan's arms for a long moment to gain her composure and slow her breathing. He'd been a considerate, yet strong lover. His kisses had excited her, and his lovemaking had thrown her into a frenzy of sensuality she hadn't dreamed existed. He'd wrapped both his arms around her and covered them with the quilt. The fire had burned low and he had fallen into a light slumber. Her body tingled from his touch, and her heart would never be the same.

However, Belle was a practical woman. This was only a brief interlude, a dream that was destined to end. She carefully removed his arm from across her body. Until last evening, no man had ever seen her completely naked. Even on her wedding night, she remained attired in her cotton nightdress. She felt like a wanton, having not only shown herself to Morgan, a man she was not married to, but made love to him with an abandonment that shocked her.

She reached the end of the bed and had just dropped a leg over the side when a hand caught her wrist. "Where are you going?" Morgan's voice was husky with sleep.

"Morgan, I have to return to my room."

"It's still night. You can go back in the morning."

Wanting one last look at him, she turned and smiled. "Rosalind and Beth are in my bed. If either of them wakes and finds me gone, they'll wake up the entire household."

He carried her hand to his lips and planted a moist kiss to her palm. "I forgot you have responsibilities. Will you come back tomorrow night? Or is it already tomorrow?"

Her heart pounded out of control. "I don't know."

"We'll be discreet, Belle. No one need know, if that's what you're worried about."

How could she refuse him? "I'll see. Now I've got to gather my clothes and get back." Since the fire had died down, the room had grown colder. She shivered.

Morgan threw his legs over the edge of the bed and stood naked in all the glory of his bold masculinity. He reached into a carved armoire and pulled out a handsome velvet robe. "Wear this." He held the heavy garment until she slipped her arms into the sleeves and tied the belt in front. The sleeves reached over her hands and the hem dragged the floor.

Warmed by his robe, she set about retrieving her clothing that had been tossed from one end of the room to the other. She looked at the garments in her hands. Her gown was virtually ruined since Morgan had ripped off the buttons, and her corset was beyond repair. It was an old dress anyway, since she'd changed after the wagon ride. And she didn't like corsets. The destruction to her clothing was a small price to pay for the wonderful time she'd spent in Morgan's arms.

Still completely nude, Morgan crossed over to the door. He kissed her gently on the lips, then stepped aside to allow her to leave. "Sleep well, but if you get lonely, I'll be here."

She garnered one last look at him and raced through the doorway. If she didn't get away quickly, she would end up back in his bed. And take a chance on being caught in a terribly compromising, yet exciting, position.

Careful not to make a sound, she crept up the rear stairs. As she neared her room, she spotted a thin slash of pale light in the hallway. Lightning fast, the glow disappeared in the click of a door. She watched, not certain where the light had come from. Had it come from Abby's room, or had Rory or Jerome sneaked a glimpse of her? Who had spied on her and found her returning to her room wearing Morgan's robe? Her cheeks heated. How would she ever explain her midnight tryst? On a sigh, she shoved open the door to her room, and slipped inside.

In the privacy of her room, she determined to put Morgan out of her mind. However, she knew full well she could never put him out of her heart.

Chapter 11

Belle was up very early the next morning. She didn't know if she wanted to see Morgan or not. What would he say to her? How would she react to him? Every time she thought about him, her skin tingled and her body heated. Yet, her feelings confused her.

She'd made love with him—given herself completely and fully. Freely. But no words of love were spoken, no promises made. In the bright light of day, she wondered if she'd made a mistake. How could she face him and not give her emotions away. Belle had never been one to hide her feelings. Surely they were written on her face and in her eyes. It would never do to let anybody know what had happened between them the previous night.

As the hours passed, Belle grew more agitated. It seemed all her worry was for naught. Morgan hadn't shown his face all day. She wondered if Morgan was trying to avoid her. Nobody seemed to know where he'd gone. Her nerves on edge, she became aware of a different kind of tension filling the house. Abby barely spoke to Belle, only answering in one-word responses when questioned. Belle supposed she was upset about Dan Sullivan's interest in Belle. If the young woman only knew what had transpired between her and Morgan, her fears would be relieved.

To keep her mind off Morgan, she decided to give her room a thorough cleaning. She'd moved her things in, but hadn't fully removed the last traces of her late husband's belongings. Rory and Rosalind were in school, and Jeb had promised to pick them up on his way back from town. Jerome and Beth were playing outdoors, and Belle took the opportunity to work off some of her frustration. The dark, heavy furniture wouldn't have been her choice, but it was well made, and with just a few personal touches she would make the room suitable for her needs.

She rearranged her clothing in the large armoire and neatly folded her underwear in the drawers. The dress she'd worn the evening before was in a sad state of disrepair, thanks to Morgan's impatience. She'd stuffed the ruined corset in the corner of a drawer until she could dispose of the tattered garment. She hid Morgan's robe under one of her gowns until she could return it without being seen. Someone, probably Louise, had removed James's clothing and left only a few personal effects.

Belle sifted through the items remaining on the bureau—a ring with a small diamond, his shaving kit with his initials on the mustache cup, and a small jackknife, much like the one Morgan owned. She pulled out the lower drawer of the bureau to stash away his things. Perhaps his daughter would like them someday as a memento of her father.

As she pulled on the drawer, it only opened halfway. Belle knelt on the floor and shoved her hand into the drawer to see what had it blocked. There didn't seem to be anything there, so she jerked harder. The restraining object loosened, and Belle landed on her bottom. As she started to return it to the correct slot, she noticed that the drawer seemed smaller than the oth-

ers—not nearly as deep. She examined it, and saw that the
sides appeared to be cut down.

Curious, she pulled out the next drawer and measured the
two together. Sure enough, the lower drawer was a good six
inches shorter than the other. When she tried to switch the
drawers, the longer one stuck out from the front of the furniture.
By then, her interest was piqued. Reaching into the empty
space, she encountered a board, a false back to the bureau.
Surely she was mistaken. She'd heard about hidden compart-
ments in furniture, but they were mainly in desks.

Although she doubted that anything of importance was hidden in the space, Belle wouldn't rest until she knew what James,
or perhaps the former owner of the piece, had hidden there. It
took all her strength to shove the bureau away from the wall
just far enough for her to get a peek. The back of the bureau
was smoothly finished, as pristine as the front. She ran her
hand along the smooth mahogany. At the spot where the drawer
was, she felt a line, a place where the wood had been cut and
then put back together. She thought for a moment about how
to access the space, short of knocking a hole in the wood with
a hammer. But that would make too much noise, and Belle felt
the need for secrecy.

Her gaze fell on her correspondence on the small secretary
in the corner. Surely if there was a hidden compartment, it
would be in the desk. But she knew little about her late husband,
and she doubted that James did what was expected.

Picking up her letter opener, she listened for noise in the
hallway. She chided herself for thinking she was doing something illegal or illicit. After all, it was her property. Careful
not to mar the finish, she slipped the tip of the steel knife into
a narrow crack. She pried, and to her surprise, a rectangular
panel popped out into her hands.

She gasped. Shoving in her hand, she removed two cloth
bags and an envelope. A smaller bag was shoved into the corner.

She retrieved it and carried her newly found treasures to the bed. The larger bags were heavy, as if they contained rocks.

Feeling like a sneak thief, she dumped the objects on her quilt. Sure enough, there were rocks of a sort. Tiny specks of metal glinted in the sunlight from the window. She'd never seen gold or silver ore, but instincts told her that it could be valuable if James had seen fit to conceal it. She opened the envelope and read carefully. It was an assayer's report on the ore that James Jordan had brought to be tested. Although she knew little about mining, according to the report, it was a very rich mine. One worth a fortune. The next words shocked her. The ore had come from the J & T Mine—Eden vein.

Belle recoiled in shock. Morgan had told her that the mine was played out. Even Corbett had confirmed it. But what did this new discovery mean? Was Morgan lying, or had James discovered another vein and kept it from his partner? She seemed to recall Louise or somebody mentioning that James had tried to buy Morgan out of the partnership, but Morgan refused to sell. Confused by the situation, she decided that until she knew exactly whom to trust, she would keep this bit of information to herself.

She opened the last bag, and nearly cried aloud when the few pieces of jewelry fell into her hand along with a number of gold coins. She touched the cameo Mr. Robinson had given her when she graduated school, the ring that had been her mother's, and the string of pearls she'd saved to buy for herself. James had stolen her few treasures when he'd also taken her money and deserted her.

Why had he kept these pieces all these years? She'd assumed he'd sold them that very day. Was there a bit of affection or goodness somewhere in the bottom of his black heart? What about the coins? She counted close to two hundred dollars. Had he left it here for her? She tied the strings of the bag and shoved it into her apron pocket. It belonged to her, and she intended to keep what was hers. The other items would be safer in their own hiding place. She returned the bags of ore and the report to the cavity and replaced the panel.

Footsteps rang in the hallway. Hurriedly, Belle shoved the bureau against the wall and replaced the drawer. No sooner had she straightened than her door burst open. Rosalind raced into the room and flung herself at Belle.

Icy tears tracked down the little girl's pink cheeks. Jerome and Beth followed at a slower pace. "Darling, what's wrong?" Belle knelt down to eye level to her daughter.

"Mama, it's Rory."

"Rory?" Belle's heart twisted. "Did he do something to you?"

"No, Mama. The teacher was mean to us today. She called us names, and she punished Rory and said he can't leave school until you go to fetch him." The child buried her face in Belle's shoulder.

"Love, what kind of names did the teacher call you?"

Rosalind shook her head. "She said we were bad."

"Did you do anything bad?" Her shy daughter had never before been spoken to harshly.

"No, Mama. I promise. I was good. She don't like us."

Belle could well imagine why. After the froward looks they'd gotten the day before at church, she could guess what the teacher thought of the new residents of Eden House. It didn't matter if the children were as pure as newly driven snow, they were guilty by association.

"What's all the commotion in here?"

Belle stared at Morgan standing bold as brass in the doorway. Beth darted into his arms. He wore his heavy sheepskin jacket over faded denims and work shirt. He picked up the child and tossed her into the air.

Belle stood, keeping her hand on her daughter's shoulder. "Rory has been punished and the teacher wants to see me."

The smile on his face vanished. "Then let's go see what the old biddy wants."

"Morgan, really, I can handle it myself."

He set the toddler in the middle of the wide bed. "You can't drive the wagon, and I've let Jeb go for the day. I'll take you myself."

Having no other recourse, Belle reached into the armoire for her cape. The sooner she got it over with, the better for them all. "Rosie, sweetheart, will you and Jerome watch Beth? You can stay in here where it's nice and warm. When I get back, I'll give you some of the pie left from yesterday."

Rosalind wiped her cheeks with the back of her hand. "Yes, Mama. But don't be too mad at Rory. He didn't mean to get in trouble."

Jerome folded his thin arms over his chest. "I'll keep watch over them, Miz Belle. You ain't got to worry about nothing."

"Thank you, darlings. I don't know what I would do without you." She kissed all three children, then followed Morgan into the hallway.

He paused at the stairway. "Let me go first, in case you trip again."

There was no point in arguing that she had been pushed. "Okay." She hadn't seen him all day, and her heart beat a little faster as she stared at his wide back and the top of his shiny black hair.

"It will only take a minute to hitch up the team. You can wait for me in the kitchen where it's warm." He proceeded ahead of her to the rear door. Abby and Mrs. Franklin were in the kitchen preparing dinner. The housekeeper greeted Belle, but Abby kept her back to her.

"I'll go with you. I don't want to waste any time."

Morgan held the door and together they went into the chill afternoon. It hadn't snowed since the day she'd gone out to the ranch, and then only in the mountains. So far, the weather had remained rather mild, although after spending her entire life in the deep South, to Belle it felt as cold as the Arctic.

She waited patiently as Morgan hitched up the horses. Forcing her thoughts away from the man, she focused her mind on Rory. Whatever offense he'd committed must have been serious for the teacher to keep him after school and request Belle's presence.

When he finished, he led the team from the stable and helped Belle into the seat. He shoved her over and climbed up beside her. With a shake of the lines, the horses took off at a trot. They'd gone a short way when Morgan dipped into his pocket and pulled out his fist.

"You left something last night," he said, a smile in his voice.

Belle's chest constricted. She'd left her heart, but he would never know. She held out her palm.

He opened his fist and dropped a handful of buttons and hairpins into her hand. "I'll keep one as a memento, if you don't mind." He tucked a single round button into his shirt pocket.

Her emotions ran wild. Was a button the only thing he wanted of her, a token to remember their affair? And that's exactly what it meant to him—an affair with a lonely woman. She shoved her selfish concerns aside. Rory was what was important, not she and not Morgan. They were adults, and they were responsible for their own actions. It was up to her to see that the youngsters in her care grew up to be trustworthy adults.

"Thank you." She dropped the offending objects in her apron pocket along with the bag of her jewelry.

It took only minutes to reach the schoolhouse. It was growing dark, too late for a youngster to walk home from school. Belle jumped down as soon as Morgan drew the team to a stop. She didn't wait for him. This was her problem, and she intended to handle it her way.

Lamps glowed in the large room, but the fire in the Burnside stove had burned out. She shivered more from the harsh expression on Miss Lessman's face than the cold.

Bundled in a heavy coat, the teacher signaled Belle into the room. Rory was seated in a corner, his arms folded across his chest, a belligerent look on his face. He dropped his gaze when he spotted Belle.

"Well, Mrs. Jordan. It is about time you got here."

"Miss Lessman, I came as soon as I learned there was a problem. Will you be so kind as to tell me what Rory has done?"

The woman lifted her gaze and her eyes widened when Morgan entered the room. He approached and stood beside Belle. "*He* is the devil incarnate." She pointed a ruler at Rory. Belle fully expected the child to stick out his tongue at the teacher. Fortunately, he kept his temper and minded his manners.

Belle approached the dais that elevated the teacher above her class. "That is no way to speak about a child. I'd appreciate your holding your tongue."

She gasped as if she'd been slapped. "Madam, I speak as I will. What can you expect out of a boy being raised in that den of iniquity? He's surrounded by sinners and reprobates. I won't even speak the words that describe those women."

Morgan made a move toward the teacher. Belle stopped him with her hand on his arm. "Exactly what did Rory do?"

"I caught him behind the school smoking a cigar. And he was passing it to the other boys. Corrupting their morals as well as his own."

"A cigar? Wherever did he get a cigar?" She slanted a glance at Morgan. He kept a humidor in his office. "Never mind, that isn't important. I'm sure he meant no harm. However, I'll see that he's properly chastised, and he will not corrupt your other students again."

"Rory McGinnis," she called. "You may go home. Another offense, and I'll have you expelled from school."

The boy opened his mouth to speak, but stopped at Belle's hard stare. "I can assure you he will be on his best behavior.

Rory, please button your coat and put on your hat. Mr. Travers and I will take you home.''

''Mrs. Jordan.'' The woman stood and glared at the trio. ''I hope you realize that it is imperative that the boy obey orders. I'll not have him offend the other parents by his mischief. It is no wonder he's the devil's own spawn, since he resides in a house with women of questionable virtue.''

This time it was Morgan who stopped Belle from lashing out at the woman. ''No use arguing, Belle. She won't listen.''

Head held high, she draped her arm across Rory's narrow shoulders and led him out of the school. Once the cold, fresh air hit her face, she realized she'd been holding her breath. She wanted to curse and scream, but that would be a sorry example for the boy.

Silently, they loaded into the wagon, Rory bundled in the blanket in the rear. Once her temper cooled, Belle spoke. ''Rory, where did you get the cigar?''

''I found it.''

''Where?''

''Don't remember.''

Morgan chuckled under his breath.

''Morgan, this is not funny,'' she declared.

''Sorry. I think he found it in my office. I keep a supply in the humidor.''

She slanted a glance over her shoulder. ''Did you steal it from Mr. Morgan?''

''I didn't steal it. I found it.'' Rory buried his face in the collar of his jacket.

''You realize that you've broken at least three of my rules. Stealing, smoking, not to mention lying about it.'' She drew a deep breath. ''What am I going to do with you?''

''I didn't mean to do nothing wrong. I just wanted to show those bumpkins a thing or two.'' The youngster sounded more sorry because he'd gotten caught than because he'd done wrong.

"Belle, why don't you let me handle Rory?" Morgan pulled his hat low on his eyes.

"It's really my problem, not yours."

"He stole from me, and I'm afraid I'm partially responsible by setting a poor example."

After a moment's thought, she agreed it would be best to let a man handle the boy. "Okay, we'll do it your way. You won't draw blood, will you?" In her heart she knew Morgan wouldn't lift a hand to the boy. However, it wouldn't hurt to let Rory squirm a little.

"No. We'll deal with this man to man." By then they'd reached the house. When Rory started to jump out of the wagon, Morgan stopped him. "You'll help me with the horses, then we'll go in and talk about the cigar."

As much as she hated to admit the truth, there were some things only a man could handle. With one last glance over her shoulder, she lifted her skirt and headed back to the house.

Morgan wasn't sure how he was going to handle the situation into which he'd been thrust. He hadn't planned to become a father so quickly, and he wasn't ready or qualified to take on that kind of responsibility. However, as long as they were under his roof at Eden House, he felt the need to at least offer a man's viewpoint.

In a lot of ways, Rory was very much like Morgan as a youngster struggling to find his own way as a man. No doubt Belle had been very lenient with Rory, probably in an effort to compensate for a turbulent childhood. He'd seen how upset and disappointed she'd been when she'd learned the boy needed to be disciplined. The woman had taken on too much responsibility in trying to raise all these orphans without a man's help.

As they drew up to the stables, Morgan shoved aside his turbulent thoughts. Just because he'd made love with Belle didn't mean there was anything deeper between them. He wasn't about to step in and take the place of the husband who'd deserted her years ago, even if that man had been his own flesh and blood.

Oh, but he'd enjoyed their lovemaking. Belle was as hot as a Louisiana summer afternoon and as giving as a saint. After she'd slipped out of his bed, he'd never felt lonelier in his life. Needing time to study on the subject, he'd gone out to the ranch and spent the better part of the day thinking about her. When he couldn't stand not knowing how she felt about things, he returned to the house and into a hornet's nest.

"What are you gonna do to me?" Rory's trembling voice broke into his reverie.

He jumped down from the high seat. "I honestly don't know. Maybe a man-to-man talk might help, or could be you have too much free time on your hands. You might need to do some chores to keep you busy. Then, you ought to have to pay for the cigar you took. They don't come cheap."

Morgan unhitched the team and led the horses into their stalls. He picked up a wide leather strap and slapped it against his hand. The youngster's eyes widened and he cowered a step backward.

"If you're gonna wallop me, I'll take my punishment like a man." Defiant eyes gazed into Morgan's without flinching.

The kid had guts, Morgan had to give him credit. "I don't intend to touch you. I don't believe in striking somebody smaller than me. Now if you were a man full grown, I'd probably beat you to a pulp for causing Miss Belle so much grief."

"I didn't mean to do nothing to her. I just wanted to show those bumpkins that I was better than them."

"Did you?"

"They don't matter no how. None of them knows how to smoke a good cigar. All old Sammy Summers knows is how to smoke corn silk in an old pipe. It stinks to high heaven."

Morgan bit back laughter. This was no time to show any

sign of humor. "What you did really upset Miss Belle. She thought she'd taught you not to steal or lie."

"I didn't steal it. The cigar was lying smack in the middle of that little table in the big parlor. I thought you didn't want it, so I just picked it up."

Morgan tossed the boy a brush. "Help me curry these horses, then we'll go inside and discuss this like men."

On a sigh of relief, Rory worked on the animal until the coat gleamed. Morgan leaned back against a post and watched. He plucked a long, thin cheroot from his pocket and bit off the end. "These are mighty good. Better than that cigar. After you finish mucking out the stalls, you and I will have a little talk."

"Is Miss Belle real mad at me?"

Morgan lit the end and took a deep draft. "No, son, she was mad because she had to go to school and face that teacher."

The boy picked up a shovel and began the odious task. The stable was reasonably clean, as Jeb had mucked it earlier.

"Rosie said the teacher called you names. Can you tell me what she said?"

Rory shrugged his narrow shoulders. "She said that we're bad because we live at Eden House. She don't like Rosie either. Told the other kids to be careful around us."

The wicked old biddy. Morgan clamped his teeth down on the cheroot. "Don't pay them any mind. Miss Belle is a good and respectable woman. And Rosalind is a sweet girl." He took a deep draw to clear his mind. If the teacher were a man, Morgan would show him a thing or two. However it wouldn't do either Belle or the children any good for him to interfere. "Now you, I'm not so sure of."

"I don't like them kids neither. I wish we would never have come here."

"Don't you like Colorado?"

He jabbed the shovel into the ground. "No. I don't like the cold and I sure as hel. . .heck don't like cleaning up after horses."

Morgan clamped a hand on the boy's shoulder. "Son, even in the city somebody has to clean out the stables and scoop up when the horses and mules leave their calling cards."

"I don't ever intend to do that." He wrinkled his nose.

"If you don't get an education, that might be the only job you can get." Morgan shoved open the door and stepped into the growing darkness. "Let's go into the study. I want to teach you a thing or two about being a man."

They passed through the kitchen. Belle was sitting at the table with Jerome and Rosalind. Several books and slates were in front of the children. She looked up, a question in her gaze.

"I'm taking Rory to the study to talk to him. Call us when supper is ready."

Once inside the study, Morgan closed the door behind them. "Now, you've proved to be a fine worker, Rory. I suppose all you need is a man to teach you a few things." He gestured to one of the two chairs fronting the fireplace. Morgan knelt down and stirred up the fire and added several nice logs. "This should keep us warm."

Morgan realized that if Belle knew what he was up to, she would pitch a hissy fit of the worst kind. He smiled to think of her reaction to his methods.

He reached into the humidor and pulled out two big, fat Cuban cigars. Too bad he intended to waste one on a youngster who had no sense of appreciation for the finer things in life. He passed one to Rory. "Now to properly smoke a cigar, you have to snip off the end like so." After using the small scissors he kept on the desk, he passed it to the boy.

"You want me to smoke this cigar?" The youngster's mouth dropped.

"Sure, if you're going to smoke, you have to do it properly." Reaching for the decanter on the sideboard, he filled two small shot glasses of fine Irish whiskey. "You're Irish, aren't you, boy?"

With a brief nod, Rory stared at Morgan.

"Then you'll appreciate a drink now and then." He pressed the glass into the boy's hand. "There's nothing better than good whiskey and a fine cigar. Unless it's a . . . Well, never mind, you're too young for that."

Straightening his shoulders, the boy grinned from ear to ear. "I ain't too young, Mr. Morgan. I'm near grown."

"Good." Morgan held a match to the end of his cigar and took several good puffs. Then he passed the smoke to the boy, and took the other cigar from his fingers. "Just take a few good puffs, inhale deeply, and you'll feel the rich warmth of a good cigar."

"You sure it's okay? Miss Belle will have my hide. She don't take much to drinking and smoking."

"I'll take care of Miss Belle. Drink up." Morgan gulped his whiskey, and the boy did the same. Rory choked, but somehow he managed to swallow. Next, he shoved the cigar between his lips, and did as Morgan had instructed. A wreath of gray smoke circled his head. A bit of sympathy passed over Morgan. It was a hard lesson, and the boy would probably hate him, but it had to be done. He only hoped Belle understood his methods.

For a second, Morgan was afraid his scheme had failed. But as Rory took a second draw of smoke, his face turned a strange green color. His eyes watered, and the boy dropped the cigar into the ashtray on the table between them. He covered his mouth with his fingers and bent his head between his legs.

"Something wrong, son? You look a bit peaked."

"I think I'm gonna puke."

"Take another puff on the cigar. That should clear your head."

Rory stared at Morgan as if he'd gone mad. "I can't. That was the worst thing I've ever tasted." He flung the cigar into the fireplace and raced from the room. Morgan knew where the lad was headed. And he'd bet his bottom dollar it would be a very long time before he took another drink or stole another cigar.

He looked up to see Belle in the doorway staring at him, ire in her gaze. "What did you do to Rory? He ran out the door as if the banshees were hot on his tail."

"Just using a little male logic on the boy. I told him that if he wants to smoke, he should learn to do it properly."

"You taught that boy to smoke when you know it's against my convictions? He looked ill."

"Exactly as I'd planned. Belle, sit down. When I was a boy, James stole a watermelon from a neighbor's patch. He told the farmer that I'd stolen it. Of course, I was as guilty as he was because I ate it, too. The old man was pretty smart for a dirt farmer. He told me that if I wanted watermelon so much, that I could eat all I wanted. At first I thought it was mighty kind of him. I ate the watermelon, and when I was full, he insisted I eat another, and another, and another. I got so sick on watermelon, just telling this story makes me want to follow Rory outside. I've never touched watermelon since."

She smiled with a sunny warmth that could chase away the chill of the coldest winter. "So you think you taught him a lesson? That he won't try to smoke again?"

Morgan gave her a smug, self-satisfied grin. "Yup. But if it doesn't work, I can always beat him to within an inch of his life."

"You wouldn't dare."

The shocked look on her face made him laugh aloud. "Never. But a good threat works wonders."

Chapter 12

Belle didn't know whether to kiss Morgan or kick him.

Rory refused to eat, and went up to his bed early. The boy swore up and down that he would never drink liquor nor touch a smoke for the rest of his life. He'd learned a hard lesson. As much as she disagreed with his methods, Morgan had accomplished in a few minutes what days of talking would never achieve. She was forced to admit that a boy needed a man's strong hand.

After the kitchen was clean and the lessons finished, Belle retreated upstairs with the children. So far, she and Morgan had not had a single moment alone. After dinner, he had dressed and gone into the parlor with Louise and waited for their "guests" to arrive. Strangely, however, she didn't hear as much noise and laughter as the previous evenings.

At about midnight, the house was abnormally quiet. She awoke and made sure the girls were still asleep. Slipping into a robe, she checked on the boys, and found Jerome tossing and turning. His blanket had slipped off, and he shivered in the chill air. She crept to his bed and tucked a quilt over his narrow shoulders. As she lifted her hands, he opened his eyes.

"Miz Belle?" He wiped his eyes with fisted hands.

"Hush, darling. I was just making sure you and Rory were okay. You go back to sleep."

The youngster caught her fingers. "Miz Belle. I saw Earl again."

She brushed her hand across his forehead. "Your angel is always with you. The Bible tells us so."

"He says for you to be careful."

With a small smile, she nodded. The child didn't know that her greatest danger wasn't physical, but emotional. Morgan posed a threat to her heart. "You tell Earl that I'll be on my guard."

"Yes'am." He cuddled down under the quilt. "Miz Belle?"

She lifted her gaze. The child was so loving and giving, she only hoped she could provide the proper home for him. After the things that had happened in the last few days, she doubted her judgment in bringing them all to Eden House.

"Earl said that you're gonna find your treasure."

"Thank your angel for me. We'll have a fine Christmas."

" 'Night."

"Goodnight, sweetheart."

On silent feet, she slipped through the doorway, leaving it open a crack. At the head of the rear stairs, she was torn with indecision. Part of her cried out for Morgan's touch. He'd been constantly on her mind, and she blamed him for her lack of sleep. Yearnings she couldn't understand tumbled in her chest. The sensible Belle demanded she return to her lonely maiden's bed.

Voices drifted from the kitchen. She recognized Morgan's deep voice and Louise's husky tones. Since she was already awake, Belle didn't see any harm in joining them for a few moments.

Cautiously, she continued down toward the kitchen. Near the bottom of the stairs, she heard her name and stopped.

"Morgan, you've got to do something about Isabella." Louise's voice carried up the stairs.

Good manners frowned on eavesdropping. However, Belle's curiosity overran courtesy.

"What can I do, Louise? Hayes made it clear that since James left his share of the house to her, I can't very well toss her out. Not with those children."

China rattled, the sound of cups touching saucers. "I understand. I have to admit I like her, and those children need a home. But it causes a problem for us. Since they came, the men have stayed away in droves. The girls are starting to complain. We're losing money every day. You've got to do something."

"Do you have any ideas?" Morgan asked.

"We don't want to hurt the children, so you'll have to get her to leave of her own accord."

"Isabella has settled in. She's decided to stay, and short of chasing her out with a shotgun, I'm not sure she'll leave." The chair scraped and heavy footsteps marched across the floor.

Belle flattened against the wall to avoid being seen. She bit her lip to keep from moaning. The man who now wanted to get rid of her had only twenty-four hours ago made sweet, passionate love to her.

"I don't want you to shoot her. But she acts so proper and puritanical. You can seduce her. If she thinks her virtue won't be safe around here, she'll leave."

Morgan coughed. "Seduce her?"

Wrapping her arms around her waist, Belle nearly doubled over in pain. Morgan had already seduced her heart and soul as well as her body. And her near tumble down the stairs. Was that part of their scheme to frighten her away?

"Come to think of it, that's not a bad idea. She'll have to leave if she thinks her reputation is in danger from a rogue like

you. We both know how she believes you're like James, the
man who loved her and left her. Surely she won't take that
kind of chance with her virtue.''

"That won't work. Belle wants a home for those children
and she won't leave."

Another chair scraped. "Well, you've got to do something
At the rate we're going, the girls will leave, and Eden House
will shut down before New Year's.''

"I'll see what I can come up with."

Her stomach churned, and Belle was afraid she would be ill
On silent feet, she staggered back to her room. Tears burned
in her eyes, and pain tightened in her chest. Here she'd thought
Morgan cared for her, when all he wanted was to get rid of
her. He'd already seduced her into loving him. Now he was
throwing her love right back into her face like so much garbage

He was a worse scoundrel than his cousin. How could she
even imagine he was different? Morgan and James had been
like brothers. They were cut from the same cloth. Belle could
only blame herself for her indiscretion. She should have known
better. Even Jerome's angel had sent a message to be careful
Too bad the warning hadn't come sooner.

If they were so desperate to get rid of her, there was no
telling what they would try. Not only was she in danger, but
the children were as well. Belle would give her life to protect
them. If the price for their safety was her heart, she would let
Morgan break it and stomp on the pieces.

Setting her mind to leave Eden House as soon as possible
she settled on the rocking chair in her room. She had to make
plans. She'd promised the children a home for Christmas, and
it wouldn't do to uproot them so close to their favorite holiday
After uprooting them once, she couldn't move them again until
after the New Year. She remembered the small bag of coins
James had hidden. It would be enough to get her and the
children settled in a house in Denver, or another city far away
from Morgan.

Take A Trip Into A Timeless World of Passion and Adventure with Zebra Historical Romances!
—Absolutely FREE!

Let your spirits fly away and enjoy the passion and adventure of another time. With Zebra Historical Romances you'll be transported to a world where proud men and spirited women share the mysteries of love and let the power of passion catapult them into adventures that take place in distant lands of another age. Zebra Historical Romances are the finest novels of their kind, written by today's bestselling romance authors.

4 BOOKS WORTH UP TO $24.96—Absolutely FREE!

Take **4 FREE** Books!

Zebra created its convenient Home Subscription Service you'll be sure to get the hottest new romances delivered each month right to your doorstep — usually before they are available in book stores. Just to show you how convenient Zebra Home Subscription Service is, we would like to send you 4 Zebra Historical Romances as a FREE gift. You receive a gift worth up to $24.96 — absolutely FREE. There's no extra charge for shipping and handling. There's no obligation to buy anything - ever!

Save Even More with Free Home Delivery

Accept your FREE gift and each month we'll deliver 4 brand new titles as soon as they are published. They'll be yours to examine FREE for 10 days. Then if you decide to keep the books, you'll pay the preferred subscriber's price of just $4.20 per title. That's $16.80 for all 4 books for a savings of up to 32% off the publisher's price! Just add $1.50 to offset the cost of shipping and handling. Remember, you are under no obligation to buy any of these books at any time! If you are not delighted with them, simply return them and owe nothing. But if you enjoy Zebra Historical Romances as much as we think you will, pay the special preferred subscriber rate of only $16.80 each month and save over $8.00 off the bookstore price!

We have 4 FREE BOOKS for you as your introduction to KENSINGTON CHOICE!

To get your FREE BOOKS, worth up to $24.96, mail the card below. or call TOLL-FREE 1-888-345-BOOK

Take 4 Zebra Historical Romances FREE!

MAIL TO: ZEBRA HOME SUBSCRIPTION SERVICE, INC.
120 BRIGHTON ROAD, P.O. BOX 5214,
CLIFTON, NEW JERSEY 07015-5214

✔ YES! Please send me my 4 FREE ZEBRA HISTORICAL ROMANCES (without obligation to purchase other books). Unless you hear from me after I receive my 4 FREE BOOKS, you may send me 4 new novels – as soon as they are published – to preview each month FREE for 10 days. If I am not satisfied, I may return them and owe nothing. Otherwise, I will pay the money-saving preferred subscriber's price of just $4.20 each... a total of $16.80 plus $1.50 for shipping and handling. That's a savings of over $8.00 each month. I may return any shipment within 10 days and owe nothing, and I may cancel any time I wish. In any case the 4 FREE books will be mine to keep.

Name _____

Address _____ Apt No _____

City _____ State _____ Zip _____

Telephone ( ) _____

Signature _____
(if under 18, parent or guardian must sign)

Terms, offer, and price subject to change. Orders subject to acceptance.
offer valid in the U.S. only.

KNH9A

KENSINGTON CHOICE
Zebra Home Subscription Service, Inc.
120 Brighton Road
P.O. Box 5214
Clifton, NJ 07015-5214

If there really were gold in the mine, it would be enough to support her for the rest of her life. However, for now, it would be her secret. It was sort of an ace in the hole, a secret that would provide security for her and the children. Or she could just sell out to Corbett, and let the lawyer deal with the degenerate man. It would serve Morgan right.

Morgan was caught on the horns of a dilemma. Louise didn't know that he'd already seduced Belle. Or had Belle seduced him? Propped against the counter, he wondered how he was going to handle Belle. She wasn't easily scared, and seducing her certainly wouldn't chase her away.

Louise stood and glared at him. With the lack of "guests," they'd shut down early. Everything she'd said was true. They were losing money because the men were staying away in droves.

"What was that?" Louise glanced toward the rear stairs.

In a few long strides, Morgan was at the foot of the stairway. He'd heard a rustling, but if somebody had been there, they'd disappeared. "Nothing. Must have been the wind."

She set her cup in the dishpan. "Think about what I said. You have to do something."

"Why don't we have a party? Invite the men from town, and give them free drinks and some food. They'll see that we keep the children out of sight, and I hope out of mind."

"A party?" She eyed him suspiciously. "Those degenerates will eat our food and drink our liquor, and not spend a penny."

"I want to show our appreciation for their patronage. When they see that Eden House is open for business as usual, they'll come back with their hard-earned cash."

"Okay. I'll go along. But the girls aren't going to do anything free. If the men want their favors, I expect them to pay double."

"Sounds good. I'll get the word out for a week from now. You see that the food and drinks are flowing."

"And Mrs. Jordan? Will you take care of her, too?"

"You leave Belle to me." He hoped he could handle Belle. But there was no telling how she would react to their plans for a party.

"Good luck."

"I'm going to need it." Morgan waited until Louise retired to her room in the other wing before he trimmed the lamps and locked up the house. He stood for a long moment at the narrow rear stairway and thought about Belle. He'd been thinking about her all day, and he wondered if she would come to him that night.

A disturbing thought stopped him. What if she'd been on her way to him when she'd overheard him and Louise talking about her? Surely she would have misunderstood. He didn't want to hurt her or the kids. He just needed Eden House until he could get the ranch up and running. He'd already spent their ready cash on cattle. And without the mine, he needed the income from the house, as much as Belle hated the enterprise. There was only one way to find out if she'd been eavesdropping.

Morgan took the stairs two at a time and stopped outside her door. No glimmer of light came from under her door, and not a sound could be heard from the room. It was very late, and surely the children were asleep. He lifted his hand to knock and thought better of it. The two little girls slept with Belle, and she would have his hide if he woke them.

Morgan turned on his heels and retreated down the stairs. He would talk to her tomorrow and see if they could make arrangements for the following night. Shoving his hands into his pockets, he decided that was best. How he was going to sleep was beyond him. Especially knowing that the woman he desired was sleeping under the same roof.

Belle tossed and turned all night. She'd heard the footsteps outside her door, but she refused to let Morgan know she was awake. With the two little girls sharing her bed, she cried silently. Her misery tasted as bitter as her salty tears. So Morgan had set out to seduce her in an effort to frighten her away. Little did he know that his scheme had worked. She and the children would leave soon after the New Year.

By his own words, Morgan had admitted he cared nothing for Belle and the children. Well, two can play the same game. He'd toyed with her heart and with her life, and he wasn't going to get away with it.

Belle managed to avoid Morgan that morning by remaining busy. At midmorning, he spotted her alone in the upper hallway. He flashed a smile that would melt a glacier at a hundred yards. She set her reserve against his well-oiled charm. Before she could slip into her room, he caught her arm.

"Belle, I've missed you."

She pressed her hands against his chest to keep him at a distance. "Morgan, somebody might see us."

"Worried about your reputation?" He planted a light kiss to her cheek and wrapped his arms around her waist.

Her breath hitched. With a simple touch, Morgan had her mind spinning and her heart racing. "Yes. I've already been besmirched by living here."

"I have a solution for that. You can move out."

It didn't take Morgan long to get right to the point. He would do and say anything to get rid of her. "But I've decided to make Eden House my home." Until she made other arrangements, her plans for the future would remain unspoken.

"I like having you under this roof. I missed you last night. But do you think this is the right atmosphere for the children? Look what happened with Rory yesterday."

The seduction was starting again. If he thought to frighten her away, he was sadly mistaken. "We like it here. The house is certainly large enough for all of us. I thought I'd worked out a fine compromise."

"I looked for you last night."

She wouldn't let him know that she'd been on her way to him when she learned about his detestable scheme to get rid of her. "The children needed me."

"So did I." He pressed into her stomach, showing his desire. "Come to me tonight."

She jerked back as if she'd been burned. Indeed she had. Her heart had been scorched by his careless selfishness. "I don't think I can. What if somebody sees me?"

A frown turned down his lips. "If you come down after the kids go to sleep and the house quiets, nobody will be the wiser."

The memory of the slash of light she'd seen when she'd sneaked into her room after their last tryst came to mind. She shoved against his chest. "Somebody's coming. Wait for me." Slipping free, she darted down the stairs to the safety of the kitchen where Mrs. Franklin was preparing their dinner. Morgan could wait from now to kingdom come and he wouldn't see Belle in his room or in his bed. That would give the devil his due.

She'd no sooner reached the kitchen than somebody knocked on the rear door. Flinging it open, she spotted Sheriff Sullivan standing on the porch. "Sheriff. Is something wrong?"

"No, ma'am. I hope not." He glanced over her shoulder. "Can I speak to you for a minute?"

Surprised, she gestured him into the house. He shook his head. "Can you come out here?"

Belle glanced back at Mrs. Franklin, who was watching them with interest. She slipped outside and leaned against the door. What problem could have brought the law to Eden House?

Dan shoved back his hat and grinned. The man was as handsome as sin, and as she'd been warned, a lady-killer. "I was real disappointed that I didn't get a chance to be alone with you on Sunday. I really wanted to talk with you and to pay you back for inviting me to stay for dinner. Will you come eat with me at the Palace?"

Was the sheriff calling on her? Did he want to pay court? She thought of Morgan and his plans for her. "Why, Sheriff, I would be delighted. Please give me a moment to fetch my shawl."

Belle returned to the kitchen and raced up the stairs. In her room, she tore off her apron and changed her wrinkled blouse for a pretty pink one with a ruffle at the collar. She smoothed back her hair and added a small perk hat with a single rose. So far, the sheriff was the first male to escort her to a meal that she hadn't prepared. Satisfied with her appearance, she snatched an embroidered wool scarf and her reticule that contained the money she'd won from Morgan. While in town, she might decide to take a few minutes to shop for gifts for the children.

In the hallway, she ran into the housekeeper. "Mrs. Franklin, I'll be out for a while. Could you please ask Jeb to pick up the children from school and have them settle down and do their homework? And would you ask Abby to keep an eye on Elizabeth?"

Morgan appeared from the stairway with Beth in his arms. "Where are you going?"

She ignored his question. "Never mind. Mr. Travers will entertain the baby." Certain the child was in good hands, she started downstairs and out the door. She ran smack into the sheriff's arms.

"Whoa, Miss Belle." He steadied her with his hands on her arms. "Either you're real hungry, or, well, maybe you want to be with me."

It was neither, but Belle didn't want to burst the handsome sheriff's bubble. In truth, she wanted to get away from Morgan before he made an excuse to keep her from leaving. "I'm starved and I'm looking forward to being with you."

Dan gestured to the buggy near the steps. As Belle took his offered hand for help, the rear door burst open. She didn't have to look to know that Morgan filled the doorway.

"Where are you off to? Don't you care that the children wi be home from school soon?" Fury glittered in his eyes, an Beth clung to his neck. Jerome peered around his legs.

"They won't be back for hours. And if you can't look afte Beth, then Jerome can care for her with Abby's help. Goo day." With a curt nod, she climbed into the conveyance. Mor gan growled and slammed the door. Belle hid a smile an cuddled into her shawl. Let him stew for a while. Meanwhile she would try to get a bit of information from the sheriff abo mining and about her late husband.

Dan climbed up beside her and snapped the lines. The tear took off and the sheriff guided them toward town. "Thank for coming with me, Miss Belle. I really hate eating alone."

"Thank you for inviting me, Sheriff. I've been too busy t meet many of the townspeople. I enjoy getting out."

"Paradise must surely be different from New Orleans," h said.

She laughed. "Very different. All of Paradise would fit righ into the French Quarter."

"Is that where you lived?"

"No. The Creoles inhabit the *Vieux Carre*. I lived in th American section called the Garden District. Our houses ar much larger with lawns and gardens. The homes in the Quarte are enclosed around a central courtyard." A twinge of home sickness settled in her chest. She shoved it away. Belle ha left that life behind, and now Colorado was her home.

"Is that where you met James?"

"Yes." Belle didn't want to talk about herself. She stil needed information about her wayward husband. "Did yo know James well?"

"We were friends." The sheriff slanted a glance at her. " found him after the accident."

She studied the sheriff. "I didn't know. How did it happen Nobody ever told me the whole story." He shifted his eyes not meeting her gaze directly.

He tightened his hands on the lines. "James had asked me to meet him out at the J & T Mine. We were near there when I found him in the overturned buggy. He'd broken his neck and was already dead."

"Why did he want to meet you at the mine? Isn't it played out?"

"That's what Morgan says. I'm not so sure you should trust him."

She wasn't sure she could trust Dan, either.

"Did he ever write to you? Let you know he was here in Paradise?"

"No. The first I heard about James was after he'd died."

"Did his will mention anything about the mine? About gold?"

"Gold?" She turned her gaze to the road. Did anybody else know about the report and the gold nuggets she'd found? "Isn't it a silver mine?" Feigning ignorance was the safest course. No telling what would happen if word of the gold got out.

"Yes. I just wondered, is all."

"Sheriff, I hadn't heard a word from James Jordan since the day after we were married. He's never written or corresponded with me in any way. I'm more a stranger to him than his acquaintances in Paradise. Nobody was more surprised than I when I learned I'd inherited his property."

"Morgan wasn't too happy about that."

"No, Morgan wasn't. However, according to Mr. Hayes, there's nothing he can do." Belle decided to try another path. "I'm thinking about selling out my interest. I don't need a partner who doesn't want me around."

He jerked around to stare at her, surprise on his face. "If you're serious about selling the mine, I might be able to help you find a buyer."

She laid her hand on his arm. His muscles tightened under her touch. "Sheriff, Morgan told me the mine is played out. I wouldn't try to swindle anybody by selling something worthless. It would be against my conscience and everything I believe in. I've always believed that honesty is the best policy.'' With that tidbit thrown out, Belle could just sit back and see what developed.

''You're right, ma'am. But sometimes investors come in and buy up mines on speculation. Never know when they'll find another vein. Maybe gold.''

Like James may have done. ''No, if I sell anything, it will be my interest in Eden House.''

''Don't reckon Morgan will like that.''

Her fingers brushed lightly on his heavy coat. ''I don't really care what Morgan likes or doesn't like. I want to do what's best for the children and me.''

His white teeth gleamed when he smiled. As handsome as the man appeared, she doubted his sincerity. Morgan's warning echoed in her ears. Was it her property, or Belle, that interested him? She would bet her bottom dollar it was the mine.

''Hope you're hungry, Miss Belle. The food at the Palace Restaurant is good. Though not as good as yours.''

Aware that her hand was still on his arm, she folded it in her lap. He stopped the buggy at the door to the Palace Hotel. There were a few hotels and restaurants in Paradise, and from what she'd heard, this was the best. Several men lingered on the boardwalk and tipped their hats as Dan escorted Belle into the hotel lobby. In the dining room, they were shown to a table that overlooked a small garden in the rear.

Belle smiled at the waiter and accepted the menu. The fare was limited to plain cooking—beef stew, steak, and a good assortment of pies. She chose the stew and asked for a cup of coffee. The men at the next table whispered among themselves, then grinned at Belle. By the time the waiter brought coffee, a commotion at the door drew her attention.

A large man stood in the doorway with a child in his arms. A young boy peeked around his legs. She nearly came up out of the chair. Morgan.

"Mr. Travers, we do not serve colored," the waiter said.

Morgan gazed over the man's bald head and caught Belle's gaze. "Calm down, Dennis. You don't have to serve him. Serve me, and I'll serve him." Shoving past the man, Morgan approached with determined steps. Dan gazed up at Morgan, his hand dropping to the gun at his hip.

The last thing Belle wanted was a battle. However, when Morgan reached the table, he nodded, and kept going. He settled at the table next to hers and set Beth on a chair. Jerome sat beside him and grinned at Belle.

"Hey, Miz Belle," he whispered.

"Mama," shouted Beth, waving her arms in glee.

"You two hush. Mama is having dinner with the sheriff. We don't want to disturb them." Morgan tucked a napkin under Beth's chin and one under Jerome's.

Belle stared at them. "Did you follow me?"

Morgan gave her an innocent, wide-eyed gaze. "Are you talking to me?"

"Who else?" she ground between her teeth.

"Why do you say that? You wanted me to look after the children, and I decided they needed a day out. We were hungry, and this is the best restaurant in town."

Dan covered her shaking hand with his. "Ignore him, Belle. He's just showing off."

"Mama," shouted Beth. "Morgie say we get candy."

The other diners stopped eating to stare. Here Belle was with one man, while the child calling her "Mama" was with another. Heat surfaced to her cheeks.

"Only if you eat all your meal," Morgan said.

"Beth eat everything." The little girl crawled to her knees and propped her elbows on the table.

All during the meal, Belle struggled to concentrate on her escort. She didn't hear a word Dan said, their conversation interrupted by either Beth or Morgan. She wished they were as quiet and unassuming as Jerome. From time to time Beth called for "mama" to watch her. The child waved a spoonful of peas to show Belle, and proceeded to toss them all over Dan. The sheriff grunted and wiped the mush from his shirt.

Belle shot an angry glare at Morgan. He smiled back at her. "Bethie, you shouldn't play with your food. The sheriff doesn't want to wear your peas. Now if you don't eat all your dinner, you won't get those bon-bons I promised."

By then, Belle's meal sat in a heavy lump on her stomach. Everything she'd eaten agitated in her stomach like butter in a churn. She felt the way she had when she was expecting her daughter, and the nausea didn't go away for six months. Morgan was that kind of illness. He did everything in his power to upset her.

As if things couldn't get more complicated, she'd taken one bite of her apple pie when a shadow fell over the table. Both Dan and Morgan looked up at the newcomer. Belle followed their gazes.

"Mrs. Jordan, how good to see you again." Corbett Hayes stood over them with Reverend Steward at his side. The minister glared down at Belle as if she wore horns and was out to snatch away his soul.

If she had wanted to make an impression on the good people of Paradise, she'd failed miserably. She was dining with one man, while another sat nearby with her children. The third man who'd wanted to court her looked down his nose at her. Belle was the epitome of the fallen woman, Eve, tempting the men of his town into sin.

Dan jumped to his feet. "Afternoon, Reverend. How're things at the church?" The sheriff flushed, as if embarrassed by the commotion.

For his part, Morgan remained rooted to his chair and ignored the by-play at the next table.

The minister nodded to Belle and stuck out his hand for Dan. "Sheriff, Mrs. Jordan." The snub cut through Belle like a knife.

"Good afternoon, Reverend Steward. That was quite a message last Sunday. I'm sorry I couldn't remain for the entire service." She offered her hand. The minister took her fingers in a grip weaker than a small child's. It was like holding a dead fish.

The minister shifted his gaze from Belle to Beth at the next table. Her little girl stuck out her tongue at the reverend and leaped into Morgan's lap. "Man scare Beth." She buried her face in her protector's shoulder.

"Don't worry, sweetheart, Morgan won't let anybody hurt little Beth." He hugged the child to his chest.

He was pouring the guilt on thick as molasses on pancakes. Belle bit her lip to keep from groaning aloud. What had started out as a pleasant dinner with a handsome man had turned into a circus.

Belle ignored the minister and Morgan and offered her hand to Corbett. "Mr. Hayes, it's so good to see you again."

The lawyer graciously bowed over her hand. "Mrs. Jordan, it's a joy to see you again. I'd planned to ride out to Eden House this afternoon to call on you. Will you be available?"

Morgan stood with Beth against his shoulder. "I'm afraid she'll be busy, Hayes. We promised to take the children shopping for new coats this afternoon."

Belle opened her mouth to deny his statement. His hard glare prevented her rebuke. "I'm sorry, but I'd forgotten." She rose and picked up her shawl. "Thank you for dinner, Dan." Turning her gaze to the lawyer, she again offered her hand. "I hope we can get together soon, Corbett. I have legal arrangements I'd like to discuss with you."

"I'll come out to Eden House this evening, if you're agreeable." Corbett carried her hand to his lips and kissed her knuckles.

She shot a quelling glance at Morgan, daring him to contradict her again. "That will be fine. About seven?" By that time,

Morgan should be busy with his customers and out of her hair. She removed her fingers from the lawyer's grip and reached for Beth.

"I'm looking forward to seeing you." With her brightest but totally phony smile, Belle turned to the minister. "Reverend Steward, we'll see you in church next Sunday. With Christmas approaching, the children are wondering if you'll be doing a pageant or special service?"

The man puffed up his chest like a bantam rooster. "We don't observe the Lord's birth with pagan rituals."

"You mean no tree, or carols?"

"I do not believe in the heathen traditions of such nonsense. These desecrate the sacred event. We will have service as usual, and remember our Lord in quiet observation." The man's cheeks bulged out like a blowfish.

"I'm very sorry," Belle said, not sorry at all. She fully intended to observe Christmas with joy and festivities. She owed the children as much.

"Good day, Mrs. Jordan." The man touched a finger to the brim of his bowler hat and totally dismissed Belle.

Morgan took her arm and guided her toward the doorway. "Pompous ass," he whispered for her ears only.

She waited until they were on the boardwalk and out of earshot of the others before she turned on him. "Morgan, as usual your behavior was reprehensible. The man was no worse than you. You've told me more than once that you do not believe in celebrating Christmas."

"I have my reasons, and they aren't anything like his hypocritical ramblings. He preaches the commandments, then breaks half of them. More than a few times I've caught him half drunk behind the livery. As for adultery, I won't even mention where he spends an evening about once a month."

Belle's mouth gaped. "What someone else does is no excuse for lying. We made no plans to look for coats for the children."

He lifted Beth from her shoulder. "It's getting colder and they all will need to bundle up against the weather. I thought it was how you planned to spend the money you won from me."

"Then let's go. Your coins are burning a hole in my pocket."

Chapter 13

"She thinks I'm her blasted errand boy," Morgan groused under his breath.

He'd spent the past hour loading boxes from the general store into the back of the wagon. When he'd dragged Belle away from Dan on the pretext of buying coats for the children, he hadn't expected her to take this shopping expedition so seriously.

She'd restocked supplies for both Eden House and the ranch—more food than they'd bought in the past month. With five additional mouths to feed, he supposed it was necessary. When they'd argued about how many sacks of sugar and flour she ordered, she'd informed him in no uncertain terms that it was time to begin her Christmas baking. He added his own list of goods for the upcoming party, mainly cases of liquor. At the Palace Restaurant, he ordered two large hams and two fat turkeys to be prepared and delivered the day of the party.

The wagon loaded, he entered Nelson's Emporium. Belle was in the ready-to-wear section selecting new winter coats for the children. When Beth spotted him, she proudly modeled her new blue coat with a black velvet collar. Jerome wore a sheepskin-lined jacket a size too big. To grow into, he informed Morgan in the grown-up voice he often employed.

Belle ignored him and selected a similar blue coat for Rosalind and a jacket for Rory. He leaned against the counter. Arms crossed over his chest, he watched her fuss over the youngsters. His heart tripped at the concern and love she showed for the orphans in her care.

Few women he knew would take in the children of strangers and rear them as her own. His mother had taken in James, but only because he was family. The old man was eager to have another hand to work in his fields.

"So that's James's wife," Stanley Nelson whispered.

Morgan gritted his teeth. He was getting sick and tired of the way the people looked at Belle as if she were some kind of curiosity to be studied and pitied. And the way the men looked at her as if she were a mare in the corral. She surely didn't need another suitor. The pair who were sniffing after her were already two too many.

"She sure is pretty," the shopkeeper continued. He removed his canvas apron and slicked back his hair. A bachelor, Stanley ran the store with his maiden sister, who was currently assisting another customer. From time to time Miss Nelson and the woman she was serving glanced at Belle, then whispered with their heads together.

"She's only been widowed a few months. She'll be in mourning for a mighty long time."

"I didn't mean no offense, Morgan. And there ain't no harm in looking." He stepped away from Morgan and approached Belle. "Need any help, Mrs. Jordan?"

Belle glanced at the shopkeeper. "We'll take these coats. I believe the children would like to wear them home. Would you kindly wrap their old ones along with these two?"

"My pleasure. Can I show you anything else? I just got a ne shipment of silks, ribbons and goods from the East."

She looked from Stanley to Morgan. "Would you mind king the children over to that candy counter and letting them lect a few treats? I would like to pick up a few more things."

"Morgie, you promised Beth candy." The little girl grabbed is leg and tugged him toward the other side of the store.

What choice did he have? Even a rogue like Morgan wouldn't isappoint children. "Don't be long. I told Jeb we would pick p the children at school."

Belle shooed him away with a wave of her hand. "Now, Ir. Nelson, I'd like to see some of that ribbon."

With a wide smile, Nelson escorted Belle to a counter out f sight of the candy shelf. Morgan strained to hear what they ere saying, but Beth's chatter drowned out any other sound. Ie allowed the kids to select a peppermint stick and bonbons. emembering the children at school, he chose an equal amount f goodies for them. Beth devoured her candy within minutes, nd stuck out her hand for more. The soft touch that he was, Iorgan filled another sack with treats for the little girl who'd vrapped him so neatly around her little finger. Jerome licked is peppermint stick slowly enough to last a week.

As he waited for Belle, he wondered what had happened to im in the past week. Never in his wildest dreams would he ave imagined he would be escorting a widow and playing ursemaid to children. At the rate he was going, Morgan was kely to lose his place in the scoundrel's gallery.

Just as he was about to go drag Belle away from the shop-eeper, she appeared from around a stack of overalls. "Thank ou, Mr. Nelson. Will you tally my purchases?"

Stanley set a half dozen packages wrapped in brown paper n the counter. "Certainly, Mrs. Jordan." Seconds later he anded her a slip containing her total.

Morgan snatched it out of his fingers before Belle could each out. "Just put it on my account."

"No, thank you." She plucked it from him. "I'll take care of my own expenses."

"That isn't necessary, Isabella. We have an account, and I' settle up at the end of the month."

"Mr. Travers, these are my purchases, and I fully intend t pay for them myself."

Stanley's gaze bounced back and forth like a swaying pendulum. "Mrs. Jordan, may I offer a compromise? You're welcome to open your own account."

Ignoring the merchant, she dug into her reticule. "I do no believe in owing any man. I will settle my debt now."

Morgan shrugged. "Don't argue, Stanley. You won't win."

She nodded, and pulled out the necessary gold and silver coins to satisfy the merchant. "Did you add in the candy?"

"I've already paid for it. At least let me do something nice." Morgan picked up the small sacks for the other children.

"Did you thank Mr. Morgan?"

Jerome dipped his dark head. "Yes, ma'am. We remembered our manners."

"Dank you, Morgie." Beth planted a sticky kiss on his cheek.

"Are you ready?" he asked, hefting two of her packages by the string.

"I'll carry these out, Mrs. Jordan," Stanley offered.

"Thank you, Mr. Nelson. I'll be back in a few days to pick up those other items."

They stepped onto the boardwalk. The wind whipped Beth' skirts, and she nuzzled Morgan's neck. "What did you buy?" he asked.

"Morgan, it's much too close to Christmas to ask questions You'll see when everybody else does." She climbed up into the wagon unaided and took the little girl from his arms.

"You know how I feel about Christmas."

"I do. And I believe I've made my wishes clear. Let's not argue in front of the children."

Morgan climbed beside her. "Then let's discuss it tonight." His blood warmed at the thought of finally being alone with her—even if it was under false pretenses. "After the children are in bed."

Her cheeks pinked as prettily as a child's. "I don't believe there's anything to discuss. We will celebrate Christmas in my half of Eden House. What you do in your section is strictly up to you."

He bit the inside of his cheeks to hold back a string of curses. "Tonight, Belle." With a snap of the reins, the horses took off with a jolt.

She squared her shoulders in the stubborn stance he'd come to recognize. What she didn't know was that Morgan was every bit as determined. He hadn't survived this long by being a milquetoast. When he set his mind for something, neither hell nor high water would stop him. And he wanted Belle in the worst way possible.

Belle set her mind to thwart Morgan's plans if she had to build a wall between her section of the house and his. However, she knew unless she built a protective barrier around her heart, she wouldn't survive in their declared battle of wills.

He stopped at the schoolhouse and met the children. If possible, Rory was more surly than usual. Rosalind cuddled in Belle's arms, and buried her face in her shoulder. That, too, was odd.

"Did something happen at school today?" She rubbed her daughter's back.

The child shook her head in the negative. "Everything was okay."

Belle glanced over her shoulder at Rory. "How did you fare today?"

He grunted. "I hate school, I hate those bumpkins, and I hate that stupid old teacher."

"Give it time, Rory. Once you make friends, you'll enjoy

school." Belle smiled in a futile effort to console the boy. Rory had never liked school, and being in a new situation had taken its toll.

"I don't want none of them for friends. I like my old friends."

His old friends had been borderline delinquents. "That's too bad. We're living here and until we leave, you'll have to learn to get along."

Morgan dug into his coat pocket. "This should help you forget your troubles." He tossed a small paper package to the boy, and passed one to Rosalind. "For you, princess."

"Thank you, sir." The little girl hugged the treats to her chest.

Rory tore into the wrapper and pulled out a large peppermint stick. He stuck the candy into his mouth. After a sharp glance from Belle, he remembered his manners. "Thanks," he grunted. "What's in all these packages?"

"Young man, it is too close to Christmas to get curious about packages."

"Are we gonna have a real Christmas at Eden House? With a tree and decorations and all?" Rosalind asked, lifting her face from Belle's shoulder.

Belle ignored Morgan's stiff shoulders. "Yes. Tonight we can start baking our special cookies, and you can all help."

"Me, too," shouted Beth. The child stood up in the rear of the wagon and wrapped her small arms around Morgan's neck. "Morgie help make cookies."

"Sorry, sweetheart, Morgan will be busy." The frown on his face spoke volumes. He hated Christmas and wanted no part of the celebration. Whatever his feelings, Belle vowed not to let his ill temper ruin the holidays for her children.

They reached home and hurriedly unloaded the wagon. While Morgan set the boxes of foodstuffs in the kitchen, Belle carried her special purchases up the stairs to her room. She'd managed to purchase a few gifts for the children, things she hoped would brighten their Christmas. These she would add to the things she'd made and brought from New Orleans.

Belle vowed to do everything within her power to make their holiday joyful. Never would she allow her own emotions to ruin their celebration. And she would shoot Mr. Morgan Travers before she would let him throw a damper on their enjoyment.

Their gifts stashed away in the armoire, she returned down the stairs. The children were seated at the table drinking milk and eating the cake Mrs. Franklin had made for them. The housekeeper had left for the day, and the dinner was warming in the oven.

Morgan stood at the stove filling a cup from the pot heating on the fire. "Coffee, Belle?"

Abby stood nearby, fiddling with a teapot. "Maybe Miss Belle would rather have tea?"

"Tea sounds wonderful. I'm not too fond of coffee that has sat on a stove all day."

"The water in the kettle should be hot by now." The young woman set the china pot on the counter and turned away. "Can you fill the teapot, Miss Belle. I burned my fingers this morning."

Belle nodded, moving past Morgan to reach for the kettle. Her chest brushed against his arm, and delightful shivers raced through her. Instantly, he stepped back as if he'd felt the same heat of awareness.

"I'll fill the pot and let the tea steep." She hated the way her words hitched whenever she came near Morgan. In an effort to calm her racing pulse, Belle reached for the enameled kettle. She wrapped a small towel around the handle and lifted the heavy pot from the stove.

As she started to pour the hot water, the handle shifted and pulled loose from the pot. The pot tilted, splashing boiling water on the counter and on the front of Belle's gown. She squealed and dropped the kettle. It clattered to the floor, splattering hot water everywhere. Morgan caught her by the waist and lifted her up. He deposited her several feet away, out of harm's way. Puddles of hot water spread across the linoleum floor covering.

Rory jumped from the table and tossed several large towels onto the floor. "Lordy, Miss Belle, you okay?"

Morgan caught her fingers in his. "Did you get burned?" He examined her hands and clutched them tight in his grip.

"No. I don't think so." She stared at the mess. "I don't know what happened. It slipped out of my hands."

He pulled her against his chest. "You scared me half to death."

She inhaled the clean scent of his shirt. "Your quick thinking saved me from being badly burned."

Rosalind wrapped her arms around Belle's waist. "Mama, Mr. Morgan saved your life."

"I wouldn't exactly say that, princess. Her thick skirts probably would have protected her legs."

Belle wasn't so sure about that. "I can't believe I was so clumsy."

"You weren't clumsy, Miss Belle." Rory held up the kettle. "Look how the handle is broken off on this side."

Morgan released Belle and took the kettle from the boy's hand. "Looks as if it's been pried loose."

Abby clasped her palms to her cheeks. "I'm so sorry, Miss Belle. I should have thrown out that old kettle. I didn't know it was broke."

"Just clean up the mess, Abby." Morgan shot a hard glance at the young woman.

"It isn't your fault. No harm done." Belle shook out the water from the hem of her gown. "I'm soaking wet. I'll go up and change."

Knees shaking, she hurried toward the narrow rear stairs. Two accidents in the past days and both times Morgan had saved her from injury. One would think she was accident prone. Glancing over her shoulder, she spied Jerome staring at her with wide, frightened eyes. *Earl said for you to be careful.* The child's warning rang like a gong in her ears.

Belle always prided herself on being cautious and not taking unnecessary chances. Were these unavoidable accidents, or was somebody trying to frighten her into leaving Eden House? Both times Morgan had been right there. Who but he would profit by her going away? Except Louise.

Slowly, she climbed the stairs, clutching the banister for balance. Of course it had been Louise's idea to frighten her into leaving. She'd suggested that Morgan seduce her. Belle's stomach knotted. Had he told the woman they'd already become lovers? Little did Louise know that the seduction, instead of forcing Belle to leave, made her want to remain forever in Morgan's arms.

She paused at the top of the stairs. Except for Abby and Louise, none of the other women had shown any sign of animosity toward Belle. Morgan had mentioned that the young woman was sweet on Dan Sullivan. On Sunday when the sheriff had come home from church with her, he'd all but ignored Abby. Belle suspected he'd had an ulterior motive for following her home, such as calling on Belle. Then he'd shown up today and taken her to dinner. Could Abby be jealous? If she only knew how Belle felt about Morgan, she would rest assured that she had no interest in the handsome sheriff.

In the privacy of her room, she stripped from the sodden gown and slipped into a simple gray muslin garment. Old and faded, and horribly unattractive, the dress suited her mood. Looks didn't matter to Belle. The gown was modest, and perfect for the cookie-baking evening with the children. In front of the bureau mirror, she shoved pins into her hair, smoothing back the loose strands.

Her gaze shifted to the drawer where the gold nuggets were hidden. Why had Dan mentioned gold? Something about the sheriff bothered her. He was kind, courteous, a true gentleman, yet she was uncomfortable in his company. She'd only gone to dinner with him to aggravate Morgan. Maybe the irksome man was right. Dan was younger than she, and surely he had his choice of women. Could it be he really was interest in Belle's inheritance—especially the possibility of her owning a gold mine?

The idea that none of the men she'd met cared at all for her stung worse than the attack of an angry wasp. Morgan had seduced her to get rid of her, Dan was interested in gold, and Corbett? There was no telling what he wanted. Probably all of it.

Then there were the accidents. She squared her shoulders and strengthened her resolve. More and more she realized she and the children would have to leave Eden House. They weren't wanted here, and staying would only make them miserable. Judging by the accidents, staying could prove dangerous. Never would she allow the children to remain where they weren't wanted. And she would protect them with her life to keep them safe.

Immediately after the New Year, she would make plans to leave. Until then, she would pretend that everything was hunky-dory. It wouldn't be fair to upset the children. She'd promised them a happy Christmas, and she would give it to them if she had to fight the entire town of Paradise, Colorado, including Morgan Travers if necessary.

Belle rubbed her temples. She'd hoped to make a life for the children, and it looked as if she'd walked right into a hornet's nest. The "good people" of the town couldn't accept them because they lived at Eden House. Here she was an outsider because she interfered with the depraved activities going on right under the same roof.

A tear slipped from her eye. Was Belle destined to live as an outsider, never having a home of her own? Years before she'd hoped to find a home with James Jordan. That dream had died when he'd deserted her. When she'd lost the house in New Orleans, she'd hoped to find a home in Colorado—to finally have the home her husband had promised. That dream had burst like soap bubbles in the wind.

That was the ugliest dress he'd ever seen.

Morgan caught his breath when he spotted Belle in the kitchen. The gray, nearly colorless thing hung on her like a sack. In fact, he suspected it had been made from an old gunnysack. The frayed collar framed her face, now flushed from the warm kitchen, and her nose was dusted with flour. Loose strands of hair clung to her skin, damp from the kitchen heat.

She was the most enticing woman he'd ever seen.

He tugged on his silk waistcoat and adjusted his necktie. It was all he could do to keep from dragging her into his arms and licking the icing off her cheek and learning if her mouth tasted like the chocolate at the corner of her lips.

"Morgie." Beth darted toward him, her sugar-coated hands lifted high.

Belle caught the little girl around the waist before she wiped her hands clean on his black suit. "Hold it, missy." Her gaze shifted to Morgan. "Oh, is it five o'clock, already?"

"Actually, it's close to six." He checked his gold watch, then shoved it back into his pocket. He'd already been in the parlor, and with only two guests, he didn't feel needed at the moment. "How is the cookie baking coming along?"

Jerome held up a slightly lopsided gingerbread man. "Real good, Mr. Morgan. I made this one by myself."

"Nice. Got any free samples?"

"You can have the one I made." Rosalind held out a star with one point missing.

"Thanks, princess." He took one bite and grinned at the child. Sometimes the little girl was the image of James. She had her father's blue eyes and dark hair. Too bad his cousin was such a scoundrel. He'd missed knowing the beautiful little girl he'd sired.

"We're going to hang our cookies on our Christmas tree. We're going to make bells and hearts, and diamonds, and balls." It was the most the child had spoken to him since she'd arrived.

"What if you eat them all?"

"Then Mama will make more. Mama said we can cut snow-flakes out of white paper." The little girl returned to sprinkling red sugar on the cookies.

He hated to throw a damp towel on their plans, but there wasn't going to be a tree in Eden House. Or decorations, or any of the other reminders of the holiday. He intended to have business as usual on December 24 and 25. "These are real good."

"We gonna leave some for Papa Noel," Beth handed him half a cookie with a large bite taken out.

"Aw, what makes you think he'll find you here?" Rory shoved a warm cookie into his mouth.

"He will." The toddler set her hands on her narrow hips in a perfect imitation of Belle. Her white stockings sagged around her ankles and her pinafore was coated with sugar and chocolate. "I a good girl. Ain't I, Morgie?"

"You're a very good girl, sweetheart." His heart twisted. He remembered the many times he'd waited for a visit from St. Nicholas, and the disappointment when his stocking was as empty as a hen house after a visit from a hungry fox.

"Children, quit squabbling and decorate those cookies. We have to make many more to share with our friends and decorate the tree." Belle wiped her hands down the front of her apron.

"We ain't got no friends," Rory declared.

Jerome smeared frosting on a cookie with a knife. "We got Mr. Morgan, and Miss Louise, and Miss Savannah, and Miss Vivian and Miss Abby. They's all our friends. And Miz Franklin and Jeb."

Morgan was beginning to feel more and more like the cad he truly was. If they planned much more of their festivities, he would spend the next weeks at the ranch by himself. Only trouble with that was being away from Belle. Already he missed her in his bed. And he had yet to figure out a way to get her back there.

"Don't you have a business to operate?" Belle asked.

"Business is slow." He finished his cookie and licked the crumbs from his fingers. As if to prove him wrong, the knocker banged on the front door. "Company." He headed toward the foyer.

Behind him he heard Rosalind's thin voice. "Mama, what kind of business does Mr. Morgan and them do at night?"

Belle choked, and Rory laughed.

"It's . . . It's sort of like a club." Her voice cracked. "The men come and they have meetings. They talk and visit with Miss Louise, Miss Vivian, and Miss Savannah."

"Like a tea party?" Rosalind asked.

"Sort of, honey."

"Can I join the club when I get big?"

"Me, too?" added Beth's sweet little voice.

"Let's finish these cookies, and I'll read a story to all of you," Belle said to change the subject.

Fury welled up in Morgan. He'd tried to explain to Belle that she had to get these children away from Eden House. Now maybe she would understand the necessity. He pulled open the front door, ready to face a paying guest. Their customers were getting as rare as hen's teeth.

"Hayes? Come on in. Who're you seeing tonight?" At least the lawyer had a full pocketbook.

Corbett whipped his hat from his head. "I'm here to see Mrs. Jordan. Would you tell her that I'm here?"

Morgan's jaw dropped to his chest. "Belle?" He grabbed Corbett by the front of his shirt. "What are you talking about? You know damn good and well she doesn't work."

"Morgan! Leave Corbett alone." Belle stalked toward them. "I asked him to come see me. I have legal business to discuss."

Struggling to calm his temper, Morgan released the man. "Sorry, Hayes. I overreacted."

"You most certainly did." Belle shot him an angry glare. "Come into the rear parlor, Corbett, where we can be alone. I want to apologize for Morgan's bad manners."

"I don't hold you responsible, Belle." The lawyer offered his arm and escorted Belle down the hallway. "Travers doesn't know how to behave around a lady."

Morgan gritted his teeth and stared at their backs. Belle was flour-dusted, and in that ugly dress. He plucked a cheroot from his pocket. At least Belle hadn't primped for the lawyer. That said something about her interest in the other man and brought him a small measure of consolation.

That he cared said even more about Morgan's interest in Belle. He stalked back to the parlor. His only interest in Belle was as his partner and nemesis. The sooner he got rid of her, the better off they both would be.

He shook his head in wonder. With one breath he was trying to get her into his bed, and with the next he was trying to get rid of her.

Morgan wished he could make up his mind. What he needed was a few days at the ranch to clear his head. Tomorrow he would do just that. He'd always heard out of sight, out of mind. True or not, he would soon find out.

Chapter 14

Morgan nudged his horse into a trot. His plan hadn't worked worth a darn. After days at the ranch, Belle continued to haunt his every waking moment. Nights were even worse. Continually he dreamed of making love to her. Each morning he woke wanting her so badly he ached. He'd complained, he'd grumbled, and nothing anybody did satisfied him. His humor was so bad, Vic threatened to hog-tie him and drag him back to town behind his horse. He had no recourse but to face his needs—and Belle.

What was it about the woman that got under a man's skin? True, she was beautiful, but he'd met other women as lovely and he'd had no problem forgetting them the second they were out of his sight.

He tugged his collar close to his face. Dark clouds hung low, and he predicted snow before nightfall.

After skirting the schoolhouse, he turned toward Eden House. He was halfway between the school and home when he spotted a small figure running along the rocky road. Dark braids flew behind the little girl, and her dress was wrinkled and torn.

What was a child doing out here without a coat? Not to frighten the youngster, he drew the horse to a slow walk. The little girl stumbled and fell, then picked herself up and glanced back at him. He nearly fell from the saddle.

"Rosalind." Her name slipped from his lips.

Belle's daughter swiped her hand across her face and took off running again. Morgan jumped from the horse and in a few long strides caught up with the child.

"Rosie, princess, what are you doing out here? Why aren't you at school?" He caught her arms to stop her. "Where's your new coat?"

The girl tried to twist out of his grip. "They stole it from me. I have to tell Mama." Sobs wracked her small body. Tears streamed from her blue eyes.

"Tell me what happened." Morgan's heart twisted. Whoever had hurt the child would have hell to pay.

She tried to pull away from him. "They were mean to me."

The child's arms were icy, and her teeth were chattering. "You're freezing." He opened his jacket and pulled her into the warmth of his body. "Who was mean to you?"

"The kids." She sobbed and hiccuped, her small body shivering in the cold.

Morgan stroked her back. Never having been around children, he knew little about how to comfort them. "What did they do?"

"They called me names. They said that the ladies at Eden House are bad and that Mama is bad, and that I'm bad, too." Her words came out a jumble of sobs and grunts.

The urge to kill washed over Morgan. He forced his voice into a soft tone not to frighten the child. "Princess, you aren't bad. Why you're the nicest little girl in the world and your mama is the finest lady I've ever met." He wanted to throttle anybody who would say anything about Belle or her beautiful child. "Where's Rory?"

"He got in a fight. Teacher took a stick to him." Her voice quivered in a heartbreaking sob. "I was afraid she would hit me, so I ran away."

"Sweetheart, nobody's going to hurt you." Without a coat or scarf, the girl was running all the way home. Now Morgan wanted to get his hands on the teacher. He looked back toward the schoolhouse. His temper rose a notch. Picking up the child, he mounted the horse. Hugging her to his chest, he spurred his horse into a gallop. She clung to his shirt for warmth. Within minutes they reached the yard.

Rosalind started crying in earnest. "I don't want to go back. I want my mama."

"Sweetheart, I'm going to fetch your pretty new coat and take Rory home with us." Carrying her in his arms, he stomped into the building. He slammed the door shut with a loud bang. All eyes turned to him. Several of the older girls gasped at his sudden appearance.

At the sight that met him, his blood ran cold. Two boys twice Rory's size held him by the arms while the teacher brought a large cane pole down on his bottom. The boy yelled loud enough to shake the rafters.

Memories of his childhood flashed across his mind. He'd been the victim of that kind of abuse more times than he cared to remember. His pa beat him and James regularly for both offenses committed and just for pure hatefulness. He saw that same contemptible expression on the teacher's face as she brought the rod down on the boy's backside. Morgan set Rosalind down and raced toward the teacher.

The woman looked up at him with wide, frightened eyes. In one quick movement, he snatched the stick from her hands and broke it over his knee. He was sorely tempted to give the woman a taste of her own medicine.

"Let go of him." Morgan's furious tone matched the temper barely held in check.

The boys released Rory and raced to hide behind the desks.

"Sir, you have no business interfering with my class." Lifting her pointed chin, the woman glared at Morgan in an effort to intimidate him.

Gritting his teeth, he leaned over the woman from his superior height. "Woman, what the hell do you think you're doing?"

"Sir, please leave my class. I am disciplining a disobedient boy who needs to learn respect." She cowered back a step.

Morgan fisted his hands to keep from taking the stick to her. But he would never hit a woman, even one who needed it. "Lady, listen to me, and listen good. If I ever hear that you've lifted so much as a hand to these children, I swear I'll break your arm."

Fear glittered in her narrow eyes. "You have no right to speak to me like this. I am the teacher. I have authority over this wretched boy."

Rory slipped away toward the rear door where Rosalind was waiting. "Nobody gave you permission to beat a child. You're lucky I showed up and not Mrs. Jordan. I would fear for your life if she'd gotten hold of you. That woman would have torn you limb from limb."

"It's no wonder these children are so undisciplined and wicked. What else can one expect from someone living in that . . . that house of ill repute?"

He took a step closer. "These children are not wicked. Neither are Mrs. Jordan or the other residents of Eden House."

Before doing something he would regret, he turned on his heel. "Get your coats, kids. I'm taking you home."

Rory picked up a dirty, torn blue coat from the floor. It was the pretty garment Belle had purchased for her child, the one Rosalind had been so proud to wear. "Here, Rosie. I'm sorry." His face bruised and his eye black, the boy gently helped the little girl slip her arms into the sleeves.

Tears streaking down her cheeks, the child looked at her tattered coat. "My coat is tore. It's not pretty anymore. Mama will be mad at me." Her wails nearly broke Morgan's heart.

"Your mama won't be mad at you, sweetheart. We'll get you another. One even prettier." Morgan picked her up and cradled her to his shoulder. Rory slipped on his jacket and followed Morgan out the door.

At the doorway, Rory turned and stuck out his tongue at the teacher. Behind them the children giggled and the teacher gasped. Morgan had almost shocked the drawers off the spinster. "Let's go. You still have to face Miss Belle."

As if she needed to regain the upper hand, the teacher's shrill scream hit him in the back of the head. "Sir, if you ever set foot in this room again, I'll call the sheriff. He knows how to deal with ruffians like you."

Morgan paused. "Lady, if you were a man, you wouldn't be standing right now. Be thankful for small favors."

Belle drove her fists into the bread dough wishing it were Morgan Travers. He'd left days ago without even a by-your-leave. Vic had shown up yesterday with word that Morgan was at the ranch, driving everybody crazy with impossible demands.

The last she'd seen of the man had been when she'd escorted Corbett to the door and spied Morgan lurking in the shadows. Needless to say, she did not go to his room that night. When she'd awakened the next morning, he was nowhere to be found.

After forming the dough into loaves, she set them aside to rise. She didn't understand how Morgan could pester her thoughts even when he was miles away. He was like a determined mosquito, constantly buzzing around her head.

Why couldn't he be as mannerly as Corbett Hayes? In spite of the crude way Morgan had treated him, the lawyer had been more than courteous to Belle and the children. He'd assisted her in drafting a will, explaining how best to protect her daughter's interest in her father's estate. With the unusual accidents of the past days, she felt the necessity of making provisions for her child and the other children in her care.

When she'd mentioned the possibility of selling her interest in some of the property, he'd offered to find a buyer for the mine. Did Corbett and the sheriff share James's secret? Could there really be gold in the mine? What did Morgan know about it? Was gold the reason for their interest in a widow with four children?

On a sigh, she wiped her hands on her apron. Beth sat at the table drawing her version of bells and stars on brown paper. Belle had promised to take the children out on Saturday to cut greenery for decoration. She couldn't wait to defy her arrogant partner. He could do as he pleased with his half of the house. She fully intended to give the children their festive holiday.

"Miz Belle." Jerome darted through the kitchen door, bringing a blast of cold wind with him. Breathless, he stopped at the table. "Mr. Morgan is coming and Rosie and Rory are on his horse with him."

Belle's heart skipped a beat. Morgan had decided to show his face again. But why were the children with him? It was too early for dismissal from school. She moved to the door and watched as Rory jumped down from the horse, and Morgan dismounted slower with Rosalind in his arms.

Her breath caught. Something was very wrong. Her daughter's coat was torn and dirty, and the young boy had cuts and abrasions on his face. She raced to the door to meet them.

"What happened? Did you get into an accident?" She took her child from Morgan's embrace. The little girl's hair was loosed from her usual neat braids, her face dirty and tear-stained, and dirt and rocks clung to her palms. She looked to Morgan for an answer.

He clapped Rory on the shoulder and urged him into the kitchen. "I think Rory can explain everything." Morgan closed the door behind them.

She recognized the belligerent expression on Rory's face. It was the same look he hid behind whenever he'd gotten into trouble. "What happened to you and to Rosie?"

"Nothing."

Cradling her daughter in her arms, she settled on a chair. "Something did happen. You both look as if you tangled with a wildcat." She wiped moisture from her daughter's face with the corner of her apron. "Jerome, please fetch my medicine kit from my room."

"Yes, ma'am." The boy took off at a run.

"Does someone want to tell me why you're home so early from school?" She shifted her gaze from the children to Morgan. By the hard look on his face, she hated to think what could have caused their mishap. He'd never shown any anger toward the youngsters. Something else must have made him look as if he could spit nails.

Morgan slipped out of his coat and reached for a cup of coffee. "I found Rosie on the road without a coat and freezing. I took her back to the school and we fetched Rory."

"That hardly explains the situation." She looked into her daughter's eyes red with tears. Dirt and pebbles clung to her hands and her stockings were torn at the knees.

Rosalind's troubled blue eyes met Belle's. "Mama, I'm not bad, am I?"

Her heart twisted and she sought to soothe her child's worries. "Of course you aren't, darling? Who said you are?"

"The kids, and Miss Lessman." Her precious little girl buried her face in Belle's shoulder and wept as if her heart was breaking.

Belle struggled to control her temper. The old biddy had little business teaching children. "What did they say?"

"Never mind," Morgan interrupted. "It isn't important."

"Morgan, I want to know what was said. It had to be serious. My child has never gotten into trouble at school."

Between sobs, Rosalind managed to speak. "They called

you a name, a bad name.'' She lifted her face and sniffled. ''Just because we live at Eden House they said we're bad ladies. Then they took my coat and wouldn't give it back.'' Her tears continued as she fingered the dirt and rips on her pretty new coat.

Heat surfaced to Belle's face. She rocked her daughter to comfort her fears, as she'd done when her daughter was an infant. Belle felt her own heart breaking for the youngsters, who were thrust in a situation they couldn't control. Their classmates had only repeated what they'd heard their parents say. ''And what happened to you, Rory?''

''I got in a fight with one of the boys. Then teacher came and she accused me of starting trouble.'' With the tip of a towel, she brushed the dirt from his bruised cheek.

''Rory was helping me, and the teacher got mad at him. She was whopping him. I got scared and I ran away.'' The little girl allowed Belle to remove the tattered coat. ''Don't be too mad at us.''

''I'm not mad at either of you. I'll have a nice talk with Miss Lessman.'' After that the woman wouldn't dare lift a finger to another child.

''I've already discussed the situation with the teacher. It won't happen again.'' Morgan took the medicine kit from Jerome and doctored Rory's injuries while Belle tended to her daughter.

''Ow,'' Rory groaned when Morgan dabbed ointment on his cheek. ''It wouldn't have happened if we didn't live in this bawdy house. I hate it. I hate everybody here.''

''Rory,'' Belle said, shocked at the pain in his voice. ''You shouldn't say that. I thought you liked Miss Savannah and Miss Vivian.''

''They're whores. That's what they called you and Rosie. And they called me whore-boy.'' His voice rose to a scream.

Taken aback, Belle reached for his hand. Morgan was visibly trying to hide his anger.

Rory pulled free. "I wish we had never left home. I hate it here. I hate all of you." He grabbed his coat and ran from the kitchen. The other children stared at him, their mouths gaped.

"He don't mean it, Miz Belle," Jerome whispered.

Belle stood and started after the boy. Morgan caught her arm. "Let him go, Belle. He has to work out his anger. He'll get over it and come back in when he feels better."

"But, Morgan—"

"Belle, he was humiliated by his schoolmates. Let him nurse his wounded pride. You can't protect him forever."

She nodded, and returned to her daughter. "Let's go upstairs, darling, and I'll help you change into a clean dress."

"Mama, what about my pretty coat? It's hurt."

"We'll clean it, honey, and I can mend it so you'll never notice."

The little girl wiped the back of her hand across her eyes. "Okay, Mama."

Beth caught Rosalind's hand. "Poor Rosie. I love you. You can wear my coat."

"We all love Rosie. Come on, darling. Let's go get cleaned up, then you can have some of our special cookies and milk."

"Can Morgie have some, too?" As usual Beth wanted Morgan included in every aspect of her life. Little did the child know that it was only a matter of time before she never saw him again. After the fiasco at school, it was even more important that Belle get the children away as soon as possible. They needed to be away from Eden House, in a home of their own. Most of all, Belle needed to get away from Morgan.

"If he wants," she said.

From his spot at the window, Morgan glanced over his shoulder. "Sure, sweetheart. I'll eat cookies with you."

"We'll be right back."

*   *   *

Supper was on the table and still Rory hadn't returned to the house. Belle wished she hadn't allowed the boy to go off to sulk. Yet, she realized that the youngster was growing up, and needed time to work out his emotions. From time to time she glanced out the window looking for a trace of the boy she loved as if she'd given him birth.

He'd gotten into trouble in school by defending her honor. Morgan had filled her in on the details of the children's ordeal. When she'd heard that the teacher had actually struck the boy, Morgan had to hold her back to keep her from finishing what he'd started.

No good would come from sending the youngsters back to the school. The bigots in town had already rejected Jerome, and now they'd virtually done the same to Rory and Rosalind. Until they left Eden House, they would learn from Belle at home.

Savannah set the dining table, and Vivian and Louise had come in for the evening meal. The children settled at their places, but Rory failed to materialize.

"Miz Belle, do you want me to go fetch Rory?" Jerome offered.

"I would appreciate it," she said. "He's probably in the stable with the horses."

"Yes, ma'am." The little boy threw on his coat and darted out the door.

Belle moved to the window to watch Jerome. The boy raced across the yard, and was lost in the shadows of the late afternoon.

Morgan came up behind her. He curved his fingers on her shoulders, sharing his warmth and encouragement. "He'll come in, Belle. Boys are always hungry and never miss a meal."

She set her fingers on his, grateful for his support. "I know. I can't believe he stayed away so long."

After what seemed like forever, Jerome dashed through the doorway, Jeb close at his heels. The young man who ran the stable and did odd jobs was breathless. He removed his hat and blond hair tumbled into his eyes. "Miss Belle, Mr. Morgan, Jerome said you were looking for Rory."

Belle's heart sank. From the looks on their faces, she suspected that the pair had bad news for her. "Where is he? Did you see him?"

Jeb twisted his hat in his fingers. "Yes, ma'am. He came into the stable earlier. He told me that he had to run an errand for Mr. Morgan. He took one of the horses and went off."

"Where did he go?" Morgan asked.

The young man backed up, afraid he was in trouble. "I don't know, sir. He said you gave him permission to take the horse."

"He doesn't know how to ride." Belle's knees grew weak. If Morgan hadn't had his hands on her arms, she would have sunk to the floor.

"Yes, he does." Morgan tightened his grip on her arms. "Jeb and I have been teaching him. He's learning fast."

"I don't understand. Where could he have gone?"

"He must have been angrier than I suspected. I think he ran away."

Chapter 15

"It can't be true. He has to be here somewhere." Belle shook her head in disbelief.

Morgan's heart dropped to his knees. He pulled Belle into his chest to offer what little comfort he could. She shoved out of his grip and headed for the door. Before she reached the doorway, he caught her wrist. "No, Belle. You stay here, I'll go look for him."

"Morgan, he's my child. He needs me."

"He's only had a short head start. I know the territory. There are still a couple of hours of daylight left. I'll find him for you. I'm a pretty fair tracker."

"Morgan, I can't just stay here and do nothing."

"The other children need you. Throw some bread and cold meat into a sack. When I find him, he'll be starved." He turned to Jeb, fear on the young man's face. "Jeb, fetch Sheriff Sullivan and search the town. Rory may have gone to the railroad station. If you recognize his horse, tell the sheriff."

218   *Jean Wilson*

"I'll help," Abby said. The young woman set to work filling a sack with cold food.

The other children wrapped their arms around Belle's waist. "Mama, what's gonna happen to Rory?" Rosalind asked.

"I don't know, sweetheart." Trust and faith glittered in her amber eyes. "You have to find him, Morgan, please."

He nodded, and planted a quick kiss on her lips. "I'll check close by. He's probably just hiding in the woods."

Even Morgan didn't believe his own words. If the youngster had been furious enough to take a horse, he planned to get as far away as possible. He wanted to strangle the kid for worrying Belle like this. Yet, part of him understood the boy's emotions. If Morgan had been humiliated as the boy had been, he'd have done the same.

Louise caught her shoulders. "Let Morgan go, honey. He'll find the boy."

"I'll meet Sullivan back here in an hour. If we haven't found the boy by then, we'll get up a search party."

Tears ran in rivulets down Belle's cheeks. "Tell him we love him."

"I will." Grabbing his jacket from the peg behind the door, he raced into the chill air. In this vast country, he knew that if he didn't find the boy in the first few hours, he would be so far away they would have to wait until daylight to locate any sign of him. And if it snowed, all traces of his trail would be lost.

Morgan mounted his horse and made two slow circles around the yard. Several sets of hoof prints went off in varied directions. Most he assumed had been from the night before. As dusk began to fall and it grew darker, the wind picked up. He prayed it wouldn't snow before they found the boy.

He hated to admit failure, but he had no choice but to return to the house and make plans. Three horses waited at the hitching post, their breath blowing steam in the chill air. If Dan had brought in help, it didn't bode well for the search. He dismounted and raced into the kitchen.

The children huddled around her, Belle glanced up at Morgan. The first glimpse of hope in her gaze died when she saw he was alone. She leaped to her feet.

Morgan hated to tell her he'd failed when he'd promised to find the boy. "I don't suppose he was anywhere in town."

Dan shook his head. "We looked everywhere. Nobody's seen hide nor hair of the boy."

Two deputies braced against the counter with cups of hot coffee in their hands. Louise pressed one into Morgan's palm. "Thanks," he muttered, his thoughts on Belle.

"I brought a map." Dan spread out the plat on the table. "We can divide the territory up into quarters. We can each take a section."

Sam, the younger of the deputies, leaned over the map. "Hell, Dan, it's like looking for a needle in a haystack. The kid could be anywhere."

Morgan was tempted to shake the man out of his boots. "We'll tear that haystack up until we locate the youngster." He made a mark across half the map. "I'll start here and head toward the ranch. I'll get the boys to help, and we'll cover the northern portion. The rest of you can head to the south."

Dan rolled up the map and shoved it under his arm. He caught Belle's hands in his big palms. "Don't worry, Miss Belle. We'll find your boy."

"Thank you, Sheriff," she said, her voice husky with emotion.

"Let's go," Morgan ordered. "We still have a little daylight left. We might get lucky."

Taking only a moment to touch Belle's shoulder, Morgan sought to reassure her. He didn't know if it helped her, but it gave him the courage to continue the search. Outside, he returned to his horse tethered at the hitching post. As he put one foot into the stirrup, Jerome raced onto the porch. "Mr. Morgan," the boy said, his voice soft and shy.

He halted and returned to the steps. Hunkering down, Morgan sought to ease the boy's fears. "Don't worry, Jerome. We'll find Rory."

The youngster stared down at his scuffed boots. "That's what I want to tell you." He glanced over his shoulder as if afraid to go on.

"Tell me what? Did Rory say anything to you?"

"No, sir. He never told me nothing." He shuffled from foot to foot. "It was Earl."

"Earl? Who's that? I've never heard of anybody called Earl."

"Earl is my guardian angel. Sometimes he tells me things."

Impatience to get on his way to search for Rory roiled up in Morgan. Yet, the boy was so serious, he didn't have the heart not to listen. "What did Earl tell you?"

"He said that Rory is by a big hill, where there's lots of rocks."

Morgan sighed. This country was nothing but hills and rocks. "Did he say anything else?"

The boy nodded. "He said to look for silver. Do you know what he was talking about?"

He certainly wasn't a religious man and he didn't believe in the supernatural, especially in God and angels. Through experience he'd learned that a man could depend on nothing except himself—his skills and hard work. He glanced toward the north. Since it was on his way to the ranch, he figured the boarded-up mine was as good a place as any to start. "I think so, Jerome. You get inside and take care of Miss Belle. I'll bring Rory back."

"I'll be praying for you, Mr. Morgan."

Morgan gave the boy a gentle shove toward the kitchen. "I need it, Jerome. More than you know."

* * *

Snowflakes drifted from the low hanging clouds, making the search more difficult. Morgan trudged forward, looking for any sign that the boy had passed this way. Darkness was falling fast, and with the clouds obscuring the moon, finding the boy was indeed harder than finding a needle in a haystack. If Morgan had the sense of a jaybird, he would hole up at the ranch and head out at first light.

Even as he considered his choices, a picture of Belle's distraught face flashed across his eyes. She trusted him to find the boy. Misguided trust, but trust nonetheless. Morgan didn't have the heart to disappoint her.

He bypassed the ranch road and headed toward the mine. Within minutes it would be too dark to see his hand in front of his face, much less find a boy who might be lying injured beside the road. The idea sent a cold chill down his spine. He hoped Jerome's angel was on duty tonight. They needed all the help they could get.

Pulling his collar up over his face and his hat down on his forehead, he struggled against the wind. He hoped the boy had enough sense to hole up somewhere. As darkness fell, Morgan spotted movement in the bushes beside the seldom-used road. Since the mine had closed, nobody came this way. Cautiously he rode toward the shadow, not wanting to disturb a wildcat or stray bull.

On closer inspection he realized it was neither. A horse stood in the small copse, nuzzling aside the snow to reach the dry grass. Morgan's pulse quickened. It was the horse the boy had taken. The roan looked up as if begging to be taken home to his warm stable.

Morgan slipped from his saddle. Had Rory been thrown, and was he lying injured nearby? He tethered both horses, and began a slow, methodical search.

"Rory," he called, cupping his mouth with his hands. His

voice echoed back at him. He stepped from bush to bush, shoving aside the barren branches. There were few places to hide, but Morgan slowly worked his way around in a circle, finding no trace of the boy.

His heart sank. Morgan mounted his horse, and led the riderless horse by the reins. He had no choice but to continue toward the ranch. Vic was an expert tracker, but in the darkness even an Indian scout couldn't help.

Slowing his pace, he carefully followed the road, looking for any sign that Rory had been thrown from the horse. He'd been down the lonely road so many times, he didn't need light to find his way. As he neared the mine, the temperature dropped several degrees. Fear clutched his chest. Rory wasn't accustomed to this weather. He could easily freeze to death by morning.

Morgan needed a miracle, and he didn't believe in miracles.

He looked into the heavens, wondering if the angels ever cared about the mortals down here. If they did, he sure hoped they were on duty that night. From time to time he called for the boy. His only answer was the sound of the trees rustling in the wind.

Morgan rode through a small grove of trees. Wind as strong as a tornado swirled the snow around his horse's hoofs. He leaned against the horse's neck and trudged on. On the other side of the trees, he stopped to study his surroundings.

As if a great hand had wiped away the clouds, the moon glittered like a silver coin in the sky. He blinked and wiped his eyes. The snow had stopped, and only a light dusting remained on the ground. Reflected on the white snow, the moon cast its light like a huge lantern. Impossible, he thought. On the other side of the trees the night was as dark as the inside of a cave. Here he easily made his way toward the mine.

At the boarded-up entrance, he called again. Still no answer. Morgan stood in the stirrups and surveyed the land. Several hundred yards away, a tiny flicker of light glistened in the bushes. As quickly as the glow came, it disappeared. He spurred his horse.

"Rory," he called, his voice getting hoarse.

"Help," came back a weak reply.

The glow came again like the tiny flame of a match. "Rory?" He dismounted and raced into the bushes. "Where are you, boy?"

"Here."

A rock landed at Morgan's feet. Another followed. "Make some noise so I can find you."

A branch rustled, and the boy called out again. "I can't move."

Morgan thrashed through the bushes, and nearly tripped over a prone figure. He jerked to a halt and hunkered down beside his quarry. For a man who didn't believe in prayer, he couldn't help whispering a word of thanks.

"Rory, what happened? Where are you hurt?" Gingerly, he brushed his fingers along the boy's chilled face. Hatless, the boy was icy cold and was shivering out of control.

"I slipped down that cliff. I tried to walk, but my ankle hurts."

With gentle fingers, he worked his way along the boy's torso, arms, and legs. Rory groaned when Morgan touched his ankle. "It might be broken, or sprained. We don't want to take a chance on injuring it further." He picked up the boy in his arms, like carrying a baby. "You're freezing. I'm going to set you on my horse and wrap a blanket around your shoulders."

The boy remained silent as Morgan hoisted him into the saddle. He unwrapped a blanket from the roll at the back of his horse. "This should keep you warm until we get back home."

"Mr. Morgan, you got anything to eat? I'm real hungry."

He reached into the sack tied to the pommel and handed the boy a chunk of bread. "Miss Belle had a pretty good supper fixed, boy. You ruined it for all of us."

Rory dropped his head, his chin touching his chest. "I didn't mean no harm, honest. I just wanted to be alone, but I got lost. Then my horse ran away, and I fell and hurt myself."

"I'm tempted to thrash you for the trouble you caused. The sheriff and his deputies are out looking for you, and I was headed to the ranch to get the hands in on the search."

"I reckon I deserve it. I'll take my whipping like a man."

Morgan climbed up behind the youngster. After the hell he'd put Belle through, he was sorely tempted to teach the boy a lesson. "Son, a whipping is too easy a punishment. I'll let Miss Belle deal with you." He picked up the reins and spurred the horse into a gallop. "I'd sure hate to be in your shoes."

The instant they turned back toward Eden House, the clouds whipped across the sky and the moon disappeared as if it had never been. The night grew dark, and snow flurries drifted from the heavens.

It was the strangest thing Morgan had ever seen. If he were a man given to flights of fancy, he would wonder what had happened. Common sense told him that the wind had blown away the clouds, allowing the moon to shine through. He didn't try to explain why the clouds had returned as soon as he located the boy.

Exhaustion overtook the youngster, and he fell asleep with his head against Morgan's chest. Morgan reined in at the rear porch. As if she had been keeping a vigil at the window, Belle raced out of the doorway. Tears streamed down her cheeks as she reached for the boy.

"Morgan, you found him. Thank God."

The commotion woke Rory, and he rubbed his eyes. "Miss Belle?"

"Yes, darling. I'm here." She lifted her hands.

"He hurt his ankle. Watch he doesn't put his weight on the foot." Morgan passed the boy down, letting Belle steady him on one foot. Morgan leaped to the porch, and in one fell swoop lifted the youngster into his arms.

Belle held open the door and ushered them into the welcome warmth of the kitchen. Rory's hands were icy and his face chilled. Morgan set him on a chair. Immediately the children and women surrounded the boy. They were all talking at once, throwing questions at the boy.

Morgan stood at the perimeter of the crowd, his heart warmed by the smile on Belle's face. Louise pressed a cup of hot coffee into his hand. "Where did you find him?" she asked.

"Out toward the silver mine. He slipped down the hillside and hurt his ankle." He studied Belle as she inspected the boy's injuries. She cupped his face and kissed his forehead. The lovely woman was born to be a mother. Too bad she'd married a cad and had only one child of her own.

His own mother had lacked maternal instincts. Her first love had been the elegant and pampered plantation life. When marriage, a child and the War had robbed her of the luxury, she couldn't face her future. She'd gone into a decline and left him alone to deal with an abusive father.

Morgan shoved aside the memories. "I'd better stable the horses. When Sullivan comes back, pay him and the deputies with a couple of bottles of our finest whiskey. They deserve it after being out in the cold on a wild goose chase."

"What about you?" She took the empty cup from his fingers.

"I could use a hot bath and something to eat. Think you can handle that?"

"I'll take care of everything."

Taking one last look at Belle, he buttoned his coat and headed back into the cold. The wind slapped him in the face like a dose of reality. The soft feelings about Belle that had been sneaking up on him flew away with the chill. She belonged in a fine home with a loving husband who'd care for her foundlings and her daughter.

That man definitely was not Morgan Travers.

* * *

Belle glanced away from Rory when the door squeaked open. She caught a glimpse of Morgan's back as he stepped into the night. He deserved thanks, and more. He'd risked his life to hunt the youngster in the dark of night in the face of an impending storm. Already flakes of snow drifted against the windowpane. She would be eternally grateful to him.

First she had to deal with an errant youngster who had caused too much trouble. "Let's get you upstairs and out of these damp clothes and into bed. If your ankle is sprained, I'll help you keep your weight off it."

Turning her gaze to the children, she said, "Your prayers brought Rory back to us. So you'd better get to bed, too."

"I thought Morgan brought him back." Louise shot a hard glare at Belle.

"We believe he was guided by the Lord."

Savannah and Vivian, who had worried and prayed with Belle, picked up each of the girls. "We'll see that these pretties get to bed."

"I'll make a tray for him, Miss Belle," Abby offered.

Rory caught Belle's fingers in his cold hand. "I'm real sorry, Miss Belle. I didn't mean to cause trouble. I just wanted to be alone for a while, then my horse ran away, and I got lost. I wouldn't ever leave you."

Her heart tripped. "We'll deal with that tomorrow when you're warm and rested. Let's go upstairs."

"You look after the boy, Mrs. Jordan," Louise said. "I'll take care of Morgan."

Her heart tripped, but she refused to let the woman see how her words cut. Belle had her own ideas about Louise's intentions toward Morgan. Did she plan for Morgan to take James's place as her lover? Or had they already become intimate? The thought sent shivers down her spine. After the way Morgan had seduced Belle, it hurt to think of him with another woman. "Will you ell him I'll speak to him tomorrow? We have business to discuss."

"Certainly. Abby, when you finish there, you can help me prepare a bath for Morgan."

Wrapping an arm across Rory's shoulder, she guided him toward the stairs. Let Morgan and Louise do as they pleased. In a few weeks, Belle would be gone, and they could resume their decadent activities without her to watch.

But Belle knew that when she left, she would leave a large part of her heart behind.

Exhausted after a harrowing day, the children fell asleep as soon as their heads hit the pillows. Tomorrow Belle would have to deal with Rory and have the doctor check him over. The boy had frightened them all and put Morgan and the sheriff in danger. One thing was sure, her children would never set foot in the Paradise schoolhouse. Until they left, she would teach them herself.

Noises from the yard drew her to the window. She hugged her arms to ward off a chill. By the pale light spilling from the parlor windows, she spotted three horsemen rein in and dismount. Thank God the sheriff had come back. There was no use for him to be out in the cold when Rory was safely in his bed.

Wanting to thank the sheriff, she slipped from the room and into the hallway. An angry male voice came from the parlor, followed by softer female tones. Since she felt responsible for the problem, she hurried down the stairs.

Belle paused in the doorway. "That boy needs a good whipping to teach him a lesson." Dan Sullivan tossed down a glass full of amber liquid.

"Sheriff, I'll handle Rory in my own way," she said, stepping into the parlor. "He didn't mean any harm. But I do appreciate your assistance."

The three men turned and stared at her. "Sorry, Mrs. Jordan. Reckon we're just tired and cold." The sheriff's wide shoulders sagged with fatigue.

"Don't concern yourself, Belle," Louise said, reaching into a credenza. "Morgan said to give them each two bottles of our finest imported whiskey. That should warm their innards."

"That sounds fine. It's little enough payment for all their trouble." She took the bottles from Louise and passed them to the men.

"We'll be heading back home for some sleep. Keep an eye on that young'un, Mrs. Jordan. Next time Morgan might not be so lucky."

There wasn't going to be a next time. "I will, Sheriff. He won't try anything like that again."

The three men tipped their hats and tucked the bottles under their arms. Belle watched them leave, grateful for all their help. When the men left, Louise trimmed the lamps and headed for the stairs.

"Louise," Belle said, stopping the woman before she reached the stairs. "I appreciate all you've done for me and the children. You've been more than kind and helpful."

Louise laughed, a deep throaty sound. "Not bad for a madam, huh, Isabella?"

Embarrassed to remember the first time she'd spoken to Louise, her cheeks pinked. "I apologize for that, too. Beth and Rosie are crazy about you, and the boys adore all of you."

"They're great kids." She took one more step and stopped. "I nearly forgot. I promised to bring a tray to Morgan. He's probably starved."

"You've done enough. I'll see that he's fed."

She slanted a wry smile. "Thanks. I think I'll turn in. It's been a long day."

Belle headed for the kitchen. A large tray covered with a linen cloth waited on the table. Abby had gone to bed and Belle was the last one up. She turned down the lamps and picked up the tray.

The hallway leading to Morgan's room was dim, and Belle felt her way to his door. She wondered if she was making a mistake by going to him, but she couldn't stop herself. He'd done more for her than she'd have expected. Since he'd probably saved Rory's life, she had to let him know how much she appreciated what he'd done.

Common sense told her to wait until morning. Her heart told her to go to him. Heart won over head. She knocked gently on the door.

"Come on in," came his muffled voice.

Carefully, she shoved the door open and entered the dimly lit chamber. She stopped cold. Her hands trembled, the china rattled on the tray.

By the candlelight, she spotted the large copper tub in front of the fireplace. Wide bronzed shoulders gleamed above the water line. A dark head leaned against the back, and a hand drooped over the edge, a glass in the hand. A trail of gray smoke drifted from the cigar in his mouth.

"Set the tray down, Isabella, and come wash my back."

Chapter 16

Morgan watched the shadowy image in the mirror above the shaving stand. He recognized Belle by her silhouette from the dim light from the fireplace. She shoved the door shut with her back and moved slowly toward him. As always when he saw her, his body reacted. Desire swirled around him like the warm water of his bath.

"How did you know it was me?" Belle set the tray on a round marble-topped table.

"I heard your footsteps in the hall, and your hesitant knock. Louise would have burst right in." He took a sip of whiskey to calm his racing pulse, then he placed the glass on the table at his elbow. "And the others seldom come in here."

"Seldom?"

Let her stew in a bit of jealousy. He caught her frown in the mirror. "Only when invited."

"I . . . we . . . Louise said you must be hungry. She prepared a tray."

"Mighty considerate of you to deliver it. I'm starved." For more than food. "Bring it closer."

"You can eat after your bath. I must get back to the children." Even as she protested, she drifted toward him as if pulled by a magnet.

It was time to remind her how much she owed him. A little guilt did wonders to encourage gratitude. "How's the boy? We're lucky I found him when I did."

"He's none the worse for wear. We're all beholden to you."

"How beholden are you, Isabella?" He lifted his torso from the water. "Appreciative enough to help warm my chilled body. For a time I was afraid I would catch my death of cold out there in the snow."

"Morgan, I doubt you were in any real danger. You've been in this territory long enough to know how to survive."

"I could have tumbled down a mountain and broke my leg. Would you have come looking for me?" He poured the guilt on as thick as molasses on hotcakes.

"I would have sent the sheriff after you."

"He couldn't warm my frigid body like you could."

She moved to the tub and stared down at him. "How do you propose I do that?" Her voice turned husky and soft, as sultry as a Louisiana summer afternoon.

"You can begin by washing my back."

To his surprise, she reached out a hand. "Give me the soap and I'll see what I can do. After all, I'm experienced at washing obstinate children."

"I'm hardly a child, Belle. You should know that." Morgan stared at her small palm, and couldn't resist grasping her wrist. He carried the hand to his lips and pressed a kiss to her palm. Desire kindled a flame in his body hot enough to boil the water in the tub. Belle pulled back. Not wanting to let her go, he tugged. She tottered for a moment, then landed plop on top of him in the middle of the tub. Water splashed on the floor, on his head, and drenched the woman lying on his chest.

"Oh. Morgan, look what you've done."

He laughed. "If you wanted to join me, all you had to do was ask. I would have made room." Wrapping both arms around her, he pulled her closer.

"Let go of me." Her protests trailed away to a soft whisper. She set her hands on his bare chest and playfully rubbed the lather in the hair that circled his taut nipples.

"I'm not holding you." Lifting his soapy hands, he smeared soap bubbles in her face.

"Morgan, you're drenching me." She wiggled and shifted her bottom smack on the top of his already painful arousal.

A groan escaped his lips. He needed her, and out of his need, she'd come to him.

Belle stopped moving the instant she felt his hard maleness. She'd known better than to trust him. Yet, she couldn't help herself. After the tension and turmoil of the day, she needed to be with Morgan, if only for a moment.

Her gaze locked with Morgan's. His blue eyes turned to midnight, dark and mysterious—full of passion and promise. He cupped her cheeks and pulled her face close to his. His tongue snaked out and swiped across her lips. She breathed in the scent of him—warm water, whiskey, and man. Her heart twisted. Until this moment, she hadn't realized how much she wanted him—wanted his touch, wanted his love.

But Belle was wise enough to realize that his love wasn't available. Not to her, or to any woman. She gave up trying to analyze the situation and let emotions take control.

She lowered her eyelids, and surrendered to the desires that made her skin tingle and her blood sing in her veins.

Her mouth welcomed his kiss. His touch was gentle, as sweet and soft as a baby's kisses. Yet the feelings he inspired in her were far from innocent. With his tongue and teeth, he made love to her mouth. He touched, nibbled, and stroked her lips. His thumb brushed gently across her jaw, and his fingers tangled in her hair.

Dampness spread from her wet gown until she felt the chill
of the cool air. She trembled, not certain it was from the sodden
clothing, or from the delightful sensations that Morgan inspired.

Morgan ended the kiss, and grinned like a wildcat that had
conquered his prey. "Sweetheart, I'm trapped in here. If you'll
get up off me, we can move to a more comfortable position."

Shocked by her reckless behavior, Belle struggled to her
feet. She shook out her soggy skirts and stared at Morgan still
submersed in the water. A wet pool spread over the carpet.

Her gaze shifted from the man to the door and back. Run
or stay? Fly away alone, or soar with the man she loved. The
battle waged within her heart. If she stayed, they were certain
to make love. If she left, she would return to her lonely widow's
bed. For one night, she would take what Morgan offered, and
give of herself.

Surging to his feet, Morgan turned his back to her and
retrieved the towel from the floor. Her gaze followed the drizzle
of water from his wide back, to his narrow waist and over his
rounded buttocks. He was all hard muscles and sleek skin—a
glorious male, in all his masculine beauty.

He wrapped one towel around his waist tossed another over
his shoulder. "How about drying my back?" His charming
grin melted the last of her reserve.

Belle accepted the towel and gave in to her needs. In the
simple movement, she willingly accepted whatever Morgan
had for her. With slow circular strokes she wiped the water
from his back. His wet skin was slick and shiny. Bulging
muscles glowed like bronze in the firelight. The action was so
intimate and sensuous, her breath caught in her throat. She
touched her lips to his spine and tasted the warm water.

Morgan trembled and turned to face Belle. Her gaze dropped
below his waist. He was boldly aroused and ready. Instantly,
she returned her glance to his face. He grinned like a contented
cat with a canary in its paws. "You did that to me, sweetheart."

How had she let herself get caught in such a compromising

position? Second thoughts and misgivings flooded her. She took one step back, ready to retreat before she lost complete control of her senses.

"I thought you were hungry?" she asked, buying time to make her final decision.

Morgan caught her arm. "Food can wait, sweetheart. I'm starved for you. Don't go. Spend the night with me."

Wet skirts and petticoats trapped her in place. She met his gaze, and saw the passion glittering behind his thick eyelashes. Desire swept through Belle like the swift current in the Mississippi River sweeping everything away in its flow. She couldn't refuse him, even if it meant the damnation of her soul.

With a nod of acquiescence, she began to loose the buttons of her pink shirtwaist. In her rush to accept what Morgan so openly offered, her fingers shook. The thin towel couldn't hide his desire. Nor could her damp gown hide hers. In the chill air, her breasts tightened, the tips visible through her layers of material.

Morgan stepped closer. "Let me." His fingers brushed hers aside. While he undid the tiny buttons of her blouse, the tips of his fingers brushed her sensitive skin. "I'll be careful this time. I'm still finding those little buttons from last time."

His reminder of their impatience for each other sent a surge of heat through her. As his fingers worked slowly, tiny goose bumps tingled all over her skin. She reached down and loosed the button on her skirt, then shoved it to her ankles along with the sodden petticoats.

When Morgan had the blouse open to her waist, he shoved it off her shoulders. The damp batiste camisole was nearly transparent, revealing her breasts as if she were naked. He dropped a kiss at the base of her throat. "Delicious."

Delightful sensations sizzled from her neck clear to her toes. She threw back her head and clutched his shoulders. Her fingers dug into his hard flesh, pulling him closer. His kisses grew more ardent, covering her exposed skin with his moist lips.

"Let's get you out of these wet clothes," he whispered, his breath warming her chilled skin.

Carried away with passion, Belle didn't resist when he tossed her blouse aside. Catching the bottom of the chemise, he tugged it over her head. His hands skimmed her body, brushing gently over her breasts. The tips tingled into hard, tight nubs. With a quick tug, he loosed the ties of her drawers and worked the garment slowly down her legs. His fingers brushed her legs; his lips teased her inner thighs with gentle kisses.

He dropped to one knee and retraced his path back to her waist. A heaviness, a yearning settled in the secret place between her thighs. His tongue darted into her navel, and she swayed, afraid she couldn't control her emotions. She'd already given Morgan her body and heart. Could she afford to allow him to steal her soul?

In one surprising movement, he surged to his feet and scooped her up in his arms. He deposited her in the middle of his wide bed and came down with her. Belle opened her arms and offered her all to Morgan. With patience and care, he loved her. In her wildest dreams she hadn't imagined a man could make her feel so wonderful

She soared and floated, yet she never left the bed. Morgan's hands, his lips, his body, filled her with such powerful sensations, she thought she would burst with emotion. Her entire body was aflame from his touch. Yet, Belle found she could give as eagerly to Morgan as he gave to her.

He touched, she touched; he kissed, she kissed; he caressed, she caressed. When neither could bear the intense pleasure, they came together in a tangle of legs and arms, hearts and minds, and reached the ultimate fulfillment.

Morgan held Belle gently in his arms. He'd wakened slowly, not wanting to move or disturb her. He'd waited for days to make love to Belle, to have her in his bed. Now that she had come to him, he wondered if he had the strength to let her go. Until her, sex had been just a temporary pleasure, a relief. For the first time, his heart was involved along with his body.

He was a man who'd been alone for many years. He'd never before wanted a woman in his life on any kind of permanent basis. He still wasn't sure. Something had happened to him when Belle and her rag-tag pack had shown up at Eden House.

With one finger, he brushed a strand of golden hair from her cheek. He followed with his lips. She opened her eyes and smiled. Stretching her arms over her head, she thrust her breasts into his chest. Her movement sent another shaft of desire through him. How he could so quickly become aroused was beyond understanding. They'd already made love twice, and shared the dinner tray she'd brought. Then they'd dropped off to sleep.

He lowered his mouth to her breast and caught the tip between his teeth. She groaned, and sifted her fingers through his hair. "Morgan, what time is it?"

Lifting his head, he feigned a frown. "How can you be worried about the hour at a time like this?"

She laughed and tangled her fingers in his hair. "I don't want the children to wake and wonder what happened to me. Wouldn't it be something if they came in here and found me in the altogether?"

He glanced down at their bare and entwined bodies under the layers of quilts. "I'm as naked as a jay bird. We can just tell them we're wearing the emperor's new clothes."

With a huff of indignation, she tugged on his hair. "They'll laugh and point fingers. It's nearly dawn. I'd best leave."

Wrapping both arms around her, he rolled to his back and pulled her on top of him. "Give me a kiss and I'll let you go."

"Morgan, if I give you another kiss, I won't want you to let me go."

"What's wrong with that?" Wiggling under her, he cupped her buttocks and eased her lower on his stomach.

"I might never get back to my room." She gasped and rested her hands on his chest.

"I repeat, what's wrong with that?"

"I have to set a good example for the children. I can't have you compromise my reputation."

He laughed. *"Bella mia,* I'm afraid you were compromised when you entered Eden House the very first time."

The smile faded from her mouth and he could feel the uncertainty that washed over her. "Morgan, please, I must leave before anybody finds me here."

A thin stream of gray morning light streaked across the rug. "Everybody is still asleep. You'll be safe for a while longer."

Even the pale light didn't hide the distress on her face. "Mrs. Franklin will arrive soon to begin working, and Abby is always up early. I shouldn't have fallen asleep." She slanted a gaze toward the door.

"You needed the rest after the fright of yesterday. You slept like a lumberjack." Morgan tightened his grip. "One kiss, and I'll help you dress."

On a long sigh, she lowered her face to his and gave him a quick peck on the mouth. Morgan didn't try to deepen the kiss or stop her from rolling off him. She was right. Neither of them wanted to cause a scene by being found together. He didn't give a fig for his reputation, but he wouldn't impugn hers.

He slipped off the bed and drew on his trousers and shirt. Overnight the fire had burned down and the room was chilled. Quickly he tossed a log on the fire. It caught on the smoldering embers throwing out a small burst of warmth. Belle followed him, shivering. Her shapely body gleamed golden in the firelight. Morgan was hard-pressed not to pull her into his arms and return to bed. Instead, he drew upon his last shreds of gentlemanly control. He scooped up his velvet dressing gown and draped it over her shoulders. Only days before she'd returned it to him.

His hands lingered for a moment on her shoulders as she

shoved her arms into the sleeves and tied the belt at her waist. Unable to stop himself, he gathered her long hair from under the garment. He planted another kiss on the back of her neck. Her skin smelled of the soap he'd used, as if their bodies had blended into one.

"I think I wear your robe more than you do." Belle trembled under his touch.

He grew hard from simply being near her. He dropped her hair, letting it flow to her waist like a silken veil shimmering with golden highlights among the brown tresses. The woman was stunning. His heart constricted. He hated to let her go.

The rattle of a wagon and horses on the hard driveway snapped him out of his preoccupation with Belle.

"It must be Mrs. Franklin and Jeb." She rushed away from him and began to gather up her garments. "They can't find me here."

He bent over to help. "These things haven't dried. Wear my robe. You can bring it back to me tonight. If you hurry, you can make it up the stairs before they enter the house."

Panic glittered in her eyes. She snatched her clothing from his hands.

"I'll delay them. Go ahead, they won't see you."

Morgan slipped into the hallway and signaled her to follow. Barefoot, he hurried to the kitchen, and threw an arm across the door to prevent it from opening. The knob twisted, and somebody shoved against the door. With his weight, he held the door shut. Belle hurried up the stairs, her feet padding lightly on the wood stairs. When she was out of sight, he stepped away, and Jeb flew headlong onto the kitchen floor.

"You're in a mighty big hurry to get to work." He looked down at the young man sprawled on the floor.

"Door must have been stuck."

"Must have been." Morgan offered a hand and tugged Jeb to his feet. " 'Morning, ma'am." He touched a hand to his head in a brief salute to the woman standing in the chill air that blasted through the room. "Call me when breakfast is ready."

Damp clothing slung over her arm, Belle managed to reach her room without being seen. How had she let herself be caught in such a compromising position for the second time? She leaned against the closed door of her room and glanced to the bed.

"Mama, where were you? Me and Beth got cold." Rosalind sat up and rubbed the sleep out of her eyes.

Her heart tripped. Caught by her own child. "I'll toss some wood on the fire. We'll warm up in a minute." Dropping her wet garments on a chair, she rushed to the fireplace.

"Why are you wearing that funny wrapper? I never saw that before."

Belle ignored the embarrassing question. She had no reasonable answer. "Why are you awake so early? You usually bury your head and beg to stay in bed." After the trauma of the day before, Belle felt a touch of guilt that she hadn't spent the night with her child. Instead she'd selfishly given in to her carnal needs.

"We wanted to know if Rory was okay. Are you gonna whip him?"

"You know I never whip any of you. We'll have to decide on the proper punishment." She crawled into the bed between the girls in an effort to make up for her neglect. "We can stay here a little while. When we get up, I'll fix a very special breakfast. How would you like lost bread?"

"Yum," her daughter said. The children loved the Creole version of French toast that was a holiday treat.

Beth flung her arms around Belle's neck. "I love you, Mama."

Tears misted her eyes. "I love you, too, my sweet girls."

She snuggled both girls into her chest and kissed their heads. "Have you made your lists for Papa Noel?"

"I know what I want," Beth said, leaning closer to Belle's ears.

"What do you want, darling?"

"I wants a papa. Can Morgie be my papa?"

Belle's stomach sank. Morgan was the most unlikely candidate for fatherhood since James.

"Don't be silly, Beth," Rosalind said in the little lady voice she used around the younger child. "Papa Noel can't bring papas. I done already asked him for one, and I never got my wish. I'd rather have a dolly with a beautiful red dress."

She hugged her daughter closer. Until then, she'd never realized her child had missed having a father. A tear rolled down Belle's cheek. Neither child knew how much she missed having a man to love—and to love her back.

No matter how she felt about him, Morgan was definitely not the man her children needed. More and more she was convinced that she had to leave Eden House. Morgan had seduced her and succeeded in his plan to drive her away. As soon as Christmas was over, she would seek a new home for her children and herself.

And never see Morgan again.

When Beth began whining for breakfast, Belle rose and dressed the girls. They ran down the stairs, their thoughts on nothing but food. Belle dressed in a simple gown and hid Morgan's robe in her armoire.

Her gaze fell on her daughter's torn and dirtied coat. The child had cried more over losing her garment than over her scrapes and bruises. Belle fingered the rips. Even if she sewed and cleaned the coat, it had already lost its newness—its fresh crisp look. If it took the last of her money, funds she needed for their move, she would purchase another coat for her daughter.

Before going down she looked in on the boys. As usual, Jerome was awake and dressed. Rory remained buried under the covers.

" 'Morning, Miz Belle," Jerome said from the bedside where he watched over Rory.

"How are you this morning, dear? And how is our prodigal?"

The young sepia-skinned boy cocked his head as if not quite sure what she meant. "I'm fine, and Rory is still sleeping."

"You run on down for breakfast. I'll take care of Rory."

"Yes, ma'am." He darted for the door, leaving Belle to deal with the errant boy in private.

"You can quit feigning sleep. I know you're awake." She settled on the edge of the bed.

The youngster lowered the quilt and peeked out one eye. "You awfully mad at me?"

His woebegone expression brought a smile to her face. "No. I'm very disappointed. What if Mr. Morgan hadn't found you? I hate to think of what could have happened out there."

"I'm sorry, Miss Belle. I won't do that again." He shifted against the pillows. "But I still ain't going back to that school."

"You won't have to. I've decided to teach all of you at home." For as long as we're here, she added to herself. "How is your ankle?" She threw back the bottom of the quilt.

"It don't hurt no more." A loud sneeze shook the entire bed.

Belle hurriedly tucked the quilt around him. "You must have caught a cold out in the weather. Reckon I'll have to mix up my special elixir."

Again, he buried his head. "Not that. See, I'm not sneezing any more. Must have just been dust."

She laughed. "I'll fetch your breakfast, then we'll see if you need any medicine. Meanwhile, I want you to stay in bed."

Rory jerked upright. "But it's Saturday. Can't I go out and ride, or help Jeb?"

Setting her hands on her hips, she glared down at the youngster. "Young man, you forget that I have to punish you. You'll stay in your room and think about the trouble you caused yesterday. Besides, I don't want you up and about until the doctor checks you over."

"Aw, Miss Belle." Again he sneezed.

Belle tossed a log on the fire and left the room. Halfway down the stairs, she heard voices coming from the kitchen. Rosalind's excited voice and Beth's loud squeal echoed up the stairway. She hurried her steps, frightened that something had happened to the girls.

As she reached the kitchen, Rosalind ran smack into her, flinging her arms around Belle's waist. "Darling, what's wrong?"

"Mama, look. Mr. Morgan gave me a new coat. It's prettier than my other one." Encased in a lovely red coat, her daughter stepped away and modeled her new garment. "I love red. It's my favorite color."

"It's beautiful. You look like a princess." She lifted her gaze to Morgan and the smug look on his face. "Thank you," she mouthed the words.

Again Morgan had done something totally out of character— at least what she thought was his character. He'd risked his life for Rory, he'd befriended Jerome, he'd spoiled Beth, now he'd made her daughter a very happy little girl.

And stolen Belle's heart in the process.

Chapter 17

The morning passed in a flurry of activity. Morgan fetched the doctor who examined Rory and found him none the worse for wear. The youngster had sprained his ankle and caught a cold. The doctor ordered him off the foot for a day, but he could get up the following morning. Much to Rory's dismay, the doctor left a bottle of foul-tasting medicine for his cold. Although Belle hadn't decided on a suitable punishment for the boy, he argued that bed rest and the remedy were penalty enough.

As Belle straightened Rory's room, she brushed off the jacket he'd worn during his adventure. The pockets were stuffed with rocks of all color and size. The boy had an insatiable curiosity and often brought home rocks, leaves, and even an occasional insect. She lined up his treasures on the bureau where he could see them.

One particular rock caught her attention. Bright specks winked at her from the stone. She brushed a finger across the rock. It looked very much like the rocks she'd found hidden in James's bureau. Her heart leaped. Morgan said he'd found Rory near the abandoned mine. Could James have discovered gold and kept it a secret from his partner? She started to ask where Rory had discovered the rock, but he'd fallen fast asleep.

Belle debated whether she should tell Morgan about her finds. In spite of the intimacies they'd shared, she wasn't quite sure she could fully trust him. He'd never mentioned gold, and more than once he'd emphasized that the mine was played out. On top of that, he'd also indicated that he was willing to buy out her interests. As she pondered the situation, a knock sounded on the bedroom door. Assuming it was one of the children, she opened the door and faced the tall, handsome sheriff.

" 'Morning, Miss Belle. Hope I didn't disturb you. Just wanted to check on the boy.'' He removed his hat and flashed a wide, charming grin.

"He's doing well, Sheriff. Thank you for your concern." After the problems Rory had caused the lawman, she was surprised that he cared. She stepped aside and allowed him to enter. "The doctor judged him fit."

At the bedside he studied the sleeping boy. "He sure robbed me and my deputies of a night's sleep."

Protectively, she moved to stand between Dan and Rory. "He'll be properly disciplined, you can be sure."

In the dimly lit room, Dan turned his gaze to Belle. Something glittered in his brown eyes. Blond hair tumbled onto his forehead. He reached up a hand and stroked one long finger down her cheek. She shivered under his touch. The man was gentle and kind, yet his touch chilled rather than warmed her as Morgan's did.

"You're a beautiful woman, Belle," he whispered, his face lowering to hers. His hand moved along her jaw and tightened on her nape. Surprised at his unexpected attention, she backed toward the bed.

Her breath caught in her throat. He was going to kiss her, his intention was clear. His gaze locked on her lips. Trapped between his body and the bed, she saw no way out of the situation short of shoving him back and insulting him.

A gasp from the doorway jerked the sheriff away from Belle. She darted around him and faced Abby staring wide-eyed at them. The young woman covered her mouth with one hand. Tears simmered in her eyes. "I'm sorry. I wanted to know if Rory wanted something to eat."

"He's sleeping, I'll fetch him something when he wakes up."

Abby backed away, and darted down the hallway as if the beasts of Hades were on her tail.

Dan shook his head. He flashed a boyish grin. "What's the matter with Abby?"

Were all men as dense as the fog on the river? Either he didn't know how Abby felt about him, or he didn't care. Belle bit her lip to keep from revealing the girl's feelings. "Nothing. She's very busy since the children and I moved into Eden House."

He brushed a stray hair from Belle's face and tucked it behind her ear. "I had a real good time the other day when we had dinner together. Can we do it again sometime?"

Belle didn't want to insult the sheriff, but she had all the male problems she could handle with Morgan. "I enjoyed it, too. Perhaps . . ." She glanced at the bed where Rory was shoving aside the quilt.

"Miss Belle," Rory's voice drew her away from the sheriff's attention. "What's all this noise? I can't sleep."

"Sheriff Sullivan came to look in on you. He'll keep you company while I fetch your lunch." She slipped out the doorway, leaving Dan to look after the boy.

Mrs. Franklin cast sidelong glances at Belle while she prepared a tray for Rory. She wondered if the housekeeper suspected what had transpired between Morgan and Belle. She hoped Morgan had made sure she hadn't left any traces of her presence in his room the previous night. It would prove entirely too shameful if anybody learned about their liaison. It shocked and embarrassed her to realize she was having an affair with Morgan. After her disastrous marriage, she'd remained as celibate as a nun in an Ursuline convent. Somehow Morgan had managed to breach her defenses and she'd fallen into his arms and into his bed. She'd also fallen completely in love with him.

Abby studiously avoided Belle. The young woman was clearly upset about what she'd seen, or what she imagined had happened between Belle and Dan. Thankfully, Morgan had taken the younger children for a ride, allowing Belle to devote her attention to Rory.

A fresh tray containing bread, ham, cheese, slices of cake and coffee in hand, she returned up the stairs. As she approached the open door of the boys' room, Dan's deep voice gave her pause.

"Nice rocks, kid," he said. "Where did you get them?"

"Somewhere. I don't remember."

"Didn't Morgan find you out near the abandoned mine? Is that where this big one came from?" His tone turned cold, demanding. The sheriff stood beside the bed staring down at the boy.

"I got lost and I don't know where I was. I picked up rocks all over the place and shoved them in my pocket." He shifted away from the sheriff and spied Belle in the doorway. "I'm starved, Miss Belle. Hope you got something good for me to eat."

The sheriff dropped the rocks and spun to face Belle. His attitude bothered her. She remembered how he'd questioned her about the mine. Surely there was more to his inquiry than simple curiosity. "Yes, but after what happened yesterday, I should put you on plain bread and water."

Dan jumped away from the bureau. "Let me help you with that, Miss Belle. It looks mighty heavy."

"I'll set it on the table, Dan. I hope you're hungry, too."

"Yes, ma'am and that sure smells good."

"I brought enough for all of us. Please sit down, Sheriff. We can talk while we eat."

She'd no sooner served Rory and Dan than a light knock rapped on the door. Before she could call out, Morgan stuck his head around the facing. Beth clasped his shoulders and Rosalind and Jerome clung at his side. In one quick glance his gaze swept the room. When he spotted her seated beside Dan, his smile turned into a frown.

"What are you doing here, Sullivan?" He stepped across the threshold and deposited Beth onto the bed beside Rory.

The sheriff flashed a smug grin. "Having dinner with Belle. She was kind enough to invite me."

Belle ignored Morgan's ill humor and bad manners. She opened her arms to the other two children. "Did you have your lunch?"

"Yes, ma'am," Jerome said. "Mr. Morgan took us for a ride and Miz Franklin fixed us some food."

"Did you have a good time?" she asked, ignoring Morgan's stern stare.

"Yes, Mama." Her daughter gave Morgan an adoring glance. It seemed as if the man had charmed every female in the house. "Mr. Morgan was real nice to me." Lowering her voice, she whispered, "He gave me some of his cake."

Belle's heart tripped. They would be much better off if Morgan reverted back to the nasty scoundrel he professed to be. By his kindness, he only stood to hurt the children when they began depending on him. From experience, she knew she could not depend on him any longer it took to melt ice on the Fourth of July.

"That's very good. Come say hello to Sheriff Sullivan."

The shy little girl ducked her head into Belle's shoulder. "Hello," she muttered.

As if he had no idea how to greet a child, Dan touched her

lightly on the head. "How do, Missy? You're even prettier than your mama."

Morgan snorted like a winded horse. "How's our patient this afternoon?"

"Better. He'll be up and about by tomorrow. Just in time for church."

At the mention of church, Rory groaned. "Miss Belle, I don't think I'll be able to walk. I should stay in bed for another day."

Belle knew exactly what he was doing. The boy tried to get out of church at every opportunity. "Young man, you need church worse than anyone. You'll go if I have to carry you."

"I'll carry him for you, Belle." Dan covered her hand with his.

Morgan hovered over her, his frown deepened. "The boy may need another day's rest. He was sneezing an awful lot earlier."

On cue, Rory let out a series of coughs and sneezes that shook the rafters. "Mr. Morgan is right. I'm way too sick to go to church. I might give my cold to the other people and they would all get sick."

"Thank you for your offer, Dan. I'll decide tomorrow, and if he has to stay home, Morgan can look after him." She challenged Morgan with her eyes, daring him to protest at playing nursemaid. "And if Rory goes into a decline, Morgan can send for the doctor. Or he can just bury him."

Morgan snatched Beth from where she was bouncing on the bed. He tucked the child under his arm like a sack of flour. "Let's go downstairs, little bit, the air in here is getting mighty thick." Beth squealed with delight.

Belle jumped to her feet, annoyed at Morgan's attitude toward the sheriff. True, she wasn't pleased with Dan's attentions, but she didn't want to insult the sheriff who'd spent the better part of the night searching for Rory. "It's time for her nap. I'll take her to my room." She reached for the child.

"Not sleepy. Want Morgie," Beth protested, clinging tighter to Morgan's shirt.

"Elizabeth, behave," Belle admonished.

"I'll tote this sack of taters to your room." Morgan shifted the child to his shoulder.

"Excuse me, Dan. I'll be right back."

Morgan stopped in the doorway. "Don't we pay you to protect the town, Sullivan? Hadn't you better get back and see if outlaws are trying to rob the bank?"

Dan jumped to his feet, taking Morgan's broad hint. "Reckon I'll be leaving. Thanks for the cake, Belle. Mind if I call on you later?"

"She'll be busy." Morgan stomped from the room, leaving Belle staring at his back.

"You're always welcome, Dan. Feel free to call any time." She gestured to the doorway, only to find Abby skulking in the shadows of the hall. It seemed every time she turned around, the young woman was hovering nearby. Something about the way she glared at Belle caused the hair at her nape to stand on end. She shrugged off the feeling. Abby had been nothing but kind and helpful. "Abby, will you escort the sheriff downstairs. I have to tend to the children."

The young woman's expression brightened when she glanced at the tall, good-looking lawman. "I'd be honored, Miss Belle."

Dan bowed slightly from the waist, then settled his wide-brimmed hat on his head. He followed Abby to the stairway. "You're looking mighty pretty today, Abby. New dress?"

Her face flushed, Abby murmured a quick thanks. How could the man not see how much the girl cared for him? Belle hoped he wouldn't hurt the young woman. But with men, there were no guarantees. She knew that from experience.

After one last glance at the children who were studying the rocks Rory had found, Belle turned to her room, preparing for another encounter with Morgan.

"Don't want to sleep, Morgie. Want to play." Beth sat on the wide bed, her arms folded across her chest.

"You had better lie down before your mama gets here," Morgan lectured, standing near the headboard.

"No."

Belle entered and stared at the pair. The little girl had twisted the big man around her finger like a piece of string. "Young lady, lie down." The child opened her mouth to protest, but thought better. "If you don't take a nap every day, Papa Noel won't come on Christmas. He doesn't visit girls who don't obey their mamas."

The child looked to Morgan. "Morgie, will Papa Noel come here?"

He frowned, and shot a glance at Belle. "If you're good."

"I good." She flopped against the pillows, her arms still folded, her legs stiff.

"Now, close your eyes and go to sleep." Belle tucked a quilt over the child.

Her lip stuck out in a pout, she reached for Morgan. "Morgie take nap with Beth."

With a shrug, Morgan eased down on top of the quilt. "I didn't get much sleep last night. A nap sounds interesting." He winked boldly at Belle, his reminder of how they had spent the night. "Make room for your mama."

Beth grinned. "Come, Mama." She patted the bed so she would be sandwiched between Belle and Morgan.

Her face flushed, Belle eased down next to the little girl as she often did to encourage a nap. Morgan glanced at her over the child's head. "If you're cold, you can come over to this side. I'll warm you up."

That was exactly what she was afraid of. Around him, she grew hot within moments. Simply gazing into his heated eyes, her skin had burned as if she'd been lying in front of a roaring fire. "No, thank you. I'm fine."

"Comfortable bed. Big."

His innuendo wasn't lost on her. She glared at Morgan. "I share it with the girls."

"Lucky girls."

Belle closed her eyes in an effort to ignore Morgan lying only a foot away from her. Within moments Beth's breathing became soft and steady. Morgan's arm snaked across the child and his hand landed on Belle's side. His fingers danced along her skin, delighting her body with his touch. Her reaction was immediate and expected. And much too exciting for propriety.

She caught his fingers and tossed his hand back across the child. A soft chuckle came from the other side of the bed. The arrogant man knew exactly how his touch affected her. Belle shifted and started to rise. As she reached the edge of the bed, Beth lifted her head. "Mama," she whined, reaching for Belle.

"Go back to sleep, darling. Mama won't leave you."

The little girl slipped an arm around Belle's neck. On the other side of the bed, Morgan rolled to his side, wrapping the little girl and Belle in his embrace. His touch this time was gentle, protective, warm. Enfolded in his arm, Belle closed her eyes for only a moment. She had too many responsibilities to give in to much-needed sleep. As her mind drifted off, she cuddled under the quilt with the child. Warmed by the small body and charmed by the sweet baby smell of fresh soap, she vowed to rise as soon as Beth dropped off to sleep.

Morgan shifted and lifted one sleep-drugged eyelid. Momentarily disoriented, he studied his surroundings. A weight anchored his arm in place, and hair tickled his nose. The smell of rosewater brought him fully awake. He smiled, remembering in whose bed he was sleeping.

Some time after Belle had dropped off into a light slumber, Morgan had moved and now lay pressed into her back. Her head rested on his shoulder, trapping him in place. A delightful prison for a needy man. He could only imagine her reaction when she awoke to find herself in his arms—intimately in his embrace. By the dim light slanting between the curtains, he guessed it to be late in the afternoon. They'd been asleep for hours, together—in her bed.

Her bottom was pressed to his stomach, wreaking havoc with his libido. Although they were both fully clothed, he had grown hard by being so close to her. Unable to help himself, he gently cupped her breast in his hand. Her response was immediate. The nipple tightened and she sighed in her sleep. He bit back a groan. His fingers shifted from one glorious mound to the other, gauging her reaction by the way she nestled closer into his arousal.

Morgan smiled with contentment and nuzzled his lips against her nape. He was playing with fire, but he needed the warmth of her closeness. Her glorious hair had escaped the tight confines of her bun. The silky skeins tickled his nose, and Morgan let out a loud sneeze.

The noise woke Belle. Her eyes snapped open. Her gaze locked with his.

"Evening. Sleep well?" he asked.

"What . . . what are you doing in my bed?"

He laughed. "Don't you remember? You invited me."

At what would be the most inopportune moment, the door burst open and Rosalind raced into the room. "Mama, where are you?" The girl skidded to a halt. Her blue eyes grew wide. "I've been looking all over for you."

"Your mama was sleeping, princess. Come up here with us."

Rosalind planted her fists on her narrow hips. "Mr. Morgan, why are you in my place?"

He looked to Belle, unable to stop the grin that threatened his mouth. "I reckon we all fell asleep trying to get Beth to take her nap."

Belle shot him an angry glance. "What's wrong, honey? Did something happen?"

''Mr. Hayes came to see about Rory, and we couldn't find you.''

As the words left the child's mouth two more figures appeared in the open doorway—Corbett and Mrs. Franklin.

Chapter 18

Belle ducked under the quilt like a sneak thief caught in the middle of a burglary. Blood rushed to her face. If only she'd awakened sooner and had the good sense to tear away from Morgan's enticing embrace.

Morgan seemed to take the entire predicament with more than a little finesse. Likely this wasn't the first time he'd been caught with a woman in a compromising position—although it was certainly Belle's first.

"Looks as if you found us." The bed shook as he shifted from her side. "What do you want?"

Mortified at being found with a man in her bed, she threw back the covering and sat up. The pair standing guard in the doorway stared at her as if she'd committed the sin of the century. Mrs. Franklin gasped, and covered her heart with her hands. Her face reddened as if on the point of apoplexy. Turning on her heel, she darted down the hallway. Corbett remained statue still for a long moment.

The lawyer cleared his throat. "I heard about the boy's

accident and I wanted to offer my assistance.'' His gaze drifted from Belle to Morgan, still reclining on the covers.

He tucked his hands under his head. ''She doesn't need your help,'' Morgan declared in his usual gruff manner.

Taken aback by Morgan's harsh voice, Corbett backed up a step. ''I'll await you in the parlor, Isabella.''

''Wait, Corbett.'' She crawled over Morgan to reach the edge of the bed. ''We were only trying to get Beth to take her nap.'' She shook out her wrinkled gown.

Morgan slowly threw his long legs to the edge of the bed and stood. ''You don't owe him or anybody else an explanation. He had no business snooping into your boudoir.''

Pink tinged her cheeks. Morgan's sanctimonious words were almost funny. Surely everybody was wondering what he was doing in her boudoir and in her bed. Loose tendrils of hair escaped her chignon, clinging to her neck. Morgan's shirt was wrinkled and his hair had tumbled into his forehead. He slanted heavy-lidded eyes at her. What a sight she must be.

''Rosie, show Mr. Hayes to Rory's room. I'll join you there in a moment.'' Belle willed her voice to a normal tone.

Corbett stared at Belle, then at Morgan. ''Will you be all right, Isabella?''

''Of course she'll be okay, Hayes. What do you think is going to happen? And for your information, nothing happened in here with a child between us.''

''I would never suppose anything else of Isabella. I'll visit with the boy.'' Hayes backed out of the doorway and followed Rosalind down the hallway.

Belle buried her face in her hands. Caught by the lawyer was bad enough, but to be found out by the housekeeper was doubly alarming. No telling how far or exaggerated the story of her and Morgan would spread.

''I'll never live this down,'' she groaned. ''How will I ever face the people in church tomorrow?''

He reached out for her and drew her into his embrace. She

went willingly. "Don't worry, Bella. Mrs. Franklin isn't known as a gossip. I wouldn't have hired her at Eden House if she were. She's seen enough here to ruin half the men in the county." His touch was warm, too inviting. It was what had gotten her in this predicament to begin with. "I won't vouch for Hayes."

Realizing what she was doing, Belle shoved out of his arms. "Get out of my bedroom, Morgan. This would never have happened if you hadn't crawled into my bed."

With a wide grin, he chucked a knuckle under her chin. "Turnabout is fair play, Bella. You shared my bed, I thought it only fair to share yours."

Indignation surged through her. "This is different. We had a child between us until you moved to my side."

A soft whimper came from the bed. How the child had slept through the confrontation was beyond her. "Now you've wakened the baby."

He threw up his hands in surrender. "Next you're going to blame me for the snow falling outdoors. I'm good, but not omnipotent." He settled on the bed and gently patted the little girl's back. "Fix your hair and go see to your other suitor. First Dan, now Corbett. Nobody would ever suspect that you've only been widowed a short while."

She curled her fingers into her palms to keep from slapping the insolent look on his face. "That didn't seem to bother you last night."

"Nothing bothers a man without a conscience."

"Get out of my room and don't you dare come in here again."

"Not even to fetch my clothing?"

Reaching into the armoire, she grabbed his robe and shoved it into his chest. "I never want to see this thing again."

He flashed a smile so smug it sent her temper up a couple of notches. "I'll have it ready for the next time you need it."

"Don't hold your breath, Mr. Travers." She stalked away

from him and raced into the adjacent dressing room. Never had she met a man to raise her ire the way Morgan did. With only a look he heated her skin, with a mere touch he incited her passion, but the pompous ass angered her beyond reason.

After splashing water on her overheated face, she quickly twisted her hair into a tight bun at the base of her nape. Only when she studied her image in the mirror did she realize that the buttons of her frock were open at the neck. More of her bosom showed than she considered modest. No wonder Corbett and Mrs. Franklin had glared at her with so much condemnation in their gazes.

Belle squared her shoulders. Except for a momentary lack of judgment, she'd done nothing wrong. As much as she hated to agree with Morgan, the pair had no business entering her boudoir.

Thankfully, Morgan was gone when she returned to her bedroom, and Beth was sleeping soundly. Leaving the door open, she hastened down the hallway to the room the boys shared. "I'm so sorry to keep you waiting, Mr. Hayes," she said.

The lawyer stood at the side of the bed, balancing a large rock in his palm. He jerked his gaze from Rory to Belle. A look akin to guilt glittered in his eyes. "I don't mind, Isabella. The children and I were getting acquainted."

Rory shifted on the pillows, assisted by Jerome, who hadn't left his side. "Give me back my rock," he demanded.

"Sure, son. I was just admiring it. Where did you say you found it?" Corbett dropped the glittery stone to the coverlet.

"I told you I don't remember. It was dark, and I was lost."

The stones the boy had found seemed to cause a great deal of interest to his visitors. Only Morgan hadn't remarked on his finds. "Rory is always picking up rocks and shells. I'm sure he'll grow up to be a geologist or scientist."

"Hel . . . heck, no, Miss Belle. I don't want to spend the rest of my life in school. I'd rather be a cowboy. Mr. Morgan is teaching me how to ride a horse, and Mr. Vic said I can go on the round-up with him in the spring.''

Belle bit her lip to keep from revealing they wouldn't be there by spring. ''Young man, you won't decide your future occupation until you receive your education. Mr. Hayes can tell you what a privilege it is to attend college and get a fine education.''

''Aw, Miss Belle.'' The youngster slithered down under the quilt. ''I'm getting tired from all these questions and visitors. I want to go to sleep.''

She smoothed the quilt over the boy. ''I'll bring you a supper tray. Try to rest.'' Turning to the other two children hovering beside the bed, she stretched out a hand. ''You run on downstairs. We'll work on our cookies later.'' The youngsters took off at a run, leaving Belle with the lawyer. ''Let's go to the parlor, Corbett, where we can visit.''

Like the gentleman he was, the attorney offered his arm. Belle set her fingers on his forearm. ''I hope I didn't cause a problem by calling on you, Isabella.''

Considering he couldn't have chosen a less opportune time to call, Belle forced a smile she didn't feel. ''Of course not, Corbett. You're always welcome at Eden House.'' She guided him to the wide central staircase of the house.

Morgan stepped from the shadows and snorted. ''He used to be one of our best patrons, now you give him everything free.''

Belle stiffened her spine at his snide innuendo. ''Not *everything,* Mr. Travers. If you'll excuse us, I invited Corbett to join me in the parlor for tea.''

''Go ahead and entertain your beaus. Just stay out of the way of our *paying* customers.''

She resisted the urge to punch Morgan square in the gut. Belle couldn't remember ever striking a human being or animal in her life. Since meeting Morgan, she'd been seized with wanting nothing more than to strike out at him in the most violent manner.

What had happened to the considerate lover of the past night? Quite simply, he was acting like a jealous idiot. As if he owned her. As if she owed him something. What she owed him was a swift kick in the butt. Purposely ignoring his undeserved taunt, she tucked her arm into Corbett's and continued down the stairs. "Be sure to keep your *guests* on your side of the house."

Rory's cold worsened the next day, preventing Belle and the children from attending church. It didn't matter. She wasn't up to facing the censures and stares of the bigots in Paradise. There was always the chance she would run into Miss Lessman and not be able to control her temper. It was best that they remain home.

As she'd promised, she took the other children out into the nearby countryside and cut branches of pine, yew, and fir to decorate the house. Jeb drove the wagon and helped her load the bed with greenery and pinecones. She also found red holly berries among the bushes.

Since Eden House was closed to customers on Sunday, Louise, Savannah, and Vivian offered to help decorate the parlors. The women fell into the holiday spirit, and sang carols as they twisted the branches and twigs into wreaths and tied them with the ribbons they usually wore in their hair. Rosalind and Beth loved the festivities, and Jerome became their main helper. The young boy ran and fetched scissors and ribbons, and performed any chore the ladies requested. In spite of his runny nose, Rory ventured downstairs and lent a hand in the main parlor. That left Belle to decorate the rear parlor on her own.

After the mantles were draped with pine boughs and red ribbons, Belle returned to the kitchen to continue her baking. Every time the door squeaked open, her heart skipped a beat.

She looked up, expecting to see Morgan saunter into the kitchen, the parlor, or watch her from the hallway. So far, he hadn't shown his face. His horse remained in the stable, and the fancy buggy and matching team were also still there, as was the buckboard they used to haul goods. Belle took it to mean that he was still home, probably in his room or office plotting ways to cheat her out of her inheritance.

Between her other duties, Belle managed to bake a ham and fresh bread. Abby had gone off to church, and Belle was happy that she hadn't brought Dan home for dinner. With her varied chores, she was grateful Corbett had stayed away.

As she was preparing the ham, she decided to add some sweet potatoes to the meal. With everybody busy in the parlor, Belle slipped out to search for the vegetables in the root cellar behind the house. She moved carefully on the gravel walkway, lifting her skirt over the damp leaves that had fallen months ago. The wind was colder than she'd thought, but she planned to be gone only a few minutes. She could survive the cold while she gathered the potatoes.

She lifted the bar and tugged open the heavy doors. Looking down the steep stairs, she wished she'd brought a lantern or candle to light her way. With a shrug, she felt her way down. As long as the doors were flung open, enough light poured into the darkened interior for her to locate the produce and select what she needed to complete the meal. It took only seconds to find the sweet potatoes. She gathered up the corners of her apron and used it like a sack.

Further back in a corner, she spied a basket of bright red apples. An apple pie would make a fine addition to the meal. Belle reached a hand into the basket and selected several beautiful smooth apples. She wondered if Morgan liked apple pie. Although they'd become intimate, she knew little about him. Not that it mattered. In a matter of weeks she would be gone and out of his life forever.

Belle turned to return to the narrow steps, when the doors

at the top banged shut. The small cellar was immediately plunged into darkness. Startled, she dropped the edges of her apron and the potatoes and apples rolled across the dirt floor. She stumbled toward the stairs, guided by the thin streak of daylight that seeped between the boards of the door.

She shivered in the cold. She hadn't realized the wind was strong enough to pick up the doors and fling them shut. At the top of the narrow stairs, she shoved on the doors, expecting them to pop open at her touch. Neither door budged. Balanced on the top step, she braced her shoulder against the heavy wooden barrier. She pushed, and in her effort to dislodge the opening, her feet slipped on the damp steps and she skidded to the bottom.

A moment of hysteria bubbled up in her chest. Taking several deep breaths, she struggled to quiet her nerves. It wouldn't do to let herself panic. She needed to remain calm, and give the doors a good push. Crawling carefully on the cold steps, she applied all her strength, to no avail. She was stuck in a root cellar. Alone. In the dark.

"Easy, Belle," she told herself, her voice bouncing against the cold walls. "Make noise and somebody will hear you and come rescue you." Again she approached the doors. "Help," she yelled. "I'm down here. Can somebody hear me?"

Only the roar of the wind answered her. By then Jeb had gone home, and the others were on the opposite side of the house in the parlor. She had no idea where Morgan was. Tremors raced up her spine. What if the wind hadn't blown the doors shut? What if somebody had imprisoned her in the root cellar to frighten her into leaving? Could this be another in the series of accidents that had plagued her for the past days?

Thoughts of a sinister presence in the house chilled her soul as the cold air chilled her body. Belle removed her apron and wrapped it around her shoulders like a shawl. Surely, it was only a matter of time before she was missed and somebody searched for her. Until then, she would do her best to free herself.

Feeling her way around the dank cellar, she located a piece of wood about an arm's length. Desperate to escape, she used it as a hammer to pound it against the heavy doors. Either the wood would shatter, or she would raise enough ruckus to alert the entire community.

A tear inched down her face. She prayed that somebody missed her before she froze to death. Belle's fears weren't for herself. The children needed her. She hated to think what would happen to them without her protection and care.

Morgan tossed aside the ledger books. He didn't know why he'd even tried to balance the accounts. His mind wasn't on work, it was on one pretty little lady who had his thoughts jumbled and his equilibrium off kilter. To top it off, Belle had the entire household involved in her scheme to bring Christmas to Eden House.

He'd given up working in his office. It was too close to the parlor where the loud Christmas carols disturbed him. Every word about the blasted holiday brought back memories so painful, he wanted to drown his sorrows in drink. It was one way to forget that horrible Christmas when he'd discovered his mother lying in a pool of blood.

Thankfully, his apartment was far enough away that the noise didn't disturb him. Only his memories wouldn't go away. Liquor wasn't the answer, either. Drink wouldn't prevent him from remembering or from wanting Belle—only having her in his bed would ease the pain that haunted him.

Morgan didn't know how long he'd been staring into the fireplace when a knock sounded at the door. "Come in," he called out, his heart racing. Had she again come to him out of his musings.

The door opened, and a woman entered. His spirits dropped

when he saw it was Louise, not Belle, who stepped over the threshold. She paused for a second and looked around.

"Morgan, is Isabella here with you?"

He gestured to the room. "Not unless she's hiding under my bed."

"Don't get smart with me."

"Sorry. I haven't seen her all day. Is something wrong?"

"I don't suppose so. The children were looking for her, and I . . . never mind. I thought perhaps you knew where to find her."

He followed her to the doorway. "I'm sure she's somewhere in her half of the house. Have you looked in her room?"

Louise paused in the narrow hallway. "The children have been all over calling her name. She isn't in the house. Savannah checked the stables and she isn't there either."

Something twisted in Morgan's chest. "She has to be here. Belle wouldn't leave without telling somebody. She's too concerned for the children to worry them."

Together, they entered the kitchen and found Abby taking a loaf of bread from the oven. "Is something the matter, Mr. Morgan?" She dropped the hot loaf on the counter.

"Have you seen Mrs. Jordan?" Louise asked.

The girl looked away, not meeting Louise's eye. "No, ma'am. I just got home from church."

He studied the kitchen. "Did Belle bake that bread?"

Louise nodded. "She offered to prepare dinner. It isn't like her to put bread in the oven and go off and leave it. She might have just gone outdoors to cut some more greenery and lost track of the time."

"Without her shawl?" Morgan fingered the garment hanging on hooks behind the door.

"She could have gone upstairs and gotten her cloak." Louise leaned toward the window and glanced outside.

Morgan shivered. If he hadn't been sulking in his room, he

might have seen where she'd gone. Or been there to help her. "I'm going to look for her."

Grabbing his heavy jacket, he raced outside the house. In the yard, he looked right and left. He marched toward the woods, calling her name as he went. The wind flung his voice back in his face. With every moment, he grew more and more troubled. Something must have happened to her. Had she fallen and hurt herself? Fear gripped his heart. He circled the yard, and stopped at the rear to gather his thoughts. It wouldn't do to keep racing around in circles. He had to think.

On leaden feet he headed back toward the house. The sound of hammering stopped him in his tracks. The faint sound of a voice was nearly lost in the whistle of the wind.

He stopped and studied the house. As if pulled by magnets, his gaze shifted to the root cellar. Both wooden doors were shut, the wooden bar in place. It would be impossible for anyone to enter, then latch the doors.

As he moved toward the cellar, the hammering grew louder, as did the voice. Then abruptly, both stopped. Morgan hesitated. He must have been hearing things. He turned to go back to the kitchen. Belle must have returned by that time.

He'd taken only one step when the pounding began again. He stared at the root cellar. Something twisted in his chest. That was the one place he hadn't properly inspected. The closer he came, the louder the noise.

"Help," came the muffled voice.

"Belle?" he shouted.

With the speed of a desperate man, Morgan slid the bar from the brackets that held the doors shut. He threw open a door as a large two-by-four flew up toward him. Grabbing the board, he tugged gently.

"Belle, is it you?" He stumbled down the stairs.

"Morgan, thank God." She flung herself into his arms.

Relief gushed through him. He cuddled her in his embrace. Her face was icy and her body shivered with cold. "Are you okay?'' Unable to help himself, he pressed kiss after kiss on the top of her head.

''I . . . I think so. It . . . it's cold down here.'' Her teeth chattered, breaking her words into short gasps.

He shrugged out of his coat and wrapped it around her shoulders. ''Let's get inside where it's warm.'' Scooping her up in his arms, he hurriedly climbed the steep steps.

''Morgan, I'm not hurt. I can walk,'' she protested.

''We'll get to the warmth a lot faster this way.''

She wrapped her arms around his neck and pressed her face to his neck. ''I didn't think anybody would find me.''

His heart skipped a beat. He wouldn't admit he was every bit as frightened as she. ''Sweetheart, we've torn up the house looking for you. But what were you doing down there?''

''I was looking for sweet potatoes and apples. The door blew shut on me.''

Morgan threw a quick glimpse back at the heavy doors. The wind could have flung the doors closed, but only a person could have shoved the wooden bar into the slots.

By then they'd reached the rear door of the house. Louise flung open the door and the children surrounded them. He set her down on a chair near the stove. ''You'll be warm here.''

''Mama.'' Rosalind threw her arms around her mother's neck. ''We thought you were lost like Rory.''

Beth climbed up in her lap and hugged her. ''I knew Morgie would find Mama.''

The other women and the boys gathered around Belle huddled in Morgan's big coat. Abby pressed a cup of hot coffee into her fingers. They were all talking at once.

Louise pulled Morgan aside. ''Where did you find her?''

''In the root cellar. She'd gone to find something and got locked in.'' Morgan decided to keep his suspicions to himself. He wondered if Belle was accident prone or if somebody in the house was out to do her harm.

Suspicion nagged at the corners of his mind. It had been

Louise's idea to frighten Belle into leaving. He shot a glance at Savannah and Vivian, who were bustling around Belle. Their income had been drastically cut since Belle and the children had arrived. Then there was Abby. The young woman had a sweet, gentle nature. Yet she was infatuated with the sheriff and Dan had shown an abnormal amount of interest in Isabella.

"It's a good thing you found her, Mr. Morgan," Abby said. "I felt how cold it was getting when I walked home from church. Miss Belle might have froze to death overnight without a shawl or coat."

Morgan didn't need a reminder of the danger of being caught out in the elements. He'd been in the mountains long enough to know how dangerous the elements were. "Yeah. Thank goodness."

Chapter 19

Belle glanced up at Morgan huddled in conversation with Louise. While the children hugged and warmed Belle, she watched the pair. For the third time, Morgan had saved her from harm. As if by a miracle, he'd been there when she needed him. Distrust washed over her. How could she love a man she didn't fully trust? More than ever she felt the need to leave.

The children murmured how glad they were Mr. Morgan had found her. Belle assured them she had never been in any danger. She'd just accidentally let the doors close on her. Jerome told her that she didn't ever have to go to that root cellar again. He would be right beside her to run her errands.

The children's concern warmed her more than Morgan's jacket or the fire. Beth pressed her head to Belle's shoulder. Morgan stared at them with a strange expression in his eyes.

"Feeling better?" he asked. He hunkered down beside her and caught her fingers in his. Lifting her hands to his mouth, he kissed her fingertips.

"Much. I can't believe I was so careless." She tugged her

hands free. "If you'll all let me go, I'll get the dinner on the table."

Savannah pressed her hand to Belle's shoulder. "You sit here, Miss Belle. Viv and I will serve the meal. You've already done enough."

Morgan stood and helped Belle to her feet. She shrugged off his jacket and handed it to him. "Thank you, Morgan. Looks as if you're always rescuing me from my own clumsiness."

He flashed her a heart-stopping smile and bowed gallantly from the waist. "My pleasure, ma'am. Anytime you need rescuing, please call on me."

The children giggled. "Mama, come see how we decorated the parlor. It's real pretty." Rosalind tugged her hand.

Beth grabbed Morgan's leg. "You come see what I did, Morgie. I made a pretty star just for you."

Morgan picked up the child and tossed her in the air. "Not right now, sweetheart. Morgan is busy. I'll look in later."

The little girl squealed as he flipped her over, then set her on her feet. "Let's go, Mama. I'll show you the star Miss Vivie helped me make."

Belle glanced at Morgan. He refused to have anything to do with Christmas. Even Elizabeth couldn't convince him to participate in the celebration. What a sad thing for him. His childhood must have been worse than she'd figured.

In the parlor, she complimented the children on their decoration. The women had done a lovely job, bringing a festive look to the elegant parlor. She bit back a laugh. Who would expect a house of ill repute adorned with Christmas regalia? They showed her where they wanted to set the tree.

"A big one," Rosalind said.

"A giant one, bigger than Morgie," declared Beth.

Belle simply smiled, not wanting them to know the tree wouldn't be in the parlor, but in the smaller study at the rear of the house. They seemed so happy, she didn't want to spoil their celebration.

A few minutes later, Savannah stuck her head into the parlor and called them to supper. Surrounded by the children she adored, Belle strolled to the dining room. She noticed that Vivian set nine places at the table. Did that mean that Morgan intended to join them after he'd rejected the children's offer to share their Christmas decorations with them?

The food on the table and the children settled, one place was noticeably vacant. Beth knelt on an upholstered dining chair, and propped her elbows on the table. "Where Morgie?" She banged a silver spoon against a delicate crystal glass.

Belle seized the spoon from the little girl before she shattered the glass. "I don't suppose he's hungry."

"I'm starved. Heroes who rescue maidens in distress need nourishment." The masculine voice came from the doorway. "And that smells mighty good." He snatched Beth up in his arms and flopped to the chair with the child on his lap. The little girl squealed with delight. Belle's heart skipped a beat, while the other women laughed at his antics.

Since Morgan chose to tend to the child, Belle shoved back her chair to give him more room. He caught her wrist. "Where are you going?"

"To fetch some jelly." It was a poor excuse, but she was still tingling from the feel of his arms around her when he'd carried her from the root cellar. Her warm feeling for him came as a sharp contrast to the suspicion that flicked at the corners of her mind.

Returning to the dining room, she took the chair they'd saved for Morgan—across the table from his disturbing presence. He grinned as if he was very aware of her purpose. The children bowed their heads, and waited for Belle to pray. She stared ahead as if her mind had deserted her.

"Mama," Rosalind whispered. "Are you going to ask the blessing?"

Snapped out of her stupor, Belle recited a short prayer, then silently added a word for strength to resist Morgan's temptation.

Dinner passed amicably, the women chatting with the children. In the past weeks, they'd warmed considerably toward Belle and her charges. Morgan added an occasional remark to Belle, but mostly he related to the youngsters. All four glowed under the attention paid them by the adults. Even her shy little Rosie blossomed under the consideration shown her, especially by the handsome man.

Until Morgan had invaded their lives, she hadn't realized how much her daughter—as well as the other children—missed having a father. Now that she was free, she ought to consider marrying again. So far, she had two suitors who seemed eager for her hand, or her inheritance. She lifted her gaze to Morgan, who was sharing his food with Elizabeth. He caught her glance. Heat sizzled between them across the table.

Quickly, she turned away. It wouldn't hurt to consider Dan and Corbett as prospective husbands. Except that she didn't love either man. She loved Morgan, and he was not a contender for her hand. No, it was best to leave Paradise and look for a husband in Denver, or wherever she decided to settle.

"Mama." Rosalind nudged Belle's arm. "Are you listening to me?"

She jerked her attention to her daughter. Lost in her musings, she'd missed the ongoing conversation at the table. "Yes, dear?" No use explaining where her thoughts had wandered.

"Mr. Morgan wants to know if he can have some of our cookies to take to Mr. Vic and the other hands?"

For a man who didn't believe in Christmas, he was certainly interested in the treats she'd spent hours baking. Instead of berating him, she smiled. "Of course. And he can invite the men to Eden House for Christmas. We'll decorate the tree on Christmas Eve, and on the next day we'll have a lovely dinner."

In spite of the smile on his lips, Morgan's eyes were cold and forbidding. "They'll be working."

"It's a special holiday. Surely they can take a few hours off. Let them know they're all welcome."

Morgan clearly didn't want to argue in front of the children. "I'll relay your message."

"Thank you. When are you going to the ranch."

"Tomorrow morning. I'll be gone most of the week."

Her heart sank. Was he running away from her? Or from her Christmas preparations? "I'll prepare a basket to take with you."

The women across the table cast sly glances her way. Did they know she and Morgan were lovers? Her skin heated. As women experienced with men, they undoubtedly assumed any man and woman thrown together as she and Morgan had been couldn't help but become intimate. So much for secrets in the busy household.

"Eat up, children," she said, eager to get away from Morgan. "We'll work on our decorations before you have to go up to bed."

Rory grunted. "We don't have to go to school tomorrow. We can stay up as late as we want."

"Not so, young man. Even if you don't have to attend the Paradise school, you'll still continue your lessons at home."

"Aw, Miss Belle. I reckon I'm too sick to have lessons." He coughed and hacked as if he were on the verge of dying of consumption.

"You'll have your lessons in your room. Either way, you will continue your education."

Vivian reached over and brushed a tumble of red hair out of his eyes. "Sugar, you don't know how important it is to go to school. I never liked school, either. When my ma died and I had to stay home and tend the other young'uns, I was kind of glad. Now I'm sorry I never learned to read and write too good. Think of all the wonderful books I can't read, and all the things you know that I don't."

Rosalind lifted her gaze. "Mama can teach you, too, Miss Vivian. She's a real good teacher."

The red-haired woman snickered. "I'm too old to learn."

"No you aren't," Morgan chimed in. "You don't have anything to lose. Why not give it a try?" Again Morgan did something totally unselfish and kind.

"If that hard-headed little Irishman can learn, so can you," Belle added.

"I'll help you, Miss Vivian." Rory gazed at the pretty lady with youthful adoration.

"And you ain't nearly as old as Mama." At Rosalind's comment, everybody laughed.

"No she isn't, darling. Your mama is pushing thirty, and that's almost ancient."

"What does that make me?" asked Morgan, the twinkle returning to his eyes. "I'm nearly five years older."

"Does Methuselah sound familiar?" Louise lifted her glass in a toast.

"Thanks," he grumbled.

Jerome lifted his gaze. "We read about him in the Bible. He was the oldest man who ever lived. You ain't that old, are you, Mistah Morgan?"

Belle covered her mouth to hide her laughter. Morgan pointed a finger at her. "Don't laugh, Bella. You'll catch up before you can blink an eye."

"I'm already grunting and groaning when I overwork. I don't know how I'll survive when I reach your advanced age."

Beth flung her arms around his neck. "Morgie not old. He nice. Beth love Morgie."

On a long sigh, Belle tugged the child from Morgan's embrace. The little girl was getting entirely too attached to the man. The sooner Belle got her crew away from Paradise, the easier it would be for them to get over Morgan's disturbing influence. "Let's get cleaned up, and I'll let you work on the Christmas decorations." She dropped a cold glance at Morgan. "For my side of the house."

* * *

He had to get away before he did something stupid. He was on the verge of stealing Belle away and keeping her in his room until they both fell exhausted from making love. At dawn the next morning, Morgan mounted his horse and headed toward the ranch. He hadn't been lying when he told Belle he hated Christmas and all it stood for. At thirty-five, the painful memories still haunted him. His mother had taken her own life on Christmas Day. He and James were left in the care of a bitter, angry man without an ounce of affection for anything except the bottle.

Since that day, he'd avoided any mention of the Nativity season. His idea of celebrating was to find a willing woman and drown his memories in a bottle.

Let Belle decorate, and let her celebrate. Morgan planned to stay as far away from Eden House as possible during the next weeks.

He kicked the horse into a gallop. First he would check out the mine. Although he hadn't admitted it to anybody, he suspected the rocks Rory had found contained gold ore. As he wound his way down the mostly deserted road, he remembered how the area was once busy with activity. Then the mine played out, and he'd personally boarded it up. Had James suspected there was gold in the mine? He'd tried to buy Morgan out and keep the mine to himself. Impossible. Morgan had been through every shaft and tunnel and it was as bare as a pauper's pantry.

Morgan pulled up the collar of his jacket. It was getting colder by the minute. At least Belle and the children didn't have to go out in the weather. He was glad she was keeping them home from the schoolhouse. A frown tugged at his mouth. Home. Eden House wasn't a home, it was a whore house. And not a decent place to raise children.

That was one reason he had to get away. He was getting too

close to Belle and the kids. He was a loner, and he didn't need to be tied down to anybody. Come spring, he would turn the whole place over to Louise and live full-time at the ranch. Let Belle stay if she pleased. As long as she stayed out of his sight.

As he neared the mine, he spotted hoof prints in the snow. He jumped down and checked the tracks. Somebody had come up either yesterday or earlier today. Somebody who had no business snooping around his property.

Morgan rarely carried sidearms, but he usually kept a rifle in the holster at his saddle. With its longer range, a rifle was far more accurate a weapon. He unsheathed the Winchester, and hid his horse among the trees. Bending his head against the wind, he followed the trail toward the mine shaft.

Boards were pulled off, making an opening into the interior of the shaft. Carefully, he approached, pressing his back against the hillside. The wind whistled and stirred up the snow. The footprints would soon be covered, but Morgan had no trouble following their direction. Whoever had invaded his property was inside the abandoned mine. A horse nickered and tossed its head. The trespasser was careless. Morgan supposed that he wasn't expecting anybody to come this way. Least of all the owner of the property.

In the pale morning light, Morgan spotted a glow moving inside the shaft. A pick clanged against stone. A man swore. The voice was familiar. Still, Morgan moved with caution. To startle the invader could cause trouble.

He slipped into the shadows and entered the shaft. The lamp moved away from him down the tunnel. Morgan had been in the mine hundreds of times. He'd checked every tunnel, and he'd found no hint of anything of value. It didn't matter that the mine was worthless. It belonged to him, and he didn't like strangers on his property.

Pressing against the wall, he pointed his rifle at the figure carrying the lamp. "Stop right there. Don't try anything stupid, I've got you in my sights."

A string of expletives burst from the stranger's mouth. "Travers, it's me, Dan Sullivan."

"Sullivan. What the hell are you doing here?"

"The same as you. Looking for the gold."

"Come out where I can see you. This tunnel is unstable." Morgan backed away. He stepped over the criss-cross boards at the entrance and exited the mine. Keeping the rifle ready, he waited until the sheriff joined him in the brisk wind. Dan stepped out and dusted off his hat on his canvas trousers. "What makes you think there's gold in the mine?"

Dan shoved his hat back on his head and blew out the lamp. "You can quit lying about the mine. James knew there was gold, and the boy found a nugget up here somewhere."

"What do you know about James? He never mentioned gold to me." Morgan's stomach sank. Had his partner been cheating him all along?

"Abby found it in his room. He came out here all the time. There must have been something here."

As if a light went off in his head, Morgan glared at the sheriff. "Is that how you happened to be the one to find James dead? You followed him here, didn't you?" He tightened his grip on the rifle. "You killed James."

Dan jerked back as if he'd been punched in the gut. "I admit I was curious about the mine. But I didn't kill him."

"Then how did you happen to be there when he died?"

Hooking his thumbs in his belt, he shrugged under his heavy coat. "I followed him that day when he drove out to the mine. He must have known I was behind him, because he started driving faster than was safe. He took a steep curve and the buggy overturned. I got there right after it happened. James died on impact."

"Real convenient for you."

"Morgan, I didn't kill him." Under his night's growth of whiskers, Dan's face paled. Morgan may not like the man's interest in Belle, or in the mine, but overall the sheriff was as honest a man as could be expected.

"So you looked for the gold and never found it."

"I'd given up, until the kid showed up with that nugget. He found it up here somewhere. I swear there's gold, and James knew it."

"I've been all over this mine. For all I know, James was trying to salt the mine. I wouldn't put it past him to swindle some investors and take off with their cash." He shook his head. "And leave me holding the bag."

"Sounds like something James would do. Hell, any man who would desert a woman like Isabella is capable of anything."

The mention of the woman Morgan was trying to forget irked him worse than the man snooping around the mine. "Get back to town, Dan, you're trespassing."

"Okay, Morgan. This mine in worthless."

"I tried to tell you."

The sheriff nodded and strolled to his horse. He mounted, then turned to Morgan. "Morgan, you won't try to cheat Belle, will you?"

He narrowed his gaze. "It was James who was trying to cheat me. I'll deal honestly with her. Take my advice and stay away from her. You don't look like the type to take on four children and a stubborn woman."

Dan laughed. "Neither do you." He touched the brim of his hat and rode off to town.

Morgan watched until the sheriff disappeared from sight. The man was right. He didn't have the temperament to take on a family. However, he had no idea how he was going to solve his problem. He wanted Belle in his life, at least in his bed. And with every day, he grew closer to the children. It would be better for them all if he'd have run her off at the very beginning. Then he wouldn't have fallen in love with her.

His heart tripped. He swore under his breath. It couldn't be love. Lust, of course. Love? Morgan doubted he knew the meaning of the word.

Good, old-fashioned hard work would get her out of his mind and out of his thoughts. He ignored the snow flurries and mounted his horse. Yes, sir, a week at the ranch would get her out of his system.

Or succeed in driving him totally out of his mind.

Chapter 20

"If you eat all our cookies we won't have any to decorate our tree." Belle layered a piece of tissue between the lacy cookies she'd baked that morning. She had spent the better part of the week in the kitchen—baking and cooking. She'd begun informal classes with the children, and Vivian had joined them in the afternoon. Every moment was filled with activity preparing for the holiday. Anything to keep her thoughts from Morgan. In the days that he'd been gone, she hadn't had any more of the accidents. It hurt to think he'd loved her so passionately then tried to injure her.

"We ain't got no tree." Rory shoved another sugar cookie into his mouth. "Besides, we got all those tins full."

"We do not have a tree," she corrected. "Yet."

"That's what I said." He reached for another cookie, but stopped when he caught Belle's hard stare. "You reckon Mr. Morgan will help us cut one?"

Her heart sank. Morgan had made it clear he didn't want any part of Christmas. He'd been gone since early Monday, and she had no idea when he intended to return. Probably long after she'd gone. "I don't know. If he doesn't make it back in time, we'll have to cut it ourselves. I saw some really pretty firs when we took that ride out to the ranch."

"Mama, I want to pick it out," said Rosalind. She bit her lip as she struggled to slip the ribbon into the hole in a star she'd made out of colored paper.

"Me, too." As usual, Beth wanted to be part of every activity. She held up a cutout of an angel she'd colored with red paint. "Mama, you think Morgie likes angels?"

"Aw, he probably don't even believe in angels. Only Jerome sees angels." Rory rubbed his knuckles across the younger boy's nappy hair.

Jerome brushed Rory's hand away. "Angels are too real. Miz Belle, you believe, don't you."

"Of course I do. Angels watch over us all the time." Though at times she wondered if hers had gone on a long, long holiday. Her feelings for Morgan had her doing things she would never have dreamed she was capable of doing. It wasn't fair to blame her guardian angel for her shortcomings. She'd fallen in love and given in to temptation. Nobody was to blame but Isabella herself.

Belle placed her hands on her back and stretched. After a week cooped up in the house with the children, she needed to get out for a little while. With Christmas only a few days away, there were still a few things she needed from the general store and the mercantile. "Rory, I'm going to trust you to keep an eye on the others while I ride into town."

"Can't we go with you?" he whined.

"This close to Christmas, I believe it is best that I go alone. You'll only be bored when I look at ribbon and dress goods."

"Mr. Nelson has some really great knives and guns."

Belle didn't know how long she was going to be able to keep the boy under her control. More and more she realized the youngsters needed a father, a man capable of handling a rebellious youth. Without a doubt, Morgan was not that man. "Maybe Papa Noel will bring you one of those great gifts." Mentally, she counted her remaining coins. Surely, a knife couldn't be too expensive. A gun was out of the question. Even Morgan didn't carry side arms. "Run on out and ask Jeb to hitch up the wagon. I'll need to pick up some more flour and sugar for cakes and pies."

The boy shoved away from the table. "Yes, ma'am. You know I could drive the wagon for you."

She laughed. "Go. I have to make this trip alone."

When she entered the general store, Belle was glad she'd left the children behind. She threw off the hood of her cape and smoothed back the loose strands of hair. Like the other customers, she hurried to the stove and warmed her hands at the glowing fire. Two women who'd been sharing their news, slanted glances at her and shied away. "Merry Christmas," she said in an effort to be cordial.

Both grunted something and moved toward the counter. Another woman entered and skirted around the fire. Others turned their heads when they spotted Belle. She tamped down her growing agitation. Belle had always considered herself a friendly person who often held conversations with total strangers at the market. She found it difficult getting accustomed to the snubs of the other women in Paradise. But to show it bothered her would only lower her integrity.

With Christmas only days away, the store was crowded with customers getting ready for the holiday. An older gentleman was selecting a pipe and tobacco from the display on a shelf. Belle wrinkled her nose against the myriad of odors that permeated the general store. Coffee, tobacco, soap, candles, spices, apples, and a box of oranges were blended together into a strange perfume.

Belle turned toward the counter and bumped into a gruff-looking man. He tipped his battered hat and granted a gap-toothed grin. He rubbed his whiskered chin and eyed her up and down. "Merry Christmas, ma'am. You're that new lady at Eden House, ain't you? You gonna be at the party?"

Not sure to what he was referring, she slipped toward the barrels of goods against the wall. "I do not believe so." She certainly wouldn't be attending any affair to which he was invited.

The shopkeeper, Mr. Peterson, greeted her with a frown. That was unusual. On their last visit to the store, she and Morgan had spent enough to bring a wide smile to his round, ruddy face. "May I help you, Mrs. Jordan?"

She handed him her list, and felt somebody staring at her. Two women glanced at her, then quickly turned away. Belle tilted her nose in the air and returned her gaze to the merchant. "Mr. Peterson, will you have my purchases put into my wagon?"

He shifted a glance at his other customers, then lowered his voice. "I can deliver your order, Mrs. Jordan. I got in the things Morgan ordered. I'll have them out to Eden House this afternoon."

Although she couldn't imagine what Morgan could have needed, she was grateful the merchant was willing to accommodate her. "Thank you. That's very kind of you. Just make sure I get them today. I have a lot of baking to finish before Christmas."

"Yes, ma'am. I'll add it to your account."

"Mr. Peterson, I would appreciate your keeping my purchases separate from Morgan's. I'll pay when the goods are delivered."

The shopkeeper nodded his assent.

"Charles," a tall thin woman called from the other side of the store. "If you're finished with *that woman,* these ladies need help."

That woman. Belle gritted her teeth to keep from giving Mrs.

Peterson a piece of her mind. Because she was staying at Eden House didn't mean she was of any lower moral character than any other woman in town. Then she remembered her affair with Morgan, and she realized that maybe they were right. Belle wasn't any better than Louise, Vivian, or Savannah. If they were fallen women, so was she. Tugging her hood over her head, she stepped out into the chill December air.

She ran the few steps to Nelson's Emporium to complete her shopping. She'd already purchased gifts for the children, Mrs. Franklin, Jeb, Abby, and the ladies who had become friends. The only gift remaining was one for Morgan.

As usual, Miss Nelson ignored Belle. However, Stanley overlooked his other customers and offered Belle his undivided attention. He graciously showed the collection of knives. She selected a jackknife for Rory, a small folding knife with a carved ivory handle. For Morgan, she chose a Bowie knife with a tooled leather sheath. She studied the little fur muffs and hoods that both little girls would love. Instead, she settled on new hair combs to add to the gifts she'd made. And wouldn't the boys love the leather vests that were beyond her means?

Stanley totaled her purchases and carried them to the wagon. "I'll see you this evening, Mrs. Jordan. Have a good day." He offered a hand up, then hurried back to the warmth of his store.

Belle stared after him. What did he mean by saying he would see her? Did she have another suitor competing for her attention?

As she picked up the lines, Sheriff Sullivan stepped out of his office. He waved a hand and sauntered over to her. She hadn't seen him since the past week when he'd come to check on Rory.

The handsome man shoved his hat back off his forehead, revealing smiling dark eyes. "Afternoon, Miss Belle."

"Merry Christmas, Sheriff."

"Getting things ready for Morgan's party?" he asked.

That was the third reference to a party. Had Morgan relented and agreed to invite the townspeople for a Christmas celebration? But why didn't he tell her? There was no second-guessing Morgan. "I suppose I am. Will you be honoring us with your presence?"

"I wouldn't miss it for anything. Besides it's always good to have the law handy in case of trouble."

"We aren't expecting trouble. Christmas is a time for good will and cheer."

Dan nodded. "Sometimes men get too much 'cheer' and cause problems. I'll be there to see that nothing happens."

"Thank you, Dan. I'd best get back. I still have cakes and pies to bake."

"Do you need an escort? I'd be honored to see you safely home."

Belle laughed, her laughter carried away on the wind. "Eden House is just beyond the edge of town. I'm certain no harm will befall me."

He stepped away, and touched a finger to the brim of his hat.

It took only minutes to reach the stable at Eden House. The horses pranced, eager to reach their shelter. Jeb met her and stabled the animals. To her surprise, Morgan's horse was in its stall. Taking her packages in hand, she hurried to the house.

A strange wagon was at the rear door; a burly man unloaded several boxes from the bed. Had Mr. Peterson sent her purchase so soon? "Merry Christmas, Mrs. Jordan," the man called out his voice full of cheer. "Got Mr. Morgan's order. The hams are smoked and the turkeys roasted to perfection."

She recognized the owner of the Palace Restaurant. "Merry Christmas, Mr. Hale. That's quite an order."

"Yes, ma'am. Morgan didn't want anybody to go away hungry."

Another reference to a gathering. Did everybody but she know about the event? A sudden gust of wind swept a she of paper from the wagon. It landed at Belle's feet. Bending over, she picked up what appeared to be a flyer announcing an event. A party. At Eden House.

She read closer, her temper rising with every word. "Calling all men. Free food, free drinks, music, entertainment. Eden House shows appreciation to our loyal guests." That evening. In bold letters was printed, "FOR MEN ONLY."

Morgan's party was an orgy for the men in town. No wonder the women avoided her as if she had the plague and the men showed unwarranted attention. Heat to her face chased away the chill. Of all the nerve. He hadn't even consulted her.

Crumpling the flyer in her hand, she stomped into the kitchen. Thankfully, the children were nowhere in sight. Mrs. Franklin was at the stove stirring a pot.

"Mrs. Franklin, have you seen Morgan?" She dropped her packages on a kitchen chair.

The housekeeper glanced up and gestured toward the hallway. "Last I saw of him, he was headed toward his office. Reckon he's still there."

"Thanks," Belle said. She threw back her hood and headed to Morgan's sanctuary. "Morgan," she called. Flinging open the door, she stepped across the threshold.

Morgan sat at his desk, Beth on his knee. The child was scribbling on a piece of paper on the desk. Looking up, Morgan flashed a smile that usually curled her toes. Today, she was immune to his charm. Charm? Ha. He had all the charm of a rattlesnake.

"Afternoon, Isabella. Are you looking for me? Missed me while I was gone?"

She gritted her teeth at his arrogance. The man had not one ounce of humility. She stalked across the fine Oriental carpet and snatched the child from his lap. "Sweetheart, go find Rosie. Tell her it's time for your nap."

"Don't want nap. Want Morgie." She stomped her feet.

"Do as your mama says, honey. Morgie will see you later." His words worked wonders.

With a childish pout, Beth raced for the door. Once the child was gone, Belle slammed the door shut. She stepped forward and faced Morgan.

"Couldn't wait to see me? Come over here, I'll warm you up." He stood and opened his arms.

"You arrogant ass." She flung the flyer at his chest. "What is the meaning of this?"

He smoothed out the rumpled paper. "It's an invitation to the party. You said we should celebrate the holidays, so I've decided to have a social gathering."

"For men only?"

"Bella, our clients are men. Since business is off, I wanted to show our appreciation to our loyal customers. They're the ones keeping Eden House operating at a profit. I want to show them that we're still in the entertainment business."

"Don't you try to placate me, Morgan Travers. You're doing this to spite me, and to run me off."

His smile softened the hard lines in his face. "Now, Bella, why should I try to run you off? That would be like cutting off my . . . my toes to spite my foot."

She wanted to slap the smug look off his arrogant face. "Don't think I don't know what you've been up to? The threats, the warnings, the accidents—locking me in the root cellar." Stepping closer, she met his gaze without blinking. Being so close to him had her pulse racing. A band tightened around her chest.

Morgan moved so fast, she didn't have time to react. He caught her arms in a strong grip. "Bella, I didn't have anything to do with your so-called accidents." His fingers dug into the soft flesh through the heavy cloak. "I admit at first I wanted you to go, to keep away from my businesses. But I would never do anything to cause you harm."

"I heard you and Louise scheme to get rid of me. A seduction, you said. That should scare the spinsterish widow away."

He laughed, a self-derisive sound. "You're the one who seduced me, Bella. You and those children. Your smile drew me in. Hell, I don't know what happened to me."

It certainly wasn't the same thing that had happened to her. She'd fallen helplessly in love with him. "Temporary insanity, Morgan. As soon as we leave, you can get back to your depraved activities without us to interfere."

"What are you talking about?"

"Please remove your hands from my arms." His grip loosened, but he remained toe to toe with her. His eyes darkened, and the growth of whiskers gave him a hard and dangerous look. "I promised the children a happy Christmas, and I'll give it to them if I have to walk over you and your 'guests' to do it. As soon after New Year's as possible, we're moving out."

"Marrying one of your suitors?" His voice grew deceptively soft.

"No. I'll sell you my interest in our enterprises and move to Denver."

"What if I can't buy you out?"

"I'll sell to Corbett, or somebody else. He told me he can locate investors who'll be happy to partner with you."

"If you're determined to leave, I'll borrow the money and see that you're fairly compensated. I wouldn't want the youngsters to suffer on my account."

"That will be fine." She spun on her heel, eager to get away from Morgan before she gave away too much of her feelings. By his cavalier attitude, he'd shown exactly how much he thought of her. Little or nothing. He couldn't wait for her to get out of his sight.

Belle had taken one step when Morgan stopped her with a hand to her arm. "The party might get rather rowdy. It would be best if you keep the children on your side of the house."

"Would you prefer that we leave today?"

"New Year's is soon enough."

She shrugged out of his grip seconds before the tears of anger—not pain—rolled from her eyes. "It isn't soon enough for me."

Morgan let her go. A moment longer of touching her, he would have pulled Belle into his embrace and begged her not to leave him. He'd missed her terribly while he'd been gone. Unexpected joy had burst full bloom in his heart when she'd entered the room. He sank back into the chair at the desk. Too late, he realized he should have told her about the party. She would have been angry, but he suspected she was furious because he'd kept his plans a secret.

A chill skittered down his spine. It was the cold, he reasoned within himself. Since entering the office, he'd been too busy playing with Beth to bother lighting a fire. Now the cold seeped into his bones like death stealing away his life. Morgan shook off the morose feeling. She could go where she pleased, do what she willed, and marry whomever she desired. He'd be damned if he'd give her a moment's thought once he bought her out. He hadn't wanted a partner; now she was giving him a way out of the problem.

A niggling voice within him questioned if that was what he truly wanted. Morgan reached for the decanter of whiskey. He poured a small glass and stared into the liquor the exact color of Belle's eyes. He pictured her gazing back at him the way she'd looked the last time they'd been together, her beautiful eyes sparkled with gold flecks and darkened with passion.

He tossed the liquor down his throat. It burned clear down to his stomach. Getting her out of his thoughts would be hard enough. Death would be easier than getting her out of his heart. For once in his life he'd felt whole. Belle had given him back his soul, then snatched it away. He didn't know if a man could survive without a heart and soul. It looked as if he would soon find out.

For the remainder of the day, Morgan managed to steer clear

of Belle. Little Elizabeth hung onto his coattails, bombarding him with questions about what he was doing. It wasn't easy to tell the little girl he was having a party and she was not invited.

Morgan stocked the bar with the liquor Peterson had delivered. The liquor wasn't as fine as Morgan's private stock. Actually, he was still drinking the whiskey James had imported before his death. With the help of Savannah and Vivian, Louise took charge of the food. The spread was enough to satisfy every hungry man in town and from the surrounding ranches, customer or not. He wondered who had set the tray of cookies and the cakes on a sideboard in the dining room.

Beth tugged on his trouser leg. "Mama's cookies." The child answered his unspoken question. Then he wondered how Louise had gotten the precious treats from Belle. Beth reached out a hand and snatched a cookie from the tray. After taking a bite, she offered the half-eaten cookie to Morgan. "Morgie?" Her round blue eyes offered a gift he couldn't refuse.

Hunkering down, he took a bite. "Good. Did you help your mama?" Lord, being with this child and calling Belle "mama" seemed so natural, his heart tripped over the word. He pulled the little girl into his embrace. Belle was such a good mother, to her child and the others she'd taken in. Strangers' children—homeless waifs she cherished and loved as much as her own precious little daughter.

Pain sliced through his chest. Not only would he miss them, he doubted he would be able to sleep for worry about them. How would she manage after she left Eden House? They needed a home, and she'd hoped to settle them here, thanks to her legacy from her wayward husband. If Morgan could give her enough money, she could buy a house in Denver and support the children. Too bad there wasn't gold in the abandoned mine. She could live in luxury the rest of her life if it were true.

The child felt so small and fragile in his arms. She trusted him and loved him, although he didn't deserve either. For too many years he'd lived only for his own selfish pleasure. It surprised him to finally love and care for someone other than himself. As he accepted the child's kisses on his cheek, he realized how much he loved Belle and her charges. He didn't want them to leave. He had to find a way to win her heart and convince her to stay.

Without her he would return to the depraved creature he'd been, a man without direction or purpose. He had no desire to return to that.

Realizing their guests would arrive soon, Morgan flipped the child over his shoulder and headed for the kitchen. "Mama is going to be looking for you, little bit."

The child squealed with delight. "Want stay with Morgie."

He wanted it too. "I'll see you tomorrow." He deposited her on a chair at the table. Belle was nowhere in sight. "Abby, keep an eye on the baby. I have to bathe and change."

"Yes, sir, Mr. Morgan, I'll look after her."

Hours later, in his best black suit with the red and gold brocade vest, Morgan entered the parlor to welcome his guests. As he studied the decorations Belle had made for the mantle, he began to think the party was a bad idea. He'd offended Belle by excluding her and the children. After rejecting her idea of a party for the families in town, he'd planned one for men only. What a reprobate he proved to be.

He nodded to the pianist and fiddle player he'd hired. Both were playing softly waiting for the guests to arrive. Later there would be dancing for the hardy souls who could stand on their feet long enough.

"Looks as if you're ready for your party." Louise joined him at the sideboard that served as a bar.

He grunted and pulled a cheroot from his pocket. Louise was dressed in her finest gown. The purple creation was cut very low at the neck, showing her pearly shoulders and quite a bit of her chest. Black beads enhanced the décolletage. Her hair was piled in an elaborate chignon with strands of pale hair trailing down her neck. The woman was beautiful, but a hard life had left its mark in the lines around her eyes. Both she and Belle had been misused by his cousin. Morgan cursed his degenerate kin under his breath.

At least Louise had found Vic. The ranch foreman had been sweet on Louise long before James died. He was quickly on the way to winning the woman's heart.

"Are the girls ready for customers?" he asked.

"They've informed me that they'll attend your party and serve your guests, but their rooms are closed for Christmas."

Morgan shrugged. "Fine with me. I planned to let them keep all of their earnings, and charge double or triple for Christmas. But if that's the way they want it." He reached for a drink from the sideboard.

His hand tightened on the decanter when he caught movement from the corner of his eye. A woman in a red dress entered the parlor, followed by a lady in green. Vivian and Savannah would surely satisfy the guests. One thing about it, James knew how to pick women. He tilted the crystal container and filled a small glass. Another figure caught his gaze. Recognition hit him square in the gut.

The crystal glass slipped from his fingers and shattered on the marble-topped sideboard. Shards of glass flew everywhere. Whiskey splashed on his trousers. A stain spread across the carpet.

He ignored it all. His gaze locked on the newcomer standing in the doorway. Attired in a deep pink dress, with her hair piled on top of her head, she was the most magnificent woman he'd ever seen.

Belle was dressed for the party.

Chapter 21

Under the long form-fitting gown, Belle's knees turned to jelly. Her gaze shot to Morgan across the parlor. The shatter of crystal vibrated through the room like cannon fire. Whiskey dripped down his trousers and a stain spread across the carpet.

The look he gave her was enough to kill a deer at fifty paces. His stare started at her face, then dropped to the low neckline, past her nipped-in waist, and fell to her toes clad in the matching pink slippers. With his slow perusal, the frown on his mouth deepened and his brows drew together into a scowl.

Belle resisted the urge to cross her hands over her breasts or to run away and hide away in a convent. Instead, she gathered bravado around her like a shawl. She tilted her chin and met his hard, unrelenting glare.

As she and Morgan stared at each other, Louise jumped into action. She wiped the whiskey from the sideboard and scooped up the broken glass. Still, Morgan hadn't moved. His only visible reaction was the tell-tale twitch in his cheek. Fury shot from his eyes like lightning in a storm. Not wanting to show

how he unnerved her, Belle set her smile and forced her feet forward.

It had taken Belle every bit of the courage she could muster to don the evening gown. After she'd convinced Savannah to lend her a garment, she wasn't about to retreat like a scared rabbit. From the younger woman's collection of lavish garments, she'd chosen the rose satin. Adorned with crystal beads, the neckline dipped low between her breasts. An immodest amount of bosom swelled above the décolletage. Tiny sleeves covered her upper arms, leaving her chest and shoulders bare. She'd slipped a pink ribbon through the cameo James had stolen from her and tied it around her neck. Under the long white gloves, her palms grew damp.

Belle had never before worn such a luxurious gown. Her life as a housekeeper and mother didn't lend itself to evening attire. The way Morgan stared at her, she wondered if he thought she looked foolish—like a child playing dress-up. Or worse, a duckling pretending to be a swan.

She'd meant to defy Morgan, not embarrass herself. Torn between running upstairs and challenging Morgan, she held her ground.

For long moments neither of them moved. The loud bang of a fist at the door snapped Morgan out of his stupor. In long strides, he advanced on Belle. At the first sign of his approach, she darted back into the foyer and pulled open the door. Vivian joined her, effectively blocking Morgan from reaching her. Four men stood on the porch.

"Come in, gentlemen." Belle stepped away from the chill wind that whipped through the house. "You can hang your hats and coats on the hall tree." The normality of her voice surprised her, considering the trembling in her stomach.

Glancing over her shoulder, she spied Morgan still stalking toward her. Eager to avoid him, she looped her arm in that of the first man who'd entered. "Would you care for a drink?"

She sashayed past Morgan, her satin skirt rustling behind her in a short train. Fire blazed from Morgan's midnight blue eyes.

"Thank you kindly, Miss Belle." Only when he spoke in the soft southern drawl did she realize she'd escorted Stanley Nelson into the parlor. The merchant had slicked down his hair and was attired in a stiff pinstripe suit. The sweet smell of hair tonic wafted around him like a cloud. "Just a bit of wine, if you don't mind." His round face pinked. She wondered if he'd already indulged in some wine to get the courage to approach Eden House.

Hands trembling, Belle filled two wineglasses from the first bottle she found—a burgundy that matched the color of the merchant's face. She pressed the glass into his hand. Looking up, she found his gaze locked on the deep cut of her gown. Her skin chilled at the hunger in his eyes. Flirting was much more difficult than she'd anticipated.

As Morgan moved toward Belle, Savannah escorted another gentleman toward the sideboard and effectively sidetracked Morgan. "Oh, excuse us, Morgan. Would you be so kind as to serve Mr. Jones while I see to our other guests?"

"Certainly." He nodded his agreement. Belle stepped away to allow him room to prepare the drinks. "Mrs. Jordan, you can give me a hand, can't you?"

His request came out with the harshness of an order. The way he'd addressed her by her formal name was more an insult than a request. "Morgan, I'm already entertaining Mr. Nelson." His light touch on her arm stopped her as abruptly as if he'd shackled her in irons.

"You don't mind visiting with the other ladies, do you, Stan, old boy? I need Mrs. Jordan's assistance." His smile glinted like the snarl of a wolf. "Louise," he called. "Show Stanley to the buffet dinner."

"That was rude," Belle whispered, spinning to face him.

"The way I'm feeling, that's as polite as I can get. What do you think you're doing in that get-up?"

"I'm taking your suggestion and looking for a husband. Th[is] is an excellent way to meet and compare all the eligible me[n] in town. If I marry, I won't have to uproot the children an[d] move to Denver." She set her wineglass down. "Don't yo[u] like the way I look?" In spite of the rumbling in her stomac[h,] she tilted her head and smiled.

Backing up a step, he studied her like a stallion stalking [a] mare. His heated gaze set her blood aflame. "I like it ver[y] much. Only I hoped you would keep your treasures for m[y] eyes only. I can't help being a little jealous that you're dis[-] playing your wares for every man in town."

His arrogance spurred her on. "If I'm in the market for [a] husband, I had best let them know what they're getting. A[ ] woman with four children had best have something else to offe[r] a man."

"I won't allow you to marry any of these devils." He growle[d] like an angry dog. "Go upstairs and change into something decent. Didn't I warn you to stay in your half of the house?["]

"You ordered me to keep the children away. I'm hardly [a] child."

His predatory gaze dropped to the center of her chest. He[r] breasts tingled and heat spread up her neck to her face. "Nobody knows better than I." He reached out and twined a loose tendri[l] of her hair around his finger. His mouth dropped to her ear[.] "And Bella, you should know I'm a selfish man. I won't shar[e] what's mine."

Belle picked up a whiskey bottle, ready to smash it over hi[s] contemptible head. He snatched it away before she got a good grip. "I've already gotten a whiskey sprinkling, I don't nee[d] a baptism."

Gritting her teeth, she pulled away. By then more men had entered the parlor and several were staring at her and Morgan.

A large figure separated from the crowd. Sheriff Sulliva[n] clapped a hand on Morgan's shoulder. "Travers, you're going to hog Miss Belle's attention all evening? I've been looking forward for a chance to dance with her.''

Grateful for the chance to get away from the detestable man, she smiled up at Dan. Morgan snarled, and by the look on his face he was ready to strangle either her or the sheriff. It wouldn't have surprised her if Morgan had flipped her over his shoulder and carried her away. The sheriff stood eye to eye with Morgan as if daring him to deny his request.

The men nearest them had stopped talking to watch and listen. Had they expected a confrontation between the men? Morgan and Dan were evenly matched in size. With a pistol at his hip, Dan was much more dangerous. She slipped her arm in the sheriff's. ''I would love to dance with you.''

Leaving Morgan staring at them with his mouth agape, she and Dan moved to the center of the crowded room. ''Play 'Beautiful Dreamer,' '' he called over the din of the crowd. The piano and fiddle struck up the tune, inviting the few women and many men to dance.

His hand on her waist, Dan nodded gallantly and swept her around the room. ''You're exceptionally beautiful tonight, Miss Belle.'' He pulled her closer into his embrace than she considered proper.

She threw back her head and smiled. Over Dan's shoulder she met Morgan's furious gaze. The men from the ranch surrounded Morgan, blocking him from her view.

Within seconds a hand tapped Dan on the shoulder, and Belle found herself in Corbett's arms. The lawyer was an accomplished dancer, but at times his hand at her waist pulled her too close for propriety.

For the next hour, Belle was passed from one partner to another. Yet, more often than not, she found herself in either Dan's or Corbett's arms. The two men seemed to be in competition for her favors. They showered her with compliments and veiled propositions that she laughed off without insulting either man.

As foolish as it seemed, she rather enjoyed being the cente
of attention—the proverbial Belle of the ball, so to speak. O
course all her partners weren't as accomplished as others. A
rather shaggy prospector stomped on her toes several times. A
young cowboy tried to whisk her off into a corner.

Even the ranch hands danced with her, being careful to keep
her at arm's length. While Louise was occupied with another
man, Vic whirled her around the room. Unlike the others, he
refused to release her when another man tapped his shoulder.
With a snarl and a glare, he chased the other would-be partner
away.

"Enjoying the party, Miss Belle?" he asked. The ranch
foreman was a nice-looking man, soft-spoken and kind. She
caught him glancing over her shoulder, looking for Louise.

"Yes, I am. Everyone has been very nice."

He laughed. "Except Morgan. He looks as if he's eater
nothing but sour pickles for days." At that, he spun her around
and danced directly in front of Morgan.

She laughed and glanced at Morgan. "You're right. I think
he needs a little sugar to sweeten him up."

"From you, Miss Belle. He hasn't taken his eyes off you
all evening."

"How would you know, Vic? You haven't taken yours off
Louise since you arrived."

"You've got me there, ma'am." The music stopped, but Vic
kept his arm around Belle's waist. "May I offer you a bite to
eat?"

Locking her arm in his, he guided her to the dining room.
They had reached the door when Louise stopped them. Her
gaze shifted from Vic to Belle. If he'd made her jealous, she
showed no sign. "Vic, darling, can I bother you to lend me a
hand. I need something from the storeroom." She sidled up to
him, slipping her arm into his. "You don't mind, do you,
Isabella?"

Aware of the situation between the pair, she nodded. "Of

course, I don't mind. I think I'll have some champagne and a taste of that fine buffet dinner.''

With Vic out of the room, a half dozen men surrounded Belle, eager for her attention. A glance over her shoulder showed that Morgan hadn't moved from beside the liquor cabinet. Not once had he asked her to dance or share the meal with him.

Belle flirted, she evaded unwanted attention, she smiled, she ate, and she avoided Morgan. As hard as she tried to enjoy the company of her many admirers, she wanted Morgan to notice her. The party was still going strong at midnight when she slipped away and climbed the stairs.

She'd tried to make Morgan jealous, but nothing seemed to faze him. The last she'd seen of him, he'd been engaged in conversation with Louise. Her lips were close to his ear, and he didn't even notice that Belle was leaving.

By now she couldn't deny he only wanted Belle to warm his bed for as long as she remained at Eden House. His plan to seduce her and chase her away had worked all too well. He didn't care if she left, or where she went, so long as she was out of his hair. Morgan was no different than his cousin. James had left her stranded; Morgan would simply send her away.

Every muscle in Morgan's body ached. The tension had built up from the moment Belle had walked into the parlor looking good enough to devour in one bite. The gown emphasized her figure, drawing all eyes to her alabaster shoulders and chest. The rose color made her skin gleam and he didn't know how he managed to keep his hands off her. The woman was too beautiful for her own good—or his.

From the moment he'd spotted her, it had taken all his will power not to scoop her up in his arms and carry her off to his bed. He regretted throwing the party. Thanks to Morgan's foolishness, if she wanted to find a husband, she had more than

her share of candidates. It seemed every man in town, married
or single, young or old, had courted her favors.

Worse, she'd encouraged the attention. Her laughter shot
through him like a slug from a revolver.

Louise jabbed an elbow into his ribs. She dragged him to
the davenport to prevent him from doing something foolish.
"Don't even think of following her. At least a dozen men
would drill you through if you so much as said a cross word
to her—with Dan Sullivan first in line. And we know he never
misses."

The sheriff's gaze followed Belle from the parlor. "If he
goes after her, I'll be the one with the gun."

"Calm down, Morgan. She's too much in love with you to
give any one of them more than the time of day."

He growled deep in his throat. "If she loves me, she has a
strange way of showing it. I've never seen so much lust in one
room. It's like being in a corral with a dozen stallions and one
mare."

"Have you shown how you feel about her?"

"How I feel?" He rubbed his temples with his fingers. "I
don't know how I feel." A bald-faced lie. Morgan loved her,
but he was too afraid of rejection to tell her. Best to let her go
to Denver and find a decent husband and father for the children.

"Then you'd better find out before it's too late. I understand
she's leaving soon after the New Year."

"I'm going to buy her out and we can get back to normal."

With a deep, sexy chuckle, she stood. "Morgan, if you let
her go you'll be a bigger fool than James. He left her, and he
deceived me. You're deceiving yourself, and sending her away.
You deserve to be miserable."

"I am not miserable." He stretched to his feet.

"Tell me that next month after she's gone." She turned
away and smiled at Vic. The foreman looked as if ready to
knock Morgan's head from his shoulders. She took the man's
arm and guided him toward the dining room.

Alone, Morgan studied the room. Most of the food was gone and they'd served enough liquor to float a ship. Laughter rang out and the loud music had his head pounding. It was past midnight—time to call it a day. He moved into the foyer and spotted a figure on the stairway.

Fury swirled up in him like a tornado. Had Belle invited one of her suitors to her room? He took the stairs two at a time, ready to commit murder. He would kill any man who tried to get near her.

Near the landing, he caught the intruder by his nape. "Where do you think you're going?" He wasn't surprised to find himself face to face with Corbett Hayes.

The lawyer stumbled and glared at Morgan with frightened eyes. "I'm looking for the privy."

"It isn't up here." Sorely tempted to plant his fist in the lawyer's lying face, he shoved him toward the foyer. The man stumbled down the stairs. Any idiot would realize the man was looking for Belle. "You have one at home. Go. The party's over."

At the bottom of the stairs, Corbett stopped to straighten his coat. "What Isabella and I do is no concern of yours. You don't own her, you know."

The volcano that had been bubbling up in Morgan all evening erupted. With a roar, he rammed one fist into the lawyer's stomach and the other into his face. Blood squirted from Corbett's nose and he squealed like a stuck pig. Not yet satisfied, Morgan advanced on the man lying on the floor. Before he had a chance to finish off the predator, both Morgan's arms were wrenched behind him. He struggled against the two men immobilizing him.

"Let go of me. I'll kill the bastard."

"Morgan, calm down. He's already hurt." Louise joined Vic and Dan, who dragged Morgan back.

Like a trapped animal, Morgan fought his captors. Dan twisted his arm behind his back. "That's enough, Morgan."

"Keep that maniac away from me. I didn't do anything to him." Corbett struggled to his feet. Savannah pressed a handkerchief to his nose. "I should sue you." He backed toward the door.

"Get out of my house. And don't come back." Trapped between the two big men, Morgan tried to relax. The lawyer's words had struck a chord in his heart. A reminder that he had no claim on Belle. Worse, he never would.

A loud gasp from the top of the stairs drew one gaze after another. Morgan was afraid to look. Surely the noise had disturbed Belle. Vic and Dan loosed their hold. Belle, with Beth in her arms, stared down at the melee. Her hair hung down her back, and she was clad in a thick robe.

Morgan's heart sank. He'd made a fool of himself, and now she knew what an idiot he was.

"Isabella, you'd do well to get out of this den of iniquity," Corbett called out. "This man is violent. You aren't safe here. He doesn't care who he hurts."

The words struck like a knife to Morgan's chest. He leaped toward the lawyer, hands reaching for the man's thick throat. "You no good . . ." His hands inches from Corbett, pain slashed across his head. He staggered to his knees.

As darkness overtook him, he heard Louise's fading voice. "You boys carry him to his room. Vic, go with him and make sure he stays there."

Too dizzy to fight, Morgan slumped to the floor. Hands grabbed him, and his feet dragged the floor. His last conscious thoughts were on Belle. "Love you," he whispered.

"Yeah, I love you, too," came Vic's gruff voice. Deep masculine laughter followed him into oblivion.

Belle stood at the window and watched the snow flurries turn the ground white. It seemed she'd spent hours staring at the surrounding yard. After Morgan's confrontation with

Corbett, she'd watched one guest after another leave. Last to go were the ranch hands. She was surprised to see them load Morgan into the bed of the farm wagon and tuck blankets around him.

Whatever had possessed him to fight with Corbett? What could the lawyer have done to warrant such disgraceful behavior? Belle could not condone violence, yet it warmed her to think he'd fought over her. It had taken all her will power not to race to his aid when Sheriff Sullivan knocked him on the head with the handle of his revolver. However, Morgan had Louise, Vic and the ranch hands to take care of him. He didn't need Belle. Wrapping a shawl over her shoulders, she went downstairs to join her family.

The children were gathered around the table eating their breakfast when she entered the kitchen. Abby stood at the stove with her back to them.

"You looked like a princess last night, Mama," her daughter said, light dancing in her blue eyes. "Did you meet a handsome prince?"

Laughter stuck in her throat. The handsomest man she'd ever met wanted nothing to do with her. "Sorry, I kissed a prince and he turned into a toad."

The boys laughed, while Beth stared at her. "Morgie is the most handsomest prince in the whole wide world."

"Mr. Morgan isn't a prince," Rory said, relaying his superior knowledge. "He's just an ordinary man."

Beth stood on the chair and planted her hands on her hips. "No, he ain't. He is too a prince and he's gonna be my papa. Ain't he, Mama?"

The china cup nearly slipped from Belle's fingers. The child didn't understand the improbability of her wish. "I'm not sure that's possible, honey."

"Beth, don't you know nothing? In order for Mr. Morgan to be your papa, he would have to marry Miss Belle," Rory declared.

"He would be my papa, too," Rosalind said, not to be ignored.

"I'm too old for a papa," Rory said. "We get along good without somebody telling us what to do. I'm the man in the family."

Belle shook her head and strove to change the subject. "Let's not worry about that. Tomorrow is Christmas Eve. We still have to cut down a tree. As soon as the snow stops, we'll take the wagon and go out and pick out a good one."

"Morgie can help us." Again Beth depended on her hero.

"Mr. Morgan had to go out to the ranch. We'll have to do it ourselves." Earlier, Vic had informed her that he intended to keep Morgan out at the ranch until Christmas was over. Belle was grateful he wouldn't be there to criticize the decorations and celebration. Morgan's ill temper would spoil the entire Christmas for the children.

"We'll make popcorn tonight and string it for the tree. Then we'll sing carols like we always do. Won't that be grand fun?" She filled a cup from the coffee pot on the stove. Abby moved away. The young woman hadn't spoken a word all morning. "Abby, would you like to help us string cranberries for the tree?"

"No, ma'am. I'll be busy." She turned away and stalked from the kitchen.

Belle stared after her, surprised at the rude behavior. Perhaps they should have given her a few days off for Christmas. After the work Mrs. Franklin had done preparing the house for Morgan's party, Louise had given the housekeeper time off until after Christmas. That left most of the preparations for meals up to Belle. It didn't matter. The busier she stayed, the less time she had to think about Morgan.

As if every moment wasn't filled with thoughts of the man she loved.

For the remainder of the day she stayed busy with the children. Beth spent most of her time at the window looking for

Morgan. Belle tried to explain he was busy, but the child couldn't understand how something or anybody could be more important than she.

It hurt to realize that he could so easily put the child out of his mind. She adored him, and Belle had thought he felt the same about the little girl. Belle tried to explain that because of the snow, Morgan wasn't able to return home. Even attention from Savannah and Vivian didn't pacify Beth.

Being aware of the situation didn't make it any easier for Belle to accept. She put on a happy face, smiled, and joined in singing Yuletide carols. The other women joined them in the parlor that evening. Belle played the piano and they all sang together. It could have been much more pleasurable if Morgan had been there to participate in the festivities. By the time he returned to Eden House, Belle planned to be miles away.

With the promise to go out the next morning and cut a tree, the children went to bed early. After they fell asleep, Belle completed wrapping the gifts she'd made and those she'd selected for the children. The next evening, Christmas Eve, they would decorate the tree with the ornaments and decorations they'd made. Then, as a family, they would read the Bible story of the first Christmas. It was a tradition she'd started when she had her child. Belle's own mother had done the same when Belle was a child. Traditions were meant to be passed from generation to generation.

Her heart ached for Morgan. On the surface, he seemed to have everything—good looks, prosperity, ambition. Yet, she saw behind the mask to the lonely man underneath. He hadn't had a family for so long, he had no idea how to react to Belle and the children.

She loosed her hair and passed the brush through it. Memories of the many times her mother had brushed her hair, just as Belle now did for her two girls, flooded her heart. Belle had led a sheltered life with her housekeeper mother. Mr. Robinson had generously allowed Belle to live in the servant's quarters after James had deserted her. Now they were both gone. Her heart ached at her losses. Still, she'd been an adult when she lost her mother and the man who'd been like a father to her. She'd often dreamed that her mother's employer was her father. But she knew that was only a child's dream. Her father had died of the yellow fever when she was an infant, then a later epidemic took her mother.

Her gaze shifted to the girls asleep on the wide bed. They needed the love and attention only a father could offer. And the boys needed a man's discipline.

With her hair in a long braid, Belle slipped into the bed with the children. She cuddled next to them to share her body warmth. Memories of sleeping in Morgan's arms chased sleep away. Her heart ached with love for him. He'd been alone for so long, he didn't realize he needed Belle as much as she needed him.

She squeezed her eyes shut and tried to think about her future—a future without Morgan. As much as the children needed a father, she doubted she could fall in love again. Twice burned was enough for her. When she left Eden House, she would carefully guard her heart, and dedicate her life to making a fine home for the children.

That settled, she fell into a fitful sleep. She hoped Jerome's angel was on duty. They surely needed all the guidance he could provide.

Chapter 22

How had that brass band set up a practice session in his head? Morgan buried his face in the pillows to block out the noise. Had he drank too much the night before? He couldn't remember ever getting drunk enough to become immobile. He'd slept, then woke up, only to fall asleep again. Even in his sleep, he heard the band. He touched a tentative finger to the egg-sized knot on his scalp.

Rolling to his back, Morgan stared at the ceiling. The rough boards looked familiar, but his location escaped him. At the sound of a harsh male voice, he tried to sit up. Then he realized that he wasn't at Eden House, he was in a bed at the ranch.

His last conscious memories were of trying to kill Corbett Hayes and of Belle staring at him from the top of the stairs. He'd made a complete ass of himself by fighting with Hayes. It would serve him right if Belle never spoke to him again.

"Coffee, boss?" The Swedish accent drew his attention.

Morgan turned his head to see the blond-haired man shove a steaming mug toward him. That small action started another round of clashing cymbals. Stars flashed behind his eyes. Taking a few deep breaths, he brought the pain under control.

Not sure he could hold anything on his stomach, Morgan eased his feet over the side of the bed and sat up. Sven pressed a cup into his palm. "Thanks," he muttered.

Through the open doorway, he spied the other two hired hands staring at him. When they met his harsh glare, they busied themselves in the kitchen. The thin Swede backed away. "Feel better, boss?"

Morgan swallowed back a string of curses with the coffee. It burned all the way down his throat. Morgan glanced at his wrinkled trousers—the evening attire he'd worn to the party. "How long have I been asleep?" He shifted his gaze to the window. Little daylight showed through, and snow rimmed the panes.

"Since last night. Miss Louise told us to bring you back to the ranch with us. Vic came in a while ago. He's out in the barn."

"Since when did Louise start directing my life?"

The ranch hand backed away. "I only take orders."

Aware he was taking out his discomfort and frustration on the wrong person, Morgan bit down his agony. The coffee settled his stomach and he tried to stand. His head spun like a whirly top. He dropped back to the bed. Surely the lawyer couldn't have done this much damage to him. The man was half Morgan's size. "Vic knocked me out?" Morgan leaned forward, elbows on his thighs, the mug clutched in his hands.

"No, sir. It was the sheriff. He clobbered you real hard. You didn't even wake up when we loaded you in the wagon."

Morgan groaned. "I could have had a concussion. Didn't anybody care?"

"We cared enough to keep you from getting yourself killed." Vic entered the room. Snowflakes clung to his sheepskin jacket. "If you'd have kept it up, I reckon Miss Belle would have snatched Dan's gun and shot you herself."

"Was she mad?"

"Didn't say. But Louise advised me to keep you out here until after Christmas. Don't want you to ruin it for the young'uns." He shrugged out of his heavy jacket. "Feeling better?"

"I feel like hell. Did you drag me by a rope behind the wagon?"

With a laugh, Vic returned to the kitchen. "We considered it. Instead, we tossed you into the bed of the wagon."

This time when Morgan rose, he managed to reach the doorway without stumbling over his own two feet. "Got anything here to eat. I'm about starved." In his stocking feet, he padded across the chilled floor to the kitchen. He sank into a chair at the table.

Zack ladled up five bowls of beans and set them on the table. "Not as good as the chow we had at the party."

Morgan dug his spoon into the bowl. "Not even close." As if his brain had awakened, he remembered something Vic had said. "What was that about keeping me out here until after Christmas? I have to get back."

"Louise said you hate Christmas. You complained about the decorations and refused to allow a tree for the youngsters. They would all be better off if you stay away."

"You don't like Christmas, Mr. Morgan?" Zack asked. "My ma always made a big deal over Christmas. Said it was a special time. When miracles happen."

Les, a man nearer to Morgan's age, laughed. "Didn't Miss Belle invite all of us over to Christmas dinner at Eden House. That's a miracle. She sure is pretty. Those pies she made for the party were great."

Anguish welled up in Morgan's chest. Belle wanted them all at dinner except Morgan. Nobody was going to tell Morgan what to do. "I've got to get back. Sven, saddle me a horse." He rose to get his shoes and coat.

Vic clamped a large hand on his shoulder. "It's snowing

and getting dark. You slept most of the day away. Wait until Christmas, and we'll all go into town together.''

His head was still spinning. ''I'll wait until morning.'' But at first light, he would be on his way back to Eden House and Belle. He had a lot of fences to mend with Belle and the children.

By morning the snow had stopped. Belle inhaled the cold, crisp air, so different from the humid Louisiana climate. In New Orleans, she seldom wore anything heavier than her cloak or shawl. She pulled the hood over her head and stepped off the rear porch. Jeb waited in the wagon for her. Belle was going to get her tree if it took defying Morgan and the entire male population of Paradise to do so.

''Want me to drive you out, Miss Belle?'' the young man asked.

''That won't be necessary. The children want to select and cut their own tree. It's Christmas Eve, take the rest of the day off.''

''You sure, ma'am? Mr. Morgan won't get mad?''

''He isn't here to care. Go. Your mother may have chores for you. Stop back tomorrow and have dessert with us. Papa Noel might leave something for you under the tree.'' Belle had selected a new pair of gloves for the hard-working young man. He deserved that and much more.

''Thanks, Miss Belle. If you need me for anything, just send for me at ma's.''

''Run along. We aren't going far.''

With a finger to the brim of his hat, the young man took off at a run.

It took longer than she'd planned to get the children ready. Rosalind had insisted that they pack a picnic lunch and have a ''cutting down the tree party.'' Rory fetched an axe, convinced that he could cut down any tree they chose.

Louise watched the preparations with a worried look. "Belle, don't you think you should wait for the men? They'll be here in the morning for Christmas. They'll cut the tree for you."

"Tomorrow will be too late. We want to decorate the tree tonight. It's our tradition." She pulled on her gloves. "Besides, I don't want to depend on any of them. I can do it myself."

"What if you get lost? You don't know this territory. Morgan will have my head for letting you go off alone." The woman looked genuinely concerned.

As if Morgan would care what she did. He couldn't wait for her to leave Eden House. "I'll stay on the road, and be back in a couple of hours."

"I still don't like it. At least take Abby with you. I'll feel better if you aren't alone."

The young house maid entered the kitchen. "Yes, ma'am, I'll be glad to go with Miss Belle."

A few minutes later, Belle loaded her entourage into the wagon. The children bundled up in blankets, and Rory took over the chore of driving. He'd become expert in a short time. Living in the West had done wonders for the boy. He was growing taller and stronger from helping Jeb with the chores. Being able to drive and become more independent had given him self-confidence he'd never had before. Belle hated taking him away from this, but she would never keep the children where they were not wanted. And Morgan definitely did not want them at Eden House. He'd more than made it clear he couldn't wait for her to leave.

Her heart ached at the reminder of Morgan. Shoving away the sad thoughts, she pasted a smile on her face. "Let's sing Christmas carols," she called out.

Led by Jerome, the youngsters burst into song. Their rendition of "Jingle Bells" was loud enough to shake the snow off the trees. Rory followed the road toward the north. Belle's pulse raced to think that if they turned east, they would eventually end up at the ranch where Morgan was holed up.

"Those are nice trees," she said. Surely they'd gone far enough. Rory pulled the team to a halt. The children leapt from the wagon. The girls raced ahead. Abby followed at a slower pace.

Rory remained with the horses. "Call me when you find the right tree."

Rosalind and Beth marched around several trees, each of which would be perfect. "This one is flat on the side," Belle's daughter declared in her most grown-up voice. "And that one is too small."

Beth tugged on a branch and covered her head with snow. "Not good enough."

"The ones over there look good," Abby declared, pointing farther up the nearly nonexistent road.

Belle bit her lip. They'd already been gone longer than she'd planned. Until that moment, she hadn't noticed the gathering clouds. Before she could protest, the children had loaded up and Rory was headed deeper into the woods. It took two more tries before the girls found a satisfactory tree. About six feet tall, with a straight trunk and full, green branches, it would look lovely in the rear parlor. The wind had kicked up, but the children didn't seem to notice. Jerome grabbed the picnic basket and followed a few paces behind. Belle carried the blankets for extra warmth. The girls' coats weren't meant for this kind of weather.

Flexing his muscles, Rory lifted the axe and slammed it into the trunk of the tree. His efforts hardly made a dent in the thick fir. While he worked at the tree, the girls gathered snowballs and tossed them at one another. It was their first time to enjoy a real snowfall. Until recently they had never seen snow. A large wad of snow landed on Rory's head. He dropped the axe and joined the fun. Belle, too, became caught up in the festivities. Their snow fight lasted only a few minutes, before Beth hid behind Belle.

"That's enough," Belle called. "Let's get that tree cut down, or we won't make it back home in time for Papa Noel to visit us.''

Rory hacked at the tree until the trunk was nearly cut through. He signaled them all away and yelled, ''Timber.'' The tree tumbled to the ground, falling softly in the snow.

Everybody cheered at the accomplishment. ''Let's get it to the wagon,'' Belle said. ''It's getting colder and it might snow again this evening.''

''Aren't we going to eat our picnic?'' Jerome asked.

''We can eat in the wagon. Everybody grab a branch, and we'll tug it to the wagon.'' Belle draped blankets over the girls. They each took a branch and marched along together.

The tree slid easily on the snow. Following the trail they'd left with their footsteps, Belle led the way to where they had left Abby and the wagon. However, the wagon wasn't where she'd thought they'd left it.

''Abby,'' she called out. Perhaps the girl had moved to shelter with the animals. Belle dropped the tree, and scouted the area. She followed the ruts and hoof prints in the snow. A second set of tracks overlaid the first. Where could Abby have gone? Had the horses run away with her?

Belle's heart sank. Abby and the wagon were gone.

A shiver not related to the cold raced up her spine. Had it been deliberate? Had the girl deserted them out of misplaced hatred? Surely she wouldn't harm the children because she was jealous of Belle? Her stomach knotted.

Belle and four children were stranded in the woods.

''Where's the wagon?'' Rory dropped the axe and set his hands on his hips. ''What happened to Abby?''

''I don't know. Perhaps the horses ran away with her.''

Dark clouds gathered overhead, blocking out the light. Tiny snowflakes drifted from the sky. Wind whistled through the trees. ''I'm sure she'll be back. Something must have frightened the horses.'' The lie, or was it wishful thinking, burned on Belle's lips. The girl had deliberately abandoned them.

"I'll walk back to town and get help," Rory offered. The youngster pulled his knit cap down over his ears.

"No. It's best for us to stay together. Surely we'll be missed and somebody will come looking for us." Though who, Belle had no idea. By the time Louise realized they were missing, they could be frozen to death. "We have to find shelter, it's getting colder."

Beth reached up her arms to Belle. "Want to go home. Want Morgie."

As much as she hated to admit it, she wanted Morgan, too. But they were off the beaten path, and it was doubtful anybody would find them before morning. And she was certain Morgan wouldn't return to Eden House until well after Christmas. She wrapped the child in a blanket and cradled Beth to her chest.

"Mama, I'm cold." Rosalind shivered in her new coat and boots. "The snow is pretty, but it's wet and cold."

"I know, darling. Wrap that blanket over your head, and you'll keep nice and warm."

Only Jerome hadn't complained. "Miz Belle," the boy whispered. "I think we should go that way." He pointed toward the hills past the trees.

Rory draped a blanket over Rosalind's shoulder and drew her close to his side. "There ain't no houses up there." He turned to Jerome. "Where's that angel of yours when we need help."

Jerome ducked his head. "I asked him, and he said to go this way."

They plodded along for several more yards. "You know what? This looks like the place I came when I got lost that other time." Rory paused and surveyed the land.

"This land looks all the same. Nothing but rocks, trees and shrubs." Belle shifted Beth to her other hip. The trusting little girl buried her face in Belle's neck. With every step trudging through the snow, the child grew heavier.

"No, ma'am, I'm sure I was here before." The snow fluttered

down in soft flakes. "See that sparkling up there? I saw something shining and I found a cave. That's where I found those
rocks everybody was interested in."

Still dragging the food basket, Jerome took the lead. "We'll
be safe up there. Earl's watching over us."

This time, Rory didn't argue, but shoved through the bushes
and up the hillside. Rosalind slipped and stumbled. Rory caught
her arm. "Easy, Rosie. I'll take care of you."

Cold tears ran down her daughter's face. The children were
all exhausted, cold and hungry. "Mama, I want to go home."

"Think of this as a great adventure. Remember how Joseph
and Mary were alone on that first Christmas? Then they found
shelter in a stable. We're like them." She prayed harder than
ever that they, too, would find a safe place to spend the night.
Surely somebody would find them in the morning.

"We should have never left New Orleans," Rory groused.
"It's warm there and we wouldn't be freezing our toes off."

For the first time since coming to Colorado, Belle regretted
her move. If she'd stayed in the South, things might have
worked out. Over the years, she'd had several suitors, and now
that she was free, she could have remarried. Her heart sank.
Then she would never have met Morgan. No matter how he
treated her, her love would remain in her heart forever.

"Look up there. It looks like something shiny. We'll find
the cave there." Jerome took the lead. Their labored breaths
puffed soft clouds of steam in the cold air. "Earl is showing
us the way."

Belle glanced behind them. Already, the snow had covered
their footprints. She blinked back tears. It might be days before
they were found.

The wind howled through the trees, now decorated with
fluffy snow. The snow glittered like silver stars on the green
branches. It would be beautiful if she were in a position to
enjoy the beauty. She stopped to catch her breath. The blanket
and her thick cape kept her and the baby warm, but the wet

and cold seeped through her shoes. If she felt it so, she marveled that the other children could continue so valiantly. She hoped they reached shelter soon.

Looking ahead, she spotted a glimmer of what appeared to be a star. But it couldn't be. It wasn't dark enough for stars. And with the low-hanging clouds, no stars would be visible that night. She blinked, and the star seemed to be winking at her.

Rosalind tore away from Rory and hugged Belle's skirts. "Mama, I'm tired. Can we rest?"

Belle's arms and back ached from carrying the child, and her legs nearly crumbled from under her. The hem of her gown was soaked, dragging behind her like a ball and chain.

Rory reached out a hand. "I'll carry Beth. You can take care of Rosie." Before she could argue, the youngster took the child from her arms. "Come on, Bethie, let me carry you."

Carefully, Belle wrapped the blanket around the little girl. Though tired as she, Rory was pushing himself to help others. He was growing up and someday would be a fine, loving man. How different from the near delinquent who had come to her a year ago.

The wind stirred the trees and seemed to part a path through the bushes. Jerome continued up the steep hillside as if guided by an unseen hand. For a child who had known nothing but city life, the boy took to the countryside as if he'd been born to it. He reminded her of a chameleon able to adapt to his surroundings.

The others followed at a slower pace. Belle slipped several times, but managed to right herself before dragging her daughter down the hill. As she was beginning to doubt if she could continue, the star again winked at her. Fatigue had her imagination working overtime.

"Mama, did you see that star up there?" Rosalind asked, her voice coming in soft gasps. "It's just like the star that guided the wise men to baby Jesus. Do you think God sent it to help us?''

"Sweetheart, anything is possible at Christmas.''

Her little girl tore away from her and chased after Jerome. The blanket around her shoulders dragged behind her like the train of a bridal gown. "Jerome, I saw the Christmas star. It's here to lead us.''

Belle draped her arm around Rory's shoulder. "Does this look like where you found the cave?''

"I think it is. See the way the snow is filling up those cracks in the rock. It looks almost like a cross.''

Belle looked up to where she'd last seen Jerome. Her heart stopped beating. The boy was gone. He was no longer in sight. Then as she watched, her daughter disappeared. Had they fallen into a fissure? "Rosie, Jerome,'' she called. Heedless of the bushes dragging at her skirts, she raced ahead.

On a small ledge, the two children waved their arms. "Mama, Jerome found a cave. It's real nice.''

Hurrying her steps, she climbed to where her daughter waited. Her eyes grew wide.

Jerome ducked out of the low opening. "Yes, ma'am, it's warm in here, and I even found some sticks and things to light a fire.''

"Don't go inside. There might be a bear or wildcat in there.'' She ducked and stared into the darkness.

"It's my cave,'' Rory caught up with her. "There's nothing in there but rocks and stuff.'' He passed Beth into Belle's arms. "I'll go in first and make sure.''

Rosalind jumped up and down. "It's like a miracle, Mama. We'll be safe here until Mr. Morgan finds us just like he found Rory when he was lost.''

The snow was still falling in large fluffy flakes. Within minutes they wouldn't be able to see their hands in front of their faces. How would anybody be able to locate them? The wind whipped the snow, covering the bushes and tree branches like crystals. It also covered their trail. Seconds later, Rory exited. "It's okay to come in. I'll start a fire and we'll get warm."

Cautiously, Belle ducked and entered the low cave. Inside, the ceiling slanted upward until she was able to stand with room over her head. It was amazing. Surely an unseen hand had guided them to this refuge. They moved deeper into the cavern, out of the wind.

Jerome set down his basket and began to gather twigs and dry branches. "We can make a fire."

After spreading out the blankets, Belle settled on the ground with the girls on either side of her. Both children shivered with the cold. "We don't have matches."

Rory dug into his pockets. "I have matches."

Belle sighed with relief. "You've been wonderful, Rory. Jerome, too. We couldn't have managed without both of you."

"Us, too, Mama," her daughter said.

"Sweetheart, I couldn't do anything without my girls." Her heart leaped at the love and trust the children shared so generously. If she had to walk all the way to town, she would see that no harm came to the children.

It took only moments for the boys to get a small fire blazing. While Rory fanned the flames, Jerome gathered dry twigs. Surprisingly, there was much more wood in the cave than she'd expected to find.

As the flames grew higher, she studied their surroundings. The cave may not be the ideal shelter, but it offered refuge from the storm. The fire would keep them warm, and they were out of the wind and snow. She whispered a word of thanks for the miracle that had saved their lives.

Her gaze fell on a pickaxe propped against the wall. Somebody had been here before them. Had it been a prospector? The fire cast a glow on the walls. The rock wall formation glittered with small gold specks.

A shiver raced down her spine. "Rory, is this where you found those rocks? The ones that looked like gold?"

He stopped in his chore and glanced around. "Yes, ma'am. I think so. I was in a hurry, so I didn't look around too much."

Tucking a blanket around the girls, she stood and, by the dim firelight, inspected their refuge. Taking a few steps, she kicked something on the ground. Her gaze fell. A lantern. She reached down and picked it up. "Rory, give me one of those matches." In seconds, the wick glowed yellow. Belle lifted the lamp and stepped back into the cave. Specks of a shiny metal glittered in a streak along one wall. She reached out a finger. Looking closer, she saw something carved into the wall.

Tracing the lines, she realized it was more than random carvings. It was a name. She moved the lantern. Her breath caught. Letters formed in front of her eyes.

A name: J. Jordan. And a date: three months ago. Only weeks before James was killed.

Had her late husband located a hidden mine and was keeping it secret from Morgan? And everybody else? Was this where the samples and report she'd found had come from?

"Mama," her daughter's voice drew her out of her thoughts. "I'm hungry."

She trimmed the lamp to save the kerosene. Later, she would further explore the tunnel. "Jerome carried our basket. We'll eat our special Christmas picnic. Won't we have great fun?" She settled on the blanket with the children.

"Will you tell us the story of the first Christmas?" Rosalind asked.

She snuggled both girls to her sides. "Of course. The Lord led us to this shelter just like he led Joseph and Mary to their stable. Some Bible scholars think the stable was in a cave like ours."

Wind whipped outside, but the fire kept them warm. They had food, but best of all, they had each other. As a bonus, they may have discovered a lost gold mine.

Surely, they'd gotten a Christmas miracle.

Now all that remained was to be rescued. By Morgan.

Chapter 23

If Belle didn't toss him out on his ear, it would be the best Christmas in Morgan's life. He drove the wagon up to the door of Eden House. Lights burned in every window, welcoming him home. Home sounded better than it ever had to him. He closed his eyes and pictured Belle and the children in the parlor, busy with their decorations. If things went the way he planned, Christmas Eve would always be his favorite day of the year.

His heart sang with a joy he hadn't known in years, if ever. He'd left the ranch early that morning to complete his chores before nightfall. The headache was gone, but he still had a debt to settle with Dan Sullivan for nearly cracking his skull. But Christmas wasn't a time for revenge, it was a time for family. And by some goodness he didn't deserve, a family had been dropped into his lap. With a woman to love and cherish.

Her love had given him the strength to come to terms with his past. He'd lost his mother on Christmas, but he hoped that this holiday would bring him the love of his life.

Funny how it had taken a bash on the head to bring him to his senses.

Following a search of the woods on his property, he'd selected a perfect fir tree, one sure to please Belle and the children. He'd made such a fuss about not having any kind of celebration, he owed Belle the finest tree in Colorado. The fir lay in the back of the ranch wagon, now covered with snow that had started falling an hour or so ago.

Once the tree was cut, he'd taken a short cut into town. There, he'd all but bought out Nelson's Emporium. He hadn't thought that spending money on children could bring so much pleasure. Belle already knew the joy of giving, he'd had to learn the hard way. The store was crowded with last-minute customers, most of whom seemed to be in a holiday mood. Even the ladies who rarely gave him the time of day greeted him cordially.

Except for Stanley. The merchant had drunk and eaten too much at the party, and he showed all the signs of a hangover—two days later. Employing all the charm he could muster, Morgan convinced Miss Nelson, Stanley's sister, to assist him in selecting the proper gifts. She gladly wrapped his purchases in tissue and tied them with bright ribbon.

Sure, he'd paid through the nose, but it would be worth every extravagant dollar to see the smiles on the faces of the ones he'd wronged. That included everybody at Eden House and the ranch. Especially Belle.

He wasn't proud of his behavior, but he'd been fighting his emotions ever since Belle had barged into his life. For weeks he'd tried unsuccessfully to lie to himself. He hadn't wanted to fall in love. Somehow Belle had broken down his defenses and slammed smack into his heart. Her and that rag-tag troop of orphans. Now he was ready to lay his life at her feet and take the chance of having her stomp it into the mud.

Morgan slipped his hand into the pocket of his heavy jacket. His fingers curled around the special box. The only ring in stock at the mercantile was a small pearl set in gold. If Belle accepted his proposal, he would buy her the most beautiful ring in Denver. Heck, he would deliver the world to her on a silver platter.

In spite of the cold, his heart warmed. He'd selected fur muffs and hoods for the girls plus the largest porcelain dolls in the store. For the boys he'd found leather vests, gloves, and wide-brimmed hats. Lace Mexican mantillas with silver combs were a surprise for Louise and the ladies. For the men, he'd found a selection of fancy jackknives. And he had a brand-new Stetson hat for Vic. He felt as if he'd bought out the entire store.

He reined in at the front of Eden House. His heart pounded in anticipation as he flung open the door and shouted. "Belle. Come here."

Silence greeted him. Strange, usually when he entered the house, Beth raced into his arms shouting his name. Were they upstairs where they couldn't hear his call? "Hello? Anybody home?" He kicked the door closed against the cold afternoon.

Louise rushed into the foyer, a shawl wrapped around her shoulders. Her mouth was drawn into a frown. "Morgan, what's all this noise?"

Laughing, he picked up the woman and spun her around. When he returned her to her feet, he placed a loud kiss on her cheek. "Merry Christmas. Where's Isabella?"

She shoved out of his arms. Vivian and Savannah appeared behind her wearing odd expressions on their faces. They looked as if they were headed to a funeral. A chill raced over him. "What's wrong? Where are Belle and the children?"

"I don't know." Louise hugged her shawl to her chest.

Belle had left him. He knew it by the looks on their faces. While he was nursing his cracked skull, she'd taken a train to Denver. He'd acted the fool and she'd gone away. He caught Louise by the arms. "Did she go to Denver? I swear, I'll find her no matter where she's gone."

Louise glared at him as if he'd murdered her best friend. "No. She left this afternoon to cut a tree for the children. When you refused to help her, she took the children out to cut one down on her own."

Vivian stepped forward. "We expected her back a long time ago."

"Maybe she stopped in town to make some more purchases." Savannah bit her lip and glanced around as if looking for Belle.

"I just came from Nelson's. She wasn't there, and I didn't see her anywhere." A sinking feeling settled in his stomach. Something was not right. Belle should have been home getting ready for her special celebration.

"Louise, didn't Abby go with Belle?" Vivian asked. "She came back a while ago."

"Yes, where is she?" Louise turned toward the kitchen.

"In her room, I think." Vivian followed at Louise's tail.

Morgan climbed the stairs after them. At the young maid's door, Louise knocked gently. "Abby, are you in there?"

When there was no answer, Morgan pounded on the door. He didn't have the patience for courtesy. "Abby, open the door." He tried the knob and shoved the door open. The young woman was curled on her bed in the darkness. Soft sobs echoed in the silent room.

Louise slipped past Morgan. "Morgan, you frightened the girl."

"I don't give a damn. Ask her where's Belle?"

She sat on the edge of the bed. "Abby, where are Mrs. Jordan and the children?"

"I don't know," wailed the young woman.

"Didn't you go with her to cut the tree?" Louise brushed a gentle hand over Abby's head.

She sat up and wiped the back of her hand over her eyes. "I went with them, then I did a real bad thing. Forgive me, Mr. Morgan, I didn't mean to hurt anybody."

''What did you do to them?'' His gruff bark brought another bout of tears.

Louise grabbed the girl by the shoulders. ''Abby, quit sniveling and tell us where they are.''

Morgan curled his fingers into his palms to keep from shaking the truth out of the young woman. She looked up at him with fear in her gaze.

''When they went to cut down a tree, I took the wagon and left.''

Shivers raced over Morgan. ''You abandoned them in the woods?'' His voice dropped to a husky growl.

''I didn't mean to. I did those things to scare Mrs. Jordan into leaving. She stole Sheriff Dan from me.''

When Morgan took a menacing step toward them, Louise waved him away with a hand. ''You silly goose. Don't you know that she doesn't care about Dan? She's in love with Morgan.''

That revelation shook him to his core. He didn't dare hope that she loved him. ''Tell me where they are.''

''I don't know. I felt bad about what I did, so I went back looking for them. But it started to snow, and I couldn't remember where they were.'' She broke into hard, heart-wrenching cries. ''When I couldn't find them, I thought you might have come from the ranch and brought them back.''

''Are they toward the ranch?''

She nodded. ''Near the mine, I think. Somewhere out there, but not too close. I'm not sure.''

''I have to find them.'' He turned on his heel and headed back through the house. ''Louise, pack some food and blankets. Throw in a bottle of whiskey. They might be cold and hungry.'' He surely needed something to fortify his nerves.

At the wagon, he pulled the tree out and carried it in the house. Vivian and Savannah greeted him with mouths agape. ''What's this?''

''What does it look like? A Christmas tree. While I'm gone,

decorate it. When they come home, I want those children to have the best Christmas of their lives.'' Tentacles of fear tightened in his chest. He shoved the fear aside and forced a confidence he didn't feel. He had to find them. His life would be worthless without Belle.

Louise handed him a large bundle. ''Morgan, we'll be praying you find them. Do you want me to send for the sheriff and Vic?''

He looked into the darkening sky. ''If I'm not back with them by morning you can send out a search team.''

''We'll decorate the tree and get everything ready for a real celebration. Morgan, let your love guide you. You'll find them if you follow your heart.''

With a nod, he climbed into the high seat. ''I love her too much to lose her. We'll be back.'' He slapped the reins on the horse's backs. They took off at a trot. Morgan had to find them before it was too late. If Belle wanted to leave him, he would allow her to go with his blessings. He loved her enough to do what was best for her. If that meant giving her up, he would do it gladly to keep her safe.

According to Abby, they'd gone north. He cursed himself a thousand times for his stupidity. If he'd taken the usual road from the ranch, he might have spotted them. Instead, he'd completely bypassed the mine area in his rush to get to town. Morgan knew of several thick groves of firs in the area. The snow fell harder, slowing his progress. He wished he'd taken his horse. The strong animal could plow through drifts that would bog down the wagon. But he had a woman and four children to rescue and he needed a way to carry food and blankets. Only then had he realized that in his rush to leave, he'd left the pile of gifts in the wagon.

By the time he reached a thick copse of firs, it was growing dark. He jumped from the wagon and quickly scouted the area. There were no signs that they'd passed that way. Of course, the snow and brisk wind covered any tracks they might have left. Unless they had found shelter and a way to start a fire, they could be in serious trouble.

As he continued, Morgan realized he wasn't far from where he'd found Rory when the boy was lost. He hoped he would be as lucky again. But it wasn't luck he needed. He needed a miracle.

A mile further, he spotted something on the trail. A tree. A tree that had been cut and abandoned. His chest pounded. He jumped down and saw an axe beside the downed tree. They had come this way. But how long ago, he didn't know. Except for the tree, there was no other signs of their passing. To make matters worse, the low-hanging clouds nearly obscured the path. They could have gone in any direction.

He turned the wagon toward the abandoned mine. An old shack still stood on the property. If they'd made it that far, they would at least have found a bit of shelter. He forced the horses through the wind. Snow drifted close to a foot deep near the trees.

At the mine clearing, he leaped from the high seat. He cupped his mouth and shouted, "Belle." The howling wind flung his voice back at him. "Belle."

Bending against the wind, he approached the dilapidated shack. The door hung on one hinge and banged against the walls. His heart sank. Except for a rat that scurried across the floor, the building was empty. Next he tried the boarded-up mine. The wood he'd nailed to keep out trespassers a few days earlier remained intact. Nobody had come this way.

Morgan couldn't give up. He looked up to the sky. Where was that miracle when he needed it? Eyes closed, he repeated every prayer he'd ever heard. As he whispered his pleas, peace flooded his soul. Almost as if he heard the words aloud, he knew that Belle and the children were safe.

He opened his eyes and gazed at the dark hills in front of him. They could be anywhere in this wilderness. He owned all this land, so he knew there wasn't another dwelling within ten miles. Morgan backtracked to the spot where he'd found the felled tree.

Which way to go? He pondered the problem as he studied the dark and foreboding hillside. Like words in his heart, the wind whispered around him. A Scripture he hadn't heard since his mother's funeral rustled in his ears. *I will lift up mine eyes unto the hills, from whence cometh my help.*

Heeding the words, Morgan lifted his gaze and carefully searched for some sign in the darkness. At first he thought he was seeing things. A tiny glow flickered like a distant star. A fire? A star? Neither made sense. It was too high up the steep cliff for a campfire and too low for a star. And with the dark clouds, neither stars nor moon were visible.

Morgan blinked, and the light disappeared. Was he seeing things? He hopped down and led the horses by the bridle. His heart skipped a beat. Somebody had passed this way. He knew it as surely as if he could see the five figures trudging through the snow.

Again he glanced at the forbidding hillside. The light flickered and glowed brighter. He quickened his pace. Drifting snow impeded his progress. Soon the hillside would be frozen and too steep to climb. At the base of the hill, he stopped. Ahead was nothing but darkness. Instincts told him that Belle was near. Love made him set one fatigued foot in front of the other.

The light flickered and disappeared. From the recesses of his mind, he remembered the first Christmas when the wise men were led by a star. Had Morgan been sent a light to guide him to Belle and the children? It was Christmas Eve, and anything was possible.

"Tell us again, Mama, how baby Jesus slept in a cave like ours."

Belle smiled at her daughter. "Honey, I think it was a lot different. It didn't get this cold or snow in Bethlehem."

"And they had animals to keep them company," Beth added. Yawning, the little girl settled into Belle's arms for comfort.

Deep in the cave, they were protected from the icy wind and snow. The fire offered light and warmth. Outside, the wind howled and the snow gusted in sheets. Belle would be eternally grateful for the shelter they'd found. She'd been careful to ration the food, as they did not know how long it would take for someone to locate them. If the snow kept up, it could be days. It wouldn't do to voice her fears to the children.

"But they weren't in a gold mine." Rory had inspected the cave and was convinced that the glitter in the walls was gold.

"We aren't sure about that."

"We'll be rich, Miss Belle, and we can live wherever we please. I'll buy my own horse, and have lots of great stuff. I'll show those bumpkins in Paradise. They'll come begging to be my friend."

"But it ain't ours." Jerome strove to add a bit of sanity to the youth's dreams.

"We can stake a claim, then it will be ours."

Belle sighed. If there was gold, James had already found it and it belonged to Morgan. And her, as long as they were partners. "Let's get back to our story. Mary and Joseph were in the stable when she had her baby. The Bible tells us that she wrapped him in swaddling clothes and laid him in a manger."

Beth snuggled closer to Belle. "Was he littler than me, Mama?"

"Oh, much smaller. I remember when you and Rosie were first born and how tiny you were."

"I ain't little no more. Morgie said I'm a big girl. Tell us about the angels."

Belle smiled. "Out in the country the shepherds were watching their sheep. And lo, the angel of the Lord appeared unto them and said . . ." A noise from outside the cave stopped her in midsentence. She cowered back and reached for a long stick. They all held their breath. The fire snapped and crackled. Surely it would keep away any animals or predators seeking shelter from the storm.

"Fear not, for behold, I bring you tidings of great joy." The deep male voice came from the shadows.

"It's an angel," Beth shouted.

Deep masculine laughter filled the still interior of the cave. "I've been called a lot of things, sweetheart, but never an angel." The shadow ducked into the cave.

Belle's heart leaped to her throat. Beth jumped from her arms and flung off the blanket. In one leap, the child practically flew into Morgan's arms. "Morgie."

He wasn't an angel, but Morgan was the most welcome sight she'd ever seen. The children dashed toward him, hugging his legs, his waist, pulling him closer to the fire. They were all talking at once. He dropped a bundle to the ground.

Belle couldn't do anything but stare at him. At that moment, she knew she would love him until the day she died. A man who would risk life and limb for her and the children was worth more than any gold mine or riches.

And she loved him enough to turn all the assets over to him. If he wanted her to go, she would leave with only what she'd brought with her. The rest belonged to him.

"I didn't mean to interrupt your story." He moved toward the fire, dragging the children behind him. Morgan looked like a snowman with snow piled on his hat and coat.

Belle swallowed down the lump in her throat. Tears burned in her eyes. "You didn't interrupt. You brought good tidings of great joy by finding us."

His gaze drifted over her and the campsite. "Looks as if you didn't need rescuing. You've done pretty well on your own." He dropped Beth to the blanket beside Belle. "Reckon you don't need me. I'll just mosey on back to town."

"No," the children yelled in unison.

Belle's heart beat double time. "We could use transportation back to town. Something happened to our wagon.'' She wasn't about to accuse Abby until she had more of the facts. "You're welcome to join us. We have bread, jelly and some cookies to share.''

"I've brought something a little more fortifying. First I want to take care of the horses. There's room at the front of the cave where they'll be sheltered from the storm."

"I'll help you unhitch the team, Mr. Morgan." Rory stood and started for the entrance.

"Me, too," Jerome followed on his heels.

Morgan dipped down to eye level with Belle. "You okay?" His soft voice sent shivers of delight through her.

"I knew you would find us," Beth announced. "I told Mama.''

"We're doing as well as can be expected. I'd rather be home, but this is quite an experience for the children."

"I brought more blankets and some food. Thought you might want some of that fine dinner you promised us. I'm kind of hungry myself."

She couldn't help smiling at him. "Hurry back." His gaze lowered to her mouth. In the leaping flames from the fire, his eyes glittered with emotion. She cupped his face in her hands. His cheeks were icy, his lips white. He turned his head and pressed his lips to her warm palms. His skin was cold, but his touch brought a sizzle of warmth within her. "Thank you.''

In one quick movement, Morgan surged to his feet. Another second so close to Belle and he would have kissed her. Then he wasn't sure he would be willing to return to the chill night. He reached out to touch her when he realized his gloves were caked with ice. "Be right back."

With the assistance of the two youngsters, Morgan unhitched the team and led them into the shelter of the cave. In the back of the wagon, he found old blankets and handfuls of hay. The animals deserved that and more. In the morning these strong horses would see that Belle and the children were safely returned to Eden House. He wiped the horses down and threw the old blankets over their backs.

"Good work, men," he complimented the youngsters. "Miss Belle was mighty lucky to have both of you with her during her trials."

"Yes, sir," Jerome said. "Rory told us about the cave and a star guided us right to it."

"A star?"

"Just like in the Bible when a star led the wise men to baby Jesus."

"We would have found it. I knew it was here somewhere." As always, Rory argued the point.

"I'm glad you found it, too. No matter how you did it." He glanced outside the welcome shelter. "Looks like the storm might wear itself out by morning. We'll be home in time for Christmas dinner."

Both youngsters cheered. Guided by the firelight, Morgan found his way deeper into the cave. He was firmly convinced that his love had led him to Belle.

She'd opened the blankets and package he'd brought with him, and set the whiskey bottle aside. Thick slices of beef and bread were spread on the blanket. He dropped beside her.

"Morgan, you're soaked. Take off your jacket and gloves and join us."

Her small hands shoved the near-frozen sheepskin from his shoulders. Her hands lingered for a brief moment on his arms. Her touch sent an amazing amount of heat surging through his body. He caught her fingers in his and carried them to his mouth. "Thank you." She shivered under his touch.

"Thank you for finding us." She wrapped a blanket over him, and the two little girls crawled in with him. As much as he loved the children, he wished it were Belle's warm body crushed to his. "How did you manage to locate us out here?" Belle cuddled beside him.

He sat cross-legged and shifted each girl to his lap. "Abby said you'd come in this direction."

"I don't understand why she left us."

"Jealousy, sweetheart. She didn't want you to steal Dan Sullivan from her."

"Morgan, I'm not interested in Dan. I'm . . . never mind. But how did you locate us in the cave?"

"I don't know. I was looking for you and I saw a light."

"Our fire?"

"I don't think so. It was much higher up on the hill. It glowed and glittered like a star. The strangest part was that it seemed to move ahead of me. Then it stopped above this cave."

"The Christmas star," Jerome whispered. "It led you to us just like it led the wise men to baby Jesus. It even led us to the cave."

"Morgie, I knew you wouldn't forget about me." Beth snuggled closer into his chest. The children were so loving and trusting, he hoped he would never disappoint them. Or Belle.

"You were right, sweetheart. Morgie wouldn't let anything happen to his favorite girls." While he spoke to the child, his gaze locked on Belle. Her cheeks were red from the cold and her hair hung in golden waves down her back. He remembered how those long tresses had felt lying on his bare chest, how his fingers threaded through them, and the smell of her soap. He banked the fires that ignited his blood. A lump lodged in his throat. "Finish your story. I want to hear the rest."

Belle cleared her throat. Even the near darkness couldn't hide the moisture in her whiskey-colored eyes. Her voice trembled with emotion. "The shepherds left their flocks and hurried to Bethlehem to find Mary and Joseph and the baby lying in a manger."

Silence settled over the pilgrims finding safety in a cave. Surely their quest was as miraculous as it was nearly two thousand years ago. For a man who didn't believe in miracles,

Morgan couldn't deny that something special had happened that Christmas Eve night.

"Mr. Morgan was just like the wise men," Jerome added. "He followed the star and brought us gifts." The youngster took a bite of the meat Morgan had brought.

Morgan chuckled deep in his throat in a self-mocking tone. "I wouldn't call myself wise by any means. I've done too many really stupid things in my life." The worst was denying his love for Belle. He vowed to make it up to her a thousand times as soon as they got back to safety.

"We all have, Morgan. It was stupid of me to take these children out to cut down a tree by ourselves. I don't know a thing about surviving in the wilds."

His heart constricted. Their being lost was his fault. "I don't blame you. If I'd have offered to help you instead of criticizing you, this wouldn't have happened."

The girls dropped their heads against his shoulder and closed their eyes. They felt so sweet and trusting. He hoped he would never disappoint them again. Jerome and Rory yawned and stretched. "Let's get these young'uns to sleep." Then he might find a few minutes alone with Belle. Even if he had to risk rejection, he needed to confess his feelings. He prayed that Louise was right. That Belle did care for him.

Together they stretched out the blankets and bundled the children into makeshift pallets near the fire. As he kissed little Rosalind on the cheek, he tasted salty tears.

He brushed the dampness away with his fingers. "What's wrong, princess?"

"Will Papa Noel be able to find us here?"

The child's simple worry brought a smile to his lips. "Have you been a good girl?"

She glanced at her mother. "I think so."

Belle offered a smile that would chase the blizzard clear out of the state. "All my children have been good. But we'll have to wait until we return to Eden House to find out what Papa Noel has brought you."

Morgan leaned over and whispered for the children only. "He'll find you, no matter where you are. I promise. We won't hang stockings, but we'll line up your shoes." Hurriedly, they pulled off their shoes and handed them to Morgan.

Within minutes, their breathing became deep and even. "Morgan, you shouldn't make promises you can't keep," Belle said.

He draped an arm over her shoulder. "Sweetheart, I never make promises I can't keep. What makes you think Papa Noel won't visit them tonight?"

"Do you know something I don't?"

Laughing, he spread his heavy jacket on the ground and offered a seat to Belle. "Perish the thought that I should know something you don't. Trust me. Lie down, you're about to fall over."

"No, I'm too keyed up to sleep. I have something to show you." Standing over him, she bit her lip and hugged a shawl to her chest.

He surged to his feet. He'd already waited too long for a kiss. "First, I think you owe me something for rescuing you."

Her eyes grew wide. "What do you want of me, Mr. Travers?"

"A kiss for the start. Everything else can wait until we get home." Gently, he cupped her arms and pulled her close to his chest. Her hands eased to his shoulders. She lifted her face; her eyes drifted closed.

Like a starving man with a feast set before him, Morgan lowered his mouth to hers. Her lips parted as if as eager for the kiss as he. He slid his arms around her back, drawing her flush against his body. Heat surged through him, igniting a fire in his veins. He met her lips, tasting the sweetness that was

Belle alone. Her mouth opened to him, and he slipped his tongue into the recesses of her mouth. It was heaven being with her. Belle was the angel who'd brought life and love into his cold, solitary life.

The kiss went on and on, as if he couldn't be satisfied. Under her shawl, he stroked her back. She trembled under his touch. Common sense tugged at the back of his mind. If he didn't stop soon, he would end up taking her right there in the dark, dank cave. Belle deserved better than that. He ended the kiss, but couldn't draw the strength to set her away from him. He was aching with a need only she could satisfy. Her breathing was as labored as his when he set her gently aside.

"Sweetheart, we'll finish this when we get back home." The husky words caught in his throat.

She nodded and pressed her cheek to his chest. "I'm so glad you came. I prayed and prayed that you would care enough to rescue us."

He nuzzled his lips in her hair. "I nearly went crazy when you weren't at home. I'd have turned this entire territory upside-down to find you. Finding you and the children safe is the most important thing in the world."

"Jerome's angel was watching over us, and he delivered you directly to our camp."

"I'll be eternally thankful. Sweetheart, I have to apologize for the way I treated you. If I'd have cut your tree, you wouldn't have run off to do it yourself." He cradled her in his arms, afraid that if he let her go she would disappear out of his life.

"It was stupid of me not to wait for help."

"I don't blame you. I could kick myself for the way I complained about Christmas."

"Morgan, you don't owe me an explanation."

"But I do. I want you to know about me, about why I hated Christmas until you showed me the love of the season." He backed away and looked into her beautiful eyes. He knew he would never tire of looking at her. "Christmas was never special for us. My mother regretted the loss of her home, and my father used the holiday as an excuse to get drunk. When my mother couldn't take any more, she took her own life. On Christmas Day." His voice broke.

She gasped, and cupped his face in her hands. "Morgan, I didn't know. No wonder you were so upset."

"I had no right to take my distress out on you or the children. After tonight, Christmas will be my favorite holiday."

"Thank you for telling me." She kissed him on the chin. "I have something to show you. It will make your quest worthwhile." She shoved out of his embrace and picked up a lantern from the floor. "Have you ever explored this cave?" She struck a match to the wick and turned up the lamp.

"I thought I'd been all over these hills, but I don't think I've been here. What did you find?" Morgan didn't know how he'd missed this cave. But he was certain he'd never been there before.

"I'll show you."

Leading the way, Belle moved deeper into the tunnel. Morgan kicked the pick-axe and lifted it in his hands. "A prospector?"

"Look at this." She held the lantern to the wall.

Morgan traced the carved wall with one long finger. "J. Jordan? James was here not long before he died." Dan had been right. James had been looking for gold.

"It looks that way. Did you know he found gold?"

"Gold? You must be joshing. There's no gold . . ." His voice trailed off and his eyes grew wide. "Holy . . ." He stroked a hand along the glittery specks in the wall. "It sure looks like gold. A vein. A rich vein at that."

Morgan couldn't believe what she'd discovered. Would miracles never cease to happen? For a man who didn't believe in anything, he'd witnessed one miracle after another with his own eyes. First, he'd been led to Belle and the children, then he learned that a shaft off his played-out silver mine contained gold. High-grade he was certain.

A wide grin danced over his mouth. "Mrs. Jordan, I believe you are a very wealthy woman."

Chapter 24

Belle's heart thudded against her chest. "Morgan, are you sure? It's really gold?" She brushed a finger along the wall.

"As far as I can tell it is. We'll have to cut samples and take them to the assayer's office."

"I believe James did that already." She felt slightly ashamed that she hadn't trusted Morgan enough to tell him about her discovery. "I found chunks of rock with gold specks in a hidden drawer in the bureau. He'd already had it assayed. I didn't quite understand the findings, but from what I read, it was high-grade ore."

Morgan let out a long string of curses. "That's why James was so eager to buy me out. While I was breaking my back to build up the ranch, he was looking for gold. I can't believe he found it."

"He stole from his wife and tried to cheat his partner. What kind of man was James Jordan?" Her voice trailed off. She'd married a man and borne his child, but she'd known nothing about him.

"A totally selfish scoundrel. I don't think any of us really knew his mind. He rarely confided in anybody. If Louise knew about the gold, she never mentioned it."

"You said that I'm a very wealthy woman. Don't you mean we, Morgan? Aren't we still partners?"

His eyes turned midnight dark. "Yes. But now you won't have to stay at Eden House. You'll have enough money to live anywhere you choose—Denver, New Orleans, Europe."

Belle's heart sank. She'd hoped his love for her had sent him out in a storm to search for her, but it was only some misplaced feeling of guilt. His kiss still tingled on her lips. Did it mean nothing to him? Did he still want to get rid of her—to operate his businesses without her interference? "I only want to do what is best for the children. I promised them a home, and that's what I'll give them."

She turned away, not able to face him and let him see the pain in her eyes. All her emotions showed on her face. As much as she loved him, she couldn't let him know how she felt. All he wanted was for her to get out of his life as quickly as possible.

"What about what is best for you, Bella?" Morgan caught her arms and forced her to face him. His face was unreadable in the dark shadows of the mine. "You're too young to give up your life for the children."

"I don't see myself giving up anything for them. Since I'll be so wealthy, I'm certain I won't have any trouble getting a husband and a father for them."

His thumbs stroked gently on her inner arm. "Ah, sweetheart. How many times do I have to tell you that I won't let you marry some gigolo who'll rob you blind and leave you busted?"

Belle bit her lip. "Don't worry, Morgan. That happened to me once. I'm much older and wiser. I'll be much more selective when I choose a husband."

"I'm sorry. I didn't mean to remind you of James. He didn't deserve a woman like you."

She blinked back the tears that threatened to betray her feelings. As much as she loved Morgan, he was too much like the man who'd betrayed her. To risk her heart again would be to risk having it broken. Worse, he would hurt the children.

"Let's get back to the children. If they wake, they'll be frightened."

"And if you don't get to sleep, Papa Noel won't visit you, either." Mischief glittered in his blue eyes. He draped an arm around her shoulder and hugged her to his side.

In spite of the storm outside and their uncomfortable surroundings, the children were sleeping soundly. Morgan stretched out his thick jacket and settled on the ground. He reached out a hand. "Lie down with me. I'll keep you warm."

On a sigh, she accepted his offer. What harm would it do to enjoy the warmth of his body on the wintry night? It may be the last time she would be this close to him. Finding the gold had changed nothing. Belle still planned to leave immediately after the New Year.

She took his hand and sank to the jacket. He flung her cloak over them, and cradled her back into his chest. With his arm over her waist, she snuggled neatly into him, spoon-style. The intimacy of their position shot shivers of sensation through Belle.

"Cold, love?" His warm breath tickled her ear.

Far from it. With the hot body pressed to her, flames of desire licked at her flesh. "I'm fine," she managed to say.

Morgan nuzzled her ear. "I'm burning up." He shifted. Her thick gown and petticoats couldn't prevent her from feeling how much he desired her. The thought that he continued to want her renewed her hope that he could love her just a little. A man wouldn't risk his life in a storm if he didn't care.

After all, it was Christmas. She'd already gotten two miracles. What was one more on this special night? Smiling, she closed her eyes and welcomed sleep.

* * *

Morgan was surprised that he'd managed to sleep at all. With Belle's soft body crushed to his, he'd been sorely pressed not to risk making love to her. Discretion won out. He would control his needs until they were alone. But he'd be damned if he would let her leave after New Year's. Marrying anybody except him was out of the question. He hadn't found her in this cave to give her up easily.

Silence greeted him when he came fully awake. The wind had ceased, and only the sounds of deep breathing whispered in the cave. Morgan slipped from Belle's arms, reluctant to leave the sweet warmth of her body.

At the entrance to the cave, he'd found that the snow had stopped and the sun was pushing through the clouds. Ice crunched under his feet as he led the horses from the cave. As soon as he roused the children and Belle, they could be on their way back home.

Home. Until Belle had barged into his life, he hadn't even thought about a home. Last night, a cold cave had been more of a home than Morgan had ever known. Reaching under the seat of the wagon, he lifted the box of gifts he'd gotten from the mercantile. The paper was slightly damp and the ribbon limp. However, he doubted there would be one complaint from the children.

Quietly, he stepped into the cave. They were still asleep, looking like angels in their slumber. He set the appropriate gifts at their shoes. Digging the tiny box from his pocket, he dropped it into Belle's shoe along with the other gift he had for her. After he tossed several dry logs onto the fire, he slid under the covers with Belle.

She turned and looped an arm around his neck. "Good morning," she whispered. Her fingers brushed his face. "Your ears are cold."

"Then I suppose you'll have to warm me up."

Cupping his face, she covered his ears with her palms. "Is that better?"

"Much. If you keep that up, I might have to carry you deeper into the tunnel and have my way with you."

Before he could carry out his threat, noises came from near them. "It's Christmas." Rosalind sat up and rubbed the sleep from her eyes.

Beth followed. The little girl leaped from her pallet and fell on Morgan and Belle.

"It's Christmas. Did Papa Noel visit us last night?" She kissed him on the cheek.

"I don't know," he said. "You'll have to look around and find out."

By then the boys had wakened. They grunted and stretched. Rory reached for his boots and grabbed a wrapped package instead. "Holy cow, what's this?"

Rosalind came to her knees. "Papa Noel did come," she squealed.

Beth climbed over Belle and darted for her own shoes. "He brought me a present."

Morgan sat up and pulled Belle with him. He settled her between his thighs, her back pressed to his chest. His lips rested against her hair. The children tore into the packages, pulling out the gifts he'd so carefully selected.

Belle twisted to look at him. "How did you . . . ?"

He widened his eyes innocently. "I didn't do a thing. Blame Papa Noel."

"Then later I'll have to thank him properly."

"I'm sure he'll appreciate it."

She returned her gaze to the children. Watching their joy as they viewed the gifts brought a warmth to Morgan's heart he'd never known. The barriers he'd spent years building around his emotions cracked like crystal shattering on stone.

"Mama, look. Me and Beth got fur muffs and hoods. Aren't they beautiful?" Both girls brushed the soft fur against their faces. Tears rolled down Belle's cheeks. Morgan leaned over and kissed the droplets away.

"And we got dollies." Beth hugged her golden-haired doll to her chest. "She looks just like me."

The vests were too big for the boys, but he'd never seen children more excited. "We'll grow into them," Jerome said in his all-too-grown-up voice.

"I can wear mine when I go out with Mr. Vic to round up the cattle," Rory declared.

"And we got hats, too." His dark eyes glittered as Jerome set the wide-brimmed hat on his head. "I ain't never had nothing like this."

"Mama, did Papa Noel bring you anything?" Rosalind snuggled in her mother's lap wearing her muff and hugging her doll. Beth flung her arms around Morgan's neck.

"I don't think so."

"How do you know? Did you check your shoes?"

Beth grabbed both of Belle's boots and shook them upside down. "Look Mama."

Belle's heart was so full of love for Morgan, she didn't need a gift. By his kindness to the children, he'd endeared himself to her for all time.

"What's that?" Morgan asked, a smile in his voice. "Is that a mouse in your shoe?"

The girls laughed. "It's a key."

She picked it up. The metal was cold against her palm. "What is it for?"

"It looks like a house key—like the one for Eden House. I believe Papa Noel wants you to have it for a proper home for the children. It's all yours. We'll have a lawyer draw up the papers deeding my interest to you. And we sure won't use Hayes."

Belle laughed. Her heart sang with joy. His kindness was endearing. Maybe he didn't want her to leave after all. She folded the key into her palm and held it to her heart. "Thank you. We appreciate it."

"Mama, look, there's something else." A small box dropped to the ground.

Morgan picked up the box and held it away from Belle. "Miss Belle, have you been a good girl this year?"

She grinned at him, barely able to contain her tears. "I think so. What do you think, Morgie? Have I been good?"

He groaned. "Very good." He handed her the box. It was small and tied with narrow ribbon.

Hands trembling, she slipped off the ribbon and opened the box. A gold ring was nestled in tissue. She lifted it out and stared at Morgan.

"Put it on," he said. The children had gathered around and stared at them.

Morgan took it and slipped the ring onto her finger. At the sight of the tiny pearl set in gold, she could no longer hold back her tears. "It's lovely."

Lifting her so she was settled across his lap, Morgan carried her hand to his mouth. "I wanted to get a larger one, diamond, emerald, rubies, but it was all Nelson had in the store."

Confused, Belle didn't quite know how to take his gift. "I like pearls much better than gems."

"I have something to ask, so all of you listen up. Isabella, Rosalind, Elizabeth, Rory, Jerome, will you marry me? I'm asking all of you, because you're a family and I would like to join you. Do you want me for a husband and papa?"

Belle was certain her heart couldn't contain the love she felt for this man. But she had to find out if his commitment was real. "For how long, Morgan?" She couldn't bear to have the children deserted as she'd been.

"I'm figuring about sixty or so years. I intend to see our great-grandchildren." Moisture gathered on his long dark eyelashes.

The children had grown quiet. Except Beth. The youngest

child rained kisses all over Morgan's face. "I said Morgie was going to be my papa. I love you, Morgie."

He wrapped an arm around the child. "How about it, Isabella? Will you marry me? Will you give me a Christmas gift? The gift of your love?"

How could she refuse when he'd offered so much? He'd given up Eden House, and offered his heart. She looked at the children. All their futures were at stake. She had to do what was best for them. "What do you say? Do we take a chance on Morgan?"

"Yes," they shouted in unison. Even Rory grinned in response.

She returned her gaze to Morgan. "I suppose I'll have to accept. I promised them a home, and you've given it to them."

Morgan crushed her in his embrace and kissed her soundly on the lips. His mouth slanted over hers, filled with all the passion of his love. "I love you, Bella. I've loved you from the moment I barged into Eden House and you tried to protect the children with your body. I swear, I'll never leave you, and I'll take care of all your children including the ones we have together until the day they put me six feet under."

She laughed. "I've loved you from the same moment. When you pointed a gun at me and threatened to toss me out into the cold. I thought I was crazy to fall in love with you, but you won my heart with kindness."

"Come spring, I'll build you the finest house in Colorado at the ranch. You can do what you please with Eden House."

"I think we could turn Eden House into Eden Home—a safe haven for lost children. After all, I promised these hoodlums a home for Christmas. Next year we'll share with other homeless children."

Morgan groaned. "Can I take back my proposal?"

Surrounded by four children, Belle answered with a resounding, "No."

He wrapped his arms around all of them. "What a Christmas. We've discovered gold and love. And I've gotten a family to boot. Who said miracles don't happen?"

Jerome grinned at them. "Earl said we would get a miracle. Love is the best miracle of all."

BOOK YOUR PLACE ON OUR WEBSITE AND MAKE THE READING CONNECTION!

We've created a customized website just for our very special readers, where you can get the inside scoop on everything that's going on with Zebra, Pinnacle and Kensington books.

When you come online, you'll have the exciting opportunity to:

- View covers of upcoming books
- Read sample chapters
- Learn about our future publishing schedule (listed by publication month *and author*)
- Find out when your favorite authors will be visiting a city near you
- Search for and order backlist books from our online catalog
- Check out author bios and background information
- Send e-mail to your favorite authors
- Meet the Kensington staff online
- Join us in weekly chats with authors, readers and other guests
- Get writing guidelines
- AND MUCH MORE!

**Visit our website at
http://www.zebrabooks.com**